Perilous Gambit

A Mike Stoneman Thriller

Perilous Gambit

A Mike Stoneman Thriller

Kevin G. Chapman

Other novels and stories by Kevin G. Chapman

The Mike Stoneman Thriller Series

Righteous Assassin (Mike Stoneman #1)
Deadly Enterprise (Mike Stoneman #2)
Lethal Voyage (Mike Stoneman #3)
Fatal Infraction (Mike Stoneman #4)
Perilous Gambit (Mike Stoneman #5)
Fool Me Twice (A Mike Stoneman Short Story)

Stand-alone Novels

The Other Murder
Dead Winner
A Legacy of One
Identity Crisis: A Rick LaBlonde Mystery

Short Stories & Novellas

The Car, the Dog & the Girl
Ghost Creek (a romantic mystery novella)

Visit me at www.KevinGChapman.com

For Sharon, who keeps me honest, makes me laugh, and makes my characters so much better. All my love.

Chapter 1 — Cold Blood

December 22, 2019
Rapid City, SD

SENATOR HARLAN BUSHFIELD III wasn't worried about his ability to drive home after the fundraiser. At sixty-three, he was still in excellent shape. He wasn't worried about the two glasses of wine he had consumed over the course of the evening. He was concerned about the weather. The South Dakota plains were going to be near zero, and there was a chance of snow. Harlan knew his Blazer could handle the snow. What he didn't figure on was the flat tire.

"Oh, for Pete's sake!" the senator exclaimed as he eased over onto the wide shoulder, away from the non-existent traffic. He had just exited off Highway 44 onto 32nd Street. "I'll change it."

"You'll do no such thing!" Loretta's voice was sharper than normal. During the long night of glad-handing fundraisers, she had been the perfect senator's wife. She chatted amicably about how she had raised their three children and been the perfect homemaker, president of the PTA, and den mother for the boys in Cub Scouts. She was uniformly viewed as a model of morality and conservative virtue. Harlan needed that. He ran on a family values platform that meshed nicely with the current political atmosphere in his home state. She was the embodiment of what he stood for. The Senator tended to follow her lead—and her directions.

"Well, then what do you suggest? We can't drive home on a flat from here. We'll bend the rim."

"Isn't that why we have Triple-A?" Loretta asked irritably.

"Yes, I suppose it is." Harlan dug into the inside pocket of his suit jacket and extracted his phone. After fumbling with his address book, he pressed the button and waited for the operator to answer. Three minutes later, he put the phone away and sat back with a sigh. "We've got plenty of gas. We'll just idle here with the heat on and we'll be fine until the tow truck arrives."

"We shouldn't run the engine constantly. The carbon monoxide will build up." Loretta wrapped a red wool scarf around her neck and buttoned up her coat. "Turn it off and wait five minutes, then we can warm up again."

Harlan shrugged and snapped off the engine. There was no point in disagreeing. They sat in silence, each dozing after the long night of socializing. Neither was sure how much time had passed when Loretta startled and saw the bright headlights of a tow truck directly behind them. "Harlan!" she said more loudly than she intended.

He jerked his chin up from where it was lolling on his chest and turned on the engine. Within moments, a man wearing a large down coat walked up to the driver's side window. He wore a brown fur hat and a thick black beard. He motioned for Harlan to roll down the window. As he complied, Harlan and Loretta felt the icy wind flow into the SUV.

"Sir, please come out to the truck while we take care of

the paperwork."

Before Harlan had a chance to object, the driver walked away in the direction of his truck. "Why can't he do the paperwork in our car?" Loretta was clearly annoyed.

"How should I know?" Harlan grumbled as he opened the door, pulled the belt of his coat together, and stepped out into the frigid night. There were no other cars on the road. The bitter air stung his throat as he tried to breathe without a face covering. A few stray flakes of snow rushed past his already frosty ear. By the time he arrived at the truck, staring into the blinding headlights, he regretted not pausing to don his gloves. His fingers tingled as he gripped the handle of the passenger side door and hoisted himself up into the warm cab, where the driver was holding a clipboard.

"Why the hell—" Harlan started to scold the driver for making him leave his car. His reprobation was extinguished by the burning explosion of pain in his neck as the driver pulled a taser from behind the clipboard and gouged the tines into Harlan's skin. As the electricity surged into his tissue and paralyzed his nerves, lights flashed in his field of vision and he slumped sideways.

"You should have played ball," the driver said as he depressed the clutch. Harlan was barely conscious as the truck pulled onto the deserted road and drove past the parked Blazer, to Loretta's astonishment.

"What in the world?" Loretta reached for the door handle, but pulled back. Letting the freezing air into the car was a risk. She turned and looked out the rear window, but could see only blackness and some snowflakes that had accumulated on the glass. Was Harlan back there in the freezing darkness? What could have caused the truck driver to pull away without helping them? Why hadn't Harlan returned to their car? She pulled her coat tight around her, took out her phone, and resolutely grabbed the door handle.

As the biting wind hit her face, she held her phone in a gloved hand and engaged the flashlight function, pointing the light behind the Blazer. "Harlan!" Only silence and the wind replied.

Loretta trudged to the back of the car, holding the light low over the snow-covered pavement. She found the tire tracks the tow truck had made as it pulled onto the road, and scuffs in the snow that could have been footprints. "Harlan!"

Her nose was tingling and her fingers were starting to ache under her light gloves. She hadn't expected to be outside in her evening gown. Snow had wormed its way into her aqua pumps, making her feet feel like ice cubes. She couldn't withstand this environment much longer dressed as she was. "Harlan!" Her phone's bright light illuminated only snow and blacktop. There was no sign of her husband, and no tracks or marks in the snow to guide her.

She returned to the Blazer, spilling snow off her coat and uncovered hair as she slammed the passenger door behind her. After removing the gloves and massaging her hands inside the still-warm interior, she dialed 9-1-1.

A minute later, the tow truck reached the middle of the overpass over Rapid Creek and stopped on the shoulder next to a low metal railing. The bearded driver quickly jumped down, circled around to the passenger side, opened the door, and dragged out the limp body of Senator Harlan Bushfield, which he hoisted over the side. The Senator hit the iced-over surface fifty feet below with a crunch and a crack.

Ten minutes later, a tow truck dispatched by Triple-A arrived behind the Blazer, where Loretta was still talking to the 9-1-1 operator. A state patrol car arrived shortly after with lights flashing.

The next morning, a runner braving the near-zero conditions noticed the Senator's body lying on the ice under the shadow of the overpass.

♦♦♦

The local cops had no clues about the apparent assassination of the state's senior senator. Neither Triple-A nor Loretta had any idea where the mystery tow truck came from. Loretta could give no description, except that it had very bright headlights. She couldn't even say for sure it was a tow truck. The only certainty was the .32 caliber rifle slug lodged inside the SUV's rear tire. There were several likely locations from which a marginally accomplished shooter could have taken out the Senator's tire. The cops figured the shooter was probably the bearded man driving the mystery tow truck.

Loretta Bushfield was devastated by the unexpected and tragic events, but she held up with her typically stoic midwestern resolve. The only description of the truck driver she could provide was his thick fur hat and thick black beard. She couldn't even say for sure whether he was White.

The senator's wife could not think of anyone who would want to kill Harlan. She did not know about any recent disputes. There had been no recent death threats. But she did recall Harlan being unusually jumpy and nervous over the past few weeks. She attributed that to some upcoming votes in the senate. She gave the FBI nothing they considered a helpful lead.

The senator's murder was the big story in Rapid City and around the country. The FBI immediately assumed responsibility for the investigation. Although Harlan Bushfield liked to say South Dakota was "the safest place in America," a professional hitman could still get you. It was particularly easy for an assassin when the target drove himself home from a well-publicized political event, late at night, down a sparsely-traveled road, on the only logical route.

The funeral was televised by the local stations. The governor named a replacement, who was in Washington D.C. in time to be sworn in with the rest of the freshmen members of Congress on January 3rd.

Chapter 2 — An Alarming Discovery

Thursday, December 26
New York, NY

MIKE STONEMAN WAS PERPLEXED and getting frustrated. He was staring into the bottom of Dr. Michelle McNeill's bedroom closet. Michelle, the county medical examiner, was running late, which was unusual for her but not her fault. The new body in the morgue late that afternoon was a high priority. Michelle completed the portions of the autopsy requiring her personal attention and left the remainder to her assistant, Natalie. But, by the time she arrived at her Third Avenue apartment, she needed to hustle if she and Mike were going to make their pre-theater dinner reservation. Mike's assignment was to fetch her silver two-inch pumps. They were supposed to be on the rack on the left side of the closet.

Mike was dressed in a blue pinstriped suit that fit reasonably well on his five-foot-ten, slightly paunchy, fifty-year-old body. Normally, he wore lose-fitting slacks and his signature blue sport jacket on the job as a homicide detective. Tonight, he and Michelle were going out to a Broadway show, so he put on a full suit. He glanced into the mirror covering the inside of the left closet door and assessed himself. He had dropped a few pounds over the past year and he thought he looked pretty decent. His brown hair was less curly and a little more gray than it had been a decade earlier. He had more lines on his face, especially around his brown eyes, but Michelle didn't seem to care. He counted his blessings for the thousandth time that Michelle considered him attractive enough to be her boyfriend. It had been a good year.

When Mike could not locate the pumps, he was confused, since Michelle was the most organized person he knew. Other shoes were there, neatly arranged on the rack, but not the silver pumps. Mike opened the right side of the double door. As it swung outward, he noticed two things. The missing silver pumps where there, on the hardwood floor inside the threshold. But what caught his eye was the dress covering the entire inside surface of the closet door.

It was sheathed in clear plastic, as if just returned from the dry cleaner, hanging from a swiveling hanger draped over the top of the door. The dress was a shining white, covered with tiny white beads and lace fringes. It had long sleeves and white silk gloves dangling from its lace cuffs. There was no question. It was a wedding dress.

Mike had often seen the inside of Michelle's closet. This dress had not been there as recently as a few days earlier. He grabbed the silver shoes, carefully unhooked the dress hanger, and carried them both down the narrow hallway.

Michelle was looking into the bathroom mirror, applying makeup at an efficient but unhurried pace. Mike set the shoes down on the floor. "Here you go. And by the way," he held up the dress, "is there something you want to tell me?"

Michelle didn't look away from the mirror, where she was applying mascara. "Oh, Mike, you didn't touch Rachel's dress, did you?"

A very relieved Mike exhaled, not conscious of how tense he had been. "No. I mean, it's still in its plastic. But why is Rachel's wedding dress hanging in your closet?"

Michelle brushed eyeshadow onto her lids. "We picked it up this morning at the Vera Wang sample sale. She didn't have time to take it back to Brooklyn before her shift, so I said I'd hold it here for her. She was supposed to be here a half hour ago. I guess we're both running late. I hope she gets here before we have to leave. I'll text her as soon as I'm finished."

After returning the dress to its place, Mike walked to the living room and sat on the sofa, trying to assess why his heart was still racing after seeing the wedding gown. He glanced at his wristwatch. If they were going to make it to the restaurant in time to have dinner and still make the curtain for *Wicked*, they needed to be down on the street hailing a cab in the next few minutes. Then the house phone rang, indicating someone downstairs requesting entry to the building.

"I'll get that," Michelle called out, emerging from the bathroom wearing the silver pumps and looking ready to leave. "It's probably Rachel."

Michelle picked up the white phone hanging on the wall, looking like a leftover from the 70s. As soon as she brought the receiver to her ear, her expression changed from calm to concerned.

"Rachel, what's the matter? . . . Slow down, Honey . . . What? . . . Never mind. Just come right up."

"What's that all about?"

Michelle stood frozen, the phone receiver still in her hand, tethered to the wall unit by its short, coiled cord. "I'm not sure. Rachel's coming up. She was distraught — almost hysterical. I've never heard her sound like that. Something's very wrong."

◆◆◆

Fifteen minutes later, Mike excused himself, saying he was running down to the deli on 22nd Street to grab sandwiches since it was too late to go to a restaurant for dinner. He left Michelle and Rachel on the sofa. Rachel was crying. Michelle had one arm around her shoulders.

"Sweetie, Jason is going to be fine with this." Michelle handed over a tissue from the box on her lap.

"Everything is ruined! The dress isn't going to fit me in June. I might as well throw it away!" Rachel sniffed and accepted the tissue.

"Don't worry. It will all work out. This isn't a bad thing. You have to talk to Jason."

"I know. Oh my God, I'm late already. I'm supposed to meet him at my parents' place in Brooklyn. Oh, God – he'll see the dress. Oh, who cares now, it doesn't matter." She dissolved into tears again.

"Listen to me, Rachel. You're an EMT. You deal with crisis situations every day. You need to pull yourself together and deal with this right now and not let it make you crazy. You can leave the dress here another day. You need to talk to Jason. Make a plan. Decide whether you're having this baby—"

"I'm having the baby!"

"That's good. I know Jason and I'm sure he's going to be thrilled. Having a family is very important to him. You know that. Wouldn't you trade your new dress for a beautiful child?"

"Yes," Rachel said as she wiped away tears with a tissue.

"I'm sure Jason will feel the same way. You'll still get married – in June or some other time. Maybe you'll wait until afterwards and then you can still wear the dress."

"I don't want to have the baby without being married first!"

"I don't think you need to worry about that," Michelle soothed. "Why don't you call him right now?"

"That's wonderful!" Jason pulled Rachel into a hug, resting her head against his chin. His six-foot-three frame cradled Rachel, who was a statuesque five-eleven. After a lifetime of dating men who were shorter than her, Rachel appreciated having a fiancé as physically formidable as Jason. Being a homicide detective gave him an additional intimidating presence with most people. She sank into him, but couldn't help sniffling.

"The baby is going to be wonderful, but the wedding is ruined. I just spent a week's pay on a fabulous dress. I can't return it. I'm sorry, Jason."

"Do not ever be sorry." Jason stroked her soft hair. "Having our baby is so much more important than any dress." Jason rocked Rachel gently as she sniffed back her tears. "Listen. We're going to Vegas in two weeks, right?"

Rachel looked up into Jason's eyes. His confident demeanor always made her feel safe. "Yes, we are."

"Well, why don't you bring along the dress? I'll marry you anytime, anywhere. I don't need a big fancy wedding. We don't need six months of planning. We'll get married in Vegas."

Rachel smiled and nodded, snuggling into Jason's embrace. "You're sure you don't mind?"

"Of course not," Jason continued to stroke her hair. He smiled, knowing Rachel couldn't see his face. Avoiding six months of wedding planning and instead eloping in Vegas was actually a dream come true for him. And a baby! He was overjoyed. But soothing Rachel was job number one. "As long as you say 'I do' when the time comes, I'll be the happiest man on Earth."

Rachel squeezed her arms around Jason's torso. Then she loosened her grip so she could pull back and look up at his face. "I love you, Jason Dickson." She tilted her chin up and pulled Jason's head down for a long, lingering kiss. Then another.

The next day, Rachel met Michelle for lunch at a little Chinese place on Mott Street. It was within walking distance of Michelle's lab, which most people called the morgue. Rachel was mobile enough in her job as an emergency medical technician to make the meeting, leaving her partner to grab lunch at another Chinatown venue.

"Vegas? Wow. That's certainly different from the original plan."

"I know, but Jason thought it would be the best option. I can bring the dress and still wear it for the wedding. It won't be what we were planning, which makes me a little sad. I'm hoping Jason won't be too disappointed."

"Rachel, he's a man. He doesn't care about the wedding plans. I'm sure he'll be just as happy marrying you in Las Vegas."

"You think so?" Rachel's eyes showed signs of leaking.

"Yes. I'm sure. This is a perfect way for you two to make the best of the situation. You'll get married. You'll wear the dress. It will be beautiful." Michelle reached her hand out and squeezed Rachel's.

"Thanks, Michelle. You're the best friend I've ever had."

"Oh, Honey, I'd do anything for you."

Rachel lowered her eyes, then looked up at her mentor. "Michelle, I'm a little freaked out about all this. I know it's a good idea and it's going to be great and all. But I was wondering . . . would you and Mike consider coming with us? You could be our witnesses and stand up for us. It would be more like a real wedding if you could be there."

"Don't you want your sister to be your maid of honor?" Michelle processed the request in her head as she asked the obvious question.

"I'd love to, but she's almost eight months pregnant. She couldn't take a flight to Vegas, even if she wanted to. I need somebody to be there for me."

Michelle melted. "Of course, Sweetie. Running off to Las Vegas to get married is so romantic. I love the idea. I'm sure I could twist Mike's arm and convince him to go there for our vacation instead of driving to D.C. like we planned."

Chapter 3 — Reputation Matters

Thursday, December 26
Rapid City, SD

FBI AGENT DEREK DUMM TOSSED a greasy wrapper into the corner garbage can, leaving a damp streak on the wall. Senator Bushfield's funeral was that afternoon, and the ad hoc task force formed to investigate the presumed murder had nothing. The Rapid City police were also working the case, but the murder of a senator immediately sent the FBI into action. Unfortunately, Derek was assigned to lead the team. He should have been excited about the prospect of a nationally prominent case, but he had been looking forward to a quiet six months leading up to his long-planned retirement party. Rapid City wasn't a hot spot for federal investigations. There were few drugs, few cross-border crimes, no kidnappings, and while there were plenty of guns, most were registered and seldom used for criminal activity. It was a soft assignment. Until now.

Derek glanced over at the desk of his very junior partner, Chelsea Anne Shields. The kid was so wet behind the ears she needed a terrycloth collar. She was on the phone and speaking intently. Chelsea was loving this – her first big assignment.

Tall, with long legs, a slim waist, and a smooth belly (which he had seen in the federal building gym), she had short sandy-blonde hair, blue eyes, and a heart-shaped face. Every man in the office got weak in the knees when she entered the room. She worked her advantage like a pro. She was smart, having graduated from South Dakota State with a degree in criminal justice before joining the Bureau. Her whole life was ahead of her and she couldn't wait to get there. Derek couldn't decide if he was jealous, or pitied the kid.

"Shields!" he called out, not concerned about interrupting Chelsea's telephone conversation.

The young agent snapped her head toward her partner, mouthing, "Just a minute," as she covered the mouthpiece, despite not actually speaking. Thirty seconds later, she hung up and swiveled her chair around. "What's up, Derek?"

He scowled. He had instructed his young protégé to call him Dumm. For seven years, he had called his senior partner Schultz. If he had tried to call him James – or, God forbid, Jim – he would have received the business end of Shultz's Luger. That was the way senior partners kept their juniors in line, in the old days. Somehow, this greenhorn had not received the memo about tradition in the bureau. Maybe it was the comical sound of calling someone Dumm, but it was his damned name. "Did you talk to the tow truck dispatcher?"

Chelsea shook her head as if to say, "No," but said, "She had nothing. She sent out the regular driver – the guy we talked to – but she has no idea where the other truck could have come from."

"Figures." Derek turned back to his desk. The dispatcher had been away for a family Christmas gathering since the murder. A handwritten to-do list stared up at him from a yellow legal pad. All but two items were already crossed out.

Derek scratched a line through "dispatcher." The one remaining notation was at the top. His handwriting was infamously terrible, but almost anyone could have made out the word: "photo." He stood slowly, hearing the crack of his left knee joint, which hadn't extended quietly since he had fractured the kneecap ten years earlier. Walking past his partner's desk, he grunted, "C'mon, Rook. It's time to talk to the boss." Derek continued walking toward a glass-enclosed conference room, not waiting for Chelsea to catch up.

Once they were both settled, Derek picked up the remote control from the conference table's shiny surface and pointed it at a 60-inch flat-screen TV mounted on the wall. He navigated to the link for the scheduled video conference and entered the virtual meeting room. It had taken him a while, but he was reasonably comfortable now with the high-tech communications system the Bureau had installed a few years earlier. He was an old dog, but he could still learn a new trick or two. Seconds later, the face of their regional director, Trevor Honeycutt, appeared on the screen. He was sitting at his office desk with photos of the president and the secretary of the treasury prominently displayed behind his ears. They had a regular video conference every Thursday afternoon, but spoke more often whenever there was a big case happening. Those were few and far between for the Rapid City field office. This week they had been on the video link four times.

Derek didn't wait for any small talk. "Chief, we've run through all the leads we have – except the photo. We have to talk to Mrs. Bushfield and ask her if she knows where and when it was taken."

Honeycutt grimaced. "The director wants to avoid that."

"We know, Sir. But it's the best lead we have, and frankly, we're out of other options. We either go to her, or we go out wide with it and see if we can get a lead. I don't like the chances of that. I'd rather go to the person most likely to know, and that's his wife."

"Can we go wide with it and keep his identity quiet? There are people even higher up than the Director who want to avoid a scandal here. The guy was an icon. It's not going to be a good look if the Bureau is responsible for destroying his legacy."

Derek examined his partner, who was sitting back in her chair, legs crossed, looking like she expected a waiter to bring her a beer. Chelsea knew Derek was going to take the lead. She wasn't expected to talk, so she was relaxed. Derek said, "What do you think, Shields?"

"Huh?" Chelsea grunted, losing her balance as she tried to simultaneously sit forward, uncross her legs, and change her expression from detached observation to intense concentration. "I – I'm not sure."

"That's not what you told me an hour ago." Derek fixed a steely stare on the younger agent. The kid had felt empowered to give Derek her opinion and argue vigorously. Derek wanted to see if she had the nerve to be as forceful with the boss. "You were telling me that it would be unethical for us to withhold material information from Mrs. Bushfield."

Honeycutt said, "Is that right, Agent Shields?"

Chelsea was too flustered by the situation to be appropriately pissed off that Derek had thrown her under the bus. "Well, um, I did say it would be appropriate for us to share the information. I think she deserves to know." As she spoke, she gained confidence.

"Is that right?" Honeycutt leaned forward toward his webcam, his face filling the large screen as if he might jump through. "Well, let me explain this to you, Rookie." Honeycutt took a breath, as if stoking his internal fire. Derek smiled. He was going to enjoy this, even if it was going to make their investigation more difficult. "You and Agent Dumm are going to run this down without so much as hinting to the grieving widow that there was anything remotely embarrassing on the dead Senator's phone. If I find out you leaked the photo to her, you will be shoveling manure on the border wall for the next ten years. You got that?"

"Yes, Sir. I got it." Chelsea lowered her voice as well as her chin, appropriately chastised.

"Good!" Honeycutt shouted, finally sitting back in his chair. "Now, get the graphic IT guys to expunge the Senator's face and anything else that might identify him. Then send it around to the local offices and to the local police in the most likely cities and see if somebody can ID the room or those girls. We're going to do this confidentially. Any questions?"

Derek and Chelsea shook their heads, wanting the call to end. A few moments later, they left the conference room with their poker faces glued on. They were going to do this the hard way. Of course, it was possible the senator's wife would have no idea where the photo came from, or how it got onto his phone, or who the three showgirls were, or when the Senator was with them. The phone had been in the pocket of the senator's suit jacket. The killer apparently wasn't concerned about disposing of it, which suggested that whoever was instructing the hitman did not know the Senator had retained the picture. The photo was attached to a text message. It was a pretty sure bet he had not kept it as a souvenir. His personal assistant had given the FBI the unlock code for his iPhone, so Loretta didn't even know they were snooping around in there.

They had worked with the senator's staff to trace his movements over the past several months, not that they knew exactly when the photo had been taken. It turned out the

Senator got around. He had attended several conferences, done in-person sit-down appearances on television shows in six states, and gone on a fundraising tour to meet with major Republican donors in Colorado, Texas, Nevada, and Washington. On every trip, there were dinners and afterwards "personal time" with the donors and local dignitaries. The official records did not specify what happened, or where, during his personal time. On any one of those nights out, the Senator could have ended up in the room with the gold wallpaper and the three showgirls. The Bureau wasn't willing to commit a small army of agents to tracking down every venue the Senator had visited in the past year. And yet, Derek and his rookie partner were supposed to solve the case.

"You really think the old lady would lose her shit just because the guy was there with three babes?" Chelsea sat on the edge of Derek's desk, apparently recovered from the reprimand from their boss. "I mean, sure, one of them has her tit in his face, and one of them has her hand on his crotch, but it's not like she had his dick in her ass or something graphic."

Derek pursed his lips and shook his head slowly. "Kid, do you have a grandmother?"

"Nah. All my grandparents are dead."

"That figures. Well, let me ask you this: If you showed that snapshot to Mrs. Bushfield and she had a heart attack and dropped dead, would you be happy?"

Chelsea glared and didn't respond.

"Just take it as a given. We're not going there. We've got a picture that's obviously compromising and was being used to blackmail him. The note is pretty clear. I mean 'You know how to vote' doesn't have too many meanings. But we don't know what vote they were talking about. The metadata on the photo is wiped and the burner phone it was sent from gives us zip.

Our best chance is to get an ID on the girls and track down the blackmailers from there."

"You know they're not all girls, right?"

Now it was Derek's turn to glare. "Yeah. I saw the enlargements. That makes it even worse for the Senator. The blackmailers were pretty clever. His whole platform was family values and homophobia."

"What if we can't get an ID on the girls from anyone?"

"Don't be a pessimist, Kid. They're pretty recognizable."

"It's a shame we couldn't get a match on any of them from the facial recognition database."

"Yeah. A shame. It means none of them is a criminal or has a passport."

"Or served in the military." Chelsea held up a finger, like she had made an important point.

"Sure, there's another shocker."

"It sure seems like whoever killed him wanted us to find the body. I still think they didn't know he had the photo."

Derek dropped his head. They had covered this ground several times. "And I've told you, it makes sense they wanted him found to send a message. If we're right that whoever it is was trying to influence votes in Congress, they probably weren't limited to one senator. They would want anybody else being pressured to know that the penalty for bucking the instruction isn't just exposure of an embarrassing photo. They probably figured he would delete it, but even if he kept it as potential evidence for us, they don't care because they thought he'd never make it public. They also probably figured the Senator would follow his instructions and vote the way our blackmailers wanted, on whatever bill it was they cared about."

"That's another possible lead," Chelsea observed. "If we can figure out what vote they were interested in, maybe we could back into their identity."

"Sure." Derek stood, his creaky knee again objecting. "And there's a team of analysts in D.C. working on it. Let's get the redacted shot out on the wire. For now, we've got nothing else."

Chapter 4 — An Unusual Assignment

Friday, December 27
New York, NY

THE FRIDAY BETWEEN CHRISTMAS and New Year's was a lazy day for many workers who weren't taking the time off. For New York City cops, it could be quiet or crazy, depending on the weather and the state of the economy. On this day, the weather was cold, which tended to tamp down random crime, and the economy was booming, which made people generally happy. Mike Stoneman and Jason Dickson were taking some time off starting the following week, so they were working. Fortunately, the backlog of unresolved homicides was fairly light, putting them in a positive post-holiday and pre-vacation mood.

Mike was the senior of the four homicide detectives in the Manhattan North division and had seen his share of crazy winters over his twenty-four years on the force. Jason was the most junior, having been assigned as Mike's partner less than two years before. They had been eventful years. Visually, the partners couldn't be more different. Mike: the short, middle-aged White guy with the wrinkled jacket and scuffed shoes. Jason: the tall, muscular Black man always dressed to impress with starched shirts and immaculately knotted silk ties. After two years together, the novelty of their appearance had worn off around the station.

At the 94th Street precinct house on Manhattan's Upper West Side, Captain Edward "Sully" Sullivan convened a briefing for all his detectives. There were fourteen, including homicide, robbery, community crime, and vice. They didn't have a room large enough for them all to meet, so Sully had them gather in the bullpen on the third floor and stand around for the three minutes it would take. Sullivan was a short, stocky man who was as solid as a fireplug. He had a bulbous nose and Irish features including hair that had once been red. His complexion matched, and he tended to get even redder in his cheeks when he got angry. He was fiercely loyal to his cops, but also expected the best from them and let them know about it when they disappointed him.

Mike sat at his desk. Jason perched on the edge of the wooden frame, his pressed slacks hanging in space. Jason's crisp shirt and perfectly tied necktie stood out compared to the slovenly appearance of most detectives in the precinct. His muscular physique emphasized his slick clothes. He was always the best-dressed cop in the room. They had been discussing the wrap-up of their latest case and Jason didn't want to interrupt the flow by moving back to his own desk. At the appointed time, Sully marched out of his office with a yellow folder in his left hand.

"Listen up! Our good friends at the FBI need some help tracking down the people in a photo and their location. They give us some support – sometimes – so the Commissioner says we're going to help. I got copies of the photo here. There's one for each team and each one is marked DO NOT COPY. I'm told that if one of these photos shows up on the internet, there's some kind of micro code or meta whatsit in each shot to let the feds trace it back to who owned it and leaked it and there will be hell to pay. Each photo has the lead detective's name on it. Treat it like the Mona Lisa, and when we're done, you have to turn 'em back in. If you lose your copy, the feds will apparently cut your balls off – or something like that."

Mike couldn't hold himself back. "Sully, what's so super-secret about this picture?"

Sully glared at his most senior detective as if he had taken a dump on the bullpen floor. "We're not supposed to ask that question, Stoneman. Just take it on faith."

"So, what's in it?" Mike leaned back in his chair, happy to tweak the Captain rather than sit quietly waiting to receive his copy of the holy grail.

"It's a shot of three women, all dolled up like showgirls or Carnivale dancers or something. The feds can't get a facial recognition ID on them. They're with some guy whose face is blurred out. Don't worry about who he is. They only want to identify the girls or the room."

"So, the super-secret is who the dude is," Jason chimed in.

"No shit, Sherlock." Sully shot a disapproving look in Jason's direction. "Don't try to guess. Just try to chase down any venue in the city where this could have been taken. Each team has an assignment written on the back of the photo. See if any of your contacts can ID any of the women. We're supposed to do this ASAP, without letting anybody copy the photo. So, show it around over the next couple days. See if you get any hits. Then bring it back and turn it in. If you come up empty by the end of the day Monday, then you're done. That's it. Happy freaking New Year. Any questions?"

Nobody spoke. Sully walked around the room, handing out copies of the photos to the detectives based on whose name was on which copy. This took much longer than handing out an unmarked copy to everyone, but he eventually got around to Mike and Jason.

Mike looked at his captain with raised eyebrows. "Any restrictions on who we can show the pic to?"

"No. Just don't let it out of your sight." Sully stalked away toward his office, leaving his detectives to their work.

Chapter 5 — Striking Out

Monday, December 30
New York, NY

O N THE MONDAY OF NEW YEAR'S WEEK, Mike and Jason stood at the door of Captain Sullivan's office a few minutes before five o'clock. Sully motioned them inside.

"Turning in our top-secret photo, Captain." Mike snapped off the statement like a soldier.

"Can it, Stoneman! I'm not in the mood." Sully glared up from his chair. "I take it you whiffed on the ID like everybody else?"

Jason jumped in before Mike had a chance to make a snarky comment. "Yes, Sir. We showed it around everywhere it seemed likely to get a sniff, but nobody recognized any of the women or the venue."

"So, nothing for our Fibbie friends?"

Jason hesitated for a moment, then said, "One person said the room might be in Vegas, but she couldn't be sure."

"Great," Sully said sarcastically. "I'll make a note of it. I'm sure we've got counterparts out there looking at this, too, so they'll have a better shot than us."

Jason held up the picture as if examining it for the first time. "It would help if the faces were a little clearer."

"I'll express your criticism of the photographer to our friends in the Federal Building," Sully snapped, snatching the document and stuffed it into a yellow folder.

Mike said, "You know, Sully, the two Black girls in the picture aren't really girls. You knew that, right?"

"Yeah. I heard the same from a couple other teams. Did it help anybody ID them?" Sully glared, challenging one of them to answer. "I didn't think so. Don't worry about it. You did what you could do. It's not your problem anymore."

Mike's face grew a mischievous smile. "If you'd like us to be on the clock next week when we're in Vegas, we can put in some time asking around."

"Get out!" Sully shouted. Mike noticed the Captain fighting to suppress a grin.

Mike and Jason left and walked to Mike's desk, which was uncharacteristically organized. "How long did it take you to clean that garbage heap?" Jason asked playfully.

"It's easy when you pour it all in the trash. For a change, it's been a quiet holiday season."

"I'm looking forward to the time off," Jason said as he walked back to his desk.

"Yeah," Mike agreed. "Should be quite a trip. Rachel's gonna look great in the dress."

Jason snapped his head around and glared at Mike, before realizing he hadn't said *wedding* dress. The fact that Jason and Rachel were planning to get married while on their trip to Las Vegas was not common knowledge around the precinct. He was not embarrassed about it, but Rachel wanted it to be a secret, since she wasn't telling her parents until they got back. It wasn't like any of the cops were going to spill the beans to Rachel's mom and dad, but Jason had promised to keep it to himself.

"Do your parents know you're taking the trip to Vegas?" Mike asked innocently.

"No. It's not a big deal."

Mike considered asking a follow-up question, but Jason never wanted to talk about his family, even when he and Mike were alone in a car on a stakeout for hours at a time. It wasn't exactly a sore subject; it was no subject at all.

Steve Berkowitz strolled up as Mike was locking his bottom desk drawer, where he kept his personal items and confidential files. Berkowitz perched on the edge of the desk and asked in his heavy Brooklyn accent, "You gonna bring back a pile of poker winnings from Vegas, Mike?"

Mike chuckled. "It's always a possibility, but I'm not going to play cards. Michelle has a full schedule of shows and dinners lined up for us, and even a trip to the Hoover Dam, if you can believe that. This isn't a boys' trip to Vegas, it's a romantic vacation getaway."

"Yeah, sure," Berkowitz chuckled. "I'm sure you'll find a few minutes to sneak away to the casino. At your age, you can't spend the whole trip in bed, right?"

"Hey! Who are you calling old?"

"I know if it were me and the wife, there'd be twenty minutes of second honeymoon, and then a long nap."

Everyone within earshot laughed heartily. Berkowitz was a year older than Mike and he and his wife had been married 30 years, so jibes about his sex life were commonplace – mostly from his own mouth.

Mike decided to continue the theme. "Michelle and I are planning to spend some time with Jason and his fiancée, Rachel – but you know these young people. They may never come out of their suite."

"Suite?" asked George Mason, who had walked up to the

group. George was another homicide detective and Berkowitz's partner. "Seems like Detective Dickson is always in a suite on these trips, eh?" George was referring to the junior suite Jason and Rachel had occupied on their Bermuda cruise the summer before – the one that ended with a bullet in Jason's arm.

"It's not a big deal," Mike defended his partner. "At this hotel, every room is a suite."

"Where are you staying?"

"At the new Mardi Gras hotel." Mike couldn't help but smile as he said it. The Mardi Gras was the newest place on the Strip. Early January, it turned out, was a good time to get a room there, and Mike was looking forward to checking it out. "And speaking of that, it's about time for us to get the hell out of here before somebody brings in a new stiff. Steve, you and George have all the bodies for the next week or so."

Berkowitz and Mason both waved their hands dismissively as Mike packed up his things, grabbed his overcoat, and headed toward the door, with Jason right next to him. As Mike disappeared down the stairs, he called back over his shoulder good-naturedly, "Happy New Year, suckers!"

Chapter 6 — Oceans One Hundred

Monday, December 30
Las Vegas, NV

RICK "THE NECK" GARETTI SAT on a well-padded chair in front of a Little Mermaid-themed slot machine. The chair was bolted to the floor, but it swiveled enough for him to push the button that sent the electronic wheels spinning while still keeping an inconspicuous eye on the package. He was dressed to blend in with the degenerate slot players on the floor of the Mardi Gras casino. A black baseball cap with a Golden Knights logo hid most of his face from the overhead cameras. Blue jeans, a black t-shirt, and a motorcycle jacket made him an imposing presence, even sitting down. A cigarette smoldered in an ashtray to his left, which tended to drive away any player who might otherwise be interested in sitting in the next seat. During the week between Christmas and New Year's, the newest casino on the Strip was busy. If anyone had been watching, they would have seen Rick was playing the minimum each spin. He was in no hurry.

Rick's neck was exceptionally long and thin, hence the nickname he picked up as a teenager in Newark. Except for that anomaly, Garetti was otherwise fairly normal-looking for a big guy. His face was on the narrow side. His nose was slightly bent, having been broken twice. His lips were full, almost feminine. His dark eyes were like two onyx stones. He wore his black hair, with slivers of gray, slicked back.

Rick had met Freddy Costanzo when they were both growing up in New Jersey. When Rick graduated from high school, Freddy hooked him up with the organization where Freddy was pulling in a handsome income that was not subject to taxes. Years later, Rick followed Freddy to Kansas City, then to Las Vegas, which they both viewed as the land of opportunity. He had been Freddy's most trusted lieutenant for thirty years, and he enjoyed the role. Tonight was just another day at the office.

When the call came in from the blackmailer, Freddy was pissed. Rick was surprised anyone would be stupid enough to try to shake down Freddy Costanzo. The one-hundred-thousand-dollar demand was pretty reasonable, Rick thought, considering the circumstances. It showed that the blackmailer wasn't a complete lightweight. Just stupid. He claimed to have evidence linking Freddy to the murder of Senator Harlan Bushfield and said he would turn it over to the feds unless Freddy paid up. He didn't say exactly what the evidence was, which made Rick doubt it existed. Freddy was there that night. Rick had warned him to stay away, but the guy who owed Freddy a favor introduced him personally to the Senator. There was no way to get Bushfield to the venue unless Freddy went with him. It had been Rick's job to make sure nobody saw them together. He thought he had done his job well. Now it seemed there might have been some imperfection in the plan. Or the execution. He was slipping, and it was making him cranky.

Rick would have demanded more money. If the guy really had Freddy over a barrel, he was leaving money on the table. Of course, Rick also would have had the money wired to an offshore bank account. This shithead wanted a live money drop at the Mardi Gras casino. Rick was looking forward to explaining to the idiot what a bad idea it was to still be in Las Vegas, where Rick and his boys could put a hurting on him. If he was that stupid, he deserved what he got.

The package was a tall cocktail glass sitting on a large circular tray, which in turn was resting on a folding stand against the wall next to a support pillar. The glass was wrapped in a wet white napkin, obscuring its contents, and had another napkin stuffed into its mouth. Under the napkins, it was filled with twenty purple-and-gold casino chips, each with a face value of $5,000. Rick had deposited the glass on the tray, as directed, as soon as the cocktail waitress had swapped out an empty tray for one piled high with discarded dishes and garbage.

Rick had thought about putting hundred-dollar chips in the glass instead, but he didn't want his shithead blackmailer to see that he had not followed the instructions and bolt without trying to pick up the money. Freddy would be pissed if Rick didn't bring back the hundred grand, but he'd be more pissed if he didn't bring back this guy's balls in a bag. Letting him live as a constant threat to turn over whatever information or evidence he actually had to the feds, and use it for future extortion, was not an option.

Rick turned his head and made eye contact in sequence with each of his three companions. They had the drop location surrounded. It was go time, so they all needed to be on high alert. Ten minutes later, the tray was nearly filled with discarded glasses, dirty ashtrays, and soiled plates. The same cocktail waitress who had made the last tray exchange rounded the corner carrying a fresh brown disk. She was a tall Black woman with wide hips and a large upper body, but long, slim legs. She wore the standard Mardi Gras waitress outfit: a sequined leotard, a black patent-leather belt, and brightly colored feathers sticking up from the back of the costume, along with one curving up from the top of a tiara perched on her mound of black hair. The front of the outfit clung to her substantial chest. She easily hefted the full tray onto one hand while placing the fresh tray on the stand. Then she hurried off toward the kitchen.

The four men had no idea whether the waitress knew that the package was on her tray. She might have been performing her standard duties and would drop off the tray in the service area, where someone else would grab the glass. Or, she might be fully aware and pass off the package to an accomplice. Or, she might be their target. Anything was possible.

One of Rick's men, Eddie Alonzo, followed close behind the waitress. Eddie was younger than Rick and was paying his dues in the organization. He had the physique of a linebacker; tall with broad shoulders and substantial heft. Bobby was covering the far wall, preventing any dash toward an exit. Bobby was older and heavy. He looked like a cab driver who had spent twenty years on his ass. He wasn't going to run down anybody in a foot race, but he could block a door with the best of them. The last member of the team was a full-blooded Navajo everyone called Scout. He was tall, with a wispy beard and thin, boney shoulders, and always wore a western bolo tie around his neck. Scout was stationed next to the swinging doors that separated the gambling floor from the service area. They figured the private service bay was the most likely place for somebody to take the package, and Scout was the fastest and most agile of the group.

Rick trailed behind, watching for anyone who might swoop in and remove their napkin-wrapped glass from the tray. The waitress made a beeline for the swinging doors. When she turned backwards and used her ass to push through, Scout hustled toward the door. They were not going to let the "employees only" sign prevent them from following the hundred grand.

"Go!" Rick shouted, not worrying about who might hear.

Scout reached the door less than two seconds after the waitress, but had to stop cold when the doors swung open from the inside and a tall Black man wearing a white apron and a white chef's hat came through, carrying a huge cake on a wooden board. By the time the wedding cake cleared the doorway, another five seconds had elapsed.

"Get around to the kitchen exit on the other side of the casino floor," Rick barked at Bobby. He already had Louis watching that door, but he didn't want to take any chances. Nobody was getting out of the service bay without his guys knowing it. They had carefully cased the area before the drop and confirmed that those two doors were the only ways in or out.

Rick rushed forward through the service area door seconds behind Scout, scanning for their waitress. She was nowhere in sight. The tray she had been carrying was sitting on a steel counter. The napkin-wrapped glass was on its side. Empty. Rick waved to Scout to go left, while he ran to the right. They pushed past several annoyed staff members. One blonde waitress scolded Rick for being in a non-public area. He ignored her and rushed forward, scanning for their waitress, but she was nowhere. After patrolling the entire interior space, Rick attempted to enter the ladies' room, where he was met by a very angry middle-aged woman in a waitress costume who pushed him back and berated him, drawing a crowd. He backed off and re-grouped with Scout.

Eddie was standing by the swinging doors on the inside. He held up his hands to indicate that the waitress had not come back out his way. They figured whoever snatched the chips would probably hand them off to somebody else. It would be impossible to search every person coming in and out of the service area, and those chips could be hidden easily. But Rick figured he could still follow the Black waitress. When she left the safety of the casino's security system, they would grab her and convince her to spill the chips, or the information about what happened to them. Rick and Scout were known to be very persuasive in such circumstances.

A Hispanic man in a white apron, wielding a meat cleaver, confronted Rick, Scout, and Eddie. "Get out of here or I'll call security!" He seemed to mean business. They calmly stepped back out through the swinging doors. Rick left Scout and Eddie there while he joined their comrades, who confirmed that the woman had not emerged through the alternate door.

"She's probably in the ladies' room," Rick said.

"Sure, but she probably already handed off the chips," Bobby pointed out.

"Yeah, sure. But when she comes out, we'll find out who she gave 'em to."

They waited, covering both doors, but their waitress did not come through either. The chef who had brought out the wedding cake made another trip toward the hotel's ballroom, carrying another huge castle of frosting and frills. Waitresses came and went, except for their target. After an hour, Rick figured the woman was hiding out inside, although he wondered why the service supervisor had not yet scolded her for her dalliance. Maybe she was feigning illness. He left his men to watch the doors, while he walked around the perimeter, scanning for any other possible escape route for the waitress. Rick kicked himself for not getting a photo of her. He still expected his guys to spot her eventually. Another hour later, they were still waiting. The chef who had waved his meat cleaver at Rick came out from the kitchen and saw the guys who had invaded his domain. He walked to the nearest casino security guard and pointed out the men loitering around the service area. The guard chased Rick and his crew away. They split up and circled back to the area around the service area through different casino entrances. Two hours later, without any sign of the waitress, who could easily have slipped out while they were absent, Rick told his crew to call it a night.

Rick did not relish the upcoming report to the boss that they had lost the $100,000. He was looking forward even less to explaining how they let the blackmailer get away.

Chapter 7 — Hit List

Monday, December 30
Las Vegas, NV

FREDDY COSTANZO WAS NOT ACCUSTOMED to being shaken down. He had been looking forward to Rick's report about how the shithead begged for his life while Scout pulled his fingernails off. If the blackmailer did have evidence linking Freddy to the Senator, he could bring a volcano's worth of heat down on Freddy and his operation. Of course, it was Freddy who had created the problem in the first place by setting up the Senator for those compromising pictures. He still couldn't figure out who this guy was, or what he actually had for the feds. Whatever he had, Freddy had been confident that Rick and Scout would extract the information – before the shithead died. Now, he was dealing with disappointment. It wasn't his best self.

Freddy's last name at birth was not Costanzo; it was Costanslov. He had decided as a teen that being Italian in New Jersey was a more likely road to financial opportunity than being Russian. *The Godfather* had idealized the Italian Mafia, and Freddy wanted in. His parents were both dead, so he legally changed his name to Frederico Enrico Costanzo as soon as he turned eighteen. He studied Italian, which he spoke fluently and without a hint of a Russian accent. But he couldn't entirely fake his way around his actual family history in Jersey. So, he took the money he had saved, and six one-carat diamonds he borrowed from a safe to which he had acquired the combination, and moved to Kansas City. After a successful run there for several years, he moved on to Las Vegas at the behest of a boss there who needed some East Coast experience.

Twenty years later, Freddy was in his late 50s and looked worse for the wear. His once-thick black hair had turned starkly white. Rather than color it, he embraced the silver fox look, which made him stand out in a city where outrageous costumes made normal an anachronism. Freddy was less accepting about the spots on his skin, which had been baked in the Vegas sun for two decades; he went for regular dermatology appointments to dim the dark splotches. He usually wore slick clothes, even though his short frame didn't show them off well. But when you had money in Las Vegas, the girls didn't seem to mind if you had a few extra pounds around the waistline. Everybody in town knew who Freddy Costanzo was. He enjoyed being recognized and respected. People knew to avoid crossing him.

Freddy was sitting in a plush chair in his expansive 40th floor apartment/office at the Palms Place tower. The space was technically a condominium, but building management didn't mind Freddy using it as office space as well as for parties. The picture windows looking out toward the Strip exposed the galaxy of lights coming from the Earth, obliterating most of the stars in the heavens. It was almost midnight. The Nevada desert was in the midst of a nearly unprecedented cold spell, with nighttime temperatures hovering in the mid-30s. Rick Garetti was sweating on the sofa opposite the boss.

"Ricky, you know I trust you forever," Freddy said in the Italian-Jersey accent he had cultivated over the years. "How the fuck did you let this asshole walk away – and with my hundred grand? You said you had it covered."

"I thought so, too, Boss. I'm as pissed off as you."

"You will be when I take fifty Gs from your draw next month," Freddy said calmly. "You need to have some skin in the game, I think."

Rick fumed internally, but knew better than to show any disrespect. He inclined his head. "I understand. When I get my hands on this guy, he's going to pay us both back. Then he'll regret his poor decision."

"I expect nothing less. How do you plan to find him?"

Rick squirmed. He had no clue. He wasn't a cop or a private investigator. He could hire a PI, but he couldn't share why they needed to find the guy, or what the circumstances were, or who else was involved. That wasn't going to work. Maybe they needed to get a PI on the payroll.

The first call had come in one week earlier from someone using a voice distortion tool that sounded like it had been purchased from Toys R Us. Rick assumed the caller was a man, but couldn't be sure. It made sense that he called Rick's cell, since his number was generally available on the street. As Freddy Costanzo's right-hand man and chief fixer, people had to be able to contact him. Rick had no way to trace a phone call, and if the shithead had an ounce of sense, he would have used a burner. The guy had brass balls to threaten Freddy. Or maybe he was crazy.

The second call wasn't a call, but a text message to Rick's phone. It gave him a date and time and told him to go to the Mardi Gras and buy $100,000 in chips, then call the phone back. When he called, the same electronically modified voice gave the instructions about the money drop. Rick hadn't given the blackmailer much credit for the plan, which seemed simplistic and like it would allow Rick and his team to easily catch him, take back their casino chips, and then work him over until he spilled his information before they killed him – slowly. Now, Rick was eating crow for being overconfident.

He did have one angle to play. "The dude has to be working with one of the girls. There was nobody else there when we took the pictures, except you and me. Unless he had a hidden camera in the room, which I can't figure, it has to be one of the bitches."

"You're probably right." The boss got up from his chair and wandered to the window to watch the lights of the Strip. "Nobody knew we were going to be there." Rick noted the way Freddy avoided using Senator Bushfield's name – in case somebody was listening. Freddy had his apartment swept for electronic surveillance twice a week, but he was still careful, most of the time.

"If he had a photo of you with the mark, he would have sent it to me to prove his threat level. As it is, he probably only has information, which means either he was somewhere in . . . the establishment at the time, or he's working with somebody who was there, so it had to be one of the girls."

Freddy paced in front of the windows. "If I thought for a minute he would have gotten away from you, I wouldn't have given him any cash. I'd have called his bluff."

"He did know the name of our guy, and he knew about the photo session," Rick said quietly.

"Yeah. He did. Even if somebody saw me and the mark together going inside, that means nothing. So, I think you're right that it had to be one of the bitches. They were with him and might have recognized him – or more likely seen his mug on the news and put it together recently. That's how I figure it. One of them is working with this guy."

"In that case, I think we should talk to them and find out who they talked to about that gig."

Freddy raised an eyebrow as he turned back toward his long-time confidant. "Do you think you can handle it? Or should I bring in somebody else to clean up your mess?"

Rick sat up straight and flashed a defiantly confident smile. "I can handle it. I'll have Eddie help me talk to them and see what they know."

"Eddie?"

"Yeah. He's hot to trot. He wants to prove his worth and earn some credibility. He's smart enough, and I'll give him directions. If he does good, then fine. If he fucks up, then I'll bust him down a little, which is also fine. He's an arrogant asshole. He thinks his father's connections mean he's untouchable."

"I thought you said he was smart?"

Rick laughed. "Yeah, I know. He's smart about some things. He doesn't quite understand that his old man isn't that connected."

"Fine. It's your call. Use Eddie if you want to. Just make sure you get what you need."

"I will. And if I don't, then I'll make sure they never get another gig." Rick stood and buttoned his suit jacket. He never wore a necktie, but he liked to wear suits and nice shirts. "Leave it to me, Freddy. I'll find out who this shithead is. One of those girls will give him up."

"Don't leave any loose ends."

Rick nodded and headed for the door.

Chapter 8 — Regrets and Reservations

Tuesday, December 31
New York, NY

AT A LITTLE CHINESE RESTAURANT on 21st Street, not far from Michelle's apartment, the two couples met for a New Year's Eve dinner. With the big trip to Las Vegas coming up, neither Mike and Michelle nor Jason and Rachel wanted elaborate plans for the last day of 2019. While most restaurants in the city were decked out for revelers, the little hole-in-the-wall Szechuan place was mostly empty. They liked it that way and took their time with the informal meal.

As he held half a steamed dumpling inches from his mouth at the end of two chopsticks, Mike gestured with his other hand toward Jason. "A year ago, I was barely out of the shoulder brace and couldn't lift my arm over my head. What a year."

Jason lifted his Mai Tai glass and held it up toward Mike. "It certainly was. Michelle introduced me to this wonderful woman," he nodded toward Rachel, who was sitting on his right, "and less than a year later, we're off to Vegas to get married. Man, there's no way I would have predicted that a year ago. But I'm glad it happened." He clinked his glass against Rachel's and took a small sip.

"It's amazing that a man as smart as Jason is so easily manipulated," Rachel said, trying to keep a straight face but quickly devolving into laughter as she leaned against Jason's shoulder.

The men had dressed more casually than the ladies. Both had slacks, jackets, and no neckties. Rachel chose a silver sequined top above a black leather skirt and three-inch heels. She had her hair up in a braided knot, which showed off her slender neck and the emerald earrings dripping from her lobes. She had taken to green jewelry to match the emerald engagement ring Jason had presented to her in June. Michelle chose a gold top, complementing Rachel's silver in what was definitely no coincidence. Her slender, bare legs peeked out through the slit in a long black velvet skirt. Her short hair was practical for performing autopsies at the morgue, but it didn't lend itself to much in the way of fancy styling, so she had pinned it back and donned a sparkling tiara bearing "2020" in three-inch tall numbers. It had cost all of five dollars from a street vendor, but it lent the proper playful spirit to the evening.

Michelle took up the serial toast by standing and raising up her wine glass. She was the shortest member of the group and enjoyed being the only one standing. Her dark eyes sparkled. "Well, I for one am thrilled things have worked out so well. When I invited Rachel to come along to the Billy Joel concert last February, I thought she and Jason would be great together, and it's wonderful that it worked out." She nodded at her friend. "And it's a relief that I didn't ruin your life by setting you up with someone who might have broken your heart."

"I generally hate being set up," Jason said, "but in this case, I'm glad you decided to play matchmaker."

"I only regret that you two won't get the June wedding you

wanted, Honey." Michelle reached across the table to touch Rachel's bare arm.

"It's for a good cause," Rachel replied, patting her still-flat tummy. "I'm just glad I'll be able to wear the dress." She giggled momentarily and held up her champagne glass, filled with ginger ale.

"I'm sure Jason's not sorry to miss the big wedding party." Mike had finished chewing his dumpling and washed it down with a Chinese beer.

"Oh, we're still having the party," Rachel responded with a big smile. "Our families and friends will get the wedding party in June – just not the wedding. It would have been wonderful to have the ceremony in the summer. I'm really sorry Jay won't be able to have his parents there."

"It's fine, Sweetheart. It's worse that you won't have your parents. The father of the bride may be a little unhappy when he finds out he didn't get to walk his baby girl down the aisle."

"It's not too late to invite him and Olivia to come along," Mike suggested.

"No, Mike," Rachel cut in. "We talked about it. As soon as we start inviting anyone, then everybody else who didn't get invited feels slighted. Plus the logistics of getting people there on short notice. My sister can't fly because she's eight months pregnant, and my mom would want to be here for her in case she goes into labor. It's best to keep it to the four of us. Everybody will get to celebrate with us later."

Michelle put down her chopsticks and slid her right arm around Mike's left elbow, giving him a squeeze. "I'm glad we were able to work it out to come with you. I've always had a fantasy about flying off on the spur of the moment to elope. It's so romantic."

"It's not like we weren't already engaged." Rachel held out

her left hand, showing off her ring.

"I know. But it's still romantic and exciting. It's a small miracle we were able to get a room at the Mardi Gras. I just wish we could all travel together. Mike, can't you blow off your training class Friday so we can fly out with them?" Her pleading was accompanied by leaning her head against Mike's arm, looking up, and batting her eyelashes.

Mike laughed and squeezed her arm with his. "Hey, I took the week off, plus the Monday after, and I'm happy to get you to Vegas for a little while, but I'm not missing my class. They have the detectives' exam in two weeks. I'm not walking out on them."

When Michelle withdrew her arm and returned to her plate, Mike wondered for a minute whether she was genuinely upset that he didn't drop all his responsibilities at her request. He relaxed when she said, "Well, if we're not going out on Friday with Rachel and Jason, then you have to agree to take me to the show on Saturday night at the hotel theater. Agreed?"

Mike looked at Michelle's face and considered that Jason and Rachel were watching. "Sure," he said, although he had no clue what he was agreeing to. "Whatever you want is fine with me. If it's in Vegas, I'm sure it'll be great."

"Good!" Michelle said, looking at Rachel. "That will be a wonderful way to start the trip on the first night."

"I hope so," Rachel said hesitantly.

Michelle made eye contact with Rachel and held it as she said, "Rachel, can you tell us anything about the show?"

Rachel shook her head. "I think it's best if it's a surprise, for now."

Before Michelle could respond, Mike asked, "What are the logistics for the wedding?" He turned to his partner for the answer, but Jason shrugged and turned to Rachel, who launched happily into an explanation about the plans she and Michelle had made for the ceremony. The Mardi Gras hotel had its own wedding chapel, where they were booked on Sunday afternoon. Then they had reservations for dinner at the top of the Stratosphere, followed by a limo ride up and down the Strip. It was a night designed to make Rachel happy. Jason was glad to elope without fanfare, avoid giving input, and agree to do whatever Rachel wanted.

"Great," Mike said when Rachel was finished. "Sounds like you have it all worked out. Just tell me where to be and when and I'll be there."

"You'd better be," Michelle chided, playfully slapping Mike's arm. "I'm certainly not going alone – plus they need two witnesses."

When the happy group finally finished their leisurely dinner, they all walked back to Michelle's apartment. When the ball dropped in Times Square, marking the end of the teens and the beginning of the new decade, they all shouted, "Happy New Year!" It had indeed been an eventful year. Nobody talked about Jason losing a partner and Mike losing an ex-partner. This was a night to celebrate.

When Rachel and Jason said their good-byes and headed to Jason's apartment, Michelle turned off the television and instructed her home assistant unit to play some John Coltrane, Mike's favorite jazz. Mike sat on the sofa; his jacket tossed onto the back of a bar stool next to the kitchen pass-through. Michelle swayed to the music, thrusting her hips from side to side. Then she slowly pulled down the zipper on her skirt and allowed it to fall gracefully to the hardwood floor, while Mike sat up and made his lap easily available.

Chapter 9 — Chasing Tails

Thursday, January 2, 2020
Rapid City, SD

AGENT DEREK DUMM STARED at his computer screen, then rubbed his eyes and looked away. There were seventy-six reports in the folder titled "HB." Each of the FBI's fifty-six field offices had sent one in, along with one each from twenty municipal police forces to which they had sent copies of the photo. Derek had hoped the local expertise would drum up some leads. Instead, they had seventy-six swings and misses.

Derek called to Chelsea, sitting at her desk across the open room. "Shields! Did you get the report from the locals in Vegas?"

"Yeah, I think it came in yesterday. They said they got nothing."

"Damn! I was hoping it was Vegas." Derek slapped his open palm on his desktop, causing a container of paperclips to jingle.

"It still could be," Chelsea replied brightly, ever the optimist. "Just because they didn't ID any of them right away doesn't mean the location isn't in Las Vegas."

"Sure, it could be. Or it could be New Orleans or New York or ten other places."

Chelsea rose from her chair and sauntered over to Derek's desk. "I've been looking through the summary of Senator Bushfield's votes."

"We already got that from the D.C. boys." Derek didn't try to hide his annoyance at the prospect of covering the same ground again. Chelsea tended to speculate and spin out wild theories that only left them with dozens of improbable lines of investigation. Derek didn't like chasing down low-return leads. He lacked Chelsea's seemingly boundless energy. Nineteen and a half years with the Bureau will do that to an agent.

"I'm not talking about that. I looked at his committee votes. He's on three committees, so there's a ton of bills over the past year."

"So, why are you grinning like you solved the Lindberg baby kidnapping?"

Chelsea pulled a sheet of printer paper from behind her back and handed it to her senior partner. She pointed to the middle of the page, where some material was underlined. "Those two votes are the only ones where Bushfield changing his vote to 'yes' would have moved them out of committee. So, maybe one of those bills is the one whoever was pressuring him was interested in."

Derek scanned the paper. "You're making an assumption. Maybe the key vote was one where he voted yes, but our bad guys wanted a no."

Chelsea's gleeful expression faded instantly. "I guess I hadn't thought of that. I'll go back and look for more close votes." She reached to retrieve the sheet.

"Do that," Derek said, pulling the page back from Chelsea's hand. "But, it's possible you're right in your assumption. It's creative thinking, Shields. Have you researched these two bills?"

"Yes, I have." Her enthusiasm returned, a bit more muted. "One was a farm aid bill that would have removed a tariff cap on imported soy beans."

"Sounds pretty dull. Who would have benefited if he had voted the other way?"

"Mainly Chinese farmers and agricultural importers."

"So, the Chinese government? Setting him up in a compromising photo doesn't seem like the way the Chinese would try to pressure a senator."

"I agree. But the other bill was to push up a national authorization for sports gambling."

Derek raised an eyebrow and tilted his head. "Well, that's interesting. The bill died in committee, huh?"

"Yep."

"I can think of a few bad actors who would be in favor of more legal sports betting. Like a few guys under observation by the RICO squad. We still have a task force working on the NFL point-shaving operation, right?"

Chelsea shrugged. She hadn't been around long enough to be clued in to all the national investigations the way Derek was. Since there was no NFL team anywhere near South Dakota, manipulating the score of pro football games wasn't high on the local radar.

"Well, trust me, it was a big thing six months ago. We assume the mob guys in Vegas were involved."

"The Senator took a trip to Nevada last year."

"Yeah. I remember. He went a lot of places. This doesn't exactly provide probable cause for a search warrant."

"No." Chelsea snatched the sheet away from Derek, much to his annoyance. "But it does give me enough to push back on our guys in Las Vegas and see if they can come up with something."

"Fine. Do that." Derek sat back in his chair with a sigh. "Dumm?"

"What?"

"Maybe I don't get it, but it still seems strange. Whoever did this threatened him with the exposure of that photo, but then when he didn't comply, they didn't release the picture. They killed him instead. Why?"

"If you assume these guys are an organized operation, then Bushfield probably isn't the only person they're shaking down. Maybe they're twisting arms and making threats at the state or even local level. They could have published the photo and embarrassed the guy, but that doesn't get them the vote they wanted, and it doesn't send a message to anybody else about the consequences of non-compliance. They whacked him and dumped his body in a very findable place to make sure everyone knew about it. They're sending a message. I'm guessing it was received loud and clear."

Chelsea nodded slowly. "I hope we can find those showgirls. They might be able to place somebody involved at the scene. Somebody had to take that photo, right? If I were setting up a senator for extortion, I wouldn't trust a freelance photographer to take the picture."

"You're right, Shields. If the people blackmailing the Senator knew we had a copy of that photo, then these girls would be loose ends."

"They're also potential witnesses."

Derek pursed his lips. "Sure, if we can find them."

Chapter 10 — Dressed to Kill

Thursday, January 2
Las Vegas, NV

CRICKET WAS FIVE HOURS and fifty-five minutes into her six-hour shift at the Circus casino. Her feet were sore, and the muscles around her mouth were aching from forcing herself to smile all night. She gripped the silver pole in the center of the small, circular stage and leaned down, stretching her shoulder muscles, which felt good. She leaned back, arching her spine and neck until her long strawberry-blonde hair dragged against the black stage surface. In her inverted position, she made eye contact with a middle-aged man sitting at the blackjack table a few feet away. She raised an eyebrow suggestively as the man focused on the portions of her breasts that bulged from the tight fabric of her costume. She twisted to the side and spun herself up into a squatting position with all her weight on the balls of her feet inside her extremely high heels. She winced, then lowered herself down to the floor.

There were six blackjack tables arranged around the little stage in the center of the casino floor. Her job was to keep the gamblers' attention on her gyrating hips and her mostly exposed legs, ass, and breasts. The more they focused at her, the less they concentrated on their cards. That's what the casino bosses wanted. The "BJ Stage," as it was known, was one of the more sought-after assignments among the dancers because the patrons were close enough to toss them chips as tips, and there was a walkway where players could come up close to stuff a bill into their G-strings. They weren't allowed to actually strip inside the casino, even though nobody within eyesight was supposed to be under 21. But, while complying with the rules, she exposed as much skin as humanly possible. As tired as she was, at least her bejeweled handbag lying at the edge of the steps to the stage was bulging with accumulated tips.

Holidays in Las Vegas brought out crowds, and the day after New Year's was definitely still holiday season when it fell on a Thursday. At five minutes to three o'clock in the morning, there were only a few open seats at the nearby tables. As "All Night Long," faded out on the speakers above the stage, Cricket glanced toward the door marked "cast only" across the room. Gary Ottavino, the floor manager, stood watching the expansive space. He saw her and inclined his head toward the exit from the stage: the signal that Cricket could call it a night. She broke into her first genuine smile of the night. After gathering up the tips scattered around the base of her pole, she strutted away with exaggerated hip turns, causing her ass cheeks to squeeze together. Gary watched her approach, then patted her butt as she walked through the door.

When she had left Sequim, Washington two years earlier as Sheila Buchanan, she thought by now she would have arrived in Hollywood and been starring in a big-budget movie, or at least a Netflix miniseries. Instead, her girlfriend, Heather, who had volunteered to share an apartment, had hooked her up as a dancer in a high-end Vegas strip club. She had adopted the name Cricket Linderman, who was a real person back home whom she admired. Plus, it was a spectacular name. She and Heather worked together and made good money, although getting naked and grinding up on overweight, middle-aged men for profit was not the glamourous life she had envisioned when she left home.

When Heather got a call about dancing at Circus Circus, the two of them auditioned. The hotel was trying to compete with the newer, glitzier properties in Las Vegas and wanted the hottest dancers, which was a tall order. They were willing to pay top dollar, and the girls didn't have to strip or give lap dances. Both Heather and Cricket were thrilled to get a paycheck instead of working for tips. Six months into the gig, Cricket had saved up enough money to enroll in spring classes at UNLV. She had given up on the idea of stardom in Hollywood and instead set her sights on a degree in business. A friend had given her a copy of *Financial Feminism: A Woman's Guide to Investing for a Sustainable Future* by Jessica Robinson. While she was gyrating on the stages at the Circus Circus, she was planning her future investment portfolio. She figured a sexy woman who knew how to pole dance could get ahead in the world of high finance if she had a brain to go along with a great ass.

Ten minutes later, a very differently dressed Cricket emerged through the same door, wearing blue jeans and a bulky sweater. Her long hair was pulled into a pony tail. Another dancer, Laura Templeton, walked beside her wearing sweat pants and a denim jacket over an aqua leotard. Cricket laughed at something Laura said as they walked purposefully toward the cashier's window, where they handed over their tip money and the chips their admirers had tossed at them during their shift. This was the dancers' version of "coloring up" – exchanging a pile of singles and a stack of chips for a few crisp hundred-dollar bills and some less-soiled smaller denominations. They both left a dollar for their cashier, stuffed their nightly rolls of cash into their purses, and headed for the parking garage.

At the blackjack table facing the cast door, Eddie Alonzo pushed his chips toward the dealer to be "colored up" to the fewest number of disks as soon as Cricket left the stage. He had remained in his seat, putting down minimum bets while waiting for the dancer to emerge. Tonight, he was dressed in a shiny black silk shirt and black slacks. He looked like many other holiday party-goers, but his choice was also calculated to be difficult to see in a dark space. As he fell into an easy stride behind the two women, Eddie pulled out his cell phone and tapped his text message box, which was pre-filled with the message, "heading toward the garage." Eddie had been pretty sure Cricket would go that direction, since her 2009 Toyota Corolla was parked on the 6th floor of the parking lot in an area reserved for employees. The employee section was far away from the elevators so as not to take desirable spaces away from the guests.

Like most Las Vegas casinos, management offered all employees the option of being escorted to their cars by a security officer. The dancers seldom took advantage of the offer. Cricket and Laura felt safe, partly because of the very visible security cameras in the parking lot and partly because they were together. The security guards had to get clearance from their captain before leaving, which took ten minutes – and they often got handsy. The rumor among the dancers was that, when the guys in the booth knew one of their brothers was escorting a dancer to her car, they arranged for the camera in that area to go down for maintenance. Cricket was happy to take her chances with Laura.

Rick "The Neck" Garetti read Eddie's text message and smiled. He shut his car door on the fifth floor of the parking lot and walked toward the stairwell. He had already squirted super glue into the driver's side door lock of Cricket's car. The old model, without remote entry, was easy to disable. Rick also knew a few tricks that would work on newer cars, but they were more time-consuming and more likely to be caught by the security cameras. He exited the stairs on the sixth floor and quickly walked to the elevator lobby. After scanning the readouts above the six elevator cars, he pushed the call button and waited in front of the car that sprang to life as soon as he summoned a ride. Then he stood in the threshold, in the path of the sensor that kept the doors from closing. He watched the other displays until one lit up to indicate a car moving up from the casino level.

When the doors opposite his position opened to reveal Cricket and Laura, Rick allowed his elevator to close behind him and smiled at the ladies with what he hoped would seem like an inebriated and friendly expression.

The two women gave Rick a surprised and cautious once-over with their eyes and quickly moved toward the doors to the right leading toward their cars. Rick turned in the opposite direction to a different exit. Laura and Cricket, who had gone quiet upon seeing the unfamiliar man in the elevator lobby, resumed chatting as their sneakers padded across the polished concrete floor.

As much as the casino wanted to be an upscale location, putting money into ambiance for the parking garage had not been a priority. Like all such structures, it was barren save for signage designed to look like circus tents, marking area 6A, 6B, and so on. The lighting came from dim fluorescent strips overhead at ten-foot intervals. A faint scent of smoke hung in the unusually chilly air from distant forest fires.

As Rick hustled around the outside of the elevator lobby to follow the women, Eddie emerged from the stairwell in his black outfit, having taken the elevator to 5 and the stairs up from there to avoid being seen. He walked along the wall in the area least illuminated by the overhead lighting, keeping the remaining parked cars between him and the ladies. Rick walked a parallel path on the far side of a row of support pillars.

Laura and Cricket walked hurriedly to Laura's car, eager to escape the near-freezing temperature. Laura tapped her remote control as they approached, causing the interior lights to turn on as the horn gave a weak beep. They exchanged a quick hug before Laura closed the door and engaged the engine. Rick held up his arm for Eddie to see. This was plan A. Plan B called for Eddie to appear to help the ladies with Cricket's car problem if the women arrived at her car first. That contingency was more complicated, but not as much as the scenario where Cricket came up with a security guard.

Laura backed out of her space and drove slowly toward the exit ramp as Cricket approached her Toyota, key in hand. The January air was still. Her bare hand fumbled as she tried to get the key into the lock. "Damn!" she muttered when she dropped the small keyring, which tinkled against the smooth floor.

"Is everything OK there, Miss?" Rick made an effort to keep his voice soft and comforting, still seeming to be tipsy and harmless. He stood next to the front left headlight, careful to keep his back to the security camera on a pillar fifteen feet behind him. He had bribed the security guard already, so he expected the camera to be disabled, but he wasn't taking any chances.

Cricket looked up, immediately on guard. "You're not supposed to be in this area." Cricket kept her head up to monitor the stranger's location while fumbling for her keys. She saw Laura's tail lights disappear around a corner, heading for the down ramp toward the exit. She wished she had asked Laura to wait until she was safely in her car before leaving.

"It looks like you're having a little trouble." Rick took a slow step toward Cricket. Meanwhile, Eddie had been working his way along the wall, unnoticed. Rick smiled and held his hands out to his sides to show he was unarmed and not a threat. Cricket recognized him as the guy from the elevator lobby. He had arrived there at the same time as she and Laura had. But she didn't remember him being with them on the casino level. Of course, he might have gotten into the elevator on the basement shopping plaza level.

"I'm fine," Cricket said nervously, collecting her keys and standing back up. Rick held his ground at a safe distance and watched as she again tried to jam her key into the lock. Again, she fumbled it and it clanged to the floor. "Shit!"

"You sure you don't need some help, there?"

"No. I mean, yes, I'm sure I don't." Cricket was down on one knee now, reaching under the car for her keyring.

"OK, that's fine," Rick said, taking a step back. "How 'bout if I wait here until you get your key to work, then, just to make sure?"

Cricket relaxed a bit, seeing him back off. If he'd wanted to attack her, he would have done it by then. Maybe she did need help, since she seemingly couldn't unlock her damned car. She regained her feet, again holding her keys, and faced Rick. "Thanks. I think I'm good, but I appreciate it." She considered Rick, dressed casually with a nice sport jacket. He had well combed hair and a clean-shaven face. Something about him seemed familiar. She smiled and pivoted toward the car door, her key in her right hand. Rick nodded.

Cricket felt a sudden pressure on the side of her face as an arm circled her neck, pulling her backwards. She tried to scream, but a sweaty hand covered her mouth and muffled the attempt. The arm around her neck, covered with something smooth and soft, was pressing against her windpipe. She lashed out with her key, trying to slash her attacker, but she had no leverage and couldn't get her arm behind her head while she was being strangled.

Cricket lowered her chin and opened her mouth, biting down on her attacker's hand.

"Shit!" Eddie cried out and loosened his grip, pulling his hand away.

Cricket slumped to the cold floor. She looked up at the man who had offered her assistance. He made no move to help her now. As Eddie reached down toward her head, she flattened herself against the ground and rolled under the car. "Help!" she screamed as loudly as her compressed larynx would allow.

Rick scrambled to the ground, knocking his knee on the concrete and tearing his slacks. He swore and grabbed Cricket's leg, securing a grip on the bottom of her jeans and dragging her toward him. Cricket kicked and continued crying out to the empty garage.

The slick floor provided no resistance as Rick pulled Cricket's small body from under the Toyota. Eddie reached down and pulled her up by her sweater collar. She took a breath in anticipation of trying to scream again, but Eddie regained his strangle hold. She kicked backwards, but her sneakers found nothing solid. She couldn't breathe. Her neck hurt. She felt herself being pulled backwards, off her balance.

She fell, but instead of the hard floor, she landed softly on Eddie's lumpy body, which hit the ground first. Eddie still had her in a tight choke hold. She couldn't get in a breath. She kicked and clawed. Her keys again clattered to the floor. The hand left her mouth, but the pressure on her throat barely allowed a trickle of air as she gasped. Then Cricket felt something wet and soft covering her nose and mouth. It smelled acrid and burned her nostrils as she struggled to take in air. Rick stood before her, pressing his hand against her face. She was light-headed. She kept kicking and squirming as she slowly drifted into unconsciousness.

Chapter 11 — A Disappointing Outcome

Friday, January 3
Las Vegas, NV

FROM THE WINDOW OF HIS OFFICE, Freddy Costanzo could see the marquis of the Mardi Gras casino. It was a huge improvement over the ancient dump that had been there for the forty years before the shiny new façade went up. He smiled to himself at the thought that his real estate had become more valuable merely by virtue of somebody else's building plans. The smile faded immediately when he remembered what Rick had said a moment earlier about the dancer, Cricket. He didn't care about her name. He had hoped the only actual woman involved in their set-up job on the old senator might be their snitch. Women were generally more willing to give up information than men. He had no experience dealing with men who dressed in drag. Perhaps they would be pliable also – if necessary.

Freddy turned back from the window toward his silent lieutenant. Rick knew to keep quiet while the boss was thinking. "You're sure she didn't know anything?" Freddy's voice was calm.

"I'm very sure, Boss. Eddie was very persuasive. I can't see much chance that she was protecting somebody."

"Even herself? Even if she was the one calling the shots?"

"I don't think so."

"OK. I hoped maybe we'd get lucky on the first shot. I presume you and Eddie took care of the body?"

"Yeah. We had her car, so we made it look like an accident. She took a lot of damage while we worked on her, but a bad crash can cause that. We got a lot of alcohol in her while she was still conscious, so it should be fine."

"As long as the right team handles the case." Freddy raised an eyebrow and waited for a confirmation.

"Yeah. No problem. That's covered. And the doc will clean up anything that needs it."

"Fine. That's what we pay 'em for." Freddy walked across the room to a glass-topped bar and poured himself a finger of an 18-year-old Highland single malt. "Are you comfortable that you and Eddie are clean on the girl?"

"Yeah. No heat there. My guy on the security team at the Circus is reliable."

"So, what's the next move?"

Rick stood and stretched his back. Neither he nor Freddy were the young guns they had been when they roamed the streets of Newark together. He knew the session was about over and he wanted to get a jump toward the door. "There's a chance that whoever is behind this will get the message, take the hundred Gs they already have, and call it a scam. As much as I was hoping to tear this guy a new asshole, I'll be happy enough to let it go."

"I'm not!" Freddy put his glass down on the bar with a clang. "I think you're probably right that this shithead hasn't got anything on me. If he did, he'd have said what it is. Even if he was there, or has a witness who can put me there with our boy, it's just testimony. We can handle that. I'll come out clean. But I don't want word getting around that you can shake down Freddy Costanzo and get away with it!"

"I agree," Rick quickly pivoted. He knew from long experience that it was best to avoid contrary positions.

"This is your fuck up, Ricky." Freddy struggled to retain his composure. "You're slipping. If you had a picture of that waitress, we'd have a better idea of who we're looking for."

"I know. I'll take the blame for that. But for now, I'd suggest we wait a few days and see what happens. I'll see what I can do about tracking down our money. I've got some resources I can use. We might be able to find him cashing in those Mardi Gras chips. We can be patient. I'll find him."

"I guess we're pretty sure it's a him at this point, eh?" Freddy cocked his head to the side.

"Yeah. I guess so." Rick turned to leave. When Freddy didn't say anything to keep him there, he continued to the door and left.

Freddy tipped back his glass and finished the last drops of the succulent liquid. He had learned to enjoy the finer things in life. He knew time was working against him. There was only so much good scotch and so many young women left for him. Twenty more years would be a stretch. *Smoke 'em if you got 'em*, he thought. He liked his good Cuban cigars, and he appreciated that he could drink the good scotch. His best bottle had cost him more than three thousand dollars, but he'd gladly break it over the head of the bastard who stole his hundred grand, and he'd gladly sacrifice the money to have the guy's head on a platter. However safe he believed himself to be, he still wanted to avoid having the feds crawling around.

Chapter 12 — Foregone Conclusion

Friday, January 3
Las Vegas, NV

DETECTIVE BUZZ RICKENBACKER SAT in a well-worn leather chair behind his corner desk. As the most senior member of the department who didn't have an office, he got his pick of desk locations. He preferred the corner by the window, where he could see the top of the Stratosphere beyond the freeway. A bulky monitor connected to a six-year-old computer tower under the desk hummed softly. The desk and monitor were configured so nobody else in the large open room could see what Buzz was looking at. That was another reason he liked the corner.

"We get anything back from the lab?" Drew Maulgray always announced himself loudly when he approached Rickenbacker's desk. He had learned that Buzz was often engrossed in what he was looking at behind his big-ass monitor, and didn't like being "snuck up on" by anyone, especially his junior partner. Drew was a lanky six feet tall, with freckles, red hair, brown eyes, and soft features. He was thirty-two, but looked much younger. For years, older cops had called him "Opie" after the Ron Howard character from *The*

Andy Griffith Show, which he had never seen. He had hoped that by moving from Memphis to Las Vegas, he'd be able to lose the nickname.

Buzz pushed back from his keyboard and peered around the monitor. "Not yet, Opie. Don't be in such a rush. And don't be looking for something that isn't there." Buzz glared at the younger detective. Given the name Marvin by his parents, Buzz had been glad to adopt a nickname. As a broad-shouldered teen with a rather square head, he had kept his blond hair in a tight crewcut – hence, "Buzzcut Rickenbacker," and then later simply "Buzz." Thirty years later, Buzz was still an athletic six-foot-two and considered himself to still be in peak condition. His now-sandy hair was clipped into a tight fade above his blue eyes. The ladies fell for his former jock looks and cop attitude. He always made sure they knew he had a big gun.

"I'm not looking any harder than what's obvious, Buzz. You saw her – all bruised up around her mouth and eyes. I've seen plenty of girls beaten up. Somebody worked her over good before she got in that car. I'm thinking we need to dig a little here."

Buzz set his thin lips into a straight line of discontent. "It's cute that you're all soft for this girl, but you gotta have a thicker skin, Kid. Strippers like her are a dime a dozen in this town. She got banged up when she drove her car off that overpass. She was probably wasted. Car crashes can beat the shit out of a body. It's a traffic accident, and she's nobody special. Don't get all weepy or you'll never last in this job."

"I'm not weepy. You've got no feelings at all if you don't feel sorry for her – and she wasn't a stripper."

"Maybe not recently, but she used to be. Bet on it."

"Why? Did she grind you up somewhere? Is that how you know?"

Buzz broke into an arrogant smile. "I don't have to pay girls to grind on me, Opie. I happen to know where the Circus got all their dancers from. They were all strippers. They wanted the best to compete with the new hotels. The floor guy said she was dancing on the blackjack pole last night until three, right? She goes out, has a few too many after work, and drives her hunk of junk off the road on the way home. So what? Dime a dozen, like I said."

Drew, who had been leaning in during the discussion, stepped back. "Listen, Buzz, you're probably right. Maybe I'm overreacting since she was so young and so good looking. Unlike you, I'm not used to being surrounded by gorgeous babes. We'll see what the autopsy says."

"Sure, Kid. We'll see. Don't hold your breath. And no, we don't have any toxicology back yet. Probably won't for a while."

"OK, I guess nobody put a rush on it. Fine. I'm gonna see if her boss can get me a number for her friend, the one she left with last night. What did he say her name was?"

Buzz blew out a sigh and leaned back toward his keyboard. He had already entered his notes into the electronic case file. After a few mouse clicks, he said dismissively, "Laura Templeton."

Drew straightened up, trying to look less Opie-ish. "I'll let you know if Laura tells me anything important. And I'll see if they found the security cam video."

"You're wasting your time, dude, but fine. Go chase some shadows. It's not like we're that busy this week. For a change, the holidays haven't been a shit show on the Strip." Buzz returned his attention to his monitor screen, which was a not-so-subtle indication that Drew should go back to his own desk and stop bothering him.

❖❖❖

Gary Ottavino, the floor boss at Circus, told Drew that Cricket was in fine shape and didn't have any bruises when she left the casino the night before. He paid close attention, and he was very sure. Whatever bruises she had, she'd gotten after she left. Gary gave Drew a number for Laura, who said over the phone that she didn't think Cricket had a boyfriend and that she was fine when Laura left the parking garage. She'd assumed Cricket was right behind her, but when she thought about it, she hadn't actually seen Cricket's car come out of the garage. She had no other light to shine on the situation. What were the chances Cricket had somehow gotten beaten up right before she crashed her car? Who would have a motive to do that to a dancer, especially if she didn't have an obvious ex-boyfriend or somebody stalking her? Laura didn't know, but she admitted to not knowing Cricket well.

The security cam video didn't show anything. Cricket was on camera in the elevator lobby leading to the parking garage at 3:14 a.m. The cameras on the sixth floor, where the employee parking area was, were down for routine maintenance between 3:00 and 3:30. There was nothing on the camera at 3:30 except a deserted garage with a few remaining cars, and no sign of Cricket.

After the interview, Drew sat in his car in the parking garage, trying to decide how much he wanted to push things. He drove to the sixth floor and parked in the employee area, contemplating what could have happened to Cricket. Maybe she did bump into an old boyfriend Laura didn't know about. Maybe she stopped somewhere and got rolled for her tip money – except her purse was in the wrecked car, containing three hundred dollars and change. Buzz was right. There was nothing worth chasing. But something still bothered Drew about the situation. He'd be interested in seeing the toxicology report and the autopsy.

Chapter 13 — Friendly Skies

Friday, January 3
United Flight 2138

A HALF HOUR INTO THE FLIGHT from Newark to Las Vegas, the Boeing 737 leveled out at cruising altitude and the captain issued the standard admonition that passengers should keep their seat belts fastened when not moving around the cabin. Rachel lifted the armrest separating her seat from Jason's and snuggled against his shoulder. She didn't like flying, and she was nervous about the trip. Despite the confident, happy discussion on New Year's Eve, Rachel had sunk into a state of semi-hysteria.

"Everything is going to work out great," Jason said in his most soothing voice. "I have supreme confidence in your planning ability, and with Michelle to help you, it's a sure thing." He put his right arm around her shoulder and squeezed gently. He was hoping Rachel would fall asleep on the flight, since she had barely slept for the two days leading up to the trip.

"I'm not worried about the wedding." Rachel pushed away slightly so she could look at Jason's face. "The arrangements are all made, and the dress is packed, so that's under control, actually." She looked directly into Jason's eyes. He was used to dealing with unexpected situations. He was calm under pressure. "There is something else we should talk about before we get there."

Jason saw concern on his fiancée's face and immediately went into supportive almost-husband mode. "What is it?"

"It's about Jackie."

"Your brother?" Jason breathed an internal sigh of relief. He was worried it was going to be something more serious. "Hey, I know you've been nervous for some reason about me meeting him. Don't worry about it. I know it's a tough situation for your family with him running off to Vegas, but I don't care about that. I'm sure we'll get along fine."

Rachel smiled at Jason's instinct to be supportive and positive, without knowing any details. "I told you Jackie is a dancer, right?"

"Sure. Like you wanted to be when you were younger."

"Well . . . not exactly what I wanted."

"Don't worry. It's not like he's some young girl running off to Vegas and working as a stripper or a hooker and getting into real trouble."

Rachel's face flashed through amusement, embarrassment, and resolve. She hoped it was all too quick for Jason to decipher. "Jay, you know Michelle and I have made plans to see Jackie's show tomorrow night."

"Yeah, you mentioned it, and I think Michelle did, too. It's at the Mardi Gras, right? I'm assuming that's how you got us the room reservations. It's nice to have somebody who works there to pull some strings, huh?"

"Yes, that's right. He helped us out. But I need to let you know about the show. You see . . . it's a drag show."

Rachel held her breath, waiting for Jason's reaction. Jason furrowed his brows and pulled his head back an inch, contemplating why this information was causing Rachel such anxiety. "OK, so? It's Vegas. Everything there is wild and over the top. A drag show? Wow. I bet that will be something to see. Is your brother some kind of background dancer in the show?"

"No, Jay. Jackie is one of the drag performers." She bit her bottom lip while watching Jason's face. It remained inquisitive, but showed no signs of being upset.

"He's . . . a drag queen?"

"Yes. He's been working in drag for a few years. He's really good. I hope that doesn't freak you out."

"Does your family know?"

"Yes. Mom and Diana are great about it. But Daddy isn't. He's had a tough time accepting that Jackie's gay. Performing in drag on top of that is something Daddy couldn't handle. It's what caused the problems between them. Jackie had been performing in Manhattan, but Daddy wouldn't go see him. They had a huge fight a year ago at Thanksgiving. That's when Jackie left for Vegas. He said there's no better place to be, and he wanted to get as far away from Daddy as possible. That was a few months before we met, so you never had a chance to know him. He's a wonderful person. He's just had a tough time. I hope you aren't going to be creeped out like Daddy."

Rachel stopped talking and turned pleading eyes toward Jason. He smiled and pulled Rachel back to her position leaning against his shoulder. "Sweetheart, I'm not marrying your brother. Unless you tell me he's going to be sleeping in our bed with us, I don't care if he's gay or if he wears fake boobs and a dress. I know you love him, and that's all that matters."

Rachel relaxed her shoulders, which she hadn't even realized were tensed up during the conversation. She leaned against Jason. "Thank you. It's important to me that you're cool with him. He's doing what he loves, just like you are. It makes him happy, and that's the most important thing, right?"

"Right," Jason replied quickly, not wanting to suggest any doubt or hesitation. Rachel was going to be his wife, and what clothes her brother wore while performing on stage wasn't going to affect their lives. "Will he be dressed in drag at the wedding?"

"No!" Rachel scolded. "He'll be in a suit, like you. He performs in drag, but he's not trans."

"OK. I got it, I think," Jason said, pulling her back toward his shoulder again. "Do Michelle and Mike know we're going to a drag show?"

"Michelle knows, but I told her not to tell Mike. I wanted to tell you first. I'll tell Mike tomorrow at dinner."

"That's fine. After Mike had to keep my proposal plans secret from Michelle, it's only fair for her to have a little secret."

"You don't think Mike will have any issues with Jackie?"

"It doesn't matter – Jackie's not going to be Mike's brother-in-law. How he feels is irrelevant."

"But I want everyone to get along."

Jason stroked her hair reassuringly. "Don't worry. I'm sure Mike will be cool."

"Oh, I hope you're right. I guess I'm gun-shy because of Daddy's reaction. They haven't spoken to each other since Jackie left town. It's like he's disowned his son. It's sad, and it's a real problem for the family. I'm hoping Daddy will get past it. Maybe in June when we have our family party, Jackie will be able to come. It tears me apart to have them fighting."

"I understand. That has to suck. I'll do what I can to help – after we're married." He leaned over to give Rachel a soft kiss. "I love you, Rachel Robinson. And I will love your family, no matter how messed up their relationships are."

Rachel laughed softly and kissed Jason again. "That's what I wanted to hear. I hope your folks don't get upset about us not telling them about the wedding."

"Don't worry about that."

"I do worry. It's important to me that our families get along and that your parents aren't mad at us. They'll be grandparents next year. I know you're not close with your father. Maybe this will help you reconnect."

Jason took a deep breath before responding. "I've told you about me and my dad. That bridge is burned. I'm not going there. My mom will be fine. She's off in North Carolina with her sister and their friends for the holidays, so she's fine. She'll be happy. I just want to focus on us."

Rachel rested her head on Jason's shoulder and squeezed his hand. As her breathing became regular and she drifted toward sleep, Jason processed the new information. He was worried the situation would require him to take Rachel's side in a family feud with Ernie Robinson on the other side. He had been trying to get into his future father-in-law's good graces. Maybe he could remain neutral? No, Rachel would not stand for that. His option was to try to be a peacemaker and get Ernie over his emotional objection to his son's lifestyle and occupational choices. That could be tricky. Maybe they needed to take Ernie to see *Kinky Boots* on Broadway.

The reference to Jackie's drag show reminded Jason of the photo the FBI wanted them to track down. They had shown it to the manager of a strip club, who didn't recognize any of the faces, but said he was sure both of the Black girls were actually men in drag. He wondered if Jackie might be able to help ID one of them, if the shot was from Las Vegas. How many Black drag queens were there in the world? He realized he had no idea. There might be thousands. He now knew of at least one. He shook his head. The FBI would have sent the photo to the local cops in Las Vegas, and they would have tracked it down.

He didn't have a copy of the picture, and it wasn't something he could talk to Rachel about, since it was so ultra-confidential. He put it out of his mind. He had no obligation to ask around about drag performers while on his honeymoon. He focused on the upcoming wedding, and tried to think positive thoughts about how perfect it was going to be. Before he realized it, he was also dozing off, his arm still draped around his future wife.

Chapter 14 — Back for More

RICK "THE NECK" GARETTI WAS NOT HAPPY. He had hoped the blackmailer would back off. It would have made sense for an amateur to get cold feet once they found out about Cricket's death. Of course, if Cricket wasn't involved, then the blackmailer might not even notice. Now, that scenario seemed likely.

"I got another text from our shithead, Boss. He wants another hundred grand." Rick watched Freddy's face carefully, trying to detect his emotional reaction. He saw an eye blink that lasted longer than normal, as if Freddy were closing his eyes in disappointment – or anger. That was the only indication anything had changed in his world.

"Alright. Enough of this bullshit. There's two other girls who were there, right?"

"The drag queens. Yeah. So, not really girls."

"I don't give a shit. There were two. One of them has to be doing this, or giving the information to Shithead. Maybe both of them. They think they can threaten to go to the feds and finger me? They have to know I don't respond well to threats. You hired the girls yourself. Was there anybody else there?"

"Yeah. I arranged it through a booking agent. He brought

them in and I paid him the cash, but he never saw the mark. He dropped off the girls and left. That was maybe a half hour before you got there."

"I want you to take care of the situation, Ricky. Since Eddie did such a good job on the stripper, use him again. And anybody else you need. Whatever it takes. I want this finished."

"I understand, Boss." Rick hesitated, but figured he had to ask the next question. "Do you want to know what the text said?"

"I don't give a shit! I'm not paying this bastard any more money and I don't care what threats he wants to make. If he goes to the feds, they'll be interested in his extortion. I'm willing to call that bluff. Take care of it. We've got cover, so let's use it."

Rick nodded and turned to leave Freddy's office. He had to give the blackmailer credit for having guts – unless he was an idiot and didn't know who he was dealing with. The guy wasn't satisfied with the hundred thousand he already had. Now he wanted another. Rick would take his phone call and pretend to make arrangements. There would be no drop. He planned to take care of business before then.

Chapter 15 — Top of the World

Friday, January 3
Las Vegas, NV

RACHEL RESTED HER HEAD on Jason's naked chest. The sheets in their suite at the Mardi Gras were 1,000 thread count and felt sublime against her skin. She traced curly-cues around Jason's chest hairs and slid her leg up along his thigh. She glanced at her suitcase, still packed, sitting on the floor under the huge window looking out at the Vegas Strip. She purred and kissed Jason's nipple, sucking gently in case he was inclined to go for another round.

She had been pleasantly surprised when Jason tipped their bell hop, closed the suite door, and immediately swept Rachel into his arms. Their clothes were on the floor a few seconds later and the king-sized bed easily hosted their frantic love-making. They had avoided having sex at Rachel's parents' house. On the nights when Rachel was able to get to Jason's apartment, they were constrained by thin walls and many close neighbors. In the hotel, they didn't care who might be listening, and Rachel's voice was raw from screaming in ecstasy. They had nowhere to be until the next day and all the time in the world to please each other. They took full advantage.

An hour later, now fully unpacked and dressed in what

they expected would be appropriate Vegas clothes, they left the Mardi Gras in a Lyft car and headed for Old Towne. It had not occurred to either of them to check the weather forecast for Nevada before packing. Rachel wore a black cocktail dress with skinny straps and a low neckline. Jason donned a red silk shirt and black slacks with a black leather jacket.

They were less than eight hours removed from New York, but they were now fully on vacation. The schedule for the wedding and their work obligations back home weren't going to allow them to take a trip afterward, so they planned to use the week in Vegas leading up to the nuptials as the de facto honeymoon.

Jason took her to dinner at the Silverado Steak House at the top of Binion's Casino, which had the best steaks in Las Vegas, according to Mike. By the time they left, Jason was a believer. They toured the Mob Museum and walked around historic Freemont Street. This was not the glitzy modern Strip – it was the old Vegas, with the venues that had been there since the town was built in the 1950s. Organized crime and Las Vegas had been together since the beginning. There were fewer people crowding the sidewalks in this part of town, but it still buzzed with activity.

Later, they went up Las Vegas Boulevard to the Stratosphere, the tallest hotel in the city. From the observatory at the top, they could see all around the desert basin and all the lights of the modern mega-hotels up the Strip. They watched planes taking off from McCarren Airport and breathed in the unusually cold desert air. It was in the low 40s, but after a frigid December in New York, it felt reasonably comfortable – although they were expecting much warmer.

Jason kept an arm around Rachel's bare shoulders and repeatedly offered to give her his jacket, which she consistently refused. As they gazed at the stars from the highest point in the city, Jason twisted her around so she was facing him. He put his large hands on her shoulders, holding her at arm's length. Then he dropped to one knee, taking her hand in his.

"Rachel Robinson, will you have my baby – and marry me? Well, marry me first, then have my baby?"

Rachel suppressed a giggle. "Yes, Jason Dickson, I will gladly marry you, and then have our baby." She pulled him up to her and threw her arms around his neck as they kissed deeply, not caring who was watching. Two couples standing nearby started applauding, which prompted the entire population of the outdoor observatory space to clap and cheer, thinking they had witnessed a proposal. They waved to their adoring fans and blew kisses as they pushed through the glass doors to the much warmer indoor area of the observatory.

As Jason held the door, he overheard a woman standing nearby say, "Did you see that, Frank? That's how to stage a romantic proposal."

On a padded bench, they talked about the plans for the upcoming week. "When do I get to meet your brother?" Jason asked.

"Not until tomorrow after the show. I wanted to get together during the day, but he said he had some kind of gig in the afternoon and then he had to get ready for the early show. We'll be seeing the late show, after we have dinner with Mike and Michelle. Their plane lands at three o'clock, so we should have plenty of time to meet up with them. Before that, we can do whatever we want, but I'm looking forward to spending some time in the pool tomorrow morning."

"Sounds good to me," Jason smiled. "Is there any place you'd like to visit afterward? I assume we're meeting Mike and Michelle at the hotel, right?"

"Sure. We've got reservations at the Cajun restaurant at six, and then Jackie got us seats right up front in the theater for the nine o'clock show."

"When does Mike find out Jackie is one of the drag . . . do I call him a 'queen?'"

"Say 'performer.' That will work best," Rachel smiled at Jason's attempt at sensitivity. "He's a singer and dancer – he just happens to do it as part of a drag show."

"Fine with me. Are you sure you don't want to tell Mike until tomorrow?"

"You don't think Mike will have a negative reaction, do you?"

Jason pondered the question. He had assured Rachel that Mike would be cool about it. In their two years together as partners, Jason had observed Mike having some old-fashioned attitudes. But, in the past year, he had also shown more tolerance and sensitivity toward people who were subjected to discrimination. Gay people and drag queens certainly fell into that group. "I can't be sure, but I would bet on Mike being pretty cool with the idea. It's not like Jackie is his relative. Mike's been around New York a long time. He and Michelle didn't have any problem taking up the cause for a prostitute last spring. There's nothing to be worried about. I'm sure it would be fine to have Michelle tell him."

"No, I don't want to put that obligation on her. I'll do it myself. We'll get him a good scotch before dinner and spring it on him, then we'll go to the show and he'll see for himself what a wonderful entertainer Jackie is."

"That sounds like a perfect plan." Jason took her hand and kissed it gently. "We'll have a wonderful time this week, and we'll have a fabulous wedding. I can't wait to see how beautiful you'll look."

Rachel smiled, thinking about the Vera Wang dress. She was feeling more relaxed about everyone's reactions to Jackie's professional persona and looking forward to seeing him on a Vegas stage.

Chapter 16 — A Quick Errand

Saturday, January 4
Las Vegas, NV

JACKIE ROBINSON, IN CHARACTER as Belle de la Pomme, walked back and forth inside the cramped backstage dressing room. The early show had gone well. The audience laughed at all the jokes and applauded enthusiastically for each number. Belle hit all the marks, nailed all the dance moves, and stuck all the high notes. The adrenaline rush after a show usually calmed down after five minutes. Tonight, it was still flowing twenty minutes later. She took a seat in front of the brightly lit makeup mirror, stripped down to her underwear. This was the time to feel exhilarated and satisfied, enjoying a rest between shows. But Rachel and her hunk fiancé would be at the front center table for the late show. Making eye contact with the audience was a key to success, but the thought of looking Rachel's man in the eye brought on a fluttering tummy. He was a cop, and Belle's experience with cops had been mostly bad. With so much going on inside Belle's head, it didn't take much to create a crisis.

"Honey, I need a mascara. Can I borrow yours?" Belle was jolted from her inner thoughts, looking quickly up and to the left. Mimi LaRee stood there, still in full costume and make-up from the final number of the early show. One hand rested on her extended hip, the other held an expired mascara container in long, painted nails. Mimi tapped her shoe impatiently, as if her mascara issue were Belle's fault. She didn't hate Mimi, but being the lead diva in a show filled with drag queens was bound to generate tons of envy. Belle, like nearly every performer in the cast, thought she could rock the lead role, given an opportunity. She didn't wish for Mimi to suffer a debilitating, life-shattering injury, but twisting an ankle during a spin and having to miss a few shows wouldn't be such a bad thing.

After the show, adoring fans lined up for Mimi's autographs and pictures. Everyone wanted Mimi. Terry, their director, rotated the rest of the cast members to accompany her and pose under the bright lights for the worshipping fans and the gawking tourists who only knew Mimi's name. Belle, when being honest, wanted to be there, at the center of attention. But everyone had to pay their dues. In New York, Belle de la Pomme had developed a following. She had to start over from scratch in Vegas. Things had been going pretty well, but it was a tough town, and Mimi wasn't going to make it easy to get more time in the spotlight.

"Girl, I love you, but I hate pink-eye, so I'm not sharing my mascara. You know I can't do that." Belle unconsciously reached out and clutched the mascara container lying on the makeup table. "If I had an unopened spare, I'd give it, but I need the one I have. Ask April or Lizzy. Or, you'll just have to run out to the CVS. You have time."

Mimi scowled, but couldn't argue the point. Sharing a used mascara was terrible hygiene. With pursed lips, Mimi spun on a four-inch heel and stormed away toward April's station at the opposite end of the make-up table.

Belle immediately fell back into nervous anxiety mode and reached for a backpack on the floor under the counter. The late show would start in fifty-three minutes. She had a text from Rachel confirming that she and Jason would be at the show and were excited about watching. Belle returned the phone to the backpack and picked up the mascara. There was no real need for a touch-up, but she used a little on principle, then stashed the container. On the other side of the long, narrow dressing room, Mimi grabbed a pink jacket and a gold purse that accentuated her dark skin and headed for the exit door.

Belle leaned back and blew out a long breath. The tiny confrontation with Mimi should not have been a big deal, but everything felt huge tonight. Pushing the chair back, she extended a slender foot, resting her big toe on the edge of the makeup counter. Her legs were gorgeous; slim, smoothly muscled, and long. Her dark brown skin glistened in the spotlights without any nylons or makeup. A weekly depilatory kept them hairless and ready for the show. When not in heels, she was only five-foot-seven, but a four-inch heel and a two-inch platform sufficed to almost match Mimi's statuesque height. Rachel got the family height gene, while Jackie had the same build as their father. That was actually a good thing, as it turned out, since Ernie was perpetually skinny and had a super-fast metabolism, and he was as strong as a bear without ever developing bulging muscles. These attributes served a drag performer well. It was ironic that Ernie didn't appreciate how his son used those physical gifts.

The mascara, bulking up long fake lashes, accented her dark brown eyes. The formerly bushy black eyebrows above them had been shaved years before and replaced with artificially painted designs that varied according to the day's costume and mood. Belle's thin nose allowed for makeup that accentuated her high cheekbones. No obvious Adam's apple interfered with the feminine profile in the mirror.

"Is she here yet?" The voice belonged to Belle's roommate and best friend in the cast, Lizzy.

"No, not yet. Now shut up or you'll make me more nervous than I am already."

Lizzy placed two manicured hands on Belle's shoulders and massaged them gently. A full-length terrycloth robe hid from view whatever Lizzy was wearing, but her makeup was still in place from the early show. Lizzy's ethnicity was ambiguous; she'd been born of a Filipino father and a Hawaiian mother, and had skin nearly as dark as Jackie's. All of Lizzy's features were vaguely Asian, but growing up in Hawaii and moving to California as a teen had given her an all-American accent and attitude.

"Listen, Honey, you need to relax and enjoy. You said you hadn't seen your sister in a year, right? So this is going to be great for both of you. Didn't you tell me she was your biggest supporter back home in Brookdale or wherever?"

Belle laughed and leaned back into the massage. "You know it's Brooklyn. And, yes, Rachel was always there for me. She was the one who came and got me after I ran away the first time. You'd think a sixteen-year-old from Brooklyn would have a better plan. My mom would have come, but not without my dad, so it was Rachel. I'm dying to see her. She's engaged, and I've never met her man. He's a cop. What if he's like Dad, and every other cop, and thinks I'm a freak?"

"Does Rachel think you're a freak?"

"No. Of course not."

"So, what are the chances she's hooked up with a man who thinks differently?" Lizzy paused the massage and leaned over the top of Belle's head. "Hmmm?"

"Not good, I guess. But you know how cops are."

"Not all cops are racist homophobes. Only most of 'em.

You need to think positively here and nail your act tonight. The rest will take care of itself."

"I know. I know. I'm just all wound up. Thanks for the massage. I needed that."

"I know." Lizzy winked. "I know you're terrific. You know you're terrific. Even Terry knows. You keep doing what you're doing and everything is gonna be fine."

"You know I love you, right?" Belle looked into the mirror at Lizzy's face.

"I know. I just wish you loved me the way you love that microphone." They both broke into deep laughs. Lizzy gave Belle's shoulders a final squeeze, then padded off toward the wardrobe area, where costumes for the first number of the next show were being laid out by the stagehands.

Belle leaned forward and stared into the mirror. "I can do this."

Mimi LaRee walked quickly out the stage door into a crowded corridor. The last members of the audience from the early show who had waited in the autograph line were still filing out, mixing with the Saturday night casino crowd. Somebody shouted, "I love your show!" Mimi instinctively turned in the direction of the voice and put on a bedazzling smile. She waved, not sure who she was waving at. As she moved across the river of bodies, several more voices called out greetings and congratulations. Mimi hadn't intended to mingle with the spectators, but hearing them say how wonderful the performance had been always made her heart race.

When she reached an intersection in the walking path, the exit doors beckoned. Mimi waited impatiently for the people ahead to squeeze through the glass-and-steel entrance to the Mardi Gras and spill out onto Las Vegas Boulevard. Upon achieving the sidewalk, she hurried toward the closest shopping plaza. A band was playing in an amphitheater nearby. Street performers drew small clumps of people who clogged the walking lane. Happy tourists at the outdoor tables of a Mexican restaurant drank frozen cocktails, despite wearing jackets and hoodies because of the cold. The nighttime low was expected to be in the 50s, but the temperature did not slow down the amazing parade of Las Vegas nightlife. Mimi was part of the show. The drinkers thought she was simply another hot chick in an outrageous Vegas costume.

Past the margarita bar, a Johnny Rockets, and several souvenir shops, the big red letters of the CVS drugstore welcomed pedestrians into a small oasis of normal reality within the alternate dimension that was the Vegas Strip. Inside, Mimi made a bee-line to the make-up section against the far wall. Her platinum-blonde wig and blue sequined gown made her stand out like a neon sign inside a dark theater.

Outside on the plaza, Rick and Eddie stopped next to a kiosk selling colorful frozen drinks in thin, three-foot-long plastic glasses. They had a clear view of the only public exit from the CVS. They had been watching the stage door back at the Mardi Gras, hoping one of their two targets would come out to get something to eat or get some air between shows. Failing that, they planned to wait until after the late show and take the first one who exited. They didn't have a specific plan for how they would isolate their target. Rick was improvising.

"It doesn't look like she's getting food," Eddie said as he ogled two brunettes in matching gymnastics leotards saunter past, their ass cheeks peeking out below the tight fabric.

"He," Rick corrected.

"Whatever! I can't keep the queers straight. Looks like a chick to me, so I'm sticking with 'she.' I'm pretty sure that's how they say it." Eddie glared defiantly at Rick, who was the boss of this operation. But Eddie viewed him as merely an aging obstacle blocking him from moving up in Freddy Costanzo's organization.

"You spend a lot of time around drag queens?" Rick shot back calmly. While Eddie fumed, Rick surveyed the area and planned their move. Between the souvenir shop and the CVS, a gap in the plaza wall opened into a narrow corridor. Signs above the entrance pointed toward public restrooms that were seldom occupied, since the surrounding casinos offered much more attractive options. Rick nudged Eddie with his elbow. "Get across there and see whether there's anybody in the ladies' room. If there is, wait for 'em to leave and don't let anybody else in. When it's empty, give me a wave and then wait for me inside."

Rick watched Eddie disappear down the corridor. He kept one eye on the restroom and one on the door to the CVS as four minutes ticked by. Eddie emerged from the restroom after a woman wearing a hair net and a housekeeper's uniform and waved to Rick. Mimi had not left the drugstore. When Rick saw the platinum blonde wig bouncing away from the cash register toward the door, he made his move, intercepting Mimi outside the drugstore's awning.

"Hey, Sugar, if you got five minutes, I have a guy looking to give you five hundred for a private photo."

Mimi stopped abruptly, allowing Rick to take a step ahead before slamming on the brakes. When Rick turned back, Mimi glared through heavily painted eyes, then responded in a fully masculine voice. "You obviously have no idea who you're talking to."

"Oh, but I do," Rick replied smoothly. "You're Mimi LaRee, star of the drag revue at the Mardi Gras. You're the hottest thing going, and my guy wants to give you a big tip. You up for it? I promise he's harmless. It'll just take a minute." Rick assumed a relaxed, nonthreatening posture and held his hands at his sides, palms out.

Mimi sized Rick up skeptically. She was wary of anyone putting her in a vulnerable position, but Rick was well-dressed and didn't look threatening. "Lemme see the money." Mimi stood with her arms crossed. Rick reached into his pants pocket and pulled out a thick roll of bills with a hundred on the outside. He snapped off the rubber band and peeled off five bills, which quickly curled back into tubular form in his left hand as he returned the remainder of the wad to his pocket. He extended the money toward Mimi, who stared at the cash, thinking about the new pair of shoes she had wanted to buy the day before, but passed because of the balance in her checking account. "Where?"

Rick smiled. "Right around the corner. My guy's waiting in a private space."

Rick led the way, trusting that Mimi wouldn't run off with the money. He could hear her heels clacking heavily on the concrete behind him. Mimi opened her purse, stuffed the bills inside, and tilted up the handle of the little .22 pistol she kept handy. It wasn't much of a gun, but at close range it could do enough damage to get her out of a tight spot.

When Rick turned down the corridor and stopped in front of the ladies' room, he held the door open with a smile, inviting Mimi to step inside.

Mimi hesitated. She knew better than to step inside without knowing what was beyond the door. But the idea of a fan who had been fantasizing about her and was willing to pay so much for a brief encounter was flattering. Mimi didn't have much money in the little gold purse, aside from her recently acquired five hundred. Muggers didn't generally carry wads of cash and give out five hundred dollars before rolling their victim. But there were plenty of hateful bastards who came in all shapes and sizes. She scanned the interior, which seemed vacant. Then, a voice called out from the far corner, inside the disabled persons' stall.

"In here, Mimi."

She looked back. Rick was leaning against the door, preventing anyone from entering to interrupt the meeting. She clutched the gold purse with her left hand resting on the open top, next to the little gun.

As soon as she entered the stall and saw Eddie, holding a black pistol, she reached for her .22. Eddie saw the movement.

The flash of light and the stabbing pain occurred simultaneously. By the time Mimi's knees impacted the tile floor, a second blow from the butt of Eddie's pistol to the back of her head knocked off the platinum wig, already stained red from the flowing blood released by the first impact.

Rick rushed to the threshold of the stall and saw the crumpled figure on the floor and the spreading crimson pool forming next to Mimi's head. "We're going to have a hard time getting any information out of that now."

Eddie scowled as he reached for the roll of toilet paper and started wiping blood off his gun. "Sorry. She went for a gun. I guess her head's softer than I figured."

"*His* head," Rick shot back.

"Whatever!" Eddie replied angrily. "I don't give a shit. The boss wanted her taken out. Mission accomplished." Eddie pushed past Rick and headed to the door. Rick shrugged and grabbed the gold purse from the floor. He extracted the five hundred dollars, along with the small additional amount inside, leaving the little Saturday night special on the floor. He tossed the handbag in the trash can, then pulled a handkerchief from his jacket pocket, moistened it in the sink, and wiped down the door handle on his way out. He hadn't touched anything else.

"I'll meet you back at the Mardi Gras," Rick said as Eddie walked away toward the plaza. Rick ducked into the men's room across the corridor. He sat on a toilet and took out his phone, then sent a text to Freddy's current burner. "Hit a jackpot on first pull but waitress didn't give me her number." He then checked his Twitter and looked up the lines on Sunday's NFL games. After five minutes, the door squeaked open and a short Hispanic man rushed in and took up a position in front of a urinal. Rick zipped up and meandered to the sink to wash his hands. When the other man finished pissing, Rick asked him if he knew the time. The man said it was about 8:30. Rick noticed his hat, bearing the logo of one of the vendor kiosks from the adjoining plaza. He thanked the man, then held the door open for him as he rushed back to his customers.

Rick walked casually back out to the plaza, then back to the Mardi Gras. If anyone saw him, or if he was on a security camera, he had established an alibi with a witness who would confirm he was in the men's room. He wasn't happy Eddie had killed Mimi before they could get any information. But there was still the other one, so perhaps Freddy wouldn't be too pissed off at the end of the night.

Twenty minutes later, Belle stood behind the stage at *The*

Birdcage theater, trying to peek through the curtain to see if Rachel and her group were at the front table yet. The view was blocked by a promotional poster positioned in front of the curtain. Belle, wearing a short gold dress and a Donna Summer wig, turned away and paced. Her standard pre-show routine butterflies were heightened by the pressure of having Rachel and Jason in the audience.

Upon reaching the back wall, Belle saw Lizzy. Like her stage-namesake and idol, Lizzo, Lizzy was a heavy performer, but had boundless energy and slender legs that seemed out of place against her larger torso. Belle marveled at Lizzy's personality and how she owned her oversized fake breasts, which were always a hit on stage. Since Belle's arrival in Las Vegas, Lizzy had been a supportive confidant.

"How you doin', Baby?" Belle called out.

"Good as Hell!" Lizzy sang back – her ritual response. "Terry wants to see you!"

"About what?"

"Mimi isn't here. Nobody knows where she is. I think you may have to take her part, which means I'd get to do yours." Lizzy was bouncing with excitement. "Go find him, already!"

Belle walked quickly to the side of the stage where their director, Terrance Evans, normally lorded over his minions. Terry was talented and knew how to stage a first-class show, but he was also a slavedriver. He knew the available gigs for drag performers were limited, even in Las Vegas, and that the house held all the leverage when it came to assignments and pay. The Mardi Gras paid the cast fairly well, but if anyone wanted to move up in the pecking order, it was up to Terry. And, if Terry became unhappy with your performances, you could be looking for work quickly. He made it a point to fire someone every few months, to keep everyone on their toes.

"There you are," Terry barked. "Another minute and I was going to let Chi-Chi move up." Terry had a thin face, topped by a mound of curly black hair that contrasted his pasty white complexion, as if he never went out into the Vegas sun. He wore a purple silk shirt above tight black jeans, which compressed his already thin frame into a virtual stick figure. Belle doubted he weighed more than 130.

"What's up?" Belle knew what was happening, but it made sense to play it cool.

"Mimi is missing and we're fifteen minutes until curtain. I'm moving you into the lead spot. Can you handle it?"

Belle broke into a huge smile, thinking about how surprised Rachel would be. "I was born to handle it. Do I need a costume change?"

"No. You're fine as you are. Just hit the right marks. Lizzy will be in your spot, so help her out."

"What if Mimi shows up before showtime?" Belle knew what the answer would be, but wanted to let Terry vent a little at Mimi.

"She'll be lucky if I don't fire her fat ass!" Terry barked. "It's your show. Go take it."

Belle walked back toward Lizzy to confirm the good news for both of them. She had been in the show for eight months and had risen to a featured position based on hard work, talent, and a good amount of sucking up to the director. But Mimi blocked anyone else from the lead role. Belle, as her understudy, had performed as the lead only a few times. Mimi had been headlining drag shows in Las Vegas for five years. The Mardi Gras had recruited her to be the star of their show when the hotel opened. There were no better gigs than being a featured performer at *The Birdcage*, so Belle had kept up a positive attitude and waited for opportunities. Tonight was a break. Belle knew there was nothing Terry hated more than unexpected absences. Unless Mimi had a broken leg, there would be hell to pay for missing a performance.

Belle went back to her pre-show pacing. The excitement level was higher now. This was a big night.

Chapter 17 — Delayed Gratification

Saturday, January 4
Las Vegas, NV

MIKE WAS FUMING. He and Michelle had booked a nonstop flight to Las Vegas specifically so they wouldn't have to deal with connections or delays that might make them late for meeting up with Jason and Rachel. He didn't understand why the airline couldn't have fixed the cargo door with some duct tape. Cancelling the whole flight seemed unnecessary. Michelle, as always, had been a trooper and jumped on her phone to find them an alternate flight. The new itinerary took them to San Francisco, with a connection back to Las Vegas. The layover wasn't long, but the change had them landing four hours later than scheduled. Now, their plane was circling McCarren International Airport because of some unspecified situation on the ground leaving all planes waiting for permission to land. The whole day was basically shot, which wasn't making Mike happy.

The situation wasn't making Michelle happy, either. They were already certain to miss dinner. She had texted Rachel from San Francisco with the bad news. Now, she was worried they wouldn't make it to Jackie's show at 9 p.m. Rachel still wanted to tell Mike about the drag show herself. Michelle had texted back agreeing, but now she was having second thoughts. Of course, it wouldn't matter if they missed the show.

Their flight finally touched down at 7:31 p.m. When Mike and Michelle reached the baggage claim area, one of Mike's suitcases didn't arrive on the carousel. By the time they filed a missing luggage report and got into a cab bound for the Mardi Gras, it was 8:42. They pulled up to the opulent entrance of the huge casino hotel five minutes before the start of the show at *The Birdcage*. Michelle had been texting with Rachel furiously since they landed, trying to figure out where to meet if she and Mike arrived in time. Mike handed over their luggage to the bell captain and asked him to hold the bags until after the show. Michelle cast a longing glance at her suitcase. It killed her not to check in and unpack, but she knew how important it was to Rachel that they make it. They maneuvered through the winding walkways of the casino until they found the theater entrance at 9:02.

They were not the only ones arriving late. They fell into a line of patrons, many holding drinks. The lights were already dimmed and a uniformed usher guided them to their table at the very front of the auditorium, where Rachel and Jason waved and greeted them. "Tough trip?" Jason asked.

"Ridiculous," Mike fumed.

"At least you made it." Rachel reached across the small table to squeeze Michelle's hand.

"We would have been here sooner," Michelle explained, "except one of Mike's suitcases got lost."

"Oh, no!" Rachel exclaimed. "Your clothes for the wedding?"

Mike gave a sheepish shake of his head. "No. Not my clothes. It was the suitcase with my pillows and a few other items."

"Pillows?" Jason cocked his head to the side and got a mischievous smile on his face, wondering how much grief he could give his partner over packing his own pillows.

"It's a long story," Mike said. Before he had a chance to continue, the stage lights came on, the red-and-gold curtain lifted, and recorded music blared from speakers on the sides of the stage. Mike and Michelle settled into their seats and focused on the performance, while Rachel held up her hands toward Michelle and shrugged.

When the first number started, a booming voice announced the arrival of Belle de la Pomme, who strutted out to center stage. A giant illuminated star behind her created a silhouette. She posed as the song's intro played. Her black Donna Summer wig and sleek gold dress drew whistles and cheers from the crowd as the first strains of "Love to Love You, Baby" wafted over the room.

Rachel screamed and pointed. Mike turned to Michelle and mouthed "Why?"

Michelle leaned over and said into Mike's ear, "That's Rachel's brother, Jackie."

Mike pulled away with a puzzled expression, then sat back and focused on the show. When a waiter came around, he ordered a scotch. Over the next ninety minutes, Mike sipped his Johnny Walker Black Label – the best he could do inside the venue – and enjoyed the over-the-top spectacle that was the Mardi Gras drag revue.

Seven different entertainers took their turns as the featured performer during the show. They told jokes and belted out tunes to raucous applause and cheers. Six other performers sang backup and danced behind the lead singers. Belle carried the lead vocal for three numbers and was in duets or trios for several others. When the grand finale came around, she took the last bow and was showered with adulation. The smile on her face stretched the width of the stage. Rachel was standing, clapping, and whistling louder than anyone.

Mike leaned in and called into Michelle's ear over the tumult, "That's Rachel's brother?"

"Yes," she shouted back while clapping. "She was going to tell you before the show."

Mike shrugged. "Welcome to Vegas."

After the show, Belle spent forty minutes signing autographs and snapping photos. Most members of the audience didn't know she was not supposed to be the star. Lizzy joined the post-show meet-and-greet in order to support her roommate and get into the tourists' selfies. Rachel pulled Jason out of his chair so they could join the end of the line and she could take selfies of her own.

When they reached the front, Belle introduced Rachel to Lizzy as "My legit sister," and introduced the other performers who were part of the post-show entourage to Rachel as "My drag family." Cleo Patya was a tall Asian queen with Egyptian-styled eyeshadow and a matching wig. April May was thin and pale, wearing a yellow floor-length dress and a blonde wig teased up into spikes, as if out of a 1980s sitcom. Cleo, April, and Lizzy gushed over Jason and told Rachel how much they loved working with Belle.

While they waited for Belle to finish mugging for her adoring fans and then change out of costume, Mike and Jason dashed out to the Strip to get some food. Two platters of chicken wings were the best they could do for quick take-out. Mike needed something to soak up three scotches, but greasy chicken and hot sauce were not likely to settle his stomach later. When Jackie and Lizzy finally joined them, six chairs crowded around the little front-row table in the otherwise empty theater.

"What I wouldn't give for a basket of rolls from Flannagan's," Mike said in a hushed whisper to Jason. Jason laughed in his deep voice. They both enjoyed the bread from the iconic New York steakhouse, even if it was a hangout for organized crime figures.

Jackie joined the laughter in a pitch lower than Mike expected. Now out of costume, if Jackie had walked into the theater through the audience door instead of from the stage, Mike would not have recognized him as the star of the performance they had just enjoyed. Jackie bore a family resemblance to Rachel around his eyes and had a buzz cut, leaving his head looking like the black hairs were painted on. He appeared relaxed in a tie-dyed t-shirt and loose-fitting jeans. When he looked carefully, Mike realized Jackie was thin all around, and had smoothly toned and slender arms. He couldn't see Jackie's legs through the jeans, but recalling the long, lithe gams strutting across the stage, he could now see how his lower body could work in a dress. But there was no way he would have seen Jackie sitting at a table sucking wing sauce off his fingers and guessed "drag queen." It blew his mind. But he was doing his best to roll with it.

Jackie introduced Lizzy to the group as his roommate. He explained that Lizzy had been in the show since its inception a year before and had befriended the new kid in town. Lizzy hooked Jackie up with an agent, Alexander Lewbowski, who booked many of the entertainers for side gigs. *The Birdcage* was a great job and steady work, but even the stars didn't get paid enough to sit back and rest between shows. They all had side hustles, and took whatever performing opportunities they could get. Being booked by Lizzy's agent helped Jackie establish a positive reputation in Las Vegas, and eventually got him into the revue at the Mardi Gras.

Lizzy had chosen not to change clothes or remove her makeup and was still sporting a dazzling red top above the amazingly real-looking breasts that were sized to complement her large upper body. Mike and Jason both fumbled with pronouns until Jackie explained that they should refer to Lizzy as "she" while in costume.

"A queen is always a lady," Jackie said with a wink toward Lizzy, who nodded while trying to eat a wing without dripping on her outfit.

"You can change out of costume if you want to," Rachel offered. "We're easy."

"Yeah," Mike agreed, "if it would make things easier."

When she swallowed, Lizzy said, "Don't worry, Honey. I prefer to meet new people this way. It's my best self. Even when I'm out of drag, I'm still Lizzy."

Jackie sat on the opposite side of Rachel from Jason and Mike. He cast furtive glances at Jason, while Lizzy referred to him as "the hunk." The family stories Jackie and Rachel told were new to Jason as well as Mike and Michelle. The more they talked, the more Mike started to understand some of the difficulties of Jackie's short life.

Mike had met Ernie Robinson only a few times, but could appreciate that the patriarch of the Robinson clan was an old-school family man. Ernie's parents had survived The Great Depression and the second World War, along with decades of discrimination and economic struggle. He had named Rachel after the wife of Brooklyn Dodger great Jackie Robinson, because he had two girls and had promised his father he would name a child after Jackie. When Olivia later had their son, Ernie finally had his Jackie. Ernie's dreams of having a ballplayer in the family, or at least an athlete, or at the very least someone to take with him to ballgames, never materialized.

As a young teen, Jackie took to dance and drama rather than baseball and football. When he hadn't had a date halfway through high school, Ernie called him a "fairy." Rachel, who was dreaming of being a Broadway dancer herself at the time, came to the defense of her kid brother. That put her at odds with her father, who adored her and whom she loved deeply. Ernie had always told Rachel to follow her dream, even if a career on stage was both a difficult path and one not likely to achieve financial security. She couldn't understand why her father had a different attitude when it came to Jackie's dreams.

When Jackie came out as gay, it heightened the tension inside the Robinson family. Jackie and Ernie yelled at each other more often than not. He ran away twice, scaring his mother, Olivia, to death each time. He moved out on his eighteenth birthday. Rachel and Olivia had cried. When he started performing in drag, Ernie refused to acknowledge Jackie's budding career or see him perform. Ernie refused to acknowledge any remorse for driving his only son out of the family home.

When Rachel and Michelle excused themselves to the restroom in the theater lobby, Rachel clamped a hand onto Michelle's arm and asked, "Do you think Jason and Jackie like each other?"

"Jason is totally cool. Don't worry. Jackie seems a little nervous, but I'm sure they will be fine." They both agreed that all of Rachel's apprehension about Jason had been misplaced. Even Mike seemed reasonably comfortable.

When the ladies returned to the theater, they were surprised to see two new figures standing next to their little table. Both men had their backs to the entrance and both wore suit jackets. The taller of the two was heavier and had a light-colored crewcut. The shorter man was much thinner, with reddish hair. As they neared, Michelle picked up on the conversation. Rachel immediately noticed that Jackie's mood had worsened and his face showed serious concern.

Mike waved to Michelle as they approached, motioning for her and Rachel to take their seats, then turned back to the two standing men. "Detective Rickenbacker, I can certainly understand your interest in speaking to his fellow performers, but my partner and I were here for the whole show, since nine o'clock. Both Jackie and Lizzy were on stage almost all of the time. When we couldn't see them, they were changing costumes, so they have a couple hundred alibis."

"What about before the show started?" Rickenbacker, the tall, muscular man, shot back.

Jason leaned forward. "There was an early show, wasn't there, Jackie?"

Jackie nodded, but didn't speak. His face was blank, his eyes wide. Jason had seen that look before, usually on the family members of murder victims. He was terrified of these two cops.

"What's happened?" Michelle broke in, not able to contain her curiosity.

Mike ignored the two intruding detectives and responded to Michelle. "One of the other performers in the drag show was found dead earlier tonight, not too far away. They suspect it's a homicide. They want to talk to Jackie and Lizzy. The stiff performed as Mimi LaRee. Real name Nigel Ellington. Jason and I are trying to facilitate a conversation without anyone needing to call a lawyer."

"Why would anyone need a lawyer?" Rachel asked,

concerned.

"They don't," Jason looked into Detective Rickenbacker's eyes, "unless they're suspects. Are either Jackie or Lizzy suspects, Detective?"

Rickenbacker glanced at his partner, who had been introduced before Michelle and Rachel arrived as Drew Maulgray. The thin man hesitated before saying in a soft voice, "It's really too early to say."

"In that case," Mike said, "they need to assume they *are* suspects. I know the drill, Detective. If they weren't suspects, you'd tell them. I can't imagine how, unless there's some evidence you haven't told us about. I'm no lawyer. In fact, I usually hate having them around while I'm questioning a person of interest. But we can't in good conscience allow Jackie or Lizzy to answer any potentially incriminating questions. You understand, I'm sure."

Jason stood, positioning himself between Rickenbacker and Jackie.

Rickenbacker scowled. He was an athletic six-foot-two and was a physical match for Jason. The two men staring at each other looked like a couple of heavyweights at a weigh-in, ready to rumble.

"How about they just tell us the last time they saw the dead queen?"

Mike and Jason exchanged looks and nods, then Jason told Jackie he should answer, if he could remember.

Jackie looked like a thirteen-year-old who had been summoned to the principal's office. Then, his face morphed from fright to anger. "Why are you hassling us, instead of chasing whatever bastard killed Mimi? You should be protecting us instead of accusing us." As he spoke, Jackie gained confidence, while staying slightly behind Jason.

"Yeah!" Lizzy said, pointing at Rickenbacker. "All we ever get from you cops is grief."

Rickenbacker clenched his jaw. "Just tell me when you last saw Nigel Ellington."

"It was between shows, backstage," Jackie said. "Mimi asked if she could borrow a mascara. I told her I didn't have an extra and said she should get one from the CVS. She left. I'm guessing to go there. That's the last time I saw her."

"You mean *him*?" Rickenbacker asked in a condescending tone. Mike recognized the technique. He used it when he questioned somebody he thought was lying in order to draw out a defensive reaction.

"The performers refer to themselves in the feminine when they're in costume, Detective," Jason said in the same tone, as if it was an obvious truth that Rickenbacker should know. He extended an arm, as if shielding Jackie from Rickenbacker's glare.

Mike wasn't sure why, but Rickenbacker rubbed him the wrong way. He wondered how he would react if he were the one investigating this murder. "Was the corpse wearing a dress?"

Maulgray nodded, but then said, "We really can't discuss the case. Even with other cops."

"I understand," Mike nodded back. "I guess I can't help myself. Was there a CVS anywhere nearby?"

Maulgray started to say yes, but Rickenbacker held up his hand and pressed forward with his questions, directed toward Jackie. "So, when Ellington left, what was his – *her* – mood? Angry? Did it seem like he was nervous or worried about anything?"

"No, not that I noticed. She had a stick up her ass most of the time, so it would have been hard to tell." Jackie's description made Lizzy giggle.

"What about you?" Rickenbacker turned to Lizzy. "Did you see Ellington between shows?"

Lizzy quickly stopped laughing. "I'm sure I did at some point after the show, but I don't remember speaking to her. Mimi didn't like me much, so we didn't talk unless one of us couldn't avoid it."

"Why didn't you like – Mimi?"

"Like Jackie said, she's a bitch. I probably would be, too, if I were the diva queen."

"What does that mean?" Rickenbacker's eyes darted back and forth between Jackie and Lizzy. Mike and Jason watched the questioning carefully. They were both ready to intercede if necessary.

Jackie answered the hanging question. "Mimi was the star. She made sure every one of us knew it. She treated us all like her supporting cast. Let's just say nobody loved her."

"Anybody hate her enough to beat her to death?"

Jackie and Lizzy both gasped. Mike and Jason noted the reaction. Killers could sometimes act surprised and shocked, especially if they were psychopaths, or actors. But this seemed like genuine horror.

"Oh, hell no!" Lizzy seemed offended by the suggestion. "The bitch was a diva, but no queen here is gonna beat her. We stick together. Lord knows there's plenty of hate out there without us hating ourselves. More likely it was a cop."

Rickenbacker took a step toward Lizzy, but Jason leaned over to block any advance.

"What about somebody else?" Maulgray jumped in. "Did Mimi have any enemies you know about? Anybody in her life like a jealous lover or something like that?"

Lizzy and Jackie both shook their heads.

Mike noticed that Rickenbacker didn't ask for the names of any of the other performers, or anyone else who might have interacted with Mimi immediately before the murder. "Detective, it's pretty late, especially for those of us who woke up in New York City this morning."

Rickenbacker ignored Mike and directed another question at Jackie. "We heard you took Ellington's place in the show. Is that right?"

"What? You think I killed her to take her place? That's crazy!"

"It's interesting that you immediately thought of that," Rickenbacker said.

Jason stepped forward, using his six-foot-three frame to its fullest intimidating effect. "Detective Rickenbacker, if you're making an accusation, you need to read Jackie his rights and arrest him – if you have any grounds."

Maulgray spoke up, trying to be the voice of reason. "Now, let's all just stay calm here. Nobody is accusing anybody of anything."

"I didn't think you had any probable cause," Jason said in his deep baritone. "I think we're done here." Rickenbacker and Maulgray both stood motionless. "If you gentlemen are planning to stay, then we'll leave." Jason held out his hand to Rachel, who stood, nodding toward Jackie to do the same.

"Fine." Rickenbacker took a step back. "We'll go." He reached into his jacket pocket and pulled out a white business card, handing it to Mike. "Detective Stoneman, please call me if your . . . friends here remember anything relevant. You say you're a cop, so I'm sure I can count on you." Mike took the card as the two local detectives turned and walked out. The six original tablemates all sat back down and stared at each other.

"What the hell was that?" Jackie was trembling. Lizzy

reached out a hand toward his arm, but she was also shaking.

Mike reached for a last wing, but the platter was empty. "That, I'm afraid, was two homicide detectives questioning somebody they think is a possible suspect."

"How can I be a suspect?"

"Jackie, when cops are at the start of a murder investigation, we look for the most obvious suspects. Who had the most to gain from somebody's death? I'd probably do the same in his shoes. We don't have any facts, so it's possible this could have been a botched robbery or a sexual assault, or just a random act of violence against someone different. We should probably get you a lawyer."

"Why? I didn't do anything."

"I believe you," Mike said in his best father-figure voice. "But sometimes innocent people are the ones who most need a lawyer. Do you know any?"

Lizzy and Jackie both shook their heads.

Chapter 18 — Is There a Lawyer in the House?

MIKE AWOKE WITH THE SUN STREAMING into their suite. He rubbed the sleep from his eyes and tried to focus on the alarm clock on the end table across the bed. He had become accustomed to sleeping on the right side, since Michelle insisted on the left. It wasn't a huge sacrifice for him, but the alarm clock was too far away and angled so he couldn't see it. At least the pillows were soft. As it turned out, he hadn't needed to bring his own.

He padded to the bathroom, which was luxuriously large. Michelle had her toiletries and makeup supplies laid out in arrow-straight lines on the left side of the double sink. Mike had plenty of space for the zip-lock bag crowded with all his traveling supplies, which was tossed into the right corner. He smiled because he was getting used to sharing a bathroom with the meticulous Dr. McNeill.

It was 9:00 a.m. local time when he emerged, finding Michelle in the outer room of their suite, sipping a coffee and staring at her tiny portable laptop.

"Good morning, sleepyhead," she called brightly. "I got

you a coffee. Over there on the counter."

Mike walked to the bar-style counter. He was impressed that every room in the hotel was a suite-style layout. It was nice to have a sleeping room separated from a sitting room. He wondered what the top-shelf suites must be like, since they were in a standard room. After the first sip of what was pretty good coffee, he returned to the sofa, gave Michelle a kiss, and sat next to her. "What are you concentrating on so hard?"

Without looking up, Michelle replied, "I've been working on finding a local lawyer for Jackie. I don't want him talking to the cops alone. It's turning out to be quite a chore, but people are awake in New York and I got a reference from Dave Zimmerman."

"The Assistant DA?"

"Yes. We've worked together on a few cases and he seems like a helpful guy."

"I agree. I'm sorry I wasn't up earlier to help you." Mike stood, still sipping his coffee. He found his phone, disconnected the charger, and booted it up. "I'll make a few calls." He had chided Michelle about bringing her laptop, arguing that it was a vacation and a wedding, not a work trip. He now wished he had more than his mobile to work from.

"It's OK, Mike. I wanted to let you sleep. You needed it. I've been up since six-thirty; I guess I'm jet-lagged. Zimmerman knows a guy who knows a guy and I've been exchanging messages with a local defense lawyer named Jerome Garcia. I Googled him and he's not one of those late-night infomercial kind of guys. Seems to be pretty well respected. He's on the executive board of some kind of local criminal defense bar organization. He says he can meet Jackie today at noon."

"Fine. I'll send a note to Berkowitz and Mason back in New York to see if they can get me any background on Detective

Rickenbacker. I usually like other cops, but there's something about him that makes me want to slap his smug face."

Michelle couldn't suppress a laugh. "I'm sure some people back home would say the same thing about you."

"Really?" Mike said, genuinely puzzled. Then he shrugged. "Yeah, I suppose so. I have been known to be a little pushy. But this guy seems to have settled on Jackie as his prime suspect without any basis."

"That you know about."

"Yeah, sure. That I know about. If we were back in New York, I'd ask you to expedite the autopsy and get us some information."

"I know. I feel so helpless."

"I sure hope there isn't any actual evidence implicating Jackie. I mean, just because he's a drag queen doesn't make him a murderer. This could put a damper on the wedding."

Michelle nodded, sliding over and leaning her head on Mike's shoulder. "I don't want anything to ruin Rachel's wedding."

Mike stroked her hair. "Neither do I."

"But I don't need a lawyer!" Jackie protested for the third time since they left the hotel. He was driving his 2008 Toyota, with Jason in the seat next to him. In the tiny back seat, Mike, Rachel, and Michelle were jammed together, relieved that the old car at least had working heat. They had practically forced Jackie to agree to a meeting with the lawyer Michelle found for him. Jackie couldn't afford to pay, but the rest of the group promised to take care of the fee, if there was one. Right now, they needed to consult with somebody who knew the town, and the cops, and who could give them some practical advice about how to keep Jackie from being arrested.

Mike and Jason were both having trouble being in the position of wanting to protect a possible suspect, instead of finding ways to pressure them into a slip-up or confession. For now, they were on the suspect's side. It felt weird.

When they stopped at a red light, Jackie turned toward his future brother-in-law. "Jason, I want to tell you how much I appreciate you standing up for me and Lizzy last night. I've never had a cop protect me before."

"You haven't been hanging out with the right cops," Jason said.

Rachel leaned forward from the rear seat and put a hand on Jackie's right shoulder. "Do you think I'd be marrying the kind of cop who'd beat you up instead of taking care of you?"

"No," Jackie said quietly. "I know that. But me and all of my drag family have been hassled by cops more often than not, and they mostly look away when the haters smack us. A queen gets killed and they usually call it a suicide, like Marsha P. Johnson."

"How do you even know about Marsha P. Johnson?" Michelle asked. "That was way before your time. I was just a baby."

"We all know," Jackie said, "plus, there was a Netflix documentary a few years ago. She was not the only one who got murdered and the cops didn't care."

"You want to clue me in on what you're talking about?" Mike inquired.

Michelle turned towards Mike and took his hand in hers. "I guess they don't teach new cops. She was a Black drag queen in the early 70s who was murdered. Her case was ignored by the NYPD. It's a pretty sad commentary on law enforcement, and there might have been some New York mob involvement. I'll tell you about it another time. I remember my mother being very upset about it, even years later."

Jason craned his neck toward the back seat. "For now, all Jackie needs to know is that these two New York cops have his back." Jason turned toward Jackie, who bit his lip as he turned the old Toyota into the parking lot.

It was a few minutes before noon when the group walked through the beveled glass door of the law offices of Jerome Garcia, LLC. The office was located on the second floor of a mixed-use building with a variety of retail shops and restaurants on the ground level. The place looked like a converted shopping mall, with the second floor wrapping around the sides of a central atrium. Unlike the ground floor, which was teeming with people browsing the storefronts and enjoying the air-conditioned environment, the second floor was quiet on a Sunday afternoon. Inside, a small waiting room with an empty reception desk greeted them as a bell on the door chimed to announce their arrival.

A voice from beyond an open inner door beckoned to them. "C'mon back, folks." The voice carried a tinge of southwestern twang.

Mike motioned for the group to follow him toward the open door, which led to a short hallway. Another open door brought them into a large office with windows looking out over the building's parking lot and to the rust-colored mountains beyond. The office was decorated in a desert theme, with Navajo-style wall hangings and potted cacti. Their host walked slowly from behind a huge maple desk that dominated one end of the room. As he approached, Mike took stock of the man Michelle had found to be Jackie's lawyer.

"Mr. Garcia, I presume?" Mike held out a hand.

"Absolutely," Garcia replied with a warm smile.

"Jerry Garcia? Really?"

As he gave Mike's hand a firm shake, Garcia said, "Jerome Perez Garcia, but I discovered early on that Jerry Garcia was much more memorable." Garcia was the picture of a middle-aged hippie. His gray hair was pulled back and tied into a pony tail. He wore a white dress shirt with a tie-dyed necktie above his blue jeans and cowboy boots. There was no jacket in sight. He glanced at the group and settled his eyes on Jackie. "Is this our wrongfully accused entertainer?"

"I am," Jackie spoke up quickly. "Not hard to guess, huh, with these two butch guys the only other options?"

Garcia burst out into a belly laugh and walked up to Jackie, placing a hand gently on his shoulder. "So, your father was a baseball fan?"

Jackie dropped his head. "It was my grandfather. He was a big Brooklyn Dodger fan. That's why my dad named her Rachel," Jackie pointed to his sister. "I got Jackie."

The lawyer laughed again. "Well, listen to me, Son. You are in the cross-hairs of every kind of trouble if that snake Rickenbacker is on this. He's like a dog with a meaty bone. Unfortunately, he's just as stubborn when he's wrong as when he's right. And he's a homophobe of the first order, so I'm sure he's ready to celebrate pinning a queen's murder on another queen. I'm not sure if that rock-head is on the take, but he's a certified jerk."

"Are you saying we can't trust the local cops to be honest?" Mike was incredulous.

"Let's just say there have been rumors, and I've seen some things that made me scratch my head. I've seen some low-life hoods get released for lack of evidence when even their defense lawyers were surprised, especially if they're connected to the local mob. But let me tell you, I don't give a horse's ass what that Neanderthal thinks and I'm happy to help you fend him off. He and the rest of the Vegas Keystone Cops don't intimidate me. I'll gladly take you on as a client and fight for justice."

"That's nice to hear," Jackie said, looking less frightened. "I've had nothing but bad experiences with cops. This whole thing has me pretty freaked out."

"Don't worry, Jackie. It's normal to be frightened. The prospect of getting arrested and charged with a murder is terrifying."

"Do you think the bastard will really arrest me?" Jackie was both angry and on the edge of tears.

"Now, now, I'm sorry about my stupid comment. I've got no reason to think so. Let's take this one step at a time. The first thing is to get a small retainer and have you sign a client agreement. That way we'll establish an attorney-client relationship so what we tell each other is privileged."

Mike stepped forward, getting the lawyer's attention. "How much is the retainer?"

"Well, since Jackie here hasn't been arrested, I'm providing advice and counsel, but not appearing in court . . . Let's say one thousand dollars for now, with that amount being charged against my time at two hundred an hour."

Mike and Jason exchanged a glance and a nod. "Sounds fine. Should we call you Jerry?"

"Jerry works for everyone else in Vegas, so sure." Jerry pulled out a standard client agreement contract and handed it to Jackie, who handed it to Mike. After Mike and Jason both read it and approved, Jackie signed. When the paperwork was completed, Jerry said, "Now, I'm gonna ask all of you except for Jackie to wait in the outer lobby while I have a privileged conversation with my new client."

While the rest of the group obeyed, Mike and Michelle confirmed the schedule for the rest of the week — assuming the murder investigation didn't scuttle their plans. Michelle had booked two evening shows, but had left their plans relatively flexible leading up to the Sunday wedding. Mike and Michelle were flying back to New York on Monday at noon. Rachel and Jason were lingering an extra day alone as husband and wife.

"Doesn't leave you much time to play poker," Jason ribbed Mike.

"I'm sure there'll be a few opportunities," Mike replied, but without great conviction.

Before the discussion about the merits of time at the poker table versus time with Michelle progressed, the office door opened and the smiling face of Jerry Garcia beckoned them back inside. Jackie was sitting in a high-backed chair, looking slightly less nervous than when they arrived.

"Thank you all for puttin' up with that. There are some things a lawyer can only say to his client, and vice versa."

Mike held up an open palm. "We're cops, Mr. Garcia. We totally understand."

"Cops, you say?" The lawyer cocked his head to the side. "Now, that's the first I've heard of that. I don't recognize you."

"We're in town from New York on a vacation," Jason clarified. "Jackie is my future brother-in-law. As a matter of fact, the wedding is Sunday."

"Well now, that is a wonderful thing!" Jerry turned to Jackie. "Why didn't you tell me?"

"You didn't ask," Jackie responded flatly. "You told me I shouldn't say anything except answer your questions."

"Quite correct, Jackie. Very well done." Jerry then stopped talking and the room got quiet for several seconds. Everyone was waiting for the lawyer to speak. Finally, he lost the far-away look in his eyes and focused on Mike and Jason. "I'm wondering whether you two will help or hurt when it comes to Buzz Rickenbacker. I'm not sure. He generally dislikes easterners, but sometimes cops can talk to cops in ways that others can't."

"Based on our interaction last night, I'd say there's not much chance of us becoming buddies and doing favors for one another," Mike said.

"Well, be that as it may, we need to all be together on next steps. First, and this will be obvious to you both, do not let the police talk to Jackie without me present. I know you probably think you can protect him yourself, but it is vital that you let me know if they arrest him, or if Rickenbacker tries to question him. I've already told Jackie not to say anything."

"Mr. Garcia," Rachel spoke up for the first time, "Jackie's not in any real trouble here, right?"

"It's Jerry, please. I'll give you my non-privileged assessment: Jackie is a suspect because Herr Rickenbacker is looking for an easy target, and Jackie seems to have benefited the most from Mimi LaRee's murder. It could have been a failed robbery, or rape, or a disagreement over the price of a blowjob. It could have been any number of things, and there may be plenty of other people who wanted Mimi dead for some reason. But Rickenbacker doesn't care about that. He cares about clearing his cases, so if he can find an easy suspect and make an arrest, he's gonna be happy. If he can pin it on someone like Jackie, who he considers to be a degenerate, so much the better in his mind.

"Now, Jackie has a pretty good alibi since the show was going on and he never left the theater. There are surveillance cameras around that plaza and on the sidewalk, so if Jackie had ventured outside the Mardi Gras between shows, there would be a video record. I'm sure the local cops haven't tried to look yet, but they will have to eventually. There is a small window of time when it seems that Mimi went out to the CVS to get a mascara. I'm betting there's a clerk who worked last night who will remember selling a mascara to a person in full drag."

"We can check that," Mike volunteered.

Jerry patted Mike's shoulder. "Now, Mike, that's kind of you to offer, but it's best if you stay out of the investigation and let the cops do their job. If you question the clerk before the cops do, they'll think you're trying to tamper with the witness. We don't want that. It's best if you stand back."

"Mike's not very good at that," Michelle piped up, nudging Mike with her elbow. Everyone laughed briefly, including Mike, which broke the tension. Then Michelle said, "I'd like to see the autopsy report on LaRee. I'm sure the local ME would talk to me if I asked as a professional favor."

"You have a professional relationship with the medical examiner?"

Michelle gave the lawyer a side glance. "I'm the medical examiner for New York County."

Jerry stroked his hand across his head and pulled on his ponytail as he pondered the idea. "If Jackie were arrested and charged, we'd be able to get the report as part of initial disclosures, but at this point I don't see why we'd want to dig there. The report probably hasn't even been done yet, and it's not like we need to find the real killer here in order to protect Jackie."

Michelle's face fell into disappointment. "It's always my first instinct."

"I understand. But, like I was saying, if the cops do their job they should either uncover other suspects or rule out

Jackie. They aren't going to make an arrest without evidence, and right now they have squat. They think Jackie had a motive and might have had opportunity, but that's not nearly enough. Jackie just needs to maintain business as usual and keep quiet. Everybody understand?"

"Alright. It works for me," Mike answered. "We're planning on having an enjoyable trip. Let's hope this unfortunate situation doesn't get in the way too much."

"Amen to that!" Rachel seconded.

After everyone exchanged business cards and cell phone numbers, the group said good-bye and went back out to Jackie's car. When Mike crammed himself into the tiny back seat again, he extracted his phone and checked for an email from Berkowitz. He was happy to see one, but not happy with the content. Berkowitz had called the Vegas PD and asked to speak to a detective working the Mimi LaRee murder. When he got connected to Detective Drew Maulgray, he gave him the brush-off. So much for professional courtesy between cops. Maulgray wouldn't even confirm there had been a murder or that there was an investigation. Berkowitz said he felt like he was treated like a reporter, like maybe he was lying about being with the NYPD. He apologized for not getting more.

After Mike relayed the information to the front seat, Jason replied, "I guess we would react the same way to an out-of-the-blue phone call from somebody claiming to be a cop."

"Let's hope the two local detectives will back off when they check the surveillance cams and realize they have no evidence implicating Jackie."

"Yeah," Jason agreed. "Let's hope."

Chapter 19 — Routine Investigations

Monday, January 6
Las Vegas, NV

THE LAS VEGAS POLICE HANDLED A WIDE VARIETY of criminal matters, mostly involving out-of-town actors. There were plenty of local criminals, even aside from the organized crime figures. But it was always the "foreigners" who created the most problems.

Mimi LaRee, the dead drag queen, had lived in Vegas long enough that she almost qualified as a local. Mimi, as they nearly always referred to their stiff, had a short rap sheet that included a minor drug possession bust six years earlier and one lewd conduct misdemeanor that had been pled down from a more serious solicitation arrest. That one had involved a blow job, a visiting businessman, and an undercover cop. For the last four years, her record was blank, which corresponded to Mimi's rise to drag queen stardom.

Drew Maulgray had the file information open on his computer screen and had it mostly memorized. None of it helped him with the investigation. He and Buzz Rickenbacker were still waiting for the two teams of uniformed officers who were canvasing the businesses around the plaza where Mimi's bloody body was found Saturday night. They already had several video files, including from the CVS, but had not identified a suspect.

Mimi had certainly visited the drugstore and exited at 8:14 p.m. A figure appearing to be a White male, slightly shorter than Mimi in her platform heels, approached as Mimi walked away, but the camera focused on the CVS doorway got only a brief shot of the guy's back. None of the other cameras they had were focused on the hallway leading to the public restroom. The rest of the video images showed a typical cross-section of Las Vegas Strip visitors, giving no hint about which of the hundreds of faces might have killed Mimi.

"Buzz," Maulgray called out, seeing his partner walking by. "You got a minute?"

Rickenbacker took his time altering his course to arrive. "Yeah?"

"I've looked at all the video and there's no sign of Jackie Robinson anywhere, in drag or otherwise. We've got nothing to narrow it down to anybody else, but it's pretty clear Robinson wasn't there."

"Not that you see, right? The guy's a performer. He has access to makeup and costumes, and might be dressed like a girl. So, you can't be sure."

Maulgray shook his head, but had to admit it was impossible to be one hundred percent certain. "I'm thinking we should be looking at this as a hate crime, or a robbery. That gold purse definitely belonged to Mimi LaRee and somebody cleaned out the cash before tossing it in the trash can."

"Anybody would grab the cash and dump the purse to make it look like a robbery, so that means nothing. It could also have been a contract hit. Robinson could have paid somebody else to take out his rival queen."

"It's not like Robinson has any money, Buzz. How's it possible?"

"I don't know. Maybe a big jackpot at the slot machine. You never know. Robinson still has the motive, and the opportunity. We're still hot on that ass until we have somebody different."

Maulgray started to object – again – but let it go. He knew how stubborn his partner could be, and he didn't have enough credibility to push it. "OK, Buzz. Oh, and did you send a note to the FBI about having a dead Black drag queen? I'm guessing they'll be interested if they're still trying to ID the girls from that photograph. Two of 'em were Black."

"Yeah. I got it covered."

"OK. I also want to talk about Cricket – Sheila Buchanan. I got the autopsy results and tox back on her and there's a lot there to suggest a homicide."

"Oh, geez, Opie, are you still all moony-eyed about that dead stripper?"

"Give me a little credit, Buzz. I didn't know her, and neither did you, but I'm looking at the evidence. It's not only the facial bruising. The ME said she had defensive wounds and her alcohol level was off the chart."

"Yeah, like I figured. She was loaded."

"No," Maulgray pressed, "more than loaded. Four-point-O. She should have been long since unconscious at that level. Plus, there was a lot of undigested alcohol in her stomach. It looks like somebody force-fed her a bottle of vodka, then put her behind the wheel and ran that car off the overpass."

"That's quite a fantasy story, kid. You should write mystery novels." Rickenbacker waved his hand backwards as he walked away. "I told you to let that one lie. It's not worth chasing. We've got an active murder here, so let's focus on that. Let the traffic guys deal with the accident."

Maulgray fumed behind his desk. He wrote a note indicating a possible homicide and saved it to the file. He thought about taking the issue to their boss, the division captain, but it wasn't worth expending his limited credibility on this case. Maybe if he were a veteran like Rickenbacker, he could get away with it. For now, he was the new kid in town. He would pay his dues and keep his mouth shut. But he wasn't forgetting about it, or about Rickenbacker's seemingly irrational behavior.

♦♦♦

Monday, January 6
Rapid City, SD

Agent Chelsea Shields chewed on a fingernail while she scanned summary memos from the task force working the FBI's sports gambling case. The problem with all the memos was the absence of any hard evidence that there was a central architect of the scheme – assuming there was a scheme. They had witnesses who verified the betting, which was itself illegal but fairly routine. The juice in the case was the theory that some central actor or organization was not only taking the bets and hedging via Las Vegas Sports Books, but getting an unlawful edge by having insiders provide key information. The holy grail of the investigation would be evidence of players actually shaving points or throwing games for the benefit of the gamblers.

"It has to be centered in Vegas," she said to Dumm. "They have to be placing hedge bets in the legal Sports Book."

"You're right," Derek responded in a tired voice. They had been around and around the issues for hours. "But any organized crime operation anywhere in the world could contract with local guys in Vegas to put down their hedge bets. So, it could be anybody."

Chelsea bit her lower lip, knowing they were arguing without any real facts. "OK, but just for the sake of argument, if it were centered in Vegas, who would be the most likely guys?"

Dumm stood and stretched his back. "I don't know, Shields. I don't work Vegas. I have enough trouble keeping the wise guys from Chicago and St. Louis straight. I know the guy who runs the field office there. I'll give you his number and you can call him. If you're right and the sports betting ring is linked to Vegas, it would make sense that our photo with Bushfield would have been taken there. Since our guys and the local cops couldn't ID the girls or the venue, I'm thinking you're on the wrong track."

Chelsea gave a half-hearted laugh. "Maybe. But, maybe we'll get lucky and get a lead down there so we can take a field trip and go somewhere warmer."

"That's anywhere but here."

Chapter 20 — Chocolate Dreams

Monday, January 6
Las Vegas, NV

ON MONDAY, MICHELLE PLANNED to take Rachel out for a day of pampering. She was the bride-to-be, after all, and deserved to be indulged. Jackie and Lizzy happily volunteered to come along. They had no show on Mondays, so they were up for a pampering day for themselves, since Michelle offered to treat them.

The previous day had been reasonably pleasant for the bridal party. Michelle had booked a trip to see the Hoover Dam, and Jackie was thrilled to spend time with his big sister. The tour took up most of the afternoon and early evening. Then, the group went to see a comedy show. Mike grumbled mildly about not having any time to get to the poker table, but they had the rest of the week. Nobody received any communications from the local cops about the progress of the investigation into Mimi LaRee's murder.

For the spa day, Michelle had scoped out a venue on the internet before they left New York. But Lizzy knew a much better option off the tourist track. It was where the locals went to avoid the rude out-of-towners. Lizzy had worked there part-time two years earlier, and still knew most of the staff. They all enjoyed facials, manicures, and massages.

It was the first time Rachel and Michelle had seen Lizzy out of drag. In jeans and a black t-shirt bearing the logo of Señor Frog's Cabaret – a local club that featured a weekend drag brunch – he looked younger than his alter-ego. The Asian characteristics of his eyes were muted without the emphasizing makeup. He kept his head shaved bald, which helped with wigs during performances, and wore a baseball cap whenever they were outside in the sun. Lizzy refused to disclose the first name his parents gave him and insisted on being "Lizzy" at all times.

As they lounged in shaded mesh chairs in fluffy terrycloth robes, Jackie turned his head toward Rachel. "Sis, I know I've said this ten times already, but that man of yours is fabulous! I'm glad you finally found somebody strong enough to handle you."

Michelle laughed, while Rachel pretended to be offended. "What do you mean, handle me? I'm not looking to be handled."

"I know you're not," Jackie continued, waving a half-consumed bottle of spring water in Rachel's direction. "That's just it. You don't know what you want until you got it. Now you got it. I hope you can keep him happy."

"What's that supposed to mean?" Rachel playfully responded. She was so relaxed from the spa treatment that actually getting mad was far from her mind.

"I wonder if Jason is all-in on the baby."

Rachel stared at her younger brother, whose slim, smooth legs protruded from under his robe. She felt the familiar tinge of jealousy that Jackie's legs were more attractive than her own. "What baby?"

"Oh, girl, don't think you're not super obvious. Just

watching you with that glow, and I saw you putting ginger ale in your champagne glass. And you're always touching your belly. I can see it. And the quickie Vegas wedding? Really? How dumb do you think I am?"

"I do not touch my belly!" Rachel protested. "Michelle? I don't, do I?"

"Um, well, Sweetie, to be totally honest, I have noticed it a few times." Michelle winced as she delivered the news.

"Oh, fine. You don't think anyone else has noticed, do you? Like my mother?"

Before Michelle could answer, Jackie said, "Don't worry. Mom and Dad are probably oblivious. Besides, they only have baby-eyes for Diane now. She's due, when? Next month?"

"Yeah. Four more weeks, I think. That's partly why we didn't want to have a big deal wedding now. We'll let her get through her delivery and then I'll tell Mom and Daddy about our baby. We'll be married by then, so I'm hoping Daddy won't blow a gasket."

"Are you kidding? They'll be thrilled. They've been waiting for you to get a husband and a baby for years."

Rachel slapped Jackie's shoulder. "Oh, you!"

They all toasted to Rachel and her baby and relaxed into their soft chairs.

After another half hour, they reluctantly showered and bade the spa farewell. Rachel consented to wearing a sparkling silver sash telling every passerby that she was the "Bride to Be." The next stop was the Hershey's Chocolate Bar at the New York, New York casino hotel. Rachel thought it was ironic that they would come to Vegas only to hang out in "New York," but

Michelle said a good friend told her it was essential that they visit. It was early afternoon outside, but when they entered the windowless casino space, time lost all meaning. It would have looked the same at four in the morning. They descended a twenty-foot-wide staircase from the street down to the casino level amid the buzzing din. Above the bells of the slot machines and the clack of chips and dice, Rachel noticed the opening strains of a Whitney Houston song coming from speakers hidden throughout the cavernous space. It seemed like music was always playing in Las Vegas.

As the group reached the bottom of the stairs, they could see the marquee of the bar. The word H-E-R-S-H-E-Y-'S was spelled out in huge block letters, lit with flashing bulbs. The curving bar was mostly empty, easily allowing them to find four stools together. Rachel, wearing her sash, took the seat closest to the middle of the bar, with Michelle on her right. Jackie and Lizzy took the two seats closest to the far wall.

A dark-skinned bartender with a brass nameplate identifying him as Esteban welcomed them and handed out martini menus. As she scanned the list, Rachel noticed the song still playing over the sound system: "How Will I Know," one of her favorites. On this day, she heard it in a different way – not joyful, but doubtful. She dropped her chin and worked hard to hold back tears.

Michelle glanced up from the menu and immediately noticed. "Sweetie? What's wrong?"

Rachel tried to smile. She wiped a tear away from the corner of her eye. "Oh . . . it's Whitney. I love this song, but . . . how do I really know? What if Jason doesn't really love me? What if I put too much pressure on him? And now . . . with this baby coming. Am I rushing into this just so I can fit into the dress?"

Michelle recognized the early stages of a melt-down and assumed a calm and authoritative tone. "Jason is one of the most reliable and compassionate people I know. He absolutely adores you. Don't you remember how much trouble he went through to stage that proposal? Would he have done all that if he didn't want to do whatever it takes to make you happy?"

"I know," Rachel choked. "It's just that everything's going wrong. Even having to have the wedding here instead of at home in June like we planned. And now it's freezing cold in Las Vegas! It's like the universe is telling me something."

Before Michelle could think of an encouraging response, Esteban returned to ask for their orders. Lizzy and Jackie both ordered chocolate martinis. Michelle ordered a caramel and chocolate one for herself. When it was Rachel's turn, she asked, "What's the best thing you can make me without alcohol?" Esteban suggested a sweet-sounding concoction. Rachel agreed without enthusiasm.

An older woman sitting at the other end of the bar leaned toward Rachel. She placed a boney arm on the bar, a gold bangle bracelet clanging against the polished wood. She wore a white top with a plunging neckline, drawing Rachel's attention to the exposed top third of her breasts, pushed up by a tight bra with lace fringes. The skin of her neck and chest was tanned to the point of weathered leather below a dangling gold necklace. "I see you're the bride. Congratulations, Sweetheart, but you should try one of the real martinis here. They're the absolute best." She then ordered two of the house specials.

As Esteban turned to prepare the orders, Rachel said, "I'd love to, but right now I can't."

She raised a painted-on eyebrow. "Oh, Honey, I hope you're not pregnant. That's a damned poor reason to get married."

Rachel was dumbfounded that a total stranger would say such a thing. Before she could compose herself enough to respond, Esteban returned with two slender martini glasses, depositing them on the bar in front of the woman. She hopped off the stool, grabbed one in each hand, then sashayed away.

Rachel hung her head again as Michelle put an arm around her shoulder. When Esteban brought the drinks, he said the mocktail was on the house for the bride, which failed to improve Rachel's mood. But Whitney Houston was no longer serenading them and after a few minutes, Rachel pulled herself back into a semi-festive demeanor. She even accepted Jackie's offer to take a sip of his chocolate martini.

Jackie brought the classic cone-shaped glass over so Rachel could have a sip of the chocolate specialty. "Don't pay any attention to that skank, Sis. Trash like that is like one-dollar chips around this town. If she didn't have that push-up bra, her tits would drag on the ground."

Everyone laughed, including Rachel, who couldn't help herself. She then took a small taste. "Wow! That's so good. I'm going to make Jason take me back here after we have this baby."

Chapter 21 — High Anxiety

Monday, January 6
Las Vegas, NV

THE PAMPER-THE-BRIDE GROUP took the monorail from the New York, New York to their next stop – a ride on the big Ferris wheel at the LINQ hotel, known as the High Roller. The views were spectacular, plus there was a bar at the base so they could take more champagne – and ginger ale – into the gondola and snap selfies with their glasses at the top. The clear plastic sides of their carriage acted like a greenhouse, warming the interior against the still-chilly outside air. They laughed as other riders on the High Roller yelled congratulations and took photos of the bride and her entourage. Michelle commented that she hadn't had so much to drink before dinner since their cruise, where they had an unlimited drink plan.

They wobbled off the High Roller and walked in two pairs to the back of the LINQ and across the street toward the monorail station. The area behind the hotel and casino in the middle of the afternoon was deserted, but the four revelers paid no attention. Rachel and Michelle walked ahead of Jackie, who was leaning against Lizzy after several glasses of bubbly.

Neither noticed the large black SUV that pulled out of the valet and taxi stand when they appeared on the ramp leading from the High Roller. Ongoing construction required pedestrians to skirt along Krueger Drive in order to reach the entrance to the monorail. The hulking vehicle accelerated as Michelle and Rachel stepped from the hot asphalt back onto the sidewalk under steel scaffolding.

"Watch that curb, Jackie," Michelle called out as she turned with a chuckle toward Rachel's unsteady younger brother. The smile on her face morphed into horror in an instant. "Look out!" she screamed.

Rachel spun around, as did Jackie and Lizzy. The SUV, now traveling at three times the appropriate speed for the narrow lane, swerved toward them. Rachel screamed. Lizzy grabbed Jackie's arm and pulled as they both fell under the scaffolding.

The SUV plowed into the steel supports, which toppled like bowling pins, causing a downpour of 2x8 planks as the scaffolding collapsed. Jackie rolled away from the curb and was covered in the wooden rain. Lizzy cried out in pain as a beam hit his head. The SUV swerved back toward the street as a metal pipe crashed into its windshield, leaving an indentation and a spiderweb of cracked safety glass in front of the driver. Whoever was driving didn't stop to assess the damage or help the four pedestrians. The vehicle careened back across the narrow street, banged into a temporary retaining wall, then straightened and sped off. Its tires squealed as it fishtailed around a tight curve and disappeared out onto LINQ Lane, past the High Roller, and out of sight.

Michelle's medical training and Rachel's EMT instincts kicked in as they rushed to the aid of their fallen comrades. Several people ran to the scene from the direction of the monorail station and started pulling planks off the pile under which both Lizzy and Jackie were buried. Lizzy was the first to emerge from the debris, a bloody gash running down the side of his forehead. Rachel pulled an antiseptic wipe and some tissues from her handbag and went to work on the wound.

Two tense minutes later, a man wearing a Viva Las Vegas t-shirt and a woman whose thin arms belied her strength helped Michelle pull Jackie from under the pile. Jackie coughed and rubbed his elbow, but did not seem to have suffered any serious injuries. He sat on the cluttered curb as Michelle asked questions to try to rule out a concussion, and several bystanders who had gathered offered bottles of water. Someone had called 9-1-1, and within a minute a police cruiser pulled up under full siren.

It took another half hour for them all to give statements to the police about the crazy driver who lost control and took out the scaffolding. It was amazing that nobody was seriously hurt. Jackie and Lizzy both declined when an ambulance arrived and offered to take them to the hospital. Both insisted they were fine and didn't want to pay an exorbitant bill to be transported by ambulance. Michelle was pretty certain neither had a concussion. The rest of the day of pampering Rachel was scrapped when a passing limo driver offered to take them back to the Mardi Gras for no charge, since he was going that direction anyway.

Chapter 22 — Bad Timing

Monday, January 6
Las Vegas, NV

SINCE THE REST OF THEIR PARTY WAS SCHEDULED to be out the whole day pampering Rachel, Mike and Jason took advantage of the jacuzzi and sauna at the Mardi Gras during the morning, then walked on the Strip to a Mexican restaurant with outdoor seating for lunch. Mike knew the poker room at the nearby Venetian hosted cash games frequented by both local pros and visiting tourists who were happy to give up their bankroll while on vacation. As they settled up the lunch bill, Mike noticed the opening strains of "Hotel California" coming over the outdoor sound system that provided background music all along the Vegas Strip.

"That's one of my favorite songs," he said, taking one final sip from his margarita glass.

"Really, Mike?" Jason looked askance at his partner. "I didn't figure you for an Eagles kind of guy."

"Some songs transcend genre," Mike replied in a professorial voice. "Great is great. No use fighting it. Did you know the Eagles started out as the backup band for Linda Ronstadt?"

"No kidding?"

"Gospel truth. They were so good she won a boatload of

awards, then the record label pulled them away and made them stars on their own. Think about it. Linda Ronstadt singing lead with Glenn Frey and Don Henley singing harmony and playing guitar. I wish I'd seen them in concert."

They walked to the Venetian, past the figure of Marilyn Monroe guarding the entrance to Madame Tussauds Wax Museum, and past the large fountains on the Italian-style plaza. They went up a long ramp leading to the second-level entrance and traversed the endless curving pathways inside the mammoth casino floor looking for the poker room. Jason insisted on stopping to shoot some craps. Mike couldn't say no, having taught the game to Jason on their cruise the prior May. Forty minutes later, Jason was five hundred eighty dollars up for his session, while Mike was down seventy-five. "I'll leave you to your hot dice, Jason. Come find me in the poker room when you're done here."

"I might be a while," Jason smiled.

"We've got all afternoon. We're not meeting the girls for dinner until six." Mike walked away and finally found the poker room. He secured a rack of chips from the cashier and waited for a seat in the crowded parlor. After another fifteen minutes of waiting, his name was called and he took a seat next to the dealer at a nine-handed table. Glancing at his playing companions, he immediately saw one young-looking Asian man with a huge pile of chips in front of him, two seats to Mike's left. Not great, but he had to take the seat he was given. The rest of the players all had much smaller chip stacks, giving Mike encouragement that all he needed to do was avoid big hands with the big stack and he could make some serious profit.

Two hands into his poker session, his cell phone buzzed in his pocket. He figured it was Jason, letting him know the craps table had lost a shooter. Instead, it was Michelle, saying there had been an accident and they were on their way back to the Mardi Gras with an injured Jackie and Lizzy.

"Leaving already?" the Asian man with the big chip stack asked as Mike racked his chips.

"Unfortunately, that phone call was a bit of an emergency. I'll see you back here later." The other players all wished Mike well, sad to see a new player depart without donating chips to the group. As Mike walked out of the poker room, he got a text from Jason, who was on his way to the Cashier's window. They agreed to meet at the fountain out front, next to Las Vegas Boulevard.

"I only played two hands before the phone rang," Mike immediately lamented when Jason met him at the fountain.

"Don't worry, Mike. We're here all week."

When Mike and Jason heard the story from all four of the witnesses, they both had the same thought. "I don't believe in coincidences when it comes to attempted murder," Mike said seriously.

"Oh, Mike," Michelle tried to keep Rachel and Jackie from freaking out. "You don't really think that car was intentionally trying to run us down?"

They were sitting around a glass-topped table under a multicolored umbrella beside the pool at the Mardi Gras. As some children splashed around under the watchful eyes of parents with frozen drinks next to their lounge chairs, Jason reached out for Rachel's hand. "There's one chance in a billion that one day after Mimi LaRee gets murdered, two performers from the same show are nearly run down in the street. I have to agree with Mike. It's too much of a coincidence. We have to assume that whoever killed Mimi was trying to kill Jackie and Lizzy."

"But why?" Jackie had a Band-Aid on his elbow, but didn't otherwise look to be injured. He was clearly shaken by the experience, however. "Why would anybody want to kill us? Do they think we killed Mimi?"

Mike clasped his hands on the table in front of him. "It's hard to say, Jackie. I'm assuming you and Lizzy have not been involved in any criminal activity or anything else where you were around the kind of people who might commit a murder. Is that correct?"

Jackie's face was pensive as he thought about the question. "It's Vegas, Mike. And we're entertainers. You can't know who's in the audience when we perform. We do a lot of side gigs besides the show at *The Birdcage*. We've done some pretty wild parties. You'd be amazed how crazy a bachelor party can get. But somebody who would want to kill us – and Mimi? I try not to think about it, but there are some scary haters out there. I've seen girls get beat up when some drunk redneck hits on them and then freaks out. Now, I'm totally freaked out."

"Were you three all together at any of those side gigs?" Jason asked, falling into investigation mode along with Mike.

Jackie thought about it, as did Lizzy. "I don't think so. Mimi the diva didn't consort with us underlings much. I can think of one or two that we were both working, but not with Lizzy. Honey, can you think of any?"

Lizzy agreed. "No. Nothing. I don't think I've ever performed with Miss Mimi outside of our show."

"Well, either somebody's a terrible driver and a hit-and-runner, or Jackie needs to watch his back." Mike squinted into the late-afternoon sun. "So far, nobody has reported this to the two cops we met last night, Rickenbacker and whatshisname, right?"

Everyone shook their heads. Mike sighed. "As bad a vibe as I get from that guy, and as much as Jackie's new lawyer doesn't trust him, I think we have to report this. It could be important to the investigation. If there's a killer out there who took out the diva, and then tried to run down Jackie and Lizzy, I would want to know about that if I were the detective on the case."

Rachel looked at Jason, seemingly pleading with her eyes for her fiancé to take a contrary view of the situation. She was quickly disappointed. "I agree, Mike," Jason said with his eyes on his partner, not his future wife. "We have to tell him."

Jackie reached out and took Lizzy's hand, squeezing until his knuckles turned white. Facing an audience inside *The Birdcage* theater was nothing compared to the unknown terrors of the Las Vegas police.

The group agreed reluctantly, and nominated Mike to have the conversation so Jackie didn't have to speak directly to the local cop. They all agreed that Jerry Garcia should be included.

"OK, I'll take care of that tomorrow. You two have no show tonight, so let's all stay together. We haven't got our guns with us, but there's still safety in numbers. If there is somebody out there trying to take these two out, we shouldn't let them be alone. I'm thinking maybe we should get them a room here in the hotel, so they don't have to be alone in their apartment."

"Don't you think that's overkill?" Rachel said.

"Maybe. Jackie, what kind of security do you have at home?"

Jackie's face was as chalky as a Black man's could get. "Um, we have a deadbolt lock on the door, but the apartments are all open to the outside of the building. There's no doorman or anything. It's a cheap place."

"That figures," Mike nodded. "Well, my suggestion stands. Let me talk to the manager of the hotel and see if we can get a room for you here. Jason can go with you to get some clothes and whatever else you need from home, unless you have some more secure location you can go to?"

Lizzy and Jackie both shook their heads. The events of the week were spiraling out of control. They were singers and dancers, not soldiers or cops. The thought that somebody was targeting them for murder was far more frightening than Terry cutting them from the show if they flubbed a line on stage.

Jackie said, "Mike, I'm so glad you and Jason are here. And I'm really sorry all this is messing up Rachel's wedding week."

"Oh, Jackie." Rachel leaned over and put an arm around Jackie's shoulder, pulling him into a hug. "You're more important to me than anything, including the wedding. But I'm sure everything will be OK. You're innocent. Remember that. I'm sure Jason and Mike aren't going to let anything bad happen to you."

Jackie nodded, but didn't respond. Lizzy slid over and joined the group hug.

Michelle whispered into Mike's ear, "You think you can really protect them?"

"I'm going to do my damnedest."

Chapter 23 — Boiling Point

Monday, January 6
Las Vegas, NV

THE AFTERNOON SUN STREAMED into Freddy Costanzo's office. His fists were clenched and a vein on the side of his head throbbed ominously. Rick Garetti, who had been sitting in one of the two straight-back chairs opposite Freddy's desk, bent from the waist, putting his head against his knees. A glass ashtray sailed past where his head had been a moment earlier, exploding into shards when it collided with the corner of the marble tiled floor and the far wall. Rick sat back up, saying nothing. The boss was angry, which was understandable. Flying, breakable objects in such circumstances were not unusual.

"Do I need to hire a pro here to handle the situation?" Freddy spat out, breathing heavily after the exertion of his ashtray fastball.

"No, Boss. I don't think that's going to help. Eddie and I had no trouble tracking them today. We had a good plan, but they got lucky."

"Whaddaya mean, them?"

"The queen spent the whole day with two chicks and one of his drag fuck buddies. The women are here with two cops from New York. Rickenbacker says they're detectives, but he hasn't confirmed it. We need to isolate the guy. It's hard to deal with him with two cops nearby."

"After your screw-up today, he's gonna be on guard, right? That's not gonna help. You're slipping, Rick." Freddy rested his hand on a bronze business card holder stuffed full of gold-leaf-trimmed cards. Rick flinched, but Freddy didn't hurl the throwable object.

"I agree. We didn't get the job done today. I take responsibility for that. We were trying to make it look like an accident to keep the heat off you. But, Boss, I asked around about this Jackie Robinson queen. He's in town less than a year. He's got no record. The people I talked to say he's a quiet kid who mostly keeps to himself. I don't figure him to be our blackmailer. I don't even know if he's savvy enough to have a clue about . . . the old guy."

"It has to be that queen!" Freddy bellowed. "The other two are dead. Who else could it be?"

"I don't know, Boss," Rick conceded quietly. "I'll have Eddie on him tomorrow, and I gave a tip to Rickenbacker that he should focus his energy on Robinson. That should keep him under scrutiny. We'll stay on him, and if we get a window, we'll get the job done. You can count on it."

"Can I?" Freddy softened his voice. "You're the one guy I've always relied on, Ricky. We've been doing this hustle for a long time together. I need you to come through for me, like always."

"I know. I won't let you down, Freddy."

"You better not!" Freddy barked. "They call you the Neck and not the Brain for a reason, Ricky. Maybe I need to bring in somebody else."

"I can handle it, Boss."

"Then do it!"

"Well, we'll find out if he's involved at the next money

drop. I kinda doubt he'll be there, but you never know. I've got that situation under control."

"You're not giving Shithead any more of my money, right?"

"No. Don't worry. He's not getting it, and the bait is my money, not yours."

"How many men?"

"We're gonna have six on the inside, plus two cars outside – one in the front and one in the back. This idiot isn't getting away this time."

"I'll hold you to that." Freddy turned away and stared out the window. Rick headed for the door.

Chapter 24 — Hidden Figures

Monday, January 6
Las Vegas, NV

THE TABLE BY THE MARDI GRAS POOL HAD BECOME the de facto war room for Mike and Jason as they planned strategy for dealing with the apparent danger Jackie and Lizzy were in. They tried to tamp down the anxiety level, but everyone was on edge. Michelle and Jason tried to keep Rachel focused on the excitement of the upcoming wedding and off the possibility that somebody had tried to kill Jackie. Rachel and Michelle had an appointment the following afternoon with the wedding planner from the hotel's chapel. Rachel had booked the room at the last minute, so they were relegated to a ceremony at 6:00 p.m. on Sunday, but they were happy to have it. Rachel didn't want to go to one of the on-demand wedding mills in town – with or without a reverend dressed as Elvis. She was thrilled to get a booking at the chapel in their hotel, even if it was at an awkward time.

"In Vegas, any time is party time, right?" Rachel looked around the table for confirmation that their "reception" after the ceremony would be spectacular no matter what time it started.

"That's the truth," Mike agreed with a smile. "You can walk into any club or restaurant here at midnight on a Tuesday and it's still absolutely prime time. We can party Sunday night as late as you can stay standing."

"That might be all night!" Rachel smiled and perked up noticeably.

While the group chatted about all the places on the Strip they wanted to visit, Mike checked his email and saw a note from Detective Berkowitz. The note said Mike should call, no matter what time. Mike found a relatively secluded spot off to the side of the door leading back into the hotel from the pool deck. He would have gone back to his room, but it would have taken twenty minutes in the enormous hotel, so he settled for semi-privacy.

"Hey, Mike," Berkowitz greeted the incoming call. "I'm glad you called. I gotta tell you, these Vegas cops are pretty tight with their information. I don't have much for you, but there was something I didn't want to put in an email."

"What?" Mike clipped his words, both because he was in a public space and because he wanted to get back to Michelle.

"You remember that photo the feds sent around a week ago? The guy with the blurred-out face and the three showgirls?"

"Yeah?"

"Well, you remember how we figured that at least one of those girls wasn't really a girl, right? So since your dead dancer from Saturday was a drag queen, we started to wonder if maybe there was some kind of connection. I know it's a long shot, but we found out there was another dead dancer in Vegas last week. I don't know how often twenty-something dancers in Vegas die off, but it seemed worth looking at. The death was coded as a possible homicide, but then later changed to an accident."

"How'd she die?"

"Car accident. Drove through the guardrail over an interstate highway. Not sure why that would have been pegged as a possible homicide, but it was. Go figure. I tried to ask the local detective about it, but he said he didn't know anything."

"Who did you speak to?"

"A really rude guy named Redenbacher or something like that. Like the popcorn."

"Rickenbacker. I've met him. I guess he doesn't have good phone manners, either. I understand why you didn't get much cooperation from him. But it's not a big deal that he wasn't familiar with a car accident."

"I agree, Mike. But here's the thing. I asked him about the photo, to see if he knew about it. He said he had no idea what I was talking about."

"That doesn't surprise me. It was supposed to be a big top-secret thing, right? We didn't even get to keep copies of the picture. Even if he did see it, he wouldn't tell you over the phone."

"Yeah, Mike. I know. That's what Sully said."

"You told Sully? Geez, Steve, I wasn't planning on having the captain involved in this. He's not going to be happy to find out we got involved in a murder investigation out here. You couldn't keep that to yourself?"

"No, Mike. I had to tell the captain because of the other thing."

"I'm listening."

"I called your buddy at the FBI, Agent Forrest. I told him you were out in Vegas, that you were a witness to the murder of a drag queen and you think it might be related to their photo."

"That's not really true," Mike said, a bit concerned about his colleague lying to Agent Forrest.

"Yeah, well, a little. I said you wanted to know if it was cool for you to talk to the local homicide detective about the photo. Like, you wouldn't want to mention it unless the other guy already knew about it. So Forrest tells me Vegas was one of the first places they figured might be a match. All the homicide detectives in Vegas were privy to the picture, so it would be fine for you to talk with them about it."

"OK, I get that." Mike was getting impatient. "But that doesn't mean Rickenbacker would have admitted to knowing about it."

"Yeah, yeah. I know, Mike. But the thing is, Forrest told me the FBI team working the case didn't know about the drag queen's murder in Vegas. The local detectives hadn't reported it to the feds. He called the guy in charge of the photo case, then called me back to make sure he heard it right from me that there was a murdered Black drag queen in Vegas. I said you couldn't make that up, right? I guess it didn't make big local news in Vegas. He told me to let him know if you told me any more details about the case and I said sure. But it's mighty odd that the local guys in Vegas didn't report it, don't you think?"

"Sure. Odd. But so what? How does it help Jackie?"

"I don't know, Mike, I just thought you should know. Do you still have a copy of that photo?"

"What?" Mike stared at his phone. "You mean the photo we were told to give back to the FBI on penalty of flogging? No."

"OK. Well, I took a photo of it. I'm sending it to you in a text. You should delete the text after you save the photo, in case somebody wants to look at your phone's history. Don't tell anybody you got it from me."

Berkowitz hung up before Mike could object. A moment

later, his phone buzzed again and he saw a text message with a little paperclip icon indicating an attachment. He thought about deleting it, but clicked on the clip and scrutinized the photo. He swiped his finger across the screen to enlarge the image and stared hard at it.

He glanced around to make sure nobody was looking over his shoulder. Then he closed the photo and mumbled, "Fuck."

Chapter 25 — The Persistence of Memory

WHEN MIKE SHOWED JASON THE PHOTO, he had the same reaction.

"Holy shit, Mike. What have we stepped in here?"

"Something smelly. How did we not realize this sooner?"

Jason stared at Mike's phone, slowly shaking his head. "I'd never met Jackie before Saturday, and of course never saw the drag costume. We both saw the show Saturday night and neither of us made the connection. Maybe my memory isn't as good as I think it is."

"Can we show it to Jackie without involving the local cops?" Mike asked the question as if the answer should be "yes."

"You know we can't do that."

"I know, but listen." Mike explained his conversation with Berkowitz. When he finished, he asked again, "You still think we should tell Detective Rickenbacker?"

"No. I don't. What about going to the local feds? Let them know?"

"Yeah, we'll have to, but I'm not sure we should do it before we figure out how Jackie is involved in this. I know we're cops, but under the circumstances, I think running some interference for your bride's kid brother may be more important. It's not our case. We're civilians here. Jackie's probably innocent. Maybe he's a witness to something, which would explain a few things. We may need to get him into some kind of protective custody, and I'm not sure the local cops will be entirely protective."

"You're right about that." Jason looked over his shoulder to where Rachel and Michelle were sitting, watching the two men, who had been away from their table longer than necessary for a casual conversation. Michelle was giving Mike a concerned look.

"Do we tell Michelle and Rachel?" Jason spoke to Mike while looking toward the ladies.

"Do you want to explain to Rachel tomorrow that you knew about it and kept it from her?"

"Not for a million dollars."

Mike shrugged. "Well, then, we can choose to not tell Sully instead."

Back at the table, Jason waved to Jackie and Lizzy, who were sitting on the side of the pool, dangling their feet in the cool water. Pools in Las Vegas were often refrigerated against the blistering summer heat, so the water was too cold for the liking of the two local residents. It didn't stop the tourists from taking a dip, however. When they arrived at the table, Mike asked the questions. He and Jason figured that if there was any problem, Jason shouldn't be the one conducting the interrogation.

"Jackie, I want you to think again about any side gigs you did with Mimi LaRee, and tell me if you can remember anything unusual happening." Mike and Jason had briefed Rachel and Michelle about how they were going to handle the situation. Nobody wanted to treat Jackie like a suspect. Mike wanted to see if he would recall the event on his own, which would allow them to avoid having to disclose their possession of the forbidden photo.

"No, Mike. I really can't remember. I know we did a few, but the details are just not that memorable."

Mike pulled out his phone and showed Jackie the photo.

Jackie recognized himself in one of his favorite glam dresses and the Donna Summer wig. His face was turned to the side, but the wig and his profile were recognizable enough. Neither Mike nor Jason had ever seen Jackie before that week, and neither remembered the faces from the photo well enough to match it up, but having it right in front of them, the ID on Jackie was pretty certain. Jackie also identified Mimi LaRee in the shot.

Mike was puzzled. "That doesn't look anything like the Mimi LaRee from the poster outside the theater. How is that her?"

"It's her alternate face," Jackie explained. "Mimi didn't want people to know the diva needed to work side gigs because she wasted so much money. When she wanted to be out incognito, she wore cheek bumps and made up her face like that so nobody would recognize her. But I knew it was her."

"What about the other girl?" Mike asked.

Jackie studied the photo, then said it was probably a girl named Cricket. "It was a cute and unusual name. She said it was her real name, but I didn't believe it."

"Do you remember where it was?"

Jackie studied the shot, enlarging and reducing it several times. He then handed the phone to Lizzy, who said, "I'm pretty sure that wallpaper is from Swanky's, down near Freemont Street. It's a little club that sometimes does drag shows and private parties. Not a lot, I think, but sometimes for special people."

"It must have been a while ago," Jackie said, "but it had to be after I was in this show, because I got that dress from one of the other girls here who left."

"How could we zero in on the date?" Mike asked.

Jackie turned to Lizzy. "The Big Lewbowski would know, right? I wouldn't have had a gig like that with Mimi unless he booked it."

Lizzy nodded. "Sounds right. Looks like somebody was having fun." She pointed to the man with Cricket's exposed breast in his face and Jackie's hand on his crotch.

"Who's this Lewbowski?"

"Alexander Lewbowski, our booking agent. Lots of the girls use him, and he's got plenty of other clients around town."

"Everybody has a side hustle," Lizzy nodded. "Lew booked me for a gig just the other day and got me five hundred for a couple hours of work. He's pretty good."

"Could that have been a bachelor party?" Jason asked.

Jackie stared at the photo again, then shook his head. "Nah. That dude's old and he's not wearing anything."

"He's got a suit on," Mike noted.

"Sure, but nothing like what we'd dress a groom up in for that kind of pic. He'd have a crown or a boa or a bra or something else fun. This dude is drab city."

Michelle pulled the phone toward herself, happy to finally get a glimpse of the famous photo Mike had told her about during the investigation in New York, but never showed her. "How can you tell he's an old guy? His face is all blurred out."

"Check the ankles," Jackie said simply.

Michelle looked carefully and noticed two things, the socks and the pale, spotted skin. She nodded. "I see. No young guy wears argyle ankle socks like that, and his skin looks like a ghost."

"Uh huh," Jackie nodded.

"Does that spark any memory about who he was, or where or when this happened?"

"Nope," Jackie answered Mike. "You gotta understand, when we're in drag, it's all a show. We sing and dance, we do the schtick. We mug for the cameras and we kiss the boys – and the girls. We grind up on them and we make fun of them – in a good-natured way. It's all part of the act. The customers are like pieces of the stage set. I don't really look at them or notice them. To be honest, it's all about me, not about them. It could have been Donald Trump and I wouldn't have noticed or remembered."

"OK." Mike hung his head. "I can't let you have this picture. There's people high up at the FBI who would fry my ass if they knew I had it. But if you have any flashes of memory about this photo before tomorrow, you let me know. For now, we'll keep this all between us. Don't mention it to anyone. OK?"

"Sure," Jackie said casually.

"Seriously, Jackie. This is critically important. There may be somebody out there trying to kill you. It might have something to do with this photo. Maybe the old guy doesn't want anybody to know he was getting a crotch massage from a drag queen and wants to knock off everyone who was there."

"You think so?" Lizzy asked with fear in his voice.

"I wouldn't rule it out," Mike replied.

Jason then reached out and put a hand on Jackie's shoulder. "Don't worry, Jackie, Mike and I have your back on this. You're family to me. We're going to do whatever we have to do to keep you safe."

Jackie nodded and put his hand on Jason's. "Thanks, Jason. That means a lot to me. There aren't many people in the world who have my back."

"I always do," Rachel said firmly.

"I know, Sis. You're the best – and your man is right there with you."

Rachel beamed at Jason.

Mike struggled out of his chair. "We'll get together tomorrow morning. When is your appointment with the wedding chapel?"

"One o'clock."

"Fine. We'll have time in the morning. Let's all have breakfast here in the hotel. Jason and I will meet up with Jerry Garcia and talk to the cops. The rest of you can go to the wedding chapel."

Jackie turned to Lizzy. "Are you going to come along?"

"I'm not walking around by myself tomorrow with some crazy guy out there trying to kill me."

"They're trying to kill me, Bitch," Jackie said playfully.

"So you think. I'm not taking any chances. I'm hanging with you all as much as I can."

"Fine," Mike cut off the discussion. "Don't talk to anyone about any of this."

"Who we gonna tell?" Lizzy asked. Nobody had a witty response.

Chapter 26 — The Nose on Your Face

Tuesday, January 7
Las Vegas, NV

THE NEXT MORNING, Mike and Jason went to meet with Jerry Garcia. While they were in a Lyft car on the way to Garcia's office, Mike's phone rang. It was Steve Berkowitz in New York. After several calls and one little lie about the dead dancer in Vegas possibly having a tie-in to an investigation in New York, he was able to get a photo of the girl who drove her car off the highway overpass. "I got the impression they have her case marked very closed," Berkowitz said. "I'm sending you an email now."

Mike watched his phone screen, waiting for the email to arrive. When it did, he quickly called up the photo. Holding the screen between himself and Jason, they looked at the image while Berkowitz was still on the speaker. "Don't they have a picture of her without her face all smashed up?" Mike frowned. The woman's face was a mass of bruises and bloody scars. What she had looked like before her accident was hard to say.

"That's all they had, they said," Berkowitz responded. "I gotta go, Mike. We've got a double homicide uptown and Sully doesn't know I'm working this for you."

"No problem, Steve. Thanks for the assist." Mike punched the END button and turned to Jason. "You think?"

"Could be, but we're going to have to show this to Jackie."

"We'll do that as soon as we get back. For now, let's assume this dead girl is the other one in the picture. Let's see what our local detectives have to say."

An hour later, Mike, Jason, and Jerry marched into the Las Vegas central police building and asked to see Detective Rickenbacker. Jerry had phoned ahead to alert the detective that they wanted to talk. They scrounged for an extra chair so the three guests could sit opposite Rickenbacker's desk, with his big computer monitor partially obstructing their view.

When they described the apparent attempt on Jackie's life the day before, Rickenbacker scoffed. "There ain't no way there's somebody trying to kill your fag friend."

"There's no reason for slurs," Jason reprimanded.

"I'll call him what I like," Rickenbacker retorted. "As far as I'm concerned, he's still the prime suspect."

"What do you base that on, aside from the possible motive of starring in the show?" Jason glared at the crew-cut detective, wondering whether he was just a homophobe or also a racist.

"That's enough for me."

"Have you looked at the security cam footage around the CVS drugstore, where Mimi went between shows on Saturday?"

Rickenbacker glanced toward Drew Maulgray's desk, which was unoccupied. "I can't discuss our investigation."

"Like Hell you can't!" Jason leaned toward Rickenbacker,

who leaned toward Jason, their heads separated by three feet of gray desktop.

Mike tried to break the tension by changing the subject. "Detective, a week or so ago, we got a photo from our friends at the FBI. It showed a man whose face was blurred out in a posed shot with three showgirls. Did you get a copy of that photo from the feds?"

"I don't recall," Rickenbacker said, looking Mike right in the eyes.

"We were told it was a pretty important case, and that we had to give back the prints of the photo after we chased down any local venues that might match the picture. Does that ring any bells?"

"Not really." Rickenbacker shook his head. "Maybe somebody else here got it, but not me."

"That's too bad," Mike continued, seizing upon the opening. "Because we're pretty sure two of the showgirls in the photo were Belle de la Pomme, who is Jackie Robinson, and Mimi LaRee."

Mike and Jason both watched Rickenbacker's face. It was placid. The detective didn't seem to have any reaction at all, which was itself remarkable. This information should have been surprising and fascinating, but Rickenbacker showed no response. "Well, I'm not sure how that relates to anything."

Mike raised an eyebrow. "You don't think it's significant that one of the people in that FBI photo has been murdered, and that somebody tried to kill Jackie?"

"We don't know that somebody was trying to kill—"

"Well, let's assume for the moment that yesterday's hit and run was an attempt to kill Jackie. Then add in that the third showgirl in that photo, related to some kind of high-profile federal case, may also be dead."

Again, Mike and Jason watched Rickenbacker's face, which showed no reaction. He either had an amazing poker face, or he wasn't surprised. If he already knew, but was trying not to let them know, he would be better off feigning surprise. The poker face made little sense. Maybe the guy was just emotionless.

"What makes you think that?"

Mike shrugged. "You had a dancer who died in a car accident last week. We think she might be the other girl in the photo."

"You got a name?"

"Yeah, it's Sheila Buchanan."

"Doesn't ring a bell," Rickenbacker said, turning toward the computer monitor on his desk and tapping his keyboard.

"Are you looking her up?" Jason asked, since Rickenbacker was still staring at his monitor.

"Yeah, I think I got her here. Auto accident. Single vehicle. Suspected intoxication."

"That's consistent with our information," Mike said, moving closer to Rickenbacker's sight line to get his attention. "It seems like more than a coincidence that two of the three people in that photo are dead and somebody just tried to kill the third."

Rickenbacker looked up. "I told you, the Buchanan girl was an accident."

"She's still dead. A single-car accident is simple to stage. Wouldn't you agree?"

"In the movies, sure."

"Well, life and movies are sometimes the same."

Before the blond buzzcut could respond, Jerry Garcia reached out an arm to draw everyone's eyes to him. "Detective Rickenbacker, regardless of the specifics, I'd expect you to acknowledge that my client, Jackie Robinson, is a victim here, or at least a potential victim, and not a suspect. It's as plain as the nose on your face."

Rickenbacker glared at Jerry, seemingly trying to sever the lawyer's ponytail with the lasers emanating from his angry eyes. "I acknowledge nothing. Like the detective here said, you can stage an accident, so you can stage an attempted run-down. That would be a good way to deflect attention from yourself, wouldn't it?"

"One that almost killed Jackie and Lizzy both and could have killed Rachel and Michelle as well?" Jason wasn't buying the idea. "And where would they get an SUV and a driver to pretend to run them down? That's just crazy."

Rickenbacker turned toward Jason. "I'm not saying it's true. I'm just saying I'm not making any assumptions. The little fag is still a suspect in my book."

Jason seethed, but kept his composure. "Do you have any other suspects? Any spurned lovers or creditors? Or maybe it was a simple robbery, or a straight-up hate crime? Where did you find the body? Have you tried to find any witnesses who might rule out Jackie being there?"

Rickenbacker lost his poker face. "Detective, don't tell me how to do my job! We can handle the investigation without your advice. You may be from New York, but out here in the west we know how to catch a killer."

"What about an attempted killer? What are you doing to find the hit-and-runner?"

"We don't have an open case for that. I guess nobody ever made a complaint."

Before Jason could lose his composure, Mike jumped back in. "Do you have a report from the officers who were on the scene yesterday?"

"I don't know, I work homicide, not traffic."

"Fine. Let's go in another direction. Can you give us access to the file on the accident involving Sheila Buchanan?"

"Sorry, Detective. Those files are not public records."

"Actually, they are," Jerry piped up. "All police reports are public records in Nevada."

"Well, you can make a Freedom of Information Act request for the file." Rickenbacker shot daggers from his eyes toward the lawyer.

"Since we can get the file anyway, why not just let us see it now, out of professional courtesy?" Mike asked in as polite a voice as he could manage given his increasing dislike for this cop.

"I'm sorry, but my captain wouldn't authorize that."

"May we speak with your captain?" Jason asked.

"He's not here."

"What's his name?" Jason pressed.

Rickenbacker went silent, presumably thinking about how much trouble he could get into if he refused. "His name is Henry Whithers. I think he might be back tomorrow if you want to call for him."

Mike nodded, as if satisfied with the response. "Can I use the same number that's on your card?"

"Sure."

Mike motioned to Jason and Jerry that they should leave. As they took their first steps, Rickenbacker called out, "Hey, Garcia. I'll see you back here when I arrest your client."

Jerry didn't miss a beat. "If you have sufficient evidence to issue an arrest warrant, then by all means fax it to my office and we'll make arrangements to surrender Jackie."

Rickenbacker smirked. "When we're ready to arrest him, we'll come drag him off the stage in handcuffs."

"Why are you so fixated on Jackie Robinson, Rickenbacker? Have you got no better suspects?"

"Maybe you killed LaRee while he was sucking your dick."

"Classy as always, Detective," Jerry called out, then turned and continued with the others toward the exit.

Outside, they regrouped. Jerry advised Mike and Jason that Rickenbacker was always a prick, but that his behavior was "even more dickish than usual." They were clearly not going to get any support from him.

Mike felt oddly better about retaining the old hippy lawyer. Anybody who got under Rickenbacker's skin seemed like the right choice.

Chapter 27 — Change of Plans

Tuesday, January 7
Las Vegas, NV

AT 12:55 P.M., RACHEL AND MICHELLE PUSHED through the ornate doors of the Mardi Gras Wedding Chapel with Jackie and Lizzy right behind them. The exterior was painted to resemble a small-town church, with white wooden siding and an arched doorway with white, carved wooden double doors. Garlands of flowers decorated the archway, leading the eye to a faux stained-glass window showing a wedding scene. A cleaning crew was busy removing the rice, flowers, and streamers from a recently completed wedding.

Rachel asked one of the cleaners where she could find Ms. Marchand, and was directed to a small doorway to the left of the altar. Jackie and Lizzy said they would wait outside in the chapel seats, and Lizzy eyed one of the cleaners, who smiled back.

Rachel knocked twice, then turned the knob and walked inside. The little office was appointed with a variety of wedding-themed photographs, wreathes, and decorations, all of which were available for rental to adorn the next ceremony. Certificates from the Las Vegas Chamber of Commerce and the Nevada Marriage License Registrar hung in ornate frames.

There was an abundance of pink and white in the décor. A hint of lavender hung in the air.

As soon as they entered, a serious-looking woman in a tight pencil skirt and a white blouse topped by a string of pearls stood at her small desk and beckoned them to sit in a row of chairs facing her. Ms. Marchand had auburn hair pulled back from her face and arranged in a bun. She was in her mid-forties and attractive in a Cruella de Vil kind of way. She started speaking before Rachel's butt had settled into the soft cushion. "Miss Robinson, I'm afraid I have some bad news. We can't honor your booking for Sunday."

"What?" Rachel's face, which had shown a beaming smile, transformed into a combination of panic and rage.

The wedding planner quickly launched into a carefully rehearsed explanation, keeping an expression of compassion and empathy on her face. "I am so, so sorry, but the hotel manager has forced us to cancel all the bookings for Sunday. I'm afraid it's totally out of my control. We have a top-shelf celebrity who has booked the chapel for the entire day in order to stage a surprise wedding. I know it is just terrible for you, and for the six other parties we had booked for Sunday. We are giving you a 150% refund on your pre-payment and I can assist you in finding another venue here in town for your wedding. I understand how awful this is for you, and I'm ready to help you make the best of it." She looked across the desk at Rachel's stunned face and Michelle's disapproving stare. "Now, tell me, are you absolutely fixed on Sunday, or is there any flexibility on the date?"

Michelle couldn't reign in her anger. "This is outrageous! This was supposed to be a first-class operation. You can't just bump us because some celebrity wants our day! And why are we finding out now?"

"Mrs. Robinson, I know this is upsetting—"

"I'm Ms. McNeill, and don't patronize me. You can't do this!"

"I'm so sorry, Ms. McNeill. I assumed you were the bride's mother."

"What does it matter!" Rachel cried out. "How can you do this?"

Marchand bowed her head for a moment, then looked back up with a stoic expression. "Miss Robinson, I've had to have this conversation already with three other brides, and I've got three more later today. I know this is awful, but it's out of my hands. The contract you signed gives the hotel the discretion to cancel your booking at any time if we refund your fee. That's the standard term. Legally, the hotel can do this. It's not my decision. I just found out this morning. I really am so sorry. I want to try to help you find an alternate venue."

"This was a mistake." Rachel looked at Michelle like a teenager who had arrived at the front of the line at the big roller coaster and was about to chicken out. "We'll get married back in New York."

"Are you giving up without a fight? That's not the girl I know." Michelle's eyes flashed and she motioned Rachel to look back at the wedding planner.

Rachel, who dealt with crisis situations every day as an EMT, composed herself. "Are there any bookings available here between now and Sunday?"

"No, I'm afraid not. But there are many wedding chapels here in Vegas. This is the town where miracles happen."

Michelle reached out and clasped hands with Rachel. "We figured something would go wrong – it always does. We just didn't figure on something this big. But we'll get through it."

"This is bad," Rachel said, holding back tears. "This is

really, really bad."

"So, you're wedded to Sunday?" Marchand tried to push forward to make alternate arrangements. It was her job, and the faster she navigated her client away from anger and grief and toward planning an alternate venue, the faster the very unpleasant meeting would end.

"Um, I'm not sure. It's not like we have any other specific plans, right Michelle?"

"We're seeing Penn & Teller at the Rio on Friday, but we could skip that. Don't worry – the wedding is more important." She squeezed Rachel's hand reassuringly.

"Well, I'm sure we can work around that," Marchand said, making notes on a pad in front of her. "I'll make some calls so you don't have to start researching wedding chapels. I have the name here as Rachel Robinson, and the groom is Jason Dickson, is that correct?"

"Yes," Rachel responded with a sniff.

"I'll do my best to find you a booking around the same time on Sunday. I have a cell number for you here. Do you prefer a call or a text when I have information for you?"

"Text is better," Rachel replied. "And the time doesn't really matter. We only took that time because it was all you had. When do you think you'll have something for us?"

"It should be today. I'm working on your situation and the other six parties, but I think I'll be able to get back to you later today. Tomorrow at the latest."

Michelle and Rachel exchanged glances and resigned shrugs. There was nothing to do but leave and let Ms. Marchand get to work. They moved slowly past the bright, happy decorations toward the door.

Jackie and Lizzy were surprised by the dour expression on Rachel's face when she emerged from the manager's office.

When the group was back out in the glitzy casino, Rachel said, "Somebody tries to kill Jackie, and now the wedding plans are cancelled. What a run of bad luck. Is this a bad omen? Are we making a mistake doing this?"

Michelle put an arm around her friend and nudged her on the path back toward the pool, where they planned to wait for Mike and Jason. "This is just a bump in the road, Sweetie. Nothing can stop you and Jason from loving each other and loving the baby you're going to have together. Everything else is minor details."

"You think so?"

"I know so. This is Vegas. Like the lady said, this is where miracles happen."

Rachel laughed for the first time since they entered the wedding chapel.

Chapter 28 — Identifying Marks

Tuesday, January 7
Las Vegas, NV

JERRY SUGGESTED THAT HE GO WITH THEM back to the Mardi Gras to talk with Jackie and show him the photo of the dead dancer, Sheila Buchanan. A half hour later, they walked onto the pool deck and spotted their gang at their pool-side table. A waitress was taking food orders, so Mike motioned for Jason and Jerry to wait before talking about the situation. Lizzy and Jackie ordered cottage cheese and fruit. Mike whispered to Michelle that it must suck to be in Vegas around so much great food, but have to constantly diet to fit into their costumes. Rachel, who had ordered a cheeseburger, changed her mind and asked the waitress to bring her the low-cal fruit plate also.

"Jackie," Jerry said in a soothing, fatherly voice once the server left, "I need to show you a photo and ask you if you recognize the person in it. I'll warn you that it's a pretty disturbing picture. The woman was in a car accident and she died. This is a picture from the scene. I know it's hard, but it's important. Can you do that for us?"

Jackie reached out for a glass of ice water on the table and took a healthy swig. Then he nodded and reached for the phone containing the picture. When he first looked, he grimaced and turned away, but then forced himself to look again and study the shot. "Oh my God! Do you know who that is?"

"We think so, but we need you to confirm it."

"That's Cricket. She's the other dancer from that photo, the one with me and Mimi and the old guy. Look," Jackie pointed, "you see that pink butterfly tattoo on her neck? That's Cricket's tattoo. She told me she was going to get a cricket, but they aren't very pretty so she went with a butterfly. Oh my God! She's dead?"

"Yes. She is," Mike said, taking a serious tone. "Which means that in the past week, two of the three people who were in that picture have died. One was a clear murder. The other was a car accident, but that doesn't mean it wasn't also a murder. The detective said she was intoxicated. The question is whether she got drunk voluntarily or whether somebody got her drunk and sent the car off the overpass. We have no way to get the file, at least not very quickly. And then somebody tried to kill you, so that can't be a coincidence."

"And now," Jerry broke back in, "the detective says he's going to arrest you. I think he's bluffing and just wants you to come in for questioning. We are certainly not going to have you go in voluntarily. Now, remember what I told you. If they arrest you, immediately ask for me – for your lawyer – and say nothing, no matter what they say and no matter what they threaten you with. You have the right to remain silent and you should exercise it."

Jackie looked worried. "You really think they're gonna arrest me?"

"No, I don't," Jerry replied. "But you never know. Sometimes these cops try to pressure people. I'm sure Mike and Jason have done the same, right, gentlemen?"

"Sometimes," Mike admitted. "If we think we have the

right person, arresting them and bringing them in can be useful. But we have to have cause for that – we can't arrest somebody for no reason."

"Well, let's hope Detective Rickenbacker feels the same sense of respect for the rule of law," Jerry said, not very convincingly. He then excused himself to deal with another client, telling Jackie he would be reachable at any time if Rickenbacker showed his face.

Jason reached out and put a hand on Jackie's shoulder. "Don't worry. We're here and we're not going to let some local dick railroad you. You've got the whole team here to support you." He gestured around the table. Jackie smiled and nodded, but didn't say anything. Jason then turned to Rachel. "How did things go with the wedding planner?"

Rachel's face fell. "There's a problem." She pulled Jason off to the edge of the pool to explain the sudden cancelation.

Mike excused himself to make a call and wandered off to a corner of the pool area. He found the number of his FBI contact in New York, Agent Everett Forrest. Mike had met Forrest when their paths unexpectedly crossed during the "Righteous Assassin" investigation in the summer of 2018. Forrest's quick action had provided a critical lead. He had given some tech support to Mike and Jason the following spring, and in June of 2019 he had been a valuable liaison between the FBI and the NYPD during the investigation into the murder of quarterback Jimmy Rydell. Mike had come to think of Forrest as a friend, and would certainly do a favor for the agent if ever asked. So far in the relationship, it had been Mike doing all the asking.

Steve Berkowitz had already talked to Forrest, so he was not shocked to get Mike's call. "Stoneman. What the fuck is going on out there?"

"It's a pretty screwed up situation. Jackie, the one

surviving showgirl from that redacted photo, is the brother of Jason's fiancée, Rachel. We're out in Vegas for their wedding."

"That's nice," Forrest said. "Give Jason my congratulations."

"I will," Mike responded, "But what's the deal with that photo? Can you tell me what kind of trouble Jackie is in here? He says he has no memory of when the picture was taken or who the blurred-out guy is, but somebody is trying to kill him over it. Who is he, by the way?"

"I can't tell you," Forrest replied. "What I can tell you is the field office that's heading up the case is very interested in your information. The local cops in Vegas did not immediately report any of this. We figured Vegas was a possible location for that photo, but the local guys didn't report anything. How sure is Jackie that the venue is this Swanky's place?"

"He seems pretty sure," Mike confirmed. "Also, Jackie's lawyer thinks the detective on the murder case may be dirty. He has a reputation, apparently, and our guy thinks he may be on the take from the local mob."

Forrest was silent for ten seconds while Mike waited. "Did he mention any names?"

"No. I didn't ask him for any."

"Mike. Don't send me any texts or emails about this. I don't want you to get sucked into anything as a witness. But ask him if the name Freddy Costanzo means anything to him."

Mike repeated the name to make sure he'd remember. "I'll ask him. Who is this Costanzo guy?"

"You remember the NFL point-shaving scheme Jimmy Rydell was involved in?"

Now it was Mike's turn to pause. "Yeah. I'm not sure we ever confirmed that Jimmy was involved in that."

"Sure. Sure. Well, I talked to some of our people about that investigation after the whole thing with Jimmy. They told me one of the bosses they thought was big into it was Freddy Costanzo, who is in Vegas and was working with various connections around the country. They think he might be the main guy, but they don't have enough on him yet. I'm not sure what the connection might be between the game-fixing scheme and our photo, but I'm going to dig into it. I'll let you know after I talk to my agents in Las Vegas."

Mike said goodbye and went back to join the rest of the group at their table. Jason and Rachel were locked in a tight embrace. Rachel looked like she might have been crying. Jackie was squeezing a glass of Diet Coke and whispering with Lizzy. Mike motioned to Michelle to join him a few steps away. After giving her as much of a briefing as he could about the conversation with Agent Forrest, he said, "I'm back to wishing we were in New York. I have a feeling the other girl, Sheila, or Cricket, might have been murdered. A car accident is just too convenient, given that Mimi was whacked and somebody tried to kill Jackie. If we were back home, I'd pull some strings with a certain medical examiner I know."

"Oooh, Mike – I like it when you pull my strings," Michelle winked. "But this is no time. Didn't Jerry say he was going to make a request for the file?"

"Yeah, he did, but it's going to take a few days. I wish we could get it without waiting."

"Maybe we can," Michelle said with a twinkle in her eye.

Chapter 29 — Viva Las Vegas

Tuesday, January 7
Rapid City, SD

AGENTS DUMM AND SHIELDS EXCHANGED interested and excited eye contact. They were in the video conference room in the Rapid City field office, talking again to their Regional Director. Honeycutt had conferenced in an agent from New York neither of them had met, Everett Forrest. Also on the call was Agent Davis Perkins from the Las Vegas office. The new information was fascinating.

"Yeah, we knew the two Black, uh, people in the photo are males wearing drag costumes," Dumm confirmed. "That was pretty clear. Are you sure about the intel from your guy in Vegas?"

"I'll vouch for him. Mike Stoneman isn't chasing shadows out there. He says he and his partner have a positive ID on one of the drag queens in the photo: Mimi LaRee, who was murdered this week in Vegas. The other guy in drag is named Jackie Robinson, and Stoneman says somebody tried to kill him today. The woman in the photo may be Sheila Buchanan, went by Cricket, also recently deceased."

"Do we know any of them?" Dumm asked.

"No," Perkins responded. "None of them are on our radar.

We have no reason to think they're linked to any of the guys we're watching, or who might be connected to the Senator."

"And how is this Robinson person connected to the New York cops?"

Forrest let out a chuckle. "Somehow, Robinson is the brother of the woman Stoneman's partner is marrying. That's why they're in Vegas in the first place, to get married. Leave it to Stoneman. If there's shit in the vicinity, he'll find a way to step in it."

"Can we trust these guys?" Honeycutt asked.

"Yes. They're straight shooters. You can trust them, for sure. But they seem to have a talent for finding themselves in the middle of trouble."

"Should we reach out to the local cops?" Chelsea asked.

"Let's wait on that for a bit," Perkins jumped in. "I'm concerned they knew about the LaRee murder, and maybe the death of the Buchanan girl, but didn't reach out to tell us. It's not a hard connection to make. A Black drag queen gets murdered while we're searching for a Black drag queen, then another showgirl dies the same week? Do we know anything about this Cricket?"

Agent Forrest consulted his notes. "Not much. Just that she was a dancer. The local cops reported it as a traffic accident, not a murder. Still, two young dancers dead in the same week in Las Vegas. It doesn't seem coincidental."

"And the local cops don't think it's important enough to report to us," Perkins noted. "I have to say we've had some concerns. It's not out of the question that somebody over there is dirty. A local detective on Freddy Costanzo's payroll would not shock me."

Chelsea leaned forward, practically coming out of her shoes in her excitement. "Perkins – Freddy Costanzo is a target in the NFL investigation, isn't he?"

Perkins waited for a nod from Honeycutt before confirming.

"I just sent a memo on this to you, Sir," Chelsea addressed her boss. "I've identified a critical committee vote that Senator Bushfield had three months ago – about legalization of sports gambling. That could be our connection."

Perkins stroked his chin. "Freddy C. is more connected to the sports betting operation than anybody else we know about. It's certainly plausible."

"Do we have pictures of Sheila Buchanan or Mimi LaRee?" Dumm asked. "I'd like to see if the facial recognition folks can match one of them up to the showgirl photo."

"Stoneman got a shot of the girl from the car accident. I'll see if he can send it to me and I'll forward it. He said her face was pretty busted up, but maybe we can work with it."

"Great," Dumm said. "Mimi the drag queen has to have images online we can find. Let's hope Sheila Buchanan has a public Facebook page and we'll find a better image of her. Maybe we'll get lucky."

"Sir?" Chelsea said, to get the director's attention, "with all this happening in Las Vegas, maybe Agent Dumm and I should get down there to provide support to Agent Perkins?"

After a short discussion, the Regional Director agreed that, given the high profile of the Bushfield investigation, they should chase hard, since they had no other leads.

"What we need is a witness," Chelsea stated the obvious. "If the two dead women were in that photo, then whoever took it and used it to blackmail the Senator is trying to knock them off."

Derek scowled at his junior partner. "No shit. That also means somebody views them as a threat. If it's this Costanzo who's pulling the strings, then he's scared. Probably that one of the girls can ID him from that little photo shoot. He must have been there. That means the last one could still be a witness. That could be a huge break for us."

"Sure," Perkins said, "unless Costanzo takes Robinson out."

They all agreed that, to get to Jackie Robinson before Freddy Costanzo – or whoever was knocking off the dancers from the Bushfield blackmail photo – Las Vegas was where they needed to be. Chelsea was smiling as she led the way out of the conference room, thinking about what she would pack for the field assignment in Las Vegas and whether the Bureau would put them up at a decent hotel.

Chapter 30 — Be Prepared

Tuesday, January 7
Las Vegas, NV

BUZZ RICKENBACKER SAT IN HIS CAR in the lot outside the Las Vegas central police station. He turned off his burner phone and locked it in the glove box. It was reckless of him to have it in his car at all. He knew there was always a chance some intrepid assistant district attorney would want to search it. But, he figured if they got a warrant for his car, they would have a warrant for his apartment, so what did it matter?

Before he could open the door, his business phone chimed to announce an incoming text. He saw it was from his ex-wife. He could have ignored it, but somehow after the burner phone text he felt compelled to answer. His response was typical Buzz:

I'll get it out by Friday.

He pressed SEND before he thought about saying he was sorry for missing the child support payment. He also instantly regretted not asking about Julie. She was probably home from school for break. She was a sophomore. No, a junior. Buzz definitely didn't think he was old enough to have a daughter in college, let alone nearly ready to graduate. But these things happened when you got married young and stupid. Now, he was older and wiser. He was due to get a payment that would cover Julie's spring tuition. That was the most important thing.

Inside the station, Drew Maulgray was his usual perky self. Buzz pulled Drew into a small conference room to talk about the Mimi LaRee investigation. He explained that he'd gotten a tip from one of his local sources placing Jackie Robinson near the CVS pharmacy on the evening of the murder.

"Who's the source?"

"I can't tell you, Opie. It's somebody I've used before. A reliable source. He's my guy. You have to cultivate sources like this. Anyway, I'm going to swear out an affidavit and get us an arrest warrant for Jackie Robinson. We'll haul the queen's ass in and squeeze it until we get a confession."

Drew tilted his head and spoke in a soft, conciliatory tone. "Buzz, I gotta tell ya, I'm not comfortable gettin' a warrant based on that kind of tip without anything else. Plus, he's got a lawyer, so he's probably not going to talk to us even if we bring him in. I'd hate to taint any possible case by making it look like we're out to get him."

"If you don't want to do things my way, Opie, you can ask the Captain for a change of partners. Is that what you want?" Buzz stared down his nose at Drew.

"I'm not sayin' that, Buzz. I just want to make sure we do things by the book."

"Well, sometimes you skip to the end. I tell you what, you let me handle this. I'll take responsibility."

"OK, Buzz. Whatever you say." Drew left the room, with Buzz a few paces behind. Buzz turned left and walked through a security door into the section of the station where all the desks were occupied by people in uniforms and the volume level was higher. A third of the officers were on the phone. At the rear of the expansive space, a long desk separated a group of officers who were processing detainees, taking fingerprints, taking mugshots, collecting personal effects, and escorting arrested suspects into the holding cells in the rear of the complex. A loud buzzer sounded as the heavy door separating the booking area from the holding cells opened with a clang.

Buzz motioned to a middle-aged officer behind the counter, who excused himself and joined Buzz at a doorway leading to an emergency exit. They slipped through the door, walked down one flight to the lower level, and exited through a fire door, which they propped open behind them. An overcrowded ashtray stood on a steel pole next to the door. Both men lit cigarettes. Nobody else was using the unofficial smoking area.

"Gary, we're going to be busy. I'm going to need you to pull some strings for me."

Gary, six inches shorter than Buzz but weighing about the same, looped a thick thumb onto his belt and blew out a stream of blue-gray smoke. "Is this going to give me sleepless nights, Buzz?"

"Maybe, but it's a priority instruction."

"Sure. How much?"

"Twenty grand."

"Nice. OK, I'm in. By the way, Buzz, how's your daughter?"

"I guess she's OK. We don't talk much. She's got three more semesters of college, so I'm working on making sure she gets to the finish line."

"And the bitch?"

"Who knows. She texts me. I haven't spoken to her in close to a year. Better for both of us."

"Whatever. Is Maulgray on board?"

Buzz threw his butt on the ground and crushed it with a polished loafer. "No. Leave Opie out of it."

"If he's gonna be your partner, he's going to have to get with the program."

"Maybe. He still believes in truth, justice, and the American way. Wants to do things *by the book*, and protect the rights of the criminals. He'll learn, but for now, he's out."

"Whatever. His loss."

"Yeah, well, there's no rush to get him involved. I was like him once. Maybe I wouldn't have lost Julie and Maggie if I'd been more like Maulgray."

"And less like you?" Gary laughed at his own joke.

"Yeah. Less like me." Buzz turned and grabbed the door handle. "I'll let you know when we're going live. Probably tomorrow. We'll probably have a few people coming in. Look for me this afternoon. Got it?"

"Sure. Got it. Whatever. Like I care about these degenerates." Gary followed Buzz back inside and let the door slam closed behind him.

Chapter 31 — Professional Courtesy

Tuesday, January 7
Las Vegas, NV

RACHEL WAITED IMPATIENTLY for a call from the Mardi Gras' wedding planner. She knew Ms. Marchand had much greater knowledge of available wedding chapels in Las Vegas, but she couldn't sit and wait, so she worked her phone doing research and making calls. What she quickly discovered was that the few chapels that took specific time reservations were booked, at least the ones at the top of her Google searches.

Michelle had been doing her own research, starting with a call to Natalie, her assistant ME back in New York. The community of medical examiners and coroners was surprisingly close-knit. Michelle recalled meeting the ME from Phoenix at a conference a few years earlier and had Natalie send her a message to see if she knew the ME in Las Vegas. Michelle, meanwhile, researched where the morgue and ME's office was located. Predictably, it was near the police station, on Pinto Lane. It would be a ten-minute Lyft ride from the hotel, once she figured out who to meet with.

While Rachel was frowning at her phone as one wedding

chapel director after another advised her they could not take a reservation, Michelle narrowed her list of possible contacts. It was surprisingly difficult to determine the identity of the chief ME for Clark County. It was as if their identity was a state secret. While scrolling through the coroner's website, her phone vibrated to signal an incoming text from Natalie, reporting that the Phoenix ME had a contact in Las Vegas named Stephanie Frost. She wasn't the chief ME, but she was supposed to be super helpful. There was a phone number, which Michelle immediately dialed.

After exchanging introductions and confirming the reference from the Phoenix ME, Michelle explained that they were in town on a trip for Rachel's wedding. It was always worth mentioning there was a bride involved when you wanted cooperation.

"The thing is, Rachel's brother is a performer here and the local cops think he's a suspect in a murder . . . Mimi LaRee, the drag queen. She was killed on Saturday night . . . Blunt force trauma? That's interesting, but that's not why I'm calling. You see, there was another recent death we think is related . . . Me and my – my boyfriend, who's a homicide detective in New York. It's a long story, but there was something he saw in New York that we think is connected and the other person involved also recently died. Her name is Sheila Buchanan, but she performed under the name Cricket Linderman. She died in a car crash last week . . . Well, Mike was told it was ruled an accident and not a homicide . . . Mike's my detective boyfriend . . . Yes, Mike spoke to a local detective about it . . . Buzz Rickenbacker . . . Really? . . . Well, I won't argue that with you, he does come off as a dick . . . So, do you think you could let me see that report? Jackie's lawyer says we can get a copy since it's a public record, but we'd rather not have to wait for it . . . Well, what if I came to see you, so you could verify my identity? . . . Great. I can be there in twenty minutes."

When Michelle hung up, Rachel was staring at her, having picked up on the importance of the conversation halfway through and ceased her own calls. "Was that what I think it was?"

"Probably. I worked a few connections and spoke to Dr. Stephanie Frost, the assistant medical examiner. With any luck, she's going to let me see the report on Cricket. She told me when she prepared the preliminary autopsy report, it indicated that homicide was possible."

"What do you think it means?" Rachel lost the semi-hysterical facial expression she had been sporting ever since their visit to the wedding planner. Diving into Jackie's defense seemed to give her a more positive focus.

"Stephanie wasn't very complimentary about Rickenbacker. She didn't say anything specific on the phone, but we already know he has an unnatural fixation on Jackie, like he assumes a drag performer must be a degenerate."

"I hate it when people think that," Rachel said, suddenly more serious.

"Well, Rickenbacker is clearly an asshole, so don't let it bother you."

Rachel dropped her head and reached out to grab Michelle's hand. "I'm sorry. I'm really messed up right now. Cops sometimes have bad attitudes. Do you think Jason is cool with Jackie?"

"I know he is. You've got nothing to be worried about. He's much more progressive and tolerant than Rickenbacker – or your father."

Rachel closed her eyes.

"Oh, I'm sorry, Sweetie. I know your father and Jackie

aren't on the same page, but I also know Ernie is a good man. He'll come around."

"You think so?"

"You can count on it. Now, I have a date with Stephanie Frost and I need to scoot. You need to stay with Jackie and Lizzy. When Mike and Jason get back, they'll stay with you until the hotel wedding planner calls. Don't you worry. One way or the other, you're going to wear that dress and walk down the aisle and say 'I do' with Jason. It's going to be beautiful."

"Thanks," Rachel said, fighting back tears. "It's just that everything is so not what I wanted. I'm not sorry to be pregnant, but it's like this baby is starting out on the wrong foot, you know?"

"Don't be so sure, Rachel. Sometimes things happen that you think are terrible at the time, but they turn out to be for the best."

"You're just trying to make me feel better."

"I am, but it's also true. I told you about my college boyfriend. I was practically engaged to him when we were in college. But, if you recall, he turned out to be a drug addict and he hit me, so I left him. Leaving that jerk was the best thing that ever happened to me. I never would have thought that at the time. So, you never know. Just roll with it and love Jason."

They both stood and hugged, while both worked hard to not cry.

Over dinner, Michelle recounted her meeting. Dr. Frost had been reluctant to share details at first, but Michelle explained the potential importance of the information, without mentioning the FBI photo. Frost said that the detective on the case – Maulgray, not Rickenbacker – had originally flagged it as a potential homicide because of the bruising, which he thought could have been a beating before the accident. Frost had agreed the lacerations and bruises on her face could have occurred before the car went over the overpass. She also said she was suspicious about the extraordinarily high blood alcohol level that came back on the toxicology screen. The level was way beyond the legal limit for intoxication, which would have left most people unconscious and near death. On top of that, Dr. Frost found an unusually high volume of undigested alcohol in her stomach during the autopsy. Between the stomach contents and the extremely high blood alcohol level, she suspected that Sheila Buchanan was force-fed the vodka.

"So, what happened?" Mike's impatience was showing.

"Dr. Frost flagged the issues, of course, but then the case got closed and it was determined to be an accident. She raised her suspicions with her boss, but he didn't do anything with it."

Mike cocked his head skeptically. "Does that sound odd to you?"

"It does. I'm not sure what we do with the information, but it's sure suspicious."

Rachel was interested in the information, since it concerned Jackie's possible defense. But she kept checking her phone, hoping for a message from Ms. Marchand about finding an alternate wedding chapel. The message didn't come.

Chapter 32 — A Night at the Circus

Tuesday, January 7
Las Vegas, NV

AFTER A LITTLE DIGGING, it was Rachel who first found a Facebook page for Sheila Buchanan. Actually, it was a Facebook page for Cricket Linderman, exotic dancer. Sheila seemed to keep her real identity behind appropriate privacy walls on the internet, but her alter ego, Cricket, was an extrovert who was happy to post photos and videos of herself in action. Rachel expertly navigated to portions of Cricket's profile that Mike and Jason would never have known existed and came up with a lead for the detectives.

Cricket worked in several venues around Las Vegas, but her main gig was at the Circus Circus casino. There were many photos of her wearing elaborate, skimpy costumes. That would have been helpful in itself, but Rachel also discovered a photo of Cricket with two other dancers, named Laura Templeton and Heather Simpson, at what was captioned as Laura's twenty-second birthday a month earlier. They were wearing matching costumes, indicating Laura also worked at the Circus Circus.

"That's terrific work, Rachel. You should be an

investigator," Mike praised her. Jason gave her a long kiss.

The events of the day had left Michelle and Rachel happy to forego their original plans for Tuesday night. Michelle had mapped out a walk up and down the Strip to see all the light, water, and performance shows at the various huge casinos. As it was, they were planning to watch Jackie and Lizzy in their show at the Mardi Gras. As Jackie explained it, the show was different every night and there were still many songs and routines Rachel hadn't seen yet. Jackie and Lizzy had already left for the theater for some much-needed rehearsal now that the show was being retooled without Mimi LaRee. So, Rachel and Michelle were not at all put off by the idea that Jason and Mike would go chasing down a lead – especially if it might help take the heat off Jackie.

It was 9:30 p.m. when Mike and Jason walked into the Circus Circus. It was not one of the more modern hotels on the Strip, but it had a unique charm with decorations and performance venues simulating a big top. There was less glitz than at the new hotels, but it harkened back to a time when the flying trapeze, jugglers, and clowns were all the entertainment a crowd could want. That, and some blackjack tables and slot machines. They passed by a performance ring where acrobats were performing tricks on a trampoline, and a raised circular stage where a magician in a top hat was making something disappear to the delight of a small crowd. They finally managed to find a casino boss, who directed them to the manager of the dancers and waitresses.

"I'm Detective Mike Stoneman. This is my partner, Detective Dickson. We understand you're the boss for the dancers, is that right?"

Gary Ottavino sighed and shook his head slightly before responding. "I already spoke to the other detectives. Is it really necessary to go through it again?"

"We have a couple of follow-up questions we need to ask of Laura Templeton or Heather Simpson. Are either of them working tonight?" Mike glanced around the floor, hoping to spot one and make it more difficult for Gary to brush them off.

"Yes. Laura's working. Right now she's over on the stage by the food court."

"You don't mind if we take her away from her duties for five minutes, do you?" Jason asked in his most intimidating tone.

Gary sighed again. "Fine. It's still early. Just make it quick." He turned away and waved an arm emphatically toward someone Mike couldn't see. Having obtained the permission they needed, Mike motioned to Jason and started walking in the direction Gary seemed to have been looking when he mentioned the food court.

Five minutes and two wrong turns later, they found the food court and the stage where two dancers were facing each other at opposite ends. From the Facebook picture, they easily identified Laura as the petite brunette with the thin nose and high cheekbones, and not the tall blonde with the tattoo between her breasts. They waited until "Don't Stop Believin'" finished playing and the dancers took a pause, then walked purposefully up to the edge of the stage where Laura was smiling at the passing patrons, some of whom were depositing bills and chips at her feet.

When the last of the oglers had walked past, Mike motioned to Jason, who stood at his full height and called out above the general casino cacophony, "Miss Laura Templeton? I'm Detective Jason Dickson. We need to talk to you for a moment. Can you come down to the floor please? We already spoke to Gary and he said it was alright for you to take a short break."

Laura eyed Jason suspiciously, but shrugged and walked around to the tiny stairway leading down from the stage. When she reached the bottom, Mike flashed his badge, which he always had on him even while traveling. It helped smooth out issues at the airport and provided shelter from overly enthusiastic traffic cops on the road. "Miss Templeton, we're investigating the death of Sheila Buchanan, or Cricket Linderman. We understand you two were friends."

Laura immediately started to tear up. "Yeah. We were. I mean, not really close or anything, but we hung out sometimes since we both worked here. I already talked to the other detective. The red-haired guy."

"We know," Jason quickly cut in. "We're working a different angle. Do you know whether Cricket ever worked side gigs with drag performers?"

Laura leaned her head to the side, then circled it around, stretching her neck. "I don't know. I mean, we all have side hustles. It's not like this gig pays all the bills. I've done parties with drag queens, so Cricket probably did, too. Those girls are fun. You should talk to The Big Lewbowski. He'd know for sure."

"The agent?" Mike asked.

"Yeah? You know him? He books all our side gigs. If Cricket did a drag party, it would have been through him. He takes a cut of everything, but he gets us lots of work."

Jason reached into his inside jacket pocket, where he normally kept a note pad, but it wasn't there. "Where can we find this Big Lewbowski?"

"Wait a minute." Laura scampered over to the stage and reached to the base of her dancing pole to retrieve a silver purse decorated with rhinestones. She dug around for a few seconds before finding a golden business card. She handed it to Jason. "You can keep it. I got more."

"Thanks." Jason scanned the card, which read, "Alexander Z. Lewbowski. Talent Agent." There was a phone number, an email, and a website address. "We appreciate your help, Miss Templeton."

Laura waved as she headed back up the little stairs to the stage. The first pounding chords of "Takin' Care of Business" blasted out through the sound system, which was amplified near the stage area. "I love that song," Mike said. "The Mets used to use that after victories at Shea Stadium. It always makes me think about a Mets win."

"Man, you should pick a genre," Jason scolded as they walked back toward the exit.

In the car back to the Mardi Gras, Mike composed an email to Alexander Lewbowski, saying that he needed to arrange a quick bachelor party for a buddy and wanted to meet as early in the day on Wednesday as possible.

"You're not sending that from your NYPD email address, are you?"

Mike gave his partner a reproving stare. "No. I have a personal email address I use for things like this."

"What? 'Mike the Cop?'"

"Jason, you're my partner and I trust you with all my secrets, so I'll tell you. Just don't try to hack my password. It's 'Mike from Manhattan.' I'm not dumb enough to list my occupation."

"I'd like to go with you tomorrow."

"I'd like to have you, but you may need to be with your bride-to-be and your future brother-in-law. Rachel's in a pretty bad place right now. I wouldn't make her feel like you've abandoned her."

"I know. Do me a favor and don't have too much fun without me."

Chapter 33 — Sleight of Hand

Tuesday, January 7
Las Vegas, NV

RICK "THE NECK" GARETTI BROUGHT SIX MEN to the second money drop. He wasn't going to miss the blackmailer this time. He also was not going to provide the full ransom, but that did not lessen Rick's anxiety. Freddy was not going to tolerate failure again.

The blackmailer, whom he and Freddy had started calling Shithead as shorthand, had instructed that the person carrying the money should sit at an Aladdin slot machine near the Strip exit door in the Circus Circus casino at 9:00 p.m. Rick decided to be the bag man himself. He had the money in a shoulder satchel at his feet. It was supposed to be $100,000, but it was actually only $3,000. There was a real hundred-dollar bill on the outside of each stack, making it look like $10,000. The ten stacks were separated into two bundles of five stacks each, wrapped tightly with clear tape. At a quick glance, it was impossible to tell that the rest of the bills were all singles.

Rick had been sitting at the slot machine for ten minutes, feeding the minimum bet and taking his time between pulls. Actually, they were pushes of a button. On this machine there was no handle, negating the term "one-armed bandit." He was getting impatient when he heard a cell phone ring nearby. He followed the sound to the floor behind a trash can pushed up against the wall. He grabbed the small unit, a burner, and answered. "Yeah?"

The mechanically altered voice said, "Go to the gift shop and purchase a Hello Kitty backpack with red sequins. Put the cash in the backpack. Take it to the small stage near the Emeril Grill. There's nobody dancing there. Put the backpack on the stage and walk away."

Rick knew the stage and knew his men would have it surrounded by the time he got there. After obtaining the stupid-looking backpack and putting the bundles of cash inside, Rick strolled to the drop location. The stage was a circular space about ten feet in diameter, elevated four feet off the casino floor. The surface was black vinyl. The entire circle was rimmed with silver plastic and draped in a heavy black curtain hanging to the carpeted floor. "OK, Shithead," he mumbled to himself as he placed the backpack on the empty stage, "let's see you grab this without getting your head bashed in."

Within a minute, a group of colorfully dressed performers swarmed the area. A woman in a sequined outfit showing off her long legs leaped onto the stage, followed by a man in a tuxedo and a black top hat. The man had a large black moustache and, when he removed the hat, Rick saw matching long, flowing hair, combed back from his forehead in thick waves. Three other women took up positions around the stage on the floor, beckoning casino patrons passing by to stop and watch. Rick saw two of his men join the gathering crowd, watching the man in the tuxedo. The performers ignored the backpack, which was still lying on the rear edge of the stage.

"Ladies and gentlemen," the man in the top hat bellowed out, without any artificial amplification, "gather 'round and be amazed!"

One of the women picked up the little backpack and dropped it on the floor next to the raised stage. Rick tried to keep his eyes on it, but the growing crowd blotted out his sight line. Extracting his phone from an inside pocket, he punched the button to unmute himself and turn up the volume on the conference call he and his team were all on. After the disaster of the last drop, Rick wasn't leaving anything to chance. They didn't have FBI-level earpieces and proprietary frequencies, but standard cell service, a Bluetooth earbud, and a corporate conference bridge got the job done. "Eddie – are you in the crowd around the stage?"

"I'm here," Eddie responded while the rest of the team stayed quiet. "I'm off to the side and have a good view."

"Have you got eyes on the package?"

"Yeah. It's on the floor next to the stage. One of the girls put it there when the dude in the tux showed up. They don't seem to be paying any attention to it."

Rick frowned. This was definitely not what he anticipated. "Stevie – where are you?"

"I'm standing over by the craps table, on the opposite side from Eddie."

"Good. Stay there and stay ready. Everybody else, stay on those exits. I don't want anybody getting past us with that stupid backpack."

On the stage, the man in the tux continued. "Ladies and gentlemen, welcome to the Circus Circus hotel and casino. I am The Amazing Lucchesi, here for your pleasure and amusement. Watch, and be amazed!"

With a flourish, The Amazing Lucchesi pulled a red silk cape from his sleeve and began a magic show. Rick tried to keep his attention on the crowd and the surrounding area.

"Stay sharp!" he barked into the microphone attached to his earphones. "Shithead will probably try to grab the package during this show."

While the six members of Rick's team watched, along with forty or so casino patrons gathered around the stage, The Amazing Lucchesi went through a fifteen-minute show that featured what Rick thought was fairly decent slight-of-hand while engaging in a running banter with his audience.

Rick was getting edgy that Shithead hadn't made an appearance. He wondered whether the magic show was an unexpected interruption, or if it was part of his plan to distract Rick and his team from nabbing him. He snapped a cellphone picture of The Amazing Lucchesi and each of his lovely assistants, just in case.

When The Amazing Lucchesi announced he would have one more trick, Rick told his team to be ready for something to happen when the crowd around the stage started to disperse. He had Eddie and one other man specifically keeping an eye on the backpack. As they watched, one of the female assistants reached down, grabbed the backpack, and tossed it up to the magician on the stage.

"Get ready!" Rick called out. "Move in and make sure nobody from the magic act leaves the stage area without an escort!"

The magician held up the backpack and asked for an audience member to provide something large and heavy he could put inside as part of the trick. A tall, broad-shouldered man wearing a sport jacket reached into a pocket and pulled out a Lucite cube about three inches on each side, with some kind of emblem in the middle. Probably some corporate logo paperweight from one of the conventions in town, Rick thought. He tossed it up to the magician, who opened the Hello

Kitty backpack and placed his hand inside as he appeared to drop the cube. Then he zipped the bag and put it inside a large red box with satin sides on the podium in the middle of the stage. The Amazing Lucchesi had used the box for several earlier tricks.

The magician extracted a long black wand from his jacket sleeve, stood behind the box, and tapped the wand three times. A cloud of white smoke exploded from the front of the podium. Half the crowd gasped while the other half screamed. The smoke obscured the performers momentarily.

"Get that backpack!" Rick yelled as he sprang forward toward the stage. He could not get close due to the layers of spectators, still stunned by the smoke bomb. The stage was now deserted, save for the podium and the clear cube sitting in its center. The red satin box, along with the magician, his main assistant, and the backpack, were gone. The three bedazzled women standing on the floor at the base of the stage, who had been keeping the crowd from getting too close, were still smiling, each holding one arm triumphantly in the air.

"Where'd they go?" Rick heard Eddie say in his earpiece.

"Stay on the exits!" Rick barked to his team. "Eddie, Stevie – get up there!"

Eddie was the first to push past the objections of the women around the stage and climb the stairs at the back onto the platform. The remaining audience started to boo and called for him to get down, since he was obviously not supposed to be there. He grabbed the Lucite cube and tossed it into the crowd, to the protest of its owner. Eddie picked up the podium, which was surprisingly light and thin, and looked underneath. Finding nothing but empty space, he tossed it off the back of the stage as he spun around, searching for some sign of the performers.

Stevie pushed one of the women aside and reached his hand into the plush black curtain hanging down all around the stage. He probed for a doorway or entranceway hidden behind the curtain and yelped as his fist smashed into hard wood. Eddie, above him, yelled curses as he continued to scan the audience and the surrounding casino floor. Rick joined Stevie, searching the base of the stage for some sign of a compartment underneath where the magician and his assistant could be hiding.

As he grew more frustrated with the search, Rick heard a voice in his ear say, "Ricky, one of the girls is leaving and she has the kitty backpack."

He saw one of the three women who had been controlling the crowd, her semi-covered ass wiggling as she sauntered away toward a row of blackjack tables. At the end of her long, slim right arm, the sparkling Hello Kitty backpack swung along with her stride.

"Who's got that exit?" Rick barked.

"I'm on the bitch!" came a gruff voice belonging to Tony Falsetti.

"Where's the magician?" Rick called out to the invisible team. Nobody replied. "Somebody else get over there with that girl and stay on the backpack!"

Two other members of the team rushed in that direction. The woman stopped at an empty chair in front of a five-dollar minimum blackjack table and took a seat, hanging the backpack on the chair behind her. She was out of place in her costume, but in a Vegas casino, no amount of glitz was ever truly unusual. She reached two slim fingers down the front of her bodice and extracted a one-hundred-dollar bill, which she placed on the green felt so the dealer could exchange it for chips. She focused on the dealer, ignoring the leers from two male gamblers at her table.

"Where is she?" Rick said into his microphone, squinting into the bright casino lights in the direction she had walked.

"She's at a blackjack table," Tony replied. "The backpack is on her chair. You want me to grab it?"

"Yes. Don't let anybody see you, then beat it out of here and meet me at the car."

Rick couldn't see what was happening from his place on the stage, but he noticed a casino security guard heading in his direction with a concerned expression. The crowd around the stage had vanished and he and Eddie looked conspicuous on the platform. Before the guard arrived to chase them away, they both jumped down and headed in the direction of the girl with the backpack.

Then Rick heard a high-pitched voice scream, "That guy took my bag!"

The sound of yelling voices mingled with the general din of the casino floor. The security guard who had chased Rick from the stage jogged in the direction of the noise. Rick called to his team to pull back and meet at the car.

Ten minutes later, Rick reached the Escalade in which he and four of the members of his team had arrived. Three of them were already there; Eddie, Tony, and Stevie. Tony had the backpack. It was empty.

"Fuck!" was all Rick could say.

Chapter 34 — Delivering Bad News

FREDDY COSTANZO WAS SO MAD AT RICK that he pulled out his desk gun. The oversized desk with the panoramic view of the Vegas Strip was one of his favorite places to sit and relax. But, there was only one door to his apartment, on the far side of the room. While he had pretty good security, there was always the possibility somebody would come through that door with evil intentions toward Freddy. It was natural that he'd have a Colt .45 – loaded and maintained regularly – mounted on a clip on the underside of the desk, where he could reach it easily without seeming to make any sudden moves. If someone was standing in front of the desk, Freddy could fire it without pulling it out first. It might not kill his adversary, but a .45 bullet to the groin or upper thigh would be an effective first shot. Tonight, he pulled it out and brandished it toward the ceiling, spewing expletives in the general direction of his oldest and dearest friend and confidant.

"You're fucking slipping, Ricky. I can't believe you couldn't nab this two-bit, scum-sucking bastard. I should put you out of your misery right now." Freddy pointed the gun in Rick's general direction, but Rick could tell he wasn't really in the cross-hairs. It wasn't the first time Freddy had pulled out the gun.

Rick remained calm, which was his only strategy in situations like this. "It was only $3,000, Boss, and it was my money. The magician pulled it over on us. I got no excuse. I fucked up. Again."

"Why did you put any real money in the drop?"

"Boss, I figured we were going to catch him. If he examined the bundle, I wanted it to look legit. I'm sorry. But it tells us something about Shithead."

"It's telling me that he's smarter than you!" Freddy slammed the Colt onto the desktop, making Rick flinch.

"Yeah. Well, maybe that's true for now. But we also know the drag queen wasn't there. I had a guy at the drag show and Robinson was on stage the whole time the drop was going down."

"So, the fag has people helping him. We knew that!" Freddy got up, leaving the gun, and stood by the huge window, looking out at the sparkling lights.

"Yeah. But he has a bunch. The first drop had the cocktail waitress and probably some people inside that service area. This time, the magician dude and his ladies. All different people. It's like there's a whole team working this. And for what? For two hundred grand? It seems like small potatoes for so many people to be involved. I've been asking around about our queen. He's no rocket scientist. I don't think he could be pulling this off."

"So how does he have two New York cops here protecting him?"

Rick put his hands on his knees, palms up. "I got no answer

for that, Boss. I guess he's from New York and these cops know him. Maybe the Black cop is his cousin or something. I don't know. You want me to make some calls back east to ask around about them?"

"What I wanted you to do was take care of the situation, but you're apparently not up to the task. I'm going to have somebody else take care of it."

"Fine. I don't care who gets it done." Rick stood, letting out an audible sigh to make sure Freddy would turn and see him getting ready to leave. He didn't like these meetings and wanted to get out.

"And find that hack magician. I want to personally make his fingers disappear."

Rick quietly left the suite.

Chapter 35 — The People You Meet

Wednesday, January 8
Las Vegas, NV

THE NEXT MORNING, MIKE LEFT THE MARDI GRAS early and alone. He had an appointment to meet with Jackie's lawyer. Rachel had finally heard back from Ms. Marchand and scheduled a meeting with a substitute wedding chapel. Jason and the rest of the group were going along, with Jason acting as bodyguard. Michelle and Jackie were keen on helping Rachel deal with the wedding crisis. The foray to the chapel figured to be a nice distraction for Jackie and Lizzy. They needed something to keep them from obsessing about being the targets of a potential killer.

The object of Mike's meeting with the lawyer was to plan for what they would do if Rickenbacker followed through on his threat to arrest Jackie. Mike had already filled in Jerry by phone on what they had learned about Sheila Buchanan's death. Brainstorming how to handle the possible arrest scenarios might take some time, but they figured they might be waiting a while during their trip to the Federal Building. Mike's New York FBI contact had made a call and set up a meeting for Mike with the local bureau office. He didn't want to go alone, and having a local lawyer with him seemed like a great idea. Jerry jumped at the opportunity.

Jerry suggested meeting at the Circus Circus hotel, where he had a morning meeting already scheduled with a potential new client. Coincidentally enough, Mike had arranged to meet the booking agent, Alexander Lewbowski, at the same hotel. When they were both finished with their morning meetings, Mike and Jerry would go together to the Federal Building.

When he arrived in a Lyft car back at the aging property, Mike contemplated whether he had time to get to a poker table before his meeting. But inside the main entrance, Mike noticed a large placard mounted on an easel announcing a convention taking place in the hotel. The sign was ringed in blue and orange streamers and had "Mets" in blue script letters in the center. The event was a reunion for the members of the 2018 Las Vegas 51's, the minor-league team in the New York Mets organization from 2013 through 2018. The sign was adorned with the photos of several players who had gone from Las Vegas to play in the big-leagues, including Dom Smith, Brandon Nimmo, and Pete Alonso.

"Look at that," Mike said, breaking into a big smile. "How did I miss this yesterday?" Forgetting about poker, he followed the signs toward the hotel's convention center.

The event turned out to be both a reunion of the 2018 Vegas 51's and a pre-season get-together for the younger players. The convention center was filled with fans wearing all types of jerseys and baseball caps, not all of which were blue and orange. It was a festive atmosphere as everyone looked forward to the upcoming season.

Mike strolled past tables where fans were lined up to get autographs or receive give-away items. There were hot dog, popcorn, and cotton candy vendors giving away free treats. At each exhibit station, a long-legged showgirl stood ready to snap photos with the tourists and the players. They made nice souvenirs and were so very Vegas, Mike thought. Next to one table, a tall showgirl in a flowing blonde wig made eye contact with Mike. He recognized her as one of the performers from the drag show at *The Birdcage*. Mike could not recall her name, but when Belle was taking fan photos after the show on Saturday night, this one was definitely part of the entourage. It was the wig that was most memorable.

He sidled up between photo ops and said hello. "Early gig for you today, eh?" he smiled.

"Everybody has a side hustle, Honey," she replied with an exaggerated batting of her extra-long fake lashes. Mike wondered how many of the convention patrons would realize they were posing with a drag queen.

Mike nodded and walked away without another word. He found the table where Dom Smith was signing autographs and got into the line. He glanced around for other players, hoping to see Pete Alonso. The man behind him, accompanied by a teenaged boy, said excitedly, "I heard Lenny Dykstra might be here today."

Mike grunted something intended to be noncommittal. "I'd rather see the kids."

"Yeah. We've got some good ones," the man responded, patting his son on the head. Mike dug out his phone and checked his messages to make sure there was nothing from Jerry or Lewbowski, then checked his email as he waited.

At the front of the line, Mike realized he had nothing for Dom Smith to sign. He walked behind the table to pose for a photo, handing off his phone to an assistant there for that purpose. As he stood with one arm around the big outfielder and one arm around a slender showgirl, he said to Smith,

"Looks like you're the regular left fielder this year, eh?"

"You got that right," the always jovial player responded. "No way I'm getting Pete off first base, so I've been doing a lot of shagging over the winter."

"You'll do fine," Mike said encouragingly. "I loved how you finished off last season with that grand slam. Keep swinging a hot bat and they'll always find a place for you."

"I'll do my best," Dom said as he shook Mike's hand and turned his attention to the young boy and his father, who were up next.

Mike walked away, smiling and examining the photo on his cell. As he tried to enlarge the image to see whether Dom's face was in good focus, the unit vibrated, indicating an incoming email. It was from Alexander Lewbowski, saying he was available to meet in the Sports Book.

Chapter 36 — The Big Lewbowski

MIKE WASN'T SURE WHAT TO EXPECT from the talent agent. The only person he ever knew in the profession had been pompous, arrogant, dishonest, and a raging womanizer, but he tried not to have any preconceived notions about Alexander Lewbowski. He knew the guy booked side gigs for many of the entertainers around Las Vegas. Beyond that, Lewbowski was a blank slate. Both Lizzy and Jackie had only vague things to say about him.

The email instructed Mike to meet at the Sports Book, which was off the main midway. At 11:00 a.m., there were no acrobats on the overhead flying trapeze. The Sports Book was nearly as deserted. There was a soccer game from some European venue on most of the large screens and a smattering of men watching. It was about as close as you could come to a men's club. In the bar area, outside the rail of the betting chairs, a large man lounged on a padded bench seat, his legs resting on a nearby chair. Mike waved his phone in his direction and got a half-raise of the man's arm as a confirming gesture.

Mike took a seat in the chair opposite the reclining figure. The agent had a swarthy complexion with dark features. His blue silk shirt was unbuttoned, exposing a hairy chest and a large gold medallion suspended from a thick, braided chain. Mike couldn't tell how tall he would be standing, but he was certainly shorter than Mike's five-foot-ten and had Mike covered by at least fifty pounds.

"Mr. Lewbowski, I presume?"

When the man spoke, Mike was surprised by the New Jersey accent, making him sound like an extra from a Sopranos episode. Mike wondered if it was real or part of his act. "That's correct. And I assume you're Mr. Mike."

"Right. Thanks for making time for me. I appreciate it. So, like I said, I need to stage a bachelor party on short notice. My best buddy's girlfriend just found out she's pregnant and they're getting married on Sunday. We had this trip to Vegas planned, but it wasn't supposed to be a wedding until a few days ago. I'm the best man, so I'm on the spot. I was talking to a dancer at the Circus Circus last night and she told me you were the man to see. So, again, thanks."

"What dancer?" Lewbowski asked skeptically.

"She said her name was Laura. She gave me your card."

"Laura. Nice girl. Great legs. Decent tits. Doesn't like to go down on chicks, but gives a good lap dance. You want her to be the main attraction for your buddy?"

"No. He's a big Black guy. I think he likes 'em dark and extra large. You know anybody like that, Mr. Lewbowski?"

The agent smiled, as if sensing he had a sucker in his sights. Mike thought it was a poor poker face. "Please, around town I'm known as The Big Lewbowski. The 'big' part you can figure out," he laughed at his own joke. "But my friends and clients call me Lew."

"Well, Lew, do you think you can find me some talent for tomorrow night?" Mike leaned forward, feigning anticipation.

"Maybe. First, tell me a little about you and your friend."

Mike told a semi-true version of his friendship with Jason and his impending marriage to Rachel. He left out the part about them being cops. By the time he was done, Lewbowski was treating Mike like his best friend.

"You sound like you're from New York." Lewbowski raised an eyebrow.

"And you sound like you're from Jersey."

"Touché. Well, it's been a long time since my Jersey days."

"You can take the boy out of Jersey, but you can't—"

"—take Jersey out of the boy," Lewbowski finished the joke himself. "I agree."

"You probably knew some wise guys back in the old hood, eh?"

Lewbowski tilted his head and furrowed his brow, deciding how to answer. Mike worried he had made a wrong turn, but then the agent replied, "It's not like I was the agent to the mob or anything, but I knew some guys."

"How long you been out here in Vegas?" Mike wanted to change the subject and get the man further off his guard before asking him any important questions. He seemed like a guy who liked to talk about himself, Mike thought. He was right.

The Big Lewbowski gave Mike a not-so-short personal history. After his youth in Newark, and with a degree from Rutgers, he called in a few favors and got an internship at a big talent agency in New York. From there, a regular job as a junior talent agent, which meant mostly fetching coffee and filing contracts. After several years, he started bringing in a few of his own clients, mostly through his contacts in Jersey. But when one of his clients ended up on page six of the New York

Post in bed with a candidate running for the Senate, there was some political pressure on the agency to make him the scapegoat. He understood, gracefully resigned, and moved to Vegas. One of his friends from the agency felt sorry for him and helped set him up out west.

"Well, Mike, I'm going to have to get to another appointment in a few minutes, but I think I can help you out here." The Big Lewbowski swung his ham-hock legs off the chair where they were resting and sat up straighter. "I know of a few Black girls who would put on a good show for you and your friend."

"That would be great." Mike moved to the edge of his chair and took on a more professional attitude. "But before we book this show, I have a couple of more serious questions I need to ask."

"Whaddaya mean by serious?" Lewbowski struggled to a more upright sitting posture.

"Well, Lew, my best friend really is getting married here this week, but I'm here to see you about something else. You know a girl named Cricket Linderman?"

Lewbowski's smile disappeared. "You already know I do or you wouldn't ask."

"You mean you did." Mike leveled a stare at the agent.

"Yeah, I know. She died in a car crash. Damned shame. She was a great girl. Real sweet. Did you know her?"

"No. But I know somebody who performed with her. Did you also know one of the drag queens from that show at the Mardi Gras got killed a few nights ago?"

Lewbowski hesitated. "I think I did hear about that."

"Didn't you book for Mimi LaRee?"

"I think maybe I did, not that it's anyone's business." Lewbowski looked like a man who wanted to change the subject.

"So, do you recall a gig you booked for both Cricket and Mimi to work together?"

"Who the hell are you, really?" Lewbowski leaned in and put his forearm on the little table separating them.

Mike considered his options and decided the truth was most likely to get him a real answer. "I'm a cop from New York, but that's not why I care. This is not my town and not my jurisdiction. But I have a personal interest. So, I'll ask again. Do you remember booking a gig for Cricket and Mimi together?"

"I book a lot of gigs for a lot of people. I do girls and guys and queens and jugglers and comics and magicians. I do a few dozen a week. I can't remember every gig. I guess it's possible Cricket and Mimi worked together, but I don't remember."

Before Mike could ask a follow-up question, a tall, thin man with a thick shock of black hair rushed up to the table and went straight to Lewbowski. Mike guessed this table in the Sports Book was his de facto office at this time of day. The man was agitated and ignored Mike. "Lew, what the fuck? Where's my money from last night?"

"Excuse me a moment," Lewbowski said politely to Mike, as if the man were interrupting an important business meeting rather than an uncomfortable interrogation. Then, turning to the newcomer, "Listen, Charlie. This is not the time."

"Like hell," the agitated Charlie shot back. "I did the show like you said. Tina said she saw some guys there who looked pretty fucking unhappy about something. I want the money you promised me so I can get the hell back to Reno."

"Fine," Lewbowski said dismissively. "Wait for me over at the other side of the book and I'll be with you as soon as I finish here."

Charlie sulked momentarily, then stalked away and took up a position near the entrance to the bar area, where Lewbowski would be unable to leave without passing him.

Mike seized the interruption to bore in with his questions. "Lew, I'm very close to one of your clients. Jackie Robinson. He's scared to death now because someone's trying to kill him. You booked him for a gig with Cricket and Mimi. Now, Cricket and Mimi have been murdered."

"Cricket died in a car accident!" Lewbowski protested.

"That's what somebody wants us and the local cops to think, but believe me, it was a murder. And Mimi was murdered. And yesterday somebody tried to run down Jackie with an SUV. So this is some serious shit. Everybody at that event seems to be in peril, maybe including you. Now, think! A gig with just those three – Cricket and Mimi and Jackie."

Lewbowski licked his lips and blew out the air from his mouth. Mike could smell bacon and coffee. "I'd like to help you here, Mike. I really would. I honestly can't remember. Maybe some dude got mad that he ended up with two queens when he thought he was going to have a four-way with three hot chicks. I don't know. I got no answers for you."

"Maybe you can check your records, huh? I need to know who booked the girls for that gig. Who was involved."

"For a side-gig like that, it would be all cash. I'd have no record."

"Well, I'd suggest that it's in your best interest to recover your memory."

"I'll do what I can. Now, as you saw, I have a client who needs my attention. You'll have to excuse me."

As Lewbowski hoisted himself from his chair, Mike said, "You have my phone number, from my email. If you remember anything – anything at all – you give me a call. Jackie needs his agent to be there for him.”

Mike watched as Lewbowski lumbered to the bar, where Charlie grabbed him by the elbow and escorted him away. Mike was thinking about following them, but his phone buzzed again. The text was from Jerry and said Mike needed to meet him immediately in the hotel lobby. Jerry’s text ended, “Urgent.” He got up and hurried back past the midway, where a lone juggler had drawn a small crowd. As he walked the winding path back toward the front entrance and the hotel check-in area, he ran through the conversation with The Big Lewbowski. The guy was definitely not being truthful. The question was: Why not?

As soon as Mike made eye contact with Jerry in the hotel lobby, the lawyer rose from a couch and walked toward the detective. “I got a call from my office. That dickhead Rickenbacker sent over an arrest warrant. He also said he was not going to let me bring him in. He’s going to arrest Jackie. I called him back and left a message to meet me at the Mardi Gras. Jackie’s still there, right?”

Mike shook his head. “He’s actually out with Rachel and Jason checking out a wedding chapel. But we’re supposed to hook up back at the pool for lunch at one o’clock. You think the asshole will try to grab him as he’s coming in?”

“He might. He’s that much of a dick. You think you can get a message to your group and have them come in a side door so we can at least handle the arrest on our own terms?”

“Why not take him down to the station and wait for Rickenbacker there?”

“Because he’ll probably stay away and make us wait there

for five hours before he shows up," Jerry said. "I'd rather get it over with and get Jackie booked and out on bail quickly, while the court is open, so he doesn't have to spend a night in the lockup."

"OK," Mike agreed. "Let's get back there and try to minimize the damage. You think he'll have to miss his show tonight?"

"Not if I can help it."

As they hustled toward the door, Mike said, "I guess the feds will have to wait."

Chapter 37 — An Unexpected Reunion

Wednesday, January 8
Las Vegas, NV

WHILE MIKE WAS HEADING to the circus circus to meet with Jerry Garcia, Rachel and Jason had an appointment with a wedding planner. Jackie, Lizzy, and Michelle were happy to come along, given the importance of staying together for safety. Ms. Marchand had sent Rachel a message about a chapel that had been closed for a while, but was re-opening under new management. She didn't have any relationship with the place, and couldn't vouch for it personally. But since it was re-opening, it had availability, which was all Rachel cared about.

"One chapel is the same as the next," Michelle had said. "You say 'I do' and kiss Jason and you're married. That's all that really matters."

Rachel agreed, but she wanted to make sure she had happy memories of the event. She didn't want to get married someplace trashy. They had spent some time researching the available walk-in wedding venues and were hoping for something better than the "Tunnel of Love" drive-through wedding chapel. She also did not want to wait in line at one of the on-call chapels behind whoever was doing a spur-of-the-moment wedding.

Michelle had suggested telephoning the planner from the new place, which was called The Little Jewel Chapel. Rachel preferred to speak in person and see the place for herself. The group piled into a Lyft car and arrived at The Little Jewel ten minutes before their appointed time. The small structure was made of shiny white stone, with square columns holding up the cover of an awning sheltering the double doors leading into the building. Tendrils of some kind of weed crawled up the walls near the doorway and a small cross guarded the archway.

Two workers in blue overalls were on ladders, working on the awning. At the top of one ladder, a man was hammering. At the top of the other, his partner was holding the end of a wooden sign. They could make out the word "Opening."

"It looks sweet," Michelle observed.

"Let's see the inside before we draw any conclusions," Rachel skeptically responded.

Jackie slapped Rachel playfully on the arm. "Don't get all picky and shit now, Sis. This isn't the time to have standards."

Everyone in the car, including the driver, broke out laughing.

When they exited the car and entered the chapel, Rachel's impression didn't improve. A pile of cardboard boxes leaned against one wall. The topmost box was open, with something long and pink spilling out. The center of the space was mostly empty, save for two rows of cheap-looking folding chairs arranged on either side of a central aisle. The walls were decorated with fake stained-glass windows and empty candle holders. In the front, two steps up a red velvet carpet led to a plain altar, beyond which a painted mural mixed Las Vegas images with Christian religious icons in a gaudy display.

"Can you say 'tacky?'" Rachel whispered to Michelle.

As they walked slowly down the aisle, a door off to the right of the altar opened and out walked a tall, blonde woman wearing a knee-length skirt and a cream-colored blouse. Her hair was piled up in a beehive. The blouse's buttons strained against twin mountains of breasts that overflowed into impressive cleavage. Her face was tastefully made up with dark eyeliner and deep red lipstick.

Rachel made eye contact and stopped short. Her mouth opened in surprise.

The woman stopped her approach, then broke into a wide smile and called out in a high-pitched voice, "Oh, my Gawd! Rachel Robinson and Detective Jason Dickson!"

Jason, Rachel, and Michelle stood frozen and shocked. Jackie asked the obvious question. "You know this lady?"

Before any of them could find words, their blonde host took three quick steps forward in her three-inch heels and enveloped Rachel in a full-body hug. "I saw the name Rachel on the text, but I never dreamed!" She disengaged from Rachel and moved toward Jason, who took a step back to avoid the full hug and instead held out a hand for a shake. The woman took the hand, but then pulled Jason forward and planted a kiss on his cheek, leaving behind a red smear. "I recognize you, Dr. Michelle McNeill, but who is this?" She gestured toward Jackie. "I'm guessing some relation of yours, Rachel. Am I right?"

Rachel had recovered her equilibrium and laughed. "Yes, he is." She grabbed Jackie's elbow and pulled him forward to make the introduction. "Jackie, I'd like you to meet Ms. Helene DiVito-Rosen." She paused, looking at Helene. "Did I get that right?"

"You did!" she gushed in her New Jersey accent. The last

word of every sentence raised to a higher pitch. She took Jackie's hand and gave it a firm shake. "And who is this very attractive young man?"

"I'm Jackie," he said. "I'm Rachel's brother."

"A performer. Am I right?"

Jackie did a double-take, then stammered, "Well . . . yes. That's right. How—?"

"Oh, it's easy, Honey. It's the eyebrows. No guy who's not an actor has manicured eyebrows like that." She winked, leaving Jackie to wonder what Helene was thinking.

While Helene spent a minute catching up with Rachel, Michelle gave Jackie the quick version of how they knew the tall blonde with the Jersey accent. She had been widowed when the killer called the "Righteous Assassin" murdered her husband. Then, after remarrying and having her new husband die of a heart attack, she hooked up with a foreign jeweler and ended up selling jewelry on board the cruise ship where Michelle, Rachel, Mike, and Jason had taken a vacation the prior summer. Rachel didn't know it, but Helene had sold Jason her engagement ring.

Michelle stepped forward and said, "What are you doing here? We last saw you on the cruise ship in May. What happened to your jewelry business with . . . I forget his name."

"Hendrik. Yeah. Well, we were back in Manhattan for a while, but then my sister got sick and I came out here."

"Is she OK?" Michelle asked, suddenly concerned.

Helene dropped her gaze to the floor for a moment. Jason noticed a quiver in the woman's lower lip. When she spoke, the lilting enthusiasm was gone. "She died. It was really sudden. She's – she was – older than me, but only two years. She got some kind of lung infection. She called me from the hospital and I came out, but then . . . she didn't make it. She was about to open up this place. She'd been talking about it for years. She loved weddings. She left me all her stuff since she had no kids. So, I decided to stay and take over the business. I brought Hendrick's jewelry, so now I'm his west-coast distributor." She laughed at the conceit of Las Vegas being on the coast. "Now I've got a jewelry franchise and a wedding business. I'm an entrepreneur."

Jason was the first to reply. "I'm really sorry for your loss."

"Thank you, Detective. It's been a month now, so I guess I'm getting used to it, but I miss her. I'm surprised to see you here – but I'm so happy you're getting married! I knew you two were truly in love last summer. It's wonderful, but I figured you'd get married in New York."

"Well, we had a change of plans," Jason said, looking Helene in the eyes. "We had this trip on the calendar anyway, so we decided to get married while we're here."

"But the chapel at the Mardi Gras canceled on us at the last minute," Rachel jumped into the explanation. "We were left with no venue and the planner over there said this place was re-opening and might have availability."

"I do!" Helene chirped, her lilt and pitch back to normal levels. "And I know about the big event at the Mardi Gras. I'm not supposed to tell anyone, but it's a pretty big star who's getting married there on Sunday. She spent a boatload of money to close down that chapel for the whole day. Believe me! I was hoping I'd be able to get some of the overflow, if I can be open and ready by then."

"You're not open yet?"

"Oh, Rachel, don't worry. I will be. This is so great! You'll be one of my first weddings. That's such good luck for me." Then she reached out, gently took Rachel's left hand, and leaned down to examine her engagement ring. "I knew that emerald would be gorgeous on your finger. Your fiancé has such wonderful taste. He told me you loved emeralds."

"Thank you!" Rachel beamed.

Helene turned to Jason and asked, "Detective Dickson, do you need a wedding band? I have some lovely ones in stock."

Jason chuckled. "No. I'm covered for that, Ms. Rosen."

"Oh please! Call me Helene. I feel like we're old friends."

"OK – Helene. I tell you what, though, I didn't have time to get the wedding rings engraved. I was going to do it when we got back to New York, but it would make things a little more special if you could do it."

"Of course!" She gushed. "I'm a full-service jeweler. What do you want on the inside of the bands?"

Jason guided Helene away from Rachel, explaining that he wanted the inscription to be a surprise for her. While they talked in hushed tones, Jackie sat in one of the folding chairs, tired of standing. "Sis, this is an amazing coincidence. It's like it was somehow meant to be." He looked around the room. "With some flowers and decorations, this could be pretty sweet."

Michelle and Rachel agreed and they started to speculate about what kinds of decorations would work for the ceremony. When Jason returned, he said "Rachel, Helene needs us to look at some books of colors and decorations."

"I didn't see her write down your inscription," Jackie noted.

"Don't worry," Jason smiled, taking Rachel's hand, "Helene has a photogenic memory."

Jackie opened his mouth to correct Jason, but Michelle reached out her hand and patted his leg. "Leave it alone, Honey. It's a thing."

Jackie shrugged. "Whatever. I'm just glad we have a venue

for Sunday."

The whole group crowded into Helene's office, where they spent the next hour talking about the schedule and the decorations. At one point, Jason's cell buzzed and he checked the text message, which was from Mike. His face turned serious and he excused himself, leaving the group to discuss color combinations.

Mike's message was an abbreviated version of the story, but instructed Jason not to bring Jackie in through the front entrance at the Mardi Gras when they got back. Detective Rickenbacker was planning to arrest him.

Chapter 38 — Working the System

Wednesday, January 8
Las Vegas, NV

JASON BROUGHT JACKIE INTO THE MARDI GRAS through a side entrance around the corner from the rear taxi drop-off. He was pretty sure he spotted a Vegas cop in uniform watching the main rear door and figured she had made them as her target, but at least they were inside on Jackie's home turf.

The group walked with a purpose along the winding path through the casino, past the front desk, and out to the pool deck. It was warmer than the prior few days, but still nothing like the summer blast furnace that Las Vegas was supposed to be. Guests were splashing in the pool and sunning on lounge chairs. Mike and Jerry were seated at what had become their usual pool-side table with the umbrella fully extended. Both men stood as Jason led in his group like a battalion leader reporting to his commanding officer.

Michelle rushed to Mike, gave him a quick kiss, then said, "You will never guess who we met at the wedding chapel."

"Helene DiVito-Rosen," Mike deadpanned.

Michelle spun and glared at Jason. "I told you not to tell

Mike!"

"I didn't," Jason said, holding out his hands in surrender.

"Oh, sorry," Rachel said sheepishly. "I texted Mike from the car. I didn't know you wanted it to be a surprise."

Michelle sighed. "Well, you're the bride, so you can do whatever you want this week."

Mike got Michelle's attention by pulling gently on the back of her loose-fitting sun dress, which showed off her slender legs. "I got the message, but not the explanation. What the hell is she doing here in Vegas, and at a wedding chapel? Is she getting married?"

Michelle gave Mike the quick version of the story they heard from Helene, while Jerry pulled Jackie aside and conducted a hushed but pointed conversation. Mike was dumbstruck, but managed to say, "Well, as long as you guys found an available chapel, that's the main point. The wedding is still on for Sunday, right?"

"Right!" Rachel chimed in happily. The pall that had been hanging over the wedding plans was lifted. Rachel laced her arm through Jason's and rested her head on his shoulder. Michelle sat on Mike's lap, looping her arms around his neck and planting a kiss on his cheek. For a brief moment, everything was calm.

Then, Jackie glanced toward the doors leading from the casino to the pool, following the form of a tall, muscular man with a dark tan. His smile vanished as he said, "Uh oh, look what just creeped in."

Two blue-uniformed police officers strode across the smooth stone pool deck, followed by Detectives Rickenbacker and Maulgray. Jason stood, followed quickly by Jerry and then Mike, who had to gently remove Michelle from his lap first. They waited for the officers with level stares. Jackie sat next to

Michelle and Rachel, who formed a protective flank and kept the table between them and the approaching cops.

Jerry looked back over his shoulder at Rachel and said, "Get your phone and start taking a video." Then to the newcomers, calmly, "We know why you're here, Officers. Jackie is a performer, not a killer. He's innocent, but he's ready and willing to peacefully turn himself in for arrest. I'll drive him down to the station myself and meet you. There is no need to handcuff him. He's no threat and he'll go quietly."

Rickenbacker stepped between the two uniforms, nudging one of them aside without an apology. "He's accused of a brutal murder. He's a threat to the public. We're taking him in the squad car. Step aside."

"Are you getting all this on video?" Jerry asked loudly.

"You're such a jerk," Rickenbacker said. He put a hand on Jerry's shoulder, pushed him aside, and stepped past toward Jackie, who had risen to a standing position. Rachel backed away, holding her phone up and positioning herself to keep the entire scene in frame. Rickenbacker moved in close to Jackie, using his height to intimidate. "Jack Robinson, you're under arrest for the murder of Nigel Ellington." He nodded to one of the uniformed officers to step in and cuff Jackie, who silently held out two hands, palms up. He kept his head down. His arms quivered as he tried to keep it together. The officer snapped one cuff on his left hand, then pulled his arm behind his back roughly and secured the right cuff.

Jerry called out, "Keep taking video," as he stepped up to Rickenbacker. The lawyer was a good seven inches shorter, but held his face level against the big detective's neck. "You are harassing this man. What evidence do you have to base an arrest?"

Rickenbacker's mouth curled into a sneer. "You'll read all

about it at the detention hearing, Counselor." He spat out the last word as if it were a curse.

"This arrest is unlawful and discriminatory. I will hold you personally liable for this outrageous treatment. I offered to voluntarily submit my client to you at the police station. There is no need to cuff him and drag him into a squad car. I demand that you free him from those barbaric restraints and allow him the dignity of surrendering voluntarily."

"Go fuck yourself," Rickenbacker spat out, placing a hand on the lawyer's neck. Then he remembered he was on camera and let his hand fall, stepping back. "It's my professional opinion that this person is a threat and a flight risk. I'm taking him in under restraint, according to departmental policy. Now, step aside."

Jerry took two steps back and stopped, watching Rickenbacker with a piercing stare. The officer marched Jackie away from the pool, while Rachel continued to take video. They all followed the cops through the casino and out to the front entrance, where two squad cars were parked with flashing lights. A small crowd gathered to watch Jackie get pushed into the back seat of one car, which drove away without engaging its siren. Mike and the rest of his group hopped into a yellow cab and followed the cops toward the Las Vegas police station.

Chapter 39 — Interior Designs

WHILE JACKIE WAS BOOKED, fingerprinted, and put into the general lockup, Jerry worked the system like the expert he was. Mike and Jason, along with Rachel and Michelle, sat in a public waiting room, unable to do anything but watch Jerry as he earned his fee.

After seating his companions and telling them to wait and not make any commotion, Jerry approached the Plexiglass window separating the general public from the inner sanctum and began chatting with the woman behind the partition. He smiled and reached through the small, semi-circular hole to grasp her hand warmly. Mike couldn't hear the banter, but it was clear Jerry was friendly with the uniformed woman. After a full two minutes, Jerry motioned toward the locked door, which buzzed loudly as he pushed through.

Mike and Jason, not used to being confined to the public spaces of a police station, could only wait and wonder what was happening inside. After ten long minutes, the buzz of the door jarred the consciousness of everyone in the waiting area and Jerry emerged back into the lobby. He had called his assistant back in the office to arrange for a habeas corpus petition, just in case the cops tried to hold Jackie longer than was appropriate. He had demanded a copy of the affidavit supporting the arrest warrant, which would include a summary of the evidence that supported a finding of probable cause. However, the desk sergeant inside told Jerry the detention hearing report wasn't ready and that it would be presented before Jackie's appearance before the judge. This was technically proper, Jerry explained, but was a more formal process than usual. There was nothing he could do unless the prosecutor failed to present Jackie in open court.

After two hours, he could go into court with his habeas corpus petition and demand that the police produce Jackie. Since it was still only 1:30 p.m., they had enough time before the courts closed for the day. Jerry was confident Jackie would get his detention hearing and, hopefully, get released on bail before then.

At Jerry's insistence, the group left the station and took a Lyft car down to Freemont street. They all realized they needed some nourishment, but it was a somber lunch. All the enthusiasm stemming from finding a wedding chapel was forgotten.

Jackie tried to stay calm, like Jerry had told him, but he was terrified. He had never been in trouble. Ernie Robinson did not permit his children to be lawbreakers. The inside of a holding cell felt like the surface of Mars.

Back at the side of the Mardi Gras pool, Jerry had quickly described what Jackie should expect at the police station. Jerry's instructions were to stay calm, comply with all instructions, and say nothing to anyone. That included when he was put in lockup after being booked. Anyone inside the cell could testify against him, so he should avoid any conversation.

The cops who had accompanied Rickenbacker walked Jackie inside the station, then removed the handcuffs. One of them apologized for the cuffs and gently escorted Jackie to a podium, where another officer took fingerprints and a mug shot photo. They had Jackie empty his pockets and deposited the meager contents into a manila envelope. They had frisked him at the Mardi Gras before they got into the squad car, but now conducted a much more thorough search, including a metal detector. Jackie was thankful they didn't make him strip. They didn't try to interrogate him, so he didn't have to demand that they call his lawyer or refuse to answer. Everyone involved in the process was polite, but firm.

After a half hour of processing, the same cop who had removed the cuffs led the way through two sets of locked security doors to the jail area of the station house. The officer handed Jackie over to two officers, who opened a locked cell door and motioned for him to enter. When the steel lock clanged shut, Jackie felt extremely alone, despite the presence of a half-dozen other detainees inside the large group holding cell.

Jackie looked for someplace he could sit as far away as possible from any other person. He slowly walked to the far corner of the square space. There was a metal bench running the length of a cinder-block wall. He sat in the spot farthest from the door, pushed up against the black iron bars that separated his cell from another. As long as nobody sat directly next to him, he was isolated from everyone. He pulled his legs up, resting his heels on the metal seat and hugging his knees. He took deep, regular breaths, following a yoga meditation technique Lizzy had shown him. All he had to do was sit tight and wait for Jerry to get him out.

The lawyer had explained how he would be brought into the criminal court, which was across the street. He would be allowed to meet briefly with Jerry inside the court, then he would be brought before a judge. He would plead not guilty, and bail would be set. At least, that was the hope. Jerry admitted there was a small chance that the judge would deny bail, in which case Jackie would be returned to the lockup. Though he promised that was rare, all Jackie could focus on was the worst-case scenario. He would miss the show. Would the cops even let him call Terry to let him know? Lizzy would tell the director, but missing a show could get him fired. If he was locked up for more than one day, then he would surely lose his role. Right after the big break he had been waiting for. He felt guilty that he had gladly accepted the promotion to Mimi's role, without ever grieving over the way it happened. Would Mimi have grieved for him? Jackie's mind was racing and his heart was pounding.

Over the next hour, two detainees were escorted out of the holding cell in the custody of uniformed officers, while two new men were brought in. Jackie assessed the motley group of which he was now a part. The three remaining men who had been there when Jackie arrived included an obviously homeless man with long, stringy gray hair, dirt-covered clothes, and vacant eyes. He sat alone at the opposite corner of the cell and didn't seem to be any threat. The other two seemed to know each other and sat together on the concrete floor near the middle of the cell. Each wore blue jeans and a white t-shirt and both had colorful tattoos on their exposed arms. They had glanced at Jackie when he took his seat, then returned to their private conversation.

The two new arrivals were not so innocuous. One was a tall, lean man with a blond Fu Manchu moustache. He wore a denim jacket over his jeans, with cowboy boots Jackie could tell were expensive. The scar on his neck suggested he was not somebody to talk to, so Jackie averted his eyes. The other new arrival was a burly Black man wearing a tight black shirt over baggy gray sweatpants. He looked like a lineman from a pro football team – easily six-foot-four and over 250 pounds. His shaved head made him even more intimidating. He glared at Jackie when he arrived. Even though he was the only other Black man in the cell, Jackie didn't feel any compulsion to bond with him. The bald man stood, leaning against the door to the cell and casting his gaze around the space like an eagle searching a field for a passing mouse. Jackie avoided eye contact.

As he was watching the bald man, Jackie was startled by the appearance of Fu Manchu a few feet to his right. He pulled his knees into his chest even harder and turned away.

"You don't want to look me in the eye, huh?" the tall man said with a western twang. "You don't look like much. You some kind of whore? Huh? You in here for sucking dick?" The man moved closer, standing over Jackie and scowling down at him.

"Lay off him," one of the two white t-shirts said from the middle of the cell. "Be cool and keep to yourself."

Fu Manchu turned and shouted, "Mind your own business!"

Jackie looked at the white t-shirt, happy to have somebody trying to keep the peace. Outside the holding cell, all of the uniformed officers were gone. Jackie figured they were on the other side of the security door. He couldn't remember whether one had been visible outside the cell before the bald man was brought in. When he glanced back toward Fu Manchu, he notice that the bald guy had moved in his direction.

"What have you got over here?" the big Black man asked Fu Manchu. "Looks like a little bug."

Jackie lowered his head, saying nothing.

"I think this here's a little bitch," Fu Manchu responded, reaching out to slap Jackie across the side of his head.

Jackie looked toward the door, searching again for a guard, but not seeing any blue uniforms. He thought about a snappy retort, but figured that keeping silent, like Jerry said, was the right course. He didn't look at the two men, hoping they would tire of taunting him.

The bald guy grabbed Jackie's left sneaker and pulled, ripping his leg from the chest-hug and throwing Jackie off balance. He lurched forward, falling to the concrete floor with a thud as his head smacked against the steel bench.

The two guys in the white t-shirts stood, but didn't advance. Jackie put his hands over his head and slid backwards, trying to shelter under the bench. The bald guy wasn't having it. He pulled Jackie's leg, dragging him away from the bench. Fu Manchu reached out and grabbed the back of Jackie's shirt, pulling the collar painfully around his neck and drawing Jackie to his feet. The two white shirts took a few steps toward the corner, then stopped when the big bald guy turned his head and snarled, "Back off!"

Fu Manchu grabbed Jackie by the arm, then planted a fist into his stomach. He doubled over, gasping for breath and reeling from the pain. Then Fu Manchu lifted Jackie's chin with two fingers, taunting him. "You're just my little bitch, aren't you?"

Jackie was terrified. He couldn't breathe. He tried to drop to the ground, but Fu Manchu held his arm. Jackie saw a glint of light reflecting off something thin and white in Fu Manchu's hand. He tried to cry out, but couldn't get air into his lungs.

"Help! Guard!" The words were faint croaks.

The bald guy grabbed Jackie's other arm and twisted it behind his back. He tried to scream again, but a huge hand covered his mouth. As he watched in horror, Fu Manchu pulled back his arm, a white blade extending toward Jackie. A satisfied smile spread across the tall man's face. He grunted and moved forward. Jackie closed his eyes, straining uselessly against the firm grasp of the bald mountain.

Jackie heard a soft thud. Somebody yelled, "Shit!" He felt a sting in his left side, then a burning pressure as he was pressed back into the bald guy. He tried to twist away from the pain, but he was held firm. Opening his eyes and looking down, he saw the thin white blade withdraw as a deep red stain welled up and spread across the fabric of his shirt. Again, he tried to scream, but the big hand still covered his mouth. He heard the smack of flesh against flesh and another grunt. The pressure around his face lessened and he slipped downward toward the floor, landing in a crumpled heap. He was aware of more curses and grunts and saw flashes of white and denim. He extended his legs, trying to push away, but the effort made his side burn painfully. He saw the fluorescent lights hanging from the ceiling, then closed his eyes.

Jackie heard somebody shout, "Leave him alone!" Shoes scraped along the floor next to his head. More voices yelled for help. Then, Jackie heard the buzz of the lock on the security door, then the clang of the steel cell door and shouts from several voices. He heard more grunts and groans, curses and shouts. He opened his eyes and saw a crew-cut above an angry face. "Get an ambulance!" the crew-cut called out. Jackie felt somebody press against the spot where the white knife had stuck him. He winced and turned his head, clenching his teeth and trying not to scream. He closed his eyes again and tried to slow his breathing.

Five minutes later, Jackie was on a gurney being loaded into an ambulance out the rear of the police station with two uniformed officers flanking him. The siren blasted as the paramedics drove away.

◆◆◆

Over lunch, Mike remembered to ask Jerry if he knew a guy named Freddy Costanzo.

"Everybody in Vegas knows Freddy Costanzo," Jerry explained. "He's been around for years. I heard he came to Vegas from Kansas City, but he's originally from back east somewhere. He's rumored to be involved in all kinds of shady operations. Owns a bunch of real estate."

Mike relayed the information they got from Agent Forrest. "Do you think a guy like him could have a cop in his pocket?"

"If you told me he has Vegas cops on his payroll, I'd believe it."

Jerry and the rest of the entourage returned to the police station. Jerry approached the window while the others took seats in the waiting room, but he came walking back after only half a minute.

"We're leaving," Jerry said. "Jackie's been taken to the hospital."

At the hospital, they were told Jackie was in a recovery room next to the ER. It took Jerry and Mike fifteen minutes of haggling with the hospital administrator and the officer who was standing guard over Jackie's room before Rachel was allowed to see her brother. Jerry, as the patient's lawyer, was also allowed inside. The rest of the group stayed in the ER waiting area, but not patiently. Michelle saw the ashen expression on Rachel's face when she came out, then collapsed into Jason's consoling arms. Lizzy, who was nearly as upset as Rachel, came over to join in a group hug.

They all huddled in a corner of the waiting room, surrounded by injured people waiting to be processed for treatment. Rachel and Jerry recounted the story Jackie told them of the attack inside the holding cell. The doctors assured Rachel that Jackie was going to be fine. The knife wound had resulted in a substantial loss of blood, but hadn't damaged any vital organs. They had stopped the bleeding and stitched him up under only a local anesthetic. The doctor expected Jackie to be up and around by the next day. Strenuous dancing, however, would need to cease for a few days in order for the wound to heal. Rachel reported that Jackie wasn't as shaken up about the attack as he was about not being able to perform.

The officer inside the room told Jerry that they planned to transport Jackie back to the lockup. Jerry, however, had insisted Jackie be kept in the hospital overnight for observation to make sure there wasn't any undetected internal bleeding. He threatened an immediate lawsuit if the police involuntarily removed him from the hospital. After a call to his captain, the officer relented. Jerry reported that the hospital was working on getting Jackie a normal patient room, away from the ER, where he could rest for the night.

When they stepped out of the building into the warm Las Vegas evening, Jason asked the question Mike had been thinking. "How the hell does a guy get a knife into the lockup? What kind of Mickey Mouse operation are they running over there?"

Jerry spoke softly and with concern. "Folks, I can assure you that the lockup process is no Mickey Mouse operation. I've been through there myself, and I've had plenty of clients who have told me their stories."

"Yourself?" Mike said with a raised eyebrow.

"Not important," Jerry dismissed his curiosity. "The point is that they are meticulous about searches, which include metal detectors. It might have been a ceramic knife, but even so it's next to impossible to get something like that inside a holding cell – unless a cop let them."

The two detectives stood motionless, each thinking the same thing. Mike broke the silence. "Did you ever get that warrant affidavit?"

"No. I didn't. We never filed the habeas corpus petition, and we never had an arraignment, so there's nobody I can complain to until tomorrow."

"I'll bet you never see it," Mike grumbled.

"I'm not taking that bet," Jerry responded with a wry smile.

Jason seemed skeptical. "You think Rickenbacker?"

Jerry hesitated only a few seconds. "I've heard stories. I'm admittedly biased, but some of my colleagues have told me about incidents. It seems that suspects in Rickenbacker's sights have been known to have accidents while in custody. I know of one who killed himself, but his lawyer swears that's impossible. This knife attack might not have been entirely random."

"Do we know who the perp is?" Mike asked.

"No. Not yet. I've asked my associate to dig into it, but so far I know nothing. Jackie's story is that there were two of them working together. I'll try to find out who both of them are, but it won't be tonight."

Michelle called out to Mike, who moved over to where Rachel was standing. She was shaking. All her EMS training could not overcome the emotional toll of seeing her kid brother arrested and then stabbed. The upsetting events, combined with the hormones of her pregnancy, had Rachel on the verge of tears again. Michelle suggested getting her back to the Mardi Gras as quickly as possible. They needed to get something to eat, and they needed to alert Jackie's director that his lead would be missing that night's show.

"Is there anything we can do to help at this point?" Mike asked.

"I can't think of anything," Jerry said. "We'll have to wait to see if the cops come up with something to justify another arrest warrant. If not, then presumably they'll continue the investigation. If they find some other suspect, perhaps they'll call the dogs off Jackie. But if Rickenbacker is still focused on him, we have to assume he's still at risk."

"What if we found the real killer?" Jason suggested.

"You have any leads?"

"No."

"You have any jurisdiction to interview witnesses?"

"No."

"Well, I'd be happy if you uncovered something, but I think you'd be better off concentrating on getting married."

Chapter 40 — Pointing Fingers

Wednesday, January 8
Las Vegas, NV

BACK AT THE MARDI GRAS, Michelle busied herself getting them a dinner reservation while Rachel and Lizzy went to the theater. Mike, Jason, and Jerry huddled to plot strategy for the next day. Jerry planned to file the habeas corpus petition first thing in the morning in the hope they could get a judge to set bail based on Jackie's need for medical attention. They wanted to avoid having him back in the lockup, where whoever tried to have him killed would get a second chance. It seemed certain that a cop had to have either allowed the attacker to bring the knife in, or provided it after the detainee had been through processing. They still didn't know the identity of the assailant.

"This kind of thing doesn't happen randomly," Jerry said. "No matter how much Rickenbacker might dislike Jackie, the guy wouldn't try to have him killed just because he's a homophobe. His suspect being killed in the lockup isn't going to help him close the case. And bringing in other people adds risk."

"You're right," Mike agreed. "It's going to get him into a shitstorm of inquiries and paperwork. It's probably the worst way for a cop to try to take out a suspect."

"You spend time making a list of the better ways?" Jerry chided playfully, trying to lighten the mood.

"Nah. I don't need a list. If I were a dirty cop back in New York and I wanted to make a suspect disappear, I'd put them in the river, not have some goon take them out in the lockup."

"Somebody did try to take Jackie out on the street," Jason reminded them both. "If that was the first try, then this was the follow-up. The question is why a cop like Rickenbacker would want him dead if he thought he had evidence linking him to Mimi's murder."

"I don't think it's just Rickenbacker," Mike said. "I'm betting there's somebody pulling the strings. Somebody with money. Somebody who wants Jackie silenced for some reason. They already took out Cricket and Mimi. It all links back to that photo."

"The photo you're not supposed to have, and that I never saw?" Jerry asked.

Mike and Jason looked at each other and shrugged. Mike said, "Is there any way this information could be deemed attorney-client privileged, so you could never tell anyone about it, even if there was a court order?"

Jerry thought about it. "Well, you're not my client. If Jackie had told me, then it would be privileged. It would be privileged if you were my investigator and I were paying you to help me with the case. That would make it work product."

Mike turned to Jason. "Any reason we couldn't do a little moonlighting while we're on vacation?"

"As long as Sully doesn't find out," Jason said with a smile.

Jerry pulled out his wallet and extracted two ten-dollar bills. He handed one to Mike and one to Jason. "There. You're now both officially working for me. If you make a claim for minimum wage, I'll tell your boss you're working as unlicensed

PIs in Vegas."

❧❧❧

Although Lizzy was shaken by the day's events, somebody had to step up to a more prominent role in that night's show. Terry promoted Chi-Chi to lead and Lizzy was thrilled to be filling a bigger slot – although sick about the circumstances. The director told Rachel to tell Jackie that he was suspended indefinitely. He was under arrest and accused of murdering Mimi. It seemed prudent not to have him in the show for as long as he was still a suspect. Since Jackie was under doctor's orders not to do any dancing for a few days, it was moot whether he was officially suspended or on medical leave. Either way, Jackie wasn't going to be on stage.

Mike and Jason had a few investigation duties to handle the next day, but for now there was not much to do. They'd meet Jerry at the hospital first thing in the morning to try to get Jackie released without going back to police custody. Mike contacted the local FBI agents and tentatively made arrangements for a meeting the next day, subject to Jackie's condition.

They clued in Rachel and Michelle about their discussion with Jerry. Whoever was behind all this had to have money and power – and be very frightened about that photo. It made the most sense that the person was a criminal, and Jerry said he had always suspected Rickenbacker was on the take.

"From whom?" Michelle asked.

Jason took Rachel's hand gently and said, "The Vegas Mob."

Chapter 41 — Bad Help

Wednesday, January 8
Las Vegas, NV

FREDDY COSTANZO DIDN'T DO MEETINGS, as a rule. People who needed to meet with him came to his office. People who didn't need to see him in person worked through his underlings. Still, sometimes, a face-to-face meeting was required but could not occur in Freddy's 40th-floor enclave. Today was one of those days. It wasn't making him happy.

In this case, the venue for the meeting was the plaza outside the T-Mobile Arena, where the Las Vegas Golden Knights played their games. On this day, there was no game or other event, leaving the plaza deserted except for a few homeless people who were taking advantage of the lull. Freddy left his car and walked toward the venue, then scanned the empty space. When he recognized the man he was expecting, Freddy made eye contact, then walked to an isolated spot in the shade next to an enormous concrete pillar. The day-of-game sales window was nearby, but closed.

Freddy waited with his back to the pillar until Buzz Rickenbacker slid up and leaned against the same structure at a ninety-degree angle. Neither man made eye contact with the other. Freddy spoke first, keeping his comments cryptic in case the cop was wearing a wire. The man was on the payroll, but he was still a cop.

"I'm thinking I may need to get a new department head." Freddy could see the steam from his breath as he spoke. "The employee I have has had very poor job performance recently. I'm thinking maybe I should fire him."

"Things don't always go as planned," Rickenbacker said in a quiet, even voice. "It's not possible to control all variables. Maybe you should cut your employee some slack. Give him another chance." He knew that, where Freddy Costanzo was concerned, somebody on the payroll who failed to perform wasn't let go quietly. They tended to disappear.

Freddy tilted his head up at the towering structure. He had never been inside. He considered whether attending a Golden Knights game might be an item to add to his bucket list. "I hear what you say, but there are some things that can't be overlooked. I'm going to bring in some new talent to take care of the problems in that department."

"Don't do that so fast. There are lots of factors to consider."

Freddy paused for several seconds to make the man squirm. "Is there a proposal I should think about?"

"Give your guy a few more days. Things may be a little hot right now. Sometimes you need to let things cool down, then they might get better."

"Incompetence can never be fully overlooked. I mean, suppose you hired somebody to slaughter your pig. The guy stuck the pig with a knife, but missed all the vital organs. The pig bled a little, but didn't die. So now, you have a stuck pig instead of a side of bacon. Would you hire that guy again for your next pig?"

"I probably wouldn't hire that guy again." Rickenbacker bit his lip. He wanted to curse and shout, but he had to keep under control. "But, I might give him a chance to clean up his own mess. Or, maybe remember that the guy has other talents that can still be useful."

"I'll think about that. But, like I said, I'm going to bring in some new talent to deal with my pig. I'll let you know how that works out. You got any other advice about my problems?"

Rickenbacker said nothing.

Freddy walked away, without looking back. He got back to his car, where his driver had kept the heat going. Freddy usually wanted air conditioning, but this week was upside down. "All good, Boss?"

"Yeah. I think so. We'll see. Sometimes it's hard to find good help."

Chapter 42 — Wedding Bangs

Thursday, January 9
Las Vegas, NV

JERRY GARCIA WAS DEFINITELY worth the money. The lawyer, true to his word, showed up at the hospital the next morning with a copy of the habeas corpus petition he had filed in court the moment the clerk's office had opened. Jerry was able to speak to the judge and explain that Jackie was in the hospital, having had an attempt on his life while in the lockup, and requested that he be brought directly to the courthouse so as not to be exposed to further peril. At the hospital, he explained to the officer guarding Jackie that the court had set a hearing for 10:00 a.m. and had directed that Jackie be brought directly to the courthouse's holding area for prisoners and detainees. This last statement wasn't entirely accurate. The judge said he would take the request under advisement, but Jerry was comfortable telling the officer that it was an order, which it still could be. The officer called the desk sergeant and, after some discussion, the sergeant decided that the 10:00 hearing was soon enough and it didn't make sense to bring Jackie back to the station first.

The hearing was quick. Jerry demanded to see the warrant affidavit and the evidence forming the basis for the arrest. The Assistant District Attorney, representing the state of Nevada, told the judge that the arrest warrant was based on a witness statement, but he didn't have a copy to provide to defense counsel. The judge immediately ruled the warrant invalid and released Jackie into the custody of his lawyer, with an admonition to not leave town and a warning that the police may arrest him again if they got their paperwork in order.

Jerry asked the judge to order that, if the arrest warrant were re-issued, the prosecutor should give Jerry twenty-four hours to surrender his client. Jerry described the original arrest and how he had tried to have his client surrender voluntarily, but that the police had insisted on dragging him away in handcuffs. The ADA couldn't comment on whether that was true. Jerry offered to show the judge the video recording of the arrest at the Mardi Gras, which Rachel had sent to him from her phone. After a discussion, the judge thought it was a reasonable request and issued the order.

Jackie and Rachel embraced as soon as they all exited the courthouse. Jackie wasn't out of the woods, but at least he wasn't going to be in lockup, and they didn't even need to post bail. They hopped a Lyft back to the Mardi Gras, where Jackie immediately adjourned to their suite so he could get some sleep.

♦♦♦

Jackie slept until two o'clock. Then, Michelle suggested that they had some wedding preparations to handle. After a quick bite to eat in the food court, Michelle, Rachel, Jackie, and Lizzy went to see Helene DiVito-Rosen at The Little Jewel wedding chapel, with Jason along as their security. Mike said there wouldn't be room for him in Jackie's little car. He planned to try again to get some time in at the Mardi Gras poker tables. He was still waiting to hear back from Agent Forrest, and figured he could wait for a call in a seat at the poker table just as well as by the pool or in his suite.

During the ride to the wedding chapel, Rachel tried to put Jackie's continued peril out of her mind and focus on how wonderful Sunday would be for her and Jason. Jackie was more excited than Rachel and seemed to have an easier time forgetting about Mimi LaRee's murder. Although the stitches were a constant reminder of the knife attack, Jackie was convinced the horror was in the past. Looking toward the future seemed far superior to dwelling on the possibility of a re-arrest.

After parking the little car in a lot between the chapel and the tattoo parlor next door, the group made their way up the curving sidewalk toward the welcoming shade of the awning at the front entrance. As Jason reached the door, with Rachel next to him, a black SUV with scrapes and dents on the driver's side of the front grill pulled under the white awning. Jackie watched as both the front and back windows smoothly lowered.

Behind the wheel, Jackie saw a man with a narrow face and an extremely long neck. Jackie tried to remember where he had seen that neck before, and never looked at the rear window.

On the other hand, Lizzy never looked at the driver. The SUV seemed familiar; the damage on the front grill triggered a memory. When the rear window started to lower, Lizzy moved, not waiting to see the gun.

Jason turned, recognized the impending danger, and instinctively reached for his gun, which wasn't there. Rachel screamed. Jackie felt an impact against his left side at the same instant he heard the explosion of a gunshot, then a ping as the bullet ricocheted off the concrete edge of a large planter that housed a flowering cactus. Lizzy had launched himself toward Jackie the moment the window began to lower, tackling him and driving them both to the sidewalk. The bullet had pierced only the air where Jackie had been a split-second before. Jackie screamed as the skin on his forearm scraped itself onto the pavement under Lizzy's weight.

The second shot followed the first by half a second, but was aimed more or less at the same spot, where Jackie no longer was. By the time Eddie, in the back seat, realized that his target had moved and adjusted to try a third, a thin black rectangle impacted the side of his Luger pistol, knocking it off aim as the bullet was expelled from the muzzle with another deafening crack. Jason, not finding his gun, instead found his cell phone clipped to his belt. He had grabbed it and thrown it at the assailant.

The door of the chapel opened as Rick punched the gas and accelerated away with a squeal of tires, leaving the group stunned. Helene emerged through the front door and surveyed the scene. "What happened!?" she shouted. Nobody responded immediately to the question.

Jackie and Lizzy untangled and rose from the sidewalk. Rachel took a breath, not realizing she had been holding hers. Michelle retrieved Jason's phone, which was scratched but still operating, having been protected by NYPD-issue combat casing.

Except for Jackie's skinned elbow and forearm, they were all unharmed. Lizzy apologized for being so rough, but everyone agreed it was exactly the right instinct. It had saved Jackie's life. Jackie dabbed a finger at his bleeding arm, reached his palm toward his side, where his fresh stitches ached, then slumped onto Lizzy's shoulder. The rest of the group, including Helene, rushed over and joined in a group hug, supporting Jackie. Three times in four days, somebody had tried to kill him. There was no doubt. So much for feeling like the weight of his arrest had lifted.

Chapter 43 — Reinforcements

Thursday, January 9
Las Vegas, NV

IT WAS TIME TO ESCALATE THINGS. Mike had received the call from Jason about the shooting when he was five minutes into his poker session. He expected a call from Agent Forrest, not one about another attempt on Jackie's life. After once again excusing himself only a few hands in, Mike placed a call to Forrest and left an urgent message.

As it turned out, Mike got back to the suite before anyone else and waited impatiently. When the door finally opened, Mike pulled Jason aside, leaving the rest of the bedraggled group that had spent the last hour giving statements to the local cops to slump onto the nearest chair or sofa cushion. Jason had barely started his briefing on the drive-by shooting when Mike's phone rang. He and Jason excused themselves to the bedroom to take the call.

Agent Forrest wanted the facts, so Jason re-started his briefing. When he finished, Forrest asked them to hold while he made another call. When Forrest came back on the line, he suggested a meeting at the hotel with some local FBI agents. Mike agreed and suggested they meet in Jason's suite, since everybody else was huddled in Mike and Michelle's room.

Rachel and Michelle put up a mild objection to being left

behind, but understood the limits of the FBI agents' ability to share. Jackie and Lizzy both said they were sick of talking to cops, and were happy to stay out of it.

Mike called down to the front desk to let them know that if someone came in asking for him, it was OK to give out his suite number and let them come up. Twenty minutes later, Agent Davis Perkins arrived at Mike's suite with two other agents. Perkins introduced Derek Dumm and Chelsea Shields, but didn't explain why they were there. Perkins set his phone down on the coffee table in the sitting area of the suite and engaged a Zoom video conference with Agent Forrest from New York. After Forrest vouched for Mike and Jason, and after the full briefing from the two New York cops on the events of the past four days, the agents were sympathetic about Jackie's situation. Perkins was particularly interested in the circumstantial evidence pointing at Rickenbacker. They were not surprised that Freddy Costanzo's name came up.

Jason was not able to identify the shooter at The Little Jewel Chapel. It was definitely not Rickenbacker or his partner, Maulgray, nor anyone else he had ever seen. Jason had not gotten a good look at the driver, since he had been focused on the shooter in the back.

They had called 9-1-1 after the shooting and reported it, but the responding officers couldn't immediately do much for them. They took statements, along with a description of the SUV, which did not have visible plates. Jason had looked, and Rachel snapped a cell phone picture as the truck sped away, but it was no good. Two white males in a black SUV with scratches and dents on the front driver's side was not much of a description.

When the local cops finally allowed them to leave the scene, there was still a squad there taking pictures, collecting shell casings, searching for the bullets, and canvasing the neighborhood for security cameras that might have caught some of the action.

While Jackie and Lizzy were giving their statements to the officers, Rachel and Jason had their conference with Helene about the wedding plans, which seemed trivial next to Jackie's brush with death. Two hours later than they intended, the group finally returned to the Mardi Gras and found Mike.

"It all comes back to that photo of the old guy with the three showgirls," Jason said. "We know Jackie is one of the three, and the other two are dead. That's not a coincidence, and neither are three attempts on his life. It's frustrating for us that you guys have significant information you won't share."

"How did you know who the other two girls in the photo were?" Chelsea asked, drawing disapproving stares from Perkins and Dumm. "Oh, come on – they said they already knew, and their friend is the other girl. What are we hiding?"

Agent Perkins asked Mike and Jason to hold while he and the other agents stepped out into the hallway, along with the phone streaming the video image of Agent Forrest. After five minutes, they came back with somber facial expressions. "Alright, Detectives," Agent Perkins began, "we can understand you're trying to piece the situation together without all the information. We also recognize that your friend, Jackie, is in peril and we don't want to be responsible for impeding your efforts to protect him. We're ready to share some information with you. We can't tell you everything, but we'll help. But you have to keep this all completely confidential. You can't tell anyone, including Jackie's lawyer. You're cops, and Forrest says we can trust you. Can we?"

Mike said, "I'm guessing this investigation has no local connection to New York City. We've got no jurisdiction or interest in messing you guys up."

"OK," Perkins said, "I'm turning this over to Agent Dumm."

When Dumm started speaking, both Mike and Jason noted a northern midwestern accent right out of the movie *Fargo*. If they didn't know he was with the FBI, they would have sworn he was Canadian. "The old guy in the photo is dead. I can't tell you who he is, but he's a federal official. We think he's connected to Freddy Costanzo's organization here in Vegas. There's a push in Washington to pass legislation that would legalize sports betting nationwide. Costanzo has a big interest in that; we think he's getting inside information about pro sports teams around the country, particularly in the NFL. It may even extend to outright point shaving, but we don't have confirmation of that."

Mike and Jason looked at each other. "Agent Dumm," Mike said, "before you go on, can Jason and I have a few moments?"

"Sure?"

Mike and Jason were already up from the sofa and on their way to the bedroom. Two minutes later, they were back. Mike leaned toward the federal agents. "If you guys are on the NFL point-shaving investigation, we can tell you that there are some people involved in New York, in the organization headed up by Fat Albert Gallata. They put pressure on Jimmy Rydell to shave points last season. He didn't go along with it, but he told his agent about it. They were going to go to you guys, but then Jimmy turned up dead. You probably heard about it."

"That was you?" Perkins said, seemingly impressed.

"Yeah. That was us. We don't have any evidence. I heard it from a reliable source who will deny it if you ask him, but you can take it to the bank."

"That's very interesting and helpful information, Detective Stoneman. Thank you." Perkins reclaimed the lead. Mike assumed the sports gambling case was his baby, while the other agents were on the photo. "We will certainly factor that into our investigation. In any case, we think Freddy Costanzo is involved here. We think he was trying to put pressure on the guy in the photo, but it apparently didn't work, since he's dead. Two of the three girls in that shot are dead, and somebody has tried to kill your friend. I'd give you good odds that Costanzo is trying to get rid of them because they are witnesses to the photo shoot. I would recommend getting Jackie out of town somewhere so Costanzo and his guys can't finish the job."

"That's going to be difficult. There's a court order preventing Jackie from leaving town so the police can serve a new arrest warrant. Because of our favorite cop, Buzz Rickenbacker, Jackie is a suspect in Mimi LaRee's murder."

"We can't help you with that one," Perkins said with genuine regret. "Have you notified Rickenbacker's boss about today's shooting? Maybe somebody higher up than him can take the pressure off for you. But if you can't get him out of town immediately, then get him to a secure location. Freddy C. has a reputation for not giving up easily. If he wants Jackie dead, there's a good chance he's going to end up dead."

"That's not particularly encouraging," Jason said dryly. "Can't you get Jackie into the witness protection program or something?"

"Not unless he can place Costanzo in the room when that picture was taken and testify in court. Can he do that?"

Mike and Jason both shook their heads. "No. Jackie doesn't remember anything about that day. Maybe if you put together a lineup, we might be able to get an ID, but I doubt it."

"Well, then I can't help," Perkins said. "As far as the local cops are concerned, we've suspected that there are some on Costanzo's take, but we haven't been able to develop any proof. There's an Internal Affairs Department investigation on this, but so far they don't have anything, either. I'm happy to zero in on Rickenbacker going forward, but I can't give you anything concrete to hang him right now. Sorry, Detective – we're not being very helpful."

"You're being as helpful as you can be," Mike said genuinely. "You guys didn't have to talk to us at all. We appreciate the information. I'm not sure what we'll do with it, but if we run across anything that might help you, we'll certainly let you know."

Shields piped up, speaking to Perkins. "There has to be something here, Agent Perkins. This Jackie Robinson is the target. What if we set up some kind of trap to get Costanzo's guys to take another run at him where we can grab 'em?"

Perkins glanced at Dumm, the senior agent of the team. Mike saw him give a quick eye roll. "Agent Shields, I appreciate your enthusiasm, but we don't run operations with civilians. And something like that would take time to arrange."

"I'm willing to stay," Shields said brightly, not acknowledging that her idea had been shot down. "It's a fucking freezer in Rapid City."

Dumm shot his junior partner a scolding look, which shut her up. "We might be able to arrange for some surveillance around your friend. Where does he live?"

"He's staying here in the hotel, at least this week while we're here," Jason responded. "He and his friend, Lizzy, both perform in the drag show downstairs in *The Birdcage* theater, when Jackie's not injured."

"OK, well, I tell you what. You let us know if he's ever

leaving the hotel. As long as he's here, between you two and maybe some of us, we'll try to keep him safe." Dumm handed Mike his business card.

Perkins did the same, then held out a hand toward his colleague. "Do you have authorization from HQ for this? I don't think our office has manpower to spare."

Forrest piped up, causing everyone in the room to snap their attention to the phone sitting on the small table. "Agent Dumm, I agree with you here. I'm sure we'll get the authorization. It may take a few days to move some agents around to reinforce your office, Perkins. But given the interest level in this investigation, it shouldn't be a problem."

Perkins shrugged. "OK. Well, who am I to complain about getting help. Do you think we should bring in the local cops – somebody over Rickenbacker's head?"

The agents spent several minutes discussing the issue, finally agreeing that there was a significant enough chance others within the LVPD were compromised that bringing in anyone risked the secrecy of the FBI operation. If Costanzo was going to make another attempt to kill Jackie, it would happen with or without the feds watching. Mike and Jason were happy to have the support and pledged to give their full cooperation. They agreed that leaving the local cops out of it was fine.

When the meeting broke up, Mike thanked Forrest for all his help. The agents marched to the elevators. Mike and Jason knew Rachel and Michelle would be dying to find out what had happened. They also knew they couldn't disclose much of what they had learned.

"Well." Jason sat heavily on the beige sofa. "We got some information, but I'm not sure how it's going to help us. Getting Jackie out of town isn't an option. I guess we can be his security detail as long as we're in town, but what happens when we go back to New York? This Costanzo seems like a meaner version of Slick Mick Gallata. If he's already knocked off Cricket and Mimi, he obviously has no boundaries. He needed some girls to set up the old guy, so he hired them to be his photo bombs. They took the gig not knowing it was a setup and now he's ready to kill them all. I wonder if he'll take out their agent, Lewbowski? He booked them, so he had to have some contact with somebody from Costanzo's organization. You think he was in on the setup?"

Mike thought about it. "He was evasive when I asked him about it. I guess it's possible he's on Costanzo's payroll. I'm not sure it matters at this point."

"Well, Costanzo seems to have the muscle and money necessary to pull it off. The feds are already on him, but obviously can't make an arrest. So, the guy must be plenty slippery."

"Yeah," Mike agreed. "Like any good mob boss, he insulates himself through soldiers who do the dirty work. I'm sure our federal friends are working their angles, but that's a long game. We need a short-term solution."

"You think we could get the judge to lift the travel ban if we tell him about the drive-by?"

"Not by Sunday. We can talk to Jerry, but what can the judge do as long as Rickenbacker is saying that Jackie is still a suspect? What we need is a way to get to this Costanzo guy and get him to call off his dogs. Jackie and Lizzy got a good look at Costanzo's thugs. Maybe we can use that. We can offer to have them keep quiet and forget they ever saw his guys if Costanzo will just lay off."

"Costanzo will still have a reason to want Jackie dead. And now maybe Lizzy also, not to mention Michelle and Rachel — and me. We were all witnesses to an attempted murder." Jason rose and walked to the window, tapping lightly on the thick glass as the afternoon sun streamed in to do battle with the hotel's heavy-duty air conditioning system. "The big boss doesn't care that much if we ID his goons. He'll be more interested in protecting himself. He'd probably toss those dummies under the bus in a heartbeat. I'm figuring the reason he's so worried about witnesses to that photo shoot is that he was there himself. By the way, why were those agents from South Dakota here? Does that make sense to you?"

Mike sat on the sofa, his phone open in his hands. "You picked up on Rapid City, too, eh?"

"I figured that region anyway, based on the accents, but Agent Shields made it easy. Why would Perkins bring them into this?"

After thirty seconds of searching the internet, Mike looked up. "I think I have an idea. You remember a few weeks ago, before we got the photo, there was a US Senator from South Dakota who got murdered? Guy's name was Bushfield. Old goat Republican. He was abducted from his car and then dumped on a frozen creek a few days before Christmas. It was kinda big news, although I didn't pay much attention to it at the time."

"A senator? Right. I remember reading about it." Jason tapped again on the window glass. "That would explain why the FBI is on it – and it would explain why they didn't want anyone to know it was his image in that photo. This Freddy Costanzo guy must have been blackmailing the Senator with that picture. I guess he didn't vote the way Costanzo wanted, since he's now dead. I'm not sure if that information helps us at all, or just makes things harder."

"No matter what else is going on, he still wants to kill Jackie, to prevent him from testifying about the photo shoot.

If Jackie could place Costanzo in that room with the Senator, then Costanzo could be nailed for extortion and maybe also for the Senator's murder. That's pretty high stakes."

Mike picked up his phone and searched his contacts list. "I'm beginning to have an idea, I think. But before we do anything crazy, I want to get with Jerry again. I'm no lawyer and I need to make sure I'm right."

"Right about what?"

"You know how the ADAs are always telling us to never make any statements about a case when we're going to testify? They always tell us that if we make any loose comments, the person who hears it can testify about what we said and undermine our credibility, right?"

"Right." Jason looked puzzled but interested.

"Well, what if we did it on purpose?"

"Did what? What can we say that will make Costanzo change his mind about wanting to kill Jackie?"

"Not us." Mike caught Jason's eye. "Jackie."

Chapter 44 — Strange Bedfellows

Thursday, January 9
Las Vegas, NV

MIKE MADE A CALL TO THE ONLY PERSON in his personal rolodex with a direct line to Fat Albert Gallata, the head of the most powerful organized crime family in New York. Mike had a connection to Fat Albert's operation going back to his hunt for the "Righteous Assassin." After Slick Mick Gallata was found dead in the tiger enclosure at the Bronx Zoo, Fat Albert, his son, took over the organization and ran the family business with surprising success. The prior summer, while investigating the murder of quarterback Jimmy Rydell, Mike had been summoned to a meeting with Fat Albert. The boss spoke to Mike – off the record – in order to convince him to call off the dogs on his personal assistant, a man the group called Ivan. As it turned out, Mike's investigation cleared Ivan of serious charges. Mike figured that Fat Albert owed him a favor. It was time to call it in.

Mike called the Gallata family's attorney and requested that the boss give him a call. It was urgent, Mike said.

After about an hour of waiting, Mike and Jason were back

in Jason's and Rachel's suite. Jackie more than anyone was pissed at Jason and Mike for withholding information about what they learned from the feds. What they eventually gave up to the group was the confirmation that Freddy Costanzo was the big boss behind the attempts on Jackie's life. Since Jerry had already speculated in that direction, they figured it was fair game. They explained how serious the situation was if Costanzo was gunning for him, and that they needed to be very careful. They told Jackie that the feds would be providing supplemental surveillance, but to try not to look around for them. That wasn't going to help keep him safe.

They had just decided to call Jerry and let him know what was happening when Mike's phone buzzed. Jason went to the bathroom to call Jerry, while Mike went to the bedroom to take his call.

"Thanks for reaching out for me, Alberto."

"Detective, I was very surprised to hear from you, but I will honor your request in this instance. I assume you understand."

"I do. Thanks for taking my call. How's our friend Ivan doing?"

"Thank you for asking, Mike. Ivan is doing fine. I appreciate that he was not unjustly accused during your investigation."

"I serve justice," Mike said. "I never want anyone to be unfairly accused. And speaking of that, I'm in a sticky situation I think you'll appreciate. My partner, Jason, is here in Las Vegas to get married. His fiancée, Rachel, is a terrific woman. She's an EMT in New York; a real hero. Rachel's brother, Jackie, is here in Vegas working as a performer. When we got here, somebody tried to kill Jackie. The guy behind that is, we think, a locally connected guy named Freddy Costanzo. Do you know him?"

After a pause, Fat Albert said, "I believe I have heard that name before."

"Good. Well, I won't go into all the details, but Freddy seems to be involved in betting on NFL football. I'm sure you're familiar."

"I believe I know what you're talking about, Detective, but you will understand if I don't say anything specific."

"I understand." Mike raised his eyebrows at Jason, who had quietly entered the room and was now listening in. "Let's just say Mr. Costanzo has an interest in ensuring that Jackie not have an opportunity to testify in a possible future criminal prosecution."

"I can understand that worry."

"Well," Mike pressed forward, "I can assure you that Jackie has no knowledge of anything Mr. Costanzo should be worried about. What I need is an opportunity to explain this to the man, so he can reconsider whether it's necessary to silence Jackie. You can understand. Jason is my family. Jackie is practically family to me. I feel an obligation to help."

"I understand, Mike. What can I do?"

"I need to arrange an audience with Mr. Costanzo."

"And you want me to facilitate that meeting?"

"Exactly." Mike tilted his head to the side to express that he was giving it his best shot.

"Mike, I understand. It may be possible for me to reach out to Freddy, as a personal favor for you. But if I do this, my obligation is satisfied."

"I understand. You have no obligation toward me, and I have none toward you."

"We understand each other, then. I will make a call. I can't promise anything, but if what you want is a chance to talk to the man, I think I can facilitate. Give me until tomorrow."

"Thanks. I appreciate it." Mike hung up the phone and turned to Jason. "Am I selling my soul to the Devil here?"

"No," Jason smiled, "You're selling it to someone far worse. But thank you, Mike. Let's hope Freddy Costanzo is a reasonable man."

"Yeah, let's hope."

Moments after Mike hung up with Fat Albert, Jerry called. He, Jason, and Mike spent an hour parsing through the legal issues. Jerry ultimately confirmed that Mike's plan had a sound legal basis, but he cautioned that Freddy Costanzo was not known as the kind of logical thinker who would appreciate its elegance. Costanzo might tell Mike to take his legal theory and shove it up his ass. Mike's proposed gambit was brilliant, but also dangerous.

"Do you have a plan B if this doesn't work?" Jason asked, a hint of anxiety creeping into his voice.

"Sure. In fact, I think plan B is really plan A."

After Mike and Jason met up with the rest of the group, they explained the plan to Jackie. It was risky, and Jackie was nervous about it. Rachel was opposed to putting Jackie in such jeopardy, but acknowledged the upside. Michelle was worried about Mike and Jason as much as Jackie, but didn't have any better ideas. Mike said it all might not even happen unless Fat Albert could work it out with Freddy Costanzo, but he was confident that, if the meeting could be arranged, the risk level would be low.

"These guys are vicious and have no remorse about killing people, but at the same time there's a bizarre kind of honor involved. The movies don't exactly capture it, but when a guy gives his word, it actually means something. We'll see what Fat Albert can do, but if he tells me it's safe, then it's safe. Lord knows walking around the streets without any assurance isn't safe. And then there's the wedding."

"What about it?" Rachel was immediately pensive.

Jason answered. "Well, Sweetheart, it's not a secret that we're planning to get married on Sunday at Helene's chapel. Jackie's going to be there. Anybody who is watching us knows this. Unless we figure something out before then, we're going to have to cancel the wedding. It's too risky to drive up there and walk in and stand in front of the minister. It's all so open and public. If Freddy and his guys wanted to take us all out, it would be simple."

Rachel's face went pale. "Oh my God! I didn't think of that. But, couldn't the FBI protect us? I mean, they could have the door covered so that those guys couldn't come barging in on us, right?"

"Maybe," Mike said, supporting his partner. "But there's a back entrance, and coming and going we have to go outside. I don't want to freak you out—"

"Well, you are freaking me out!" Rachel stood and started pacing.

It was Jackie who tried to calm her. "Sis, relax. We're going to do this. Your wedding is the most important thing. If Mike and Jason can work it out so you don't have to worry about these bastards ruining your day, then I'm all in on it. Besides, I don't want to spend the rest of my life looking over my shoulder, worried about somebody driving up and shooting me. I'm freaked out, too. But I keep thinking, 'What would Dad do?' Would Ernie Robinson hide in the corner and hope the bad guys didn't find him?" Jackie's eyes were blazing. Rachel had never seen him like this.

"Oh, Jackie. I don't know. I guess Daddy would probably walk outside and challenge the guys to come fight with him like men. You know how he is. He's not afraid of anything."

"Exactly! Maybe it's time for me to act a little more like him and a little less like . . . like me." Rachel held out her arms and brought Jackie in for a long hug, while everyone else remained silent. There was nothing to say. None of the group had any objections to the plan after that.

That evening, they stayed at the Mardi Gras. They didn't even go to their table by the pool for dinner, but had room service deliver it. Lizzy went down to perform in that night's shows, and the rest of the group went to the late show to cheer. They kept together the whole time, with Mike and Jason on the outside, Rachel and Michelle at the points of their diamond, and Jackie in the middle. It was awkward walking through the casino in formation like a squadron of Blue Angels, but it made them all feel better. With hundreds of hotel guests and casino patrons all around them and a phalanx of security cameras overhead, there was a minimal chance Freddy Costanzo's goons would try to take Jackie out inside the casino or the theater. Still, they took every precaution. Mike and Jason carefully stole glances around their perimeter to see if they could spot any of the feds, but never did.

Fat Albert fulfilled his obligation by reaching out to Freddy Costanzo. It was a fairly routine request: an audience with Mike Stoneman and his party, with an assurance of safety during the meeting. Nobody was guaranteeing anything about what might happen afterwards. Mike saw the message after the drag show ended: "Mr. C will call you tomorrow.

Arrangements have been made. Your safety during the discussion is promised. Good luck. Don't call again."

Chapter 45 — A Perilous Gambit

Friday, January 10
Las Vegas, NV

RACHEL EXPECTED TO BE NERVOUS two days before her wedding. She did not expect her small bridal party to be more nervous than the bride. But a meeting with an organized crime boss and the specter of another murder attempt would do that to anyone. Michelle wanted to go along with Mike, Jason, Jerry, and Jackie to provide moral support, but she conceded that the entourage would be too large. She and Rachel stayed at the Mardi Gras, holding down their table by the pool and trying unsuccessfully to relax and enjoy the relatively warmer Las Vegas afternoon.

Mike had received the phone call from one of Costanzo's men at 1:00 p.m. The meeting was set for 4:30 p.m. at Sparks steakhouse in the Fremont Street area. "What is it about these guys and steakhouses?" Mike mused to Michelle when he hung up the phone. He called Jerry, then Jason. Jackie and Lizzy were spending the day with Jason and Rachel, so there was no need to call separately. Finally, Mike called Agent Perkins and explained that they would be leaving the hotel for a private meeting and that, if there were any agents watching over them, they should stand down and not follow them. Perkins was skeptical, but Mike explained that having any feds hanging around could create a dangerous situation for everyone. Perkins objected, but ultimately agreed.

The preparation for the upcoming meeting kept Mike away from the poker tables for another day.

When they arrived at the restaurant, Rick "The Neck" Garetti met them at the reception desk. He stared at Jackie, looking for any glimmer of recognition. Jackie immediately shrank back from the man who had driven the black SUV while his companion tried to shoot him down outside The Little Jewel Chapel. Jackie grabbed onto Jason's elbow to steady a quaking hand. Mike and Jerry had coached Jackie about how to act in the face of his attackers. but the reality of confronting The Neck turned Jackie's thighs, which could hold a kick pose for a full minute, into chocolate mousse.

The Neck motioned for the group to come to a private room up a set of narrow stairs in the back of the space. At the top, they were met by two men who frisked them and swept their bodies with metal-detecting wands. Mike suspected the wands would also detect recording devices. The men tried to confiscate Mike's mobile phone, but he protested that he needed it for the meeting and that he would keep it in his hand and visible. Mike wasn't sure he'd need to show Costanzo the photo of the now-dead senator, but he wanted to keep the option available. Rick told Mike to unlock the phone, then spent a minute swiping through it to make sure there were no recording apps running. He sent himself a text message to make sure the phone was real, then powered it down and handed it back to Mike. "Leave it off, unless the boss says otherwise." Rick then led the group into the main room.

A long table, without a tablecloth or place settings,

dominated the space. Freddy Costanzo, sitting at the end, looked comfortable in slacks and a polo shirt. His signature white hair was wet, making it look like he had just come from the gym. He was flanked by two other men. One was in a business suit and was only slightly younger than Costanzo. The other was a mountain of muscle in a tight black t-shirt.

Jerry had insisted on coming to the meeting, partly to solidify the legal issues, and partly because he loved Mike's concept and wouldn't miss it for the world. He was going to have fun. He predicted that Freddy would bring his own lawyer to the meeting, too. "Mr. Costanzo, my name is Jerry Garcia." He strode to the end of the table and held out a hand to the seated boss.

Costanzo took the hand without getting up. "I know who you are. In your line of work, I could give you some business if you were interested – and if I thought you were worth it."

"I'm not looking for business. I've got a client right here." He motioned behind him at Jackie, who was doing his best to fade into the woodwork.

Costanzo looked at Mike, obviously having been briefed already. "You must be Stoneman."

"That's right. This is my partner, Detective Jason Dickson. We're in town for Jason's wedding, but you and your people have put a damper on our celebration."

"I'm sorry to inconvenience you, Detective, but you know how it is with business. Sometimes things just can't wait." He kept eye contact with Mike and maintained a placid expression. "I'm not in the habit of hosting police officers, but our mutual friend prevailed on me to hear you out, and I agreed out of respect for his father. While you're here with me, I will give you my respect as long as you do the same. After you and your associates leave here, I make no promises. You understand?"

"I understand." Mike sat in a chair, leaving one empty seat between himself and the hulking bodyguard sitting next to the boss. He motioned for the rest of the group to sit and placed his phone face up on the table. "We don't know everything that has happened to bring us to this situation. But we have a pretty good idea it involves a certain photograph."

Costanzo sat forward a few inches, signaling to Mike that he had the man's actual attention. "What photograph?"

"I understand it was taken at a club called Swanky's here in Vegas. There's an older man in the picture, along with three showgirls."

"I wouldn't know anything about that," Costanzo said calmly, sitting back again.

"I'm not here to ask you about that. I'm not here in any official capacity. I assure you that nobody here is recording this discussion. I'm just Jason's best man for the wedding. Jackie here is the brother of the bride. So, this is a family matter for me. We're hoping we can remove the reason you're concerned. I've brought Jackie's lawyer, who can explain it best."

Mike nodded to Jerry. The lawyer quickly stood and walked to the back of Mike's chair, where he had a good command of the whole room. He looked at the man in the business suit. "Hello, Arthur." Costanzo's lawyer nodded silently. "I'm glad you're here; you can verify what I'm going to do for your boss. First, I'd like for one of you gentlemen to take out your phone and start recording."

Costanzo looked puzzled. "Why would I want to record this meeting?"

"I'll explain, but it will be better if the explanation is recorded. If it's on your own device, you can delete it afterwards if you want to."

Freddy and his lawyer exchanged a whispered few words, then the lawyer shrugged, pulled out his phone, and punched the record button. He propped the device upright against a glass of water sitting in front of him, then nodded to Jerry.

"Of course, use the lawyer's phone. Protected by attorney-client privilege. That would have been my choice as well. Great. So, here we are. My name is Jerry Garcia – for the recorded record. I am the lawyer for Jackie Robinson, who is here at the table. In a minute, I'm going to have Jackie come over here so he'll be on the camera, but first I'll let you know what we're doing."

The lawyer, who had not been introduced to the group, briefly turned the phone so the camera captured all the attendees sitting at the table. Jerry continued, "If a person were a witness to a criminal act, the lawyer for the person accused would be worried about what that witness might say in court. The defense lawyer would look for potential ways to impeach that witness – to render the testimony untrustworthy. The lawyer might try to find people to whom the witness told a different version of the story, as an example. That would be effective rebuttal testimony. But what would be even better is a video recording of the witness making a statement that contradicted their trial testimony. Such a recording would destroy the witness' credibility. In fact, no prosecutor would even put that witness on the stand, knowing that the contradictory statement would make the whole case look contrived and not credible."

The lawyer holding the phone nodded his head in agreement and briefly made eye contact with Costanzo.

"Jackie?" Jerry said, motioning to his client to come forward. Mike vacated his chair so Jackie could sit directly in front of the camera. Jerry then began to question his client, as if on the witness stand. After having Jackie state his name and identify himself and his occupation, Jerry quickly got to the point. "Jackie, do you recall a private performance at which you were accompanied by a woman named Sheila Buchanan, who performed under the name of Cricket Linderman, and by Mimi LaRee?"

"I don't remember much, but I do remember we did a show together at Swanky's." Jackie shot a furtive glance toward the big bodyguard, worried that he was going to reach out and snap him in two.

"When you perform in a show like that, Jackie, do you generally pay attention to who is in the audience?"

"No. Never. When I'm strutting and singing, I'm all into the act. I don't pay attention to the crowd."

"Even if somebody from the audience comes onto the stage?"

"Nah. It's the same. Like for a bachelor party, the groom comes up and we do a whole routine with him for like ten minutes. But afterwards, I couldn't tell you what the dude looked like, or what his name was. I don't care. It's all about the act."

Arthur spoke up. "Mr. Garcia, this is all fascinating and possibly even relevant, but hardly the kind of impeachment evidence that would negate a prosecution."

"Give me a minute, Counselor." Jerry smiled affably at his adversary. In fact, they were both members of the defense bar and normally were more colleagues than opponents. "Now, Jackie, in the past week, have you seen a photograph of you, Cricket, and Mimi with an older man?"

"Yes, Mike showed me that picture."

"Good. Now, when you saw that picture, did you remember anything about that gig?"

"No, nothing."

"Did you recognize the gentleman in the photo?"

"No."

Jerry chose not to mention that the man's face was blurred out, since that fact wasn't critical and Costanzo and his lawyer did not know it. If their adversaries assumed the man's face was clear in the photo, so much the better. "If you saw that man's picture again, do you think you'd be able to recognize him?"

"No." Jackie was a little less nervous now, but Jerry had coached him to keep his answers short. Now it was time to see how well Jackie had learned his lines for this performance.

"OK, Jackie. Thank you. Now, I want you to look around this room and tell me whether anybody who is here right now was there at Swanky's the day of that gig."

Jackie made a show of looking carefully around the room. "No, I don't see anybody who was there."

"I want you to carefully look at the gentleman sitting at the head of the table. His name is Freddy Costanzo. Was he at that event, when you took that photo with the other two girls and the older gentleman?"

Jackie looked Costanzo in the eye. "No. He wasn't there."

"Do you mean you can't remember whether he was there or not? Or are you sure he was not there?"

"I don't remember much about those gigs, like I said. But this guy here, he's a good-looking man and he's got that super white hair. If he had been there, I'd remember that. There's no way he was there. I'm very sure about that."

Arthur once again nodded.

"What about this man here?" Jerry motioned toward Rick and Arthur moved the phone to capture him on the video. "Was that guy at the gig?"

Once again, as Jerry had coached him, Jackie carefully scrutinized Rick. "No. Definitely not. That dude has a crazy long neck. It looks like somebody stretched him out. He definitely wasn't there."

"Have you seen this man at any time before today?"

Jackie hesitated. Rick was unquestionably the driver of the black SUV. "Nope. I have never seen him anywhere before today. Definitely not."

"Thank you, Jackie." Jerry then looked at Arthur. "Before you stop the video, are there any questions you'd like to ask?"

Arthur paused the video, leaned over to whisper into Costanzo's ear, then sat back and pushed the red button to stop the recording. "No, Jerry. I have no questions. I understand what you've done here. This person will never be able to testify in a trial that Mr. Costanzo or Mr. Garetti were present for that event – whatever it was."

"Exactly." Jerry made eye contact with Mike, who nodded slightly. Jerry turned back toward his chair, taking Jackie with him.

"So, Mr. Costanzo," Mike took back the floor from Jerry. "That photo is in the custody of the FBI. They know who the girls are. They know two of them are dead. They already suspect that your organization may be involved. I'm sure they would love for Jackie to be a witness, to place you in that room with the girls and . . . the gentleman. But aside from that, there's nothing Jackie can tell the feds that they don't already know. We're hoping now, with that video in your pocket, Jackie will no longer be a threat to you in any way. Does that make sense?"

"Yes, Detective. I understand. That was quite ingenious of you. It took some balls to come here to see me like this and to pull this off. I respect that. Is there anything else for us to discuss?"

"One more thing. I'd like you to call off the dogs. Let your hound, Rickenbacker, know that we've made peace here and he can lay off trying to arrest Jackie."

Costanzo leaned in toward his lawyer again for a quick whisper. "I understand your request, but I don't know who this person is. Now, if there's nothing else . . ."

Everyone rose from their chairs. Mike collected his phone and both Rick and the massive bodyguard – who had never been introduced – escorted them to the door. When they were on the street in the warm Vegas air, Mike leaned in toward Jason and said, "Looks like Ivan has a brother." Jason had to laugh.

Jerry volunteered to give them a ride back to the Mardi Gras and commended Jackie on an outstanding performance.

After Jerry pulled away, Rick and Freddy emerged from the restaurant, trailed by Freddy's lawyer. Freddy shook Arthur's hand and watched him walk away. When the lawyer was out of earshot, Freddy turned to Rick. "That stunt might have worked if the little bitch boy wasn't trying to blackmail me."

"You still think so?" Rick uncharacteristically questioned his boss. "I doubt he has the balls to steal a handbag, let alone stick you up and pull off those two money drops."

"I agree, but he's got to have somebody else working with him. I don't care who the brains are, I want that little fag dead. Nobody shakes me down and gets away with it. That detective just did us a favor. They think they're in the clear now. They're going to let down their guard. If a couple New York cops get in the way of a bullet along the way, I'm sure Fat Albert won't shed any tears. Plus, they've got a wedding to distract them. Let's see how they like having a funeral instead."

Chapter 46 — Looking Up

Friday, January 10
Las Vegas, NV

THERE WAS A BIG CROWD outside the main entrance to the Mardi Gras when Jerry rolled up in his Lincoln. "This must be that celebrity wedding deal," Mike suggested.

"You didn't hear?" Jerry turned his head to the back seat as he coasted to a stop.

"Hear what?"

"It was all over the news today. Lindsay Lohan is having a big celebrity bash here tomorrow, then her wedding is Sunday. They're bringing in a couple hundred A-Listers for it. Should be a circus."

"I guess that's what happened to our venue," Jason lamented. "Just like Helene told us. Maybe if Rachel gets a selfie with some celebrity she'll feel better about it."

They waved good-bye to Jerry and made it through the gauntlet of gawkers and paparazzi to meet Rachel and Michelle at their usual pool-side table. The pool area was buzzing with hotel guests chatting about the various celebrities who were there for the big wedding.

Rachel and Michelle were dying to know what happened. All during their dinner and drinks, under intense questioning from the ladies, they told the story from their perspective. They all agreed that Jackie had done wonderfully and been incredibly brave. Michelle and Rachel both hugged Jackie multiple times.

"So, it's all settled, then?" Michelle asked Mike.

"I hope so. It's hard to get a read on a guy like him in one meeting. He and his lawyer certainly understood what we did and why. Jackie played it just right. Jerry did a nice job. He knew the other lawyer. But we'll know soon enough." Mike leaned over toward Jason. "Did you call our FBI friends?"

"Yes," Jason said, then turned back to his conversation with Jackie and Rachel.

Michelle then explained how, when Michelle and Rachel had staked out their place by the pool, Rachel was able to snap a selfie with Drake, who had come down for a dip. She already had more than a thousand retweets on the post and she was pumped. She said it was a good omen for the wedding.

The two couples had tickets to see Penn & Teller at the Rio that night. Somehow, despite everything that had happened since Michelle made the plans, not going to a show in Las Vegas seemed wrong.

Since Jackie was no longer under arrest for Mimi's murder, Belle de la Pomme was welcomed back to *The Birdcage*. She would have to tone down some of the dance moves due to her still-healing stitches, but was adamant that she would not, under any circumstances, skip the show. Jason instructed Lizzy to stay with Belle at all times, and admonished them to make sure to have as many other people nearby as possible.

The Penn & Teller show was terrific. Mike, ever the skeptic, insisted on holding one of the joke books passed around the audience during one trick. When Penn Jillette predicted the exact joke that Mike had randomly picked from the book, and then explained how he had done it, Mike was impressed. After the show, Rachel got pictures of herself and Jason with both the stars in the autograph line and told them they were to be married later that week. Mike shook Penn's hand and said how impressed he was with the show. Mike's skepticism for stage magic had been enhanced by the performance, but he had a new favorite magician.

Teller, who never spoke on stage, wished Rachel and Jason congratulations and best wishes on their upcoming wedding.

In the car back to the Mardi Gras, Mike exchanged text messages with Perkins, who reported no incidents that evening. He was genuinely starting to relax. It felt like a vacation again, instead of a Seal Team Six mission.

Back at the Mardi Gras, they slipped inside the theater as the late show crowd was filing out and waited for Jackie and Lizzy. They walked together back to the rooms, dropping off Jackie and Lizzy first. They all surreptitiously looked for any sign of the FBI surveillance, but could not see anybody who resembled an agent.

"These guys are good," Rachel whispered as they exited the elevator on their floor.

"They'd better be," Jason said in a responding whisper. "We're counting on them."

Chapter 47 — A Bridal Performance

Saturday, January 11
Las Vegas, NV

RACHEL AND JASON HELD HANDS Saturday morning as the group walked through the casino to the hotel lobby. Mike and Michelle were behind them, with Jackie in the middle. It was not quite the Blue Angel diamond formation, but it still provided maximum protection for Jackie. They might be in the clear, but they might not be, so it made sense to be careful. Mike felt good about the meeting with Freddy Costanzo. It was entirely clear that Jackie could never testify against either Freddy or Rick as long as they had a copy of that video. Without any remaining motive to want Jackie dead, he figured even the most ruthless criminal would back off and not expend resources – and subject his guys to potential prosecution if they got caught – without any tangible benefit. "He's a businessman," Mike had said before bed. "He'll make the rational business decision. I think Jackie is going to be alright and we can all enjoy the weekend – and the wedding."

As they maneuvered through the curving pathways inside the casino, Michelle marveled that the layout required guests to walk through the casino to get from the elevator bank out to the lobby and the front exit. "It's like they want everyone to stop and gamble."

Mike laughed and explained that every hotel in Vegas had the same configuration. When they reached the still-growing crowd of celebrity gawkers outside the main entrance, Jason shook his head, commenting that, even in Vegas, people would stand outside in a crowd for hours just to catch a glimpse of a movie star.

"She's more of a B-List celeb," Rachel said over her shoulder, prompting a laugh from everyone.

As they waited for their car, Jason whispered in Mike's ear, "How sure are we that it's a good idea to be out in public with Jackie?"

"Not sure, but I'll be damned if I'm going to hole up in the hotel room all day just because I'm worried. We planned a pre-wedding brunch today, and we're going to enjoy it."

"Do you think we'll have company?"

"I made the call. Perkins isn't thrilled, but he said he would give us some support. I'm not sure he's going to actually be there himself. But no matter what, we've got you and me."

"Did you tell him what happened yesterday?"

"Not exactly," Mike said. "I told him we met with one of Freddy's guys, which is true. The fact that Freddy was also there didn't come up. Anyway, I said we promised him Jackie would never testify against Freddy, and that we provided some evidence that would impeach Jackie if a D.A. ever tried to put him on the stand."

"Did that piss him off as much as it would piss me off if he was my witness?"

"Probably." Mike glanced at his phone, on which the tiny icon of a red SUV was pulling around the corner a half-block from the hotel entrance. "But if I were Perkins, I'd still be working the angle that Freddy's a wild card and might do something stupid. If he does, then I'd want to be there. If he doesn't, then we get a relaxing weekend and his men get some boring surveillance. Either way, I think we'll be fine."

Lizzy was waiting for them in the line outside Señor Frog's, holding a prime place. Several of Jackie's friends from the show would be performing during the wildly popular drag brunch inside the combination restaurant and club. Their connections got the group a front-row table, where Jackie insisted Rachel wear the "Bride to Be" sash. Before the show, Mike commented that the popularity of the venue likely stemmed from its excellent food and top-shelf open bar as much as from the drag performers. Jackie and Lizzy contested that idea, but acknowledged the quality of the food and drink.

As it turned out, there were two other bridal parties in the audience. Jason, it seemed, was the only groom present. A half hour into the show, the performers coaxed the other two brides onto the stage as their bridesmaids hooted and whistled. Rachel didn't need much encouragement; she leapt up the steps two at a time with a huge smile on her face. The drag queens did some impromptu comedy with the brides that brought on raucous laughter as well as a flurry of dollar bills tossed by the patrons.

The performer who was serving as the host then introduced a special guest and brought out Trinity K. Bonet, a tall, elegant Black queen. She came on stage wearing a red sequined gown cut slim below the waist in the style of Diana Ross and wearing a matching black wig. The crowd went wild. Jackie was standing and screaming.

"You know her?" Michelle asked.

"I wish!" Jackie yelled back over the din of the applause.

"She's my idol. I watched her on RuPaul's Drag Race when I was a teenager. God, I wish I could meet her."

Trinity was there to help judge a lip sync contest for the brides. She turned to the three smiling brides-to-be and said, "This is your chance for stardom, ladies. Now, don't fuck it up."

She then whispered into Rachel's ear the song she would be performing, Rachel burst into a huge smile. When the first notes of Whitney Houston's "I Want to Dance With Somebody" escaped from the stage speakers, Rachel reached out and grabbed the microphone from the host. She didn't lip sync the song – she sang along with Whitney as she pranced and danced with the accompaniment of several bedazzled drag performers and four scantily clad male dancers, who appeared on cue. The standing ovation from the audience nearly lifted Rachel off the stage.

After each of the three brides had their turn, Trinity polled the audience by its applause to determine the winner. Even some of the other bridal parties clapped loudly for Rachel. Trinity presented the other two brides with envelopes containing gift certificates and told them to "sashay away." Then the four muscular, shirtless men, wearing only bow ties and swim trunks, lifted Rachel onto their shoulders. They paraded her around the entire show space, as if on a litter, while she blew kisses to her adoring audience. Jason had never seen her look happier. After the parade, Trinity gave Rachel a gift certificate for a local shopping mall called the Miracle Mile.

"Did you and your friends arrange that?" Jason asked Jackie and Lizzy.

"Well," Jackie winked, "we knew there would be a lip sync competition, but everything else was all Rachel. I had no idea that Trinity K. Bonet would be here."

At 2:00 p.m., the brunch show concluded. All the audience

members had the chance to wait in line to get their pictures taken with the performers. The brides were invited to be first in line, and Rachel, Jackie, and Lizzy hammed it up with the cast, dragging Jason into the scene for a pre-wedding photo that would later draw many guffaws and catcalls back at the precinct house. Mike and Michelle joined the group for one final shot, trying to look dignified amidst the chaos.

After the photo session, Michelle approached Trinity and explained that she was Jackie's idol. Jackie had been too shy to seek out an introduction, but with Michelle's prodding, the star went to Jackie and the two talked for several minutes before Trinity was called away to join the next photo group.

"What did Trinity say to you?" Michelle asked afterwards, with Rachel and Lizzy also standing close by to hear the answer.

"She said she saw me in the show at *The Birdcage* and loved it." Jackie could hardly contain his joy. "She was so nice! She said if she had recognized me out of costume, she would have called me up to the stage. But I wouldn't have wanted to take any of Rachel's glory today." Jackie and Rachel hugged. Jackie was floating, and not just from all the booze.

After a trip to the Miracle Mile to use the gift certificate on sexy lingerie and a sparkling new purse, they arrived back at the Mardi Gras. Hotel security had set up a series of boundary lines with plush ropes to keep the celebrity-watchers from blocking the entrance. When their car door opened and Michelle stepped out, somebody shouted and pointed, calling out the name of Penelope Cruz. Several dozen people took pictures of Michelle and the entire party as they emerged from the car. They waved at the crowd as if they were actual celebrities.

Michelle and Jackie had wobbly legs after two hours of an

open bar during the drag show. Rachel had abstained from alcohol, while Mike and Jason only had light drinks. Mike had said he wanted to stay sharp, just in case. This made Michelle nervous, but she kept her concerns to herself.

Mike and Jason asked Jackie to come to their room for a few minutes. They called Jerry and put him on speaker phone so the conversation would be privileged. Then Mike showed Jackie a photo of Senator Harlan Bushfield from an online newspaper.

Jackie's reaction was immediate. "That's the dude! That's the old guy from the photo!"

"How can you be sure?" Mike asked. "You said you didn't remember."

"Well, from that photo you showed me, I didn't. But now that I see his face, it's different. I remember him because he was crazy handsy. I had to beat him off from grabbing my ass and trying to squeeze my fake tits. Oh, man, this was that guy? Wow."

They all agreed it would be best if Jackie said nothing to anyone – ever – about what he knew. Jackie was blown as a witness, but if word got out that he had been leaking information, Freddy would not take kindly to it.

"My lips are fucking sealed!" Jackie assured his lawyer and his privileged investigation team.

While Michelle adjourned for a nap, Mike decided to make a run for the poker table. His time in town was running out and he hadn't been able to get in more than a half-dozen hands. He invited Jason to join him in the casino while Rachel rested with Jackie and Lizzy, who needed to sleep off their brunch. Jason was happy to get in a little more time at the craps table while Mike hit the poker felt.

Mike was collecting his bankroll and lucky card protector coin when there was a knock on the door. A doorman stood in the entry, holding Mike's missing suitcase, which he explained had been delivered by United Airlines. Mike tipped him and put the case on his bed. It had a sticker bearing the airport code HNL. "I hope you had a nice trip," Mike mumbled before stashing the case in a closet. He'd need those pillows when he got home, but thankfully the Mardi Gras pillows had been terrific.

As Mike and Jason exited the elevator lobby and entered the casino area, the sound system was halfway through "Bohemian Rhapsody." Mike started singing along, to Jason's amusement. When the song finally ended, Mike said, "That's one of my all-time favorite songs. Don't you agree?"

"I'm sure it is, Mike. It's a great old White guy song."

Mike laughed heartily and slapped his partner on the back. "Well, maybe they'll play some Motown, which I also love."

Two hours of uninterrupted casino time later, Mike and Jason met up at a bar called Bourbon Street. Mike ordered them servings of The Macallan 18 and toasted to Jason and Rachel. He paid with a fresh hundred-dollar bill and then spent five minutes explaining the several successful poker hands that had netted him a $600 profit. "Not enough to pay for the whole trip, but enough to make me feel good about myself as a poker player."

"I'm glad you finally got the chance to play some cards. I feel like we took a gamble yesterday and I'm starting to think we came up lucky."

"I'm not counting my chickens," Mike said stoically. "We've been through enough investigations together to know how quickly situations can change."

"I know, and you're right. I guess the lead up to the wedding has me thinking more like Rachel-the-optimist."

Mike laughed. "There's a place for that. Plus, you need to get used to thinking like Rachel."

"I'm going to have to start adjusting a lot of things in my life now that we're going to be married and having a baby. It's all happening so fast."

"I'm sure you'll manage just fine, Jason. You're a pretty flexible guy."

"Thanks, Mike. But, seriously, things are going to be changing. I've always been concerned about being a husband and a cop at the same time. I figured with Rachel working as an EMT, we'd both be busy and things would stay pretty much the same, at least for a while. Having a kid was something that would come later, after we were used to being married first. This is all happening so fast now. I mean, I'm OK with it. But, Man . . ."

"I'd give you some words of wisdom, but I don't have any. This is way out of my expertise here, Jason. I'm sure you two will figure it out. People have been having babies for thousands of years and parents always figure it out."

"I know." Jason tipped back his glass and drained the last few drops of the succulent scotch. "It's just that I'm starting to really think about the future. Once this baby is born, I'm not sure I'll want to be laying my life on the line on the streets anymore. It would be worse if I were a patrol officer, I guess, but we've had some pretty hairy investigations. I'm not sure I can keep doing this."

Mike finished his own scotch and set the glass gently onto the bar. "Jason, you have to follow your heart here. I won't try to tell you what to do. I've had a bunch of partners and I'll survive without you, but I'd miss you. You've taught me a lot."

"I've taught you?"

"Sure. I wouldn't know anything about modern music without you." Mike kept a stone poker face as he kept eye contact with Jason.

"You're so full of shit."

Mike broke into a grin and the two partners laughed together. "Seriously, Jason. You've opened my eyes about a lot of things. I'm a better person since you've been my partner. I get the feeling I've still got a lot to learn from you. But, like I said, I'll be fine either way."

"So, you're giving me nothing?" Jason stared down his shorter companion.

"Not a thing. Well, I'll give you one thing. At the poker table, there's a concept called getting it in good. There's always an element of chance in anything. You've heard me call it 'variance.' You can't do anything about it. All you can do is get the money in good – in a position where the odds are in your favor and you figure to win more than you lose. If you get it in good and the other guy catches the lucky card, you can't do anything about it and you can't let it bother you. You get it in good a hundred times, you'll come out ahead. So, in the game of life, you do the same thing. You try to make good decisions and put yourself in positive situations. Life will throw you curveballs, but you have to be comfortable that you got it in good and you'll have peace of mind."

Jason looked at his mentor and friend. "So, how does that help me figure out whether I should start looking for a new career or stay a detective after the baby comes?"

Mike smiled. "You have to figure out what's good for you and Rachel. Then you go all-in on those cards and you see what happens."

"That's the worst sage advice I've ever heard, Mike."

"Probably. But that's all I've got. You want another round?"

"No. Let's get back to the girls. It's going to take me a few hours to figure out what you just said."

"I hope you're not disappointed about not getting a bachelor party."

"I'm fine with that. Plus, Jackie and Lizzy want to take us to a party after their show. It'll pass for a bachelor party."

"We could skip it. I could take you to a seedy strip club and get you wasted, then take some compromising photos of you with some half-naked dancers. How would that be?"

"I think I'd prefer the drag queen party. You think we're in the clear? Nothing happened today while we were out in the open."

"I'm staying optimistic. As you know, I'm usually a pessimist, so I would not put money on Costanzo backing off. But so far we haven't seen anything to suggest otherwise. I haven't seen our federal friends around, either, but Agent Perkins said they would be keeping an eye on Jackie. Them, I would put money on."

"Let's hope." Jason raised his empty glass in a silent salute to all the things they hoped would go right over the next twenty-four hours.

They banged their glasses on the bar, then made their way back to their suites. They had one more night in Vegas together, and they were going to try to enjoy it.

Chapter 48 — Post-Show Party

Saturday, January 11
Las Vegas, NV

THE BRIDE-TO-BE AWOKE from her post-brunch nap with an appetite. Jason convinced her that staying inside the Mardi Gras as the sun was going down would be prudent. Thankfully, there was no shortage of great restaurant choices available for their night-before-the-wedding dinner. They chose the hotel's French restaurant, where Jason happily ordered duck while Rachel chose a vegetarian option with cream and cheese. Mike, not a big fan of French cuisine, opted for a steak and a scotch. Michelle experimented with snails and frog legs, then begged some bites from Mike's beef.

After the excellent meal, they went to see the late show at *The Birdcage* theater. For Mike and Jason, the second performance was more enjoyable than the first. They cheered as loudly as Rachel when Belle came on stage in a silver gown and the Donna Summer wig. Lizzy performed "Good as Hell" as well as her namesake idol. Belle belted out "Hot Stuff," but without some of the more strenuous dance moves. The stitches were still healing.

When the last curtain call was finished and the audience stopped shouting and clapping, the group at the front table sat back down and waited for Belle and Lizzy to finish their post-show meet-and-greet. When they joined the group, April and Cleo, the performers they had first met the prior Saturday, were with them, all still in full drag. The Saturday night show was the last performance of the week; they were off on Sunday and Monday while the hotel brought in a more family-friendly act. Lizzy grumbled that the days off were because the hotel didn't want to pay the performers, but they all agreed that for the moment, it was Saturday night in Vegas and they were going out on the town. Lizzy and Belle had made arrangements for them to visit a club called Le Chic at the Venetian, across the Strip and one property down from the Mardi Gras. It was not even midnight, so things were just getting started at the club.

Jason looked at Rachel's drooping eyelids and suggested that she might want to call it a night, since she had a big day coming up on Sunday.

"You have a big day too, I believe," she chided. "Besides, that big king-sized bed would be so much nicer with you in it."

Jason put on his serious cop face. "Sweetheart, Mike and I promised to look after Jackie and Lizzy. They're going out, so we're going along. Hopefully, there's nothing to be worried about, but we're taking no chances. But you can rest up. You look tired."

"I am tired. I doubt it has anything to do with our little guy." She nodded toward her abdomen.

"Of course not," Jason said with a smile. "But tomorrow you need to be awake, so getting some sleep is probably the right call."

"Yeah. I know. You promise to be careful?"

"Hopefully there's nothing to be careful about."

Mike, who was listening in on the conversation, turned to Michelle and suggested she join Rachel and turn in early.

"Not on your life!" she responded. "My first trip to Vegas has less than 48 hours left and I plan to enjoy every minute. The gang looks like they're ready to have a crazy Saturday night and I am into it! Wild horses couldn't keep me from coming along."

Mike dropped it, despite his reservations. Jason walked Rachel back to their suite, then the group paraded through the packed casino floor and out onto Las Vegas Boulevard. The cold snap had finally moderated into more comfortable temperatures. In any other town, even New York, the wide sidewalk outside the hotel would not be packed with partying tourists at midnight in early January. Many of the revelers were carrying drinks, which was entirely legal and normal on the sidewalks of Las Vegas. Music played from speakers all along a stone wall. It was decorated to look like Bourbon Street in New Orleans, right up to the point where it changed to resemble a medieval castle parapet as the scene magically changed from the Mardi Gras property to the themed casino hotel next door. In Las Vegas, of course, next door was a quarter-mile away.

As soon as they reached the transition point, the music changed to "Livin' on a Prayer." The whole entourage broke out into a chorus. "One of your favorite songs, Mike?" Jason chided.

"You know it," Mike called out. "I love this town."

The sparkling group headed toward the escalator to the overpass above Las Vegas Boulevard. Traffic flow was always bad in Vegas, so allowing pedestrians to cross at street level was frowned upon. To get to the Venetian, they walked over the expansive, bridge-like structure, transferred to the perpendicular bridge across the wide avenue, then made their way back down to the opposite side. As they walked, the group attracted waves of attention from the other pedestrians. The four fully made-up drag queens mugged for the people who wanted to snap their photos. They periodically stopped and posed with groups of Saturday night revelers. They smiled, laughed, kissed the women, kissed the men, and generally enjoyed being the center of attention. They even collected some nice tips. Almost nobody noticed Jason, Mike, or Michelle trailing along after them.

They approached the impressive Venetian property, flanked by large fountains which were replicas of the originals in Rome. Across the street at the Mirage, the fake volcano began its eruption cycle. As blobs of red-orange gelatin exploded from the top of the artificial mountain, the crowd let out cries of excitement and burst into applause. In front of the Venetian, the pedestrians had only a partial view, but were still transfixed by the spectacle.

Mike's group stopped at a fountain nestled into the plaza's front corner. Between the fountain and the massive hotel building, a lagoon of blue water waited placidly for tourists to take rides in replica Italian gondolas. A wide pedestrian bridge over the water connected the plaza to the second floor of the hotel. Water poured down all around the fountain's circular base, where people sat on the three-foot-wide stone wall surrounding the frothing pool. It was one of the coolest places to relax on hot summer nights.

On this night, with the temperature in the mid-60s, there was plenty of empty space around the fountain and the group decided to take a seat and pose there for a group picture before going inside. Mike volunteered to take the photo, not feeling a need to be in it. Before he got the others posed for the first shot, a crowd started to gather. Mike and Jason took turns accepting cameras and phones from strangers who wanted to get their picture with the showgirls. They didn't ask whether the tourists knew that the gorgeous ladies were in drag. It didn't matter. Michelle made herself useful by organizing the line of people waiting for a turn.

After ten minutes, the line thinned out. Lizzy stood on her high heels and walked toward the back of the line, where Michelle was still satisfying her need to create order from chaos. As Lizzy approached, two men wearing jeans and tank tops stepped between them. One had a thick blond moustache hanging down, Fu Manchu-style, along the sides of his mouth. He had a thin scar on his neck. The other was clean-shaven, wearing a blue baseball cap. Both were showing off the muscles of their upper arms and shoulders.

"Well, hello, Gorgeous," Lizzy cooed. "You two hunks want a picture?"

"Hell no!" the man with the moustache spat out. "I wanna know if you're a real girl." He reached out and grabbed Lizzy's crotch. Lizzy screamed and jumped back, slapping at the man's arm.

Michelle shouted, "Get away from her!"

Fu Manchu's companion yelled, "Fucking queer!" as he stepped forward and pushed a large hand into Lizzy's chest. She fell backwards onto the stone plaza, where one turquoise heel fell off and skittered away. "Well, Bo?" he queried his friend.

"I'm not sure, Sid," the mustachioed Bo said, looking at his hand as if he had touched something toxic.

"They're in fucking drag, dude." Then, toward Lizzy, "Ain't ya?"

Bo turned his head toward the other three drag performers, still sitting on the edge of the fountain and watching closely. When he turned back to his companion, Bo didn't get a chance to give his evaluation. His head snapped back when Jason's fist connected with his jaw. He lurched to his left, but did not fall.

"You keep your redneck hands off her!" Jason shouted, glaring at Sid with his fist clenched and raised. Jason's imposing posture caused Sid to step back as his friend regained his equilibrium and launched himself toward Jason.

Jason had instantly sized up Bo and guessed he was a simplistic fighter, who used his imposing bulk and aggressive attitude to intimidate his targets. As he bull-rushed forward, Jason stepped to the side, ducked under the man's swinging fist, and planted a left hook into his midsection. Then Jason used his left leg to trip him, sending him sprawling face-first onto the sidewalk with a sickening crunch. If he'd had the breath, Bo would have cried out. As it was, he curled into a fetal position with blood pouring from his broken nose.

Sid stepped toward Jason, but hesitantly. Mike rushed over to Jason, staring down Sid, who clearly didn't want to take on both of them. Michelle rushed to Lizzy, who was still on the ground, shaken and disoriented, but not injured.

A crowd of seemingly everyone on the plaza had formed around the fight. April and Cleo got up from the edge of the fountain, where they had been frozen while watching, and walked toward the gathering spectators. Belle followed, going around the less-crowded side of the fountain toward Lizzy. After two high-heeled steps in that direction, Belle felt a sharp pain and pressure in her lower back at the same time that a rough hand covered her mouth and nose. She smelled metal and soap as she tried to cry out, but only a muffled moan escaped.

Eddie twisted Belle's head and pulled it back against his chest. Belle could see only the sweat stain under the arm of his black shirt.

Rick Garetti watched from the nearby shadows under the overpass. Out of the corner of his eye, he could see the brightly lit wax figure of Marilyn Monroe next to the entrance to Madame Tussauds.

Eddie dragged Belle backwards, away from the fountain and toward Rick's position. If any of the people on the plaza saw Belle struggling with the large White man, nobody made a move to intercede. Everyone's attention was riveted on the continuing confrontation. Rick looked back toward Mike and Jason and smiled as a uniformed police officer and his jacketed companion moved toward the small crowd.

"Vegas PD! What's this all about?" demanded Officer Gary Burkhart.

"Looks like an assault and battery," his companion, Detective Buzz Rickenbacker, responded and drew himself up to his maximum height.

"What the hell?" Jason blurted out, taking his eyes off Sid, still in a fighting posture. When Jason turned his head, Sid rushed forward. Mike stepped in, grabbed an arm, and twisted it sideways, wrenching Sid's elbow and bringing the larger man down to his knees.

Officer Burkhart grabbed the top of Mike's shoulder like a claw, secured a handful of jacket, and hauled Mike backwards as he released Sid's twisted arm. Sid groaned and remained on his knee. "Break it up! Keep your hands off him."

"These two schmucks attacked Lizzy," Mike protested. "We were protecting her. You should arrest these idiots."

"The Black guy threw the first punch," a woman standing off to the side called out. The small crowd that had initially formed when Jason took Bo down had grown larger. Several people were taking video with their phones. Cleo and April were standing at the back of the four-deep gathering. Lizzy was sticking close to Michelle. They were near the inside edge of the circle of spectators.

"Is that right?" Rickenbacker said, not really directing the question toward Jason.

Michelle called out, "He was protecting Lizzy!"

"This asshole assaulted Lizzy." Jason motioned toward Sid, who was still on one knee, rubbing his elbow. "Then his buddy shoved her in the chest. I intervened, taking action in self-defense on her behalf. I threw one punch to prevent imminent harm to Lizzy. Then the guy charged at me and I dropped him, also in self-defense."

"That's bullshit!" Sid yelled, struggling to his feet now that Mike's elbow bar had been removed. "That Black dude sucker-punched Bo and then kicked him to the ground and stomped on his face. See how he's bleedin'?"

"Alright," Rickenbacker said, clasping a strong grip onto Jason's triceps. "Turn around and give me your wrist."

"Like hell," Jason said, ripping his arm away and spinning to face the crew-cut detective. "I'm a police officer. You know that. If you don't believe me, that's fine. I'll be happy to come give a statement."

"Ten-thirty-three. Officers need assistance, Venetian plaza," Burkhart barked into a hand-held radio. "I need an ambulance and immediate back-up."

"Oh, for Pete's sake," Mike blurted out. "Stand down, Officer. Nobody needs to be arrested here."

"This asshole does," Rickenbacker said, reaching again for Jason's arm.

Jason slapped the hand away, prompting Rickenbacker to step in and reach toward Jason's neck, as if intending to go for a headlock. Jason parried by lifting his elbow and twisting toward his attacker. The crowd's general murmur increased its volume to a collective gasp as a few people shouted. Mike moved toward his partner. Burkhart grabbed Mike's jacket sleeve.

Michelle, who was now standing, yelled out above the din. "Where's Jackie?"

Everyone stopped, including the two Vegas cops. Mike and Jason spun their heads, scanning the area around the fountain, which was now mostly empty. Most of the late-night plaza patrons had gathered around the skirmish.

Before anyone could locate Jackie, a loud bang rang out over the plaza. Every head in the crowd snapped toward the Wax Museum, where the sound seemed to come from. Screaming people immediately fled in all directions as they identified the sound as a gunshot.

Chapter 49 — Unlikely Hero

MIKE SHOOK OFF BURKHART'S GRIP and took off in the direction of the gunfire. As he passed Michelle, he shouted, "Stay here!"

Jason wrenched himself away from Rickenbacker and sprinted behind Mike.

"Stop!" Rickenbacker shouted before turning to pursue, reaching for his gun as he took his first stride. Burkhart trailed behind as he called into his radio for more back-up, announcing, "Shots fired!"

The crowd that had been thick around the scene instantly dispersed in every available direction, except toward the sound of the gunshot. A few stragglers backed away to the sidewalk next to Las Vegas Boulevard, but stayed to watch the events. One or two, mostly on the periphery, were still taking cell phone videos.

As he ran, Mike could hear screaming. He glanced toward the fountain as he hurried past, looking for Cleo or April, who were nowhere to be found. Jason caught him and was a few steps ahead when they reached the overhead pedestrian walkway. A siren sounded in the distance. Mike felt a bead of sweat trickle down the side of his face as he panted. The scent of gunpowder and flint hung in the still night air.

Another gunshot echoed around the plaza, prompting more screams and more galloping feet as most of the gawkers who had been hanging around the fringes of the scene moved quickly away. Jason skidded to a stop and held out an arm. Mike ran into it. They both peered into the darkness under the overpass, beyond which the roadway curved sharply to the right.

"Freeze, motherfuckers!" Rickenbacker shouted as he and Burkhart drew close enough to stop and crouch, leveling pistols at Mike and Jason.

"Shit!" Mike barked, spinning up against a stone wall under the ramp that separated the walkway from the ultra-blue water of the gondola canal, with Jason right behind him. Basic police procedure dictated that a cop should never fire a gun in a public space toward a suspect who was not taking any threatening action. But Rickenbacker had shown himself to be unpredictable, and he was possibly corrupt. Neither Mike nor Jason took anything for granted.

They crouched in the shadows. Across the access road, now devoid of any traffic, they could see Marylin Monroe's wax figure. To their right, back toward the plaza, Las Vegas Boulevard traffic lurched along, unaware of the excitement. The sidewalk along the Strip, which had been deserted, was starting to refill with cautious onlookers. To their left, a long stretch of paved walkway ran along the side of the canal, then along the edge of the building before reaching a corner. The black gondolas were empty and motionless at this late hour. The walkway ended in shadows where it met up with the corner of the casino building.

"What the fuck is happening?" Jason reflexively reached inside his jacket where his gun would be if he had one.

"No clue," Mike panted. "Those shots didn't come from Rickenasshole or his partner. Michelle thought Jackie was missing. You think Costanzo's guys?"

"Maybe."

Before Mike could say anything else, another shot rang out, once again scattering the remaining pedestrians. This time, Mike saw the flash of the gun muzzle ahead of them at the dark corner of the walkway, next to a panel van parked at the curb. Whoever was firing those shots was not shooting toward them. The two detectives both jumped up and hurried toward the parked van, forgetting they were unarmed and that they had two local cops chasing them.

When they got close to the corner, only dimly illuminated by a floodlight over an emergency exit door, Mike slowed and called out, "Police! Put down your weapon!" Jason flashed him a quizzical look, since Mike had no authority, no gun, and no backup except for his similarly unarmed partner.

"Stoneman? Is that you?" came a voice from the shadow of the van. It sounded familiar.

Mike heard the sound of shoes pounding on the pavement behind them. Probably Rickenbacker and Burkhart. "Yeah. It's Detectives Stoneman and Dickson. Who's there?"

The voice called back, "Agent Perkins, FBI."

Mike and Jason exchanged a quick smile. "We've got company coming up our ass here!"

A moment later, Agent Perkins emerged from the shadows and greeted the two detectives, his gun drawn. Next to him, Agent Shields held her pistol in two hands, close to her chest. At the same time, Rickenbacker and Burkhart ran into the murky light.

Rickenbacker dropped to a knee and held up his pistol. "Drop the gun!"

"Relax, Rickenbacker," Perkins called back. "Agent Davis Perkins, FBI." He snapped a brown leather case from his front pocket and held out his badge. "We've got a hostage situation here, so lower your weapon and take a position over there at the front of the van."

"You've got no jurisdiction here," Rickenbacker shot back. "Gary, call for more back-up. We'll take over from here."

"No dice," Perkins replied evenly. "This is a federal scene. We're in pursuit of a suspect who has been under surveillance. You can argue about it with your boss in the morning. Now take a supporting position or get the hell out of here. Either way, lower that weapon."

Two uniformed LVPD officers had arrived on the scene and were standing ten feet behind Rickenbacker, watching. Rickenbacker scowled and shot a look toward Burkhart, then slowly lowered his gun. Burkhart called out their position into his radio so the back-up units would know where to come upon arrival. The siren they had heard before was already louder. Rickenbacker and Burkhart moved to the other side of the van, leaving the two uniforms to take up a position on the perimeter.

"What's our situation?" Mike asked.

"Our suspects are down at the end of the roadway, beyond the hotel entrance. Casino security locked the door after the first shot, so there's no way out of there – it's a turnaround for the vehicles and a dead end. They have officers on the other side of the door to make sure nobody opens it. Our perp is Rick 'The Neck' Garetti, Freddy Costanzo's right-hand man. The other guy, we think, is a dude named Eddie Alonzo, some of Costanzo's muscle. They have your friend, Jackie, as a hostage. They have no way out."

"What went down?" Jason asked, looking furtively toward

the curve in the cobbled street and the shadows beyond.

Agent Perkins turned back to where Agent Dumm was crouching next to the front of the delivery van, his gun steadied on an elbow. "We've been tailing Jackie – and you – to see if Costanzo would make a move. While you were distracted by those two dudes on the plaza, Eddie grabbed Jackie. We were too far away to intervene, but we moved in pretty quickly. Eddie met up with The Neck under the overpass. We think it's a location without any security cams. They probably planned to kill Jackie, dump the body in the canal, and disappear into the casino while you were all occupied."

"Did you fire those shots?" Mike asked.

"Not the first one. The Neck spotted us coming up on him and fired at us. I don't think he hit any bystanders. Agent Shields fired back. I guess The Neck didn't know what to do once he saw us moving in, so instead of killing Jackie, he dragged him toward the casino, but then couldn't get in. Now they're trapped back there with no way out and a hostage. One of them fired at us and hit the van, then Shields shot back again. I've instructed her to stand down with the gunfire. If I'm The Neck in this spot, I'm probably on the phone right now trying to get some help – or some advice."

"Or an Uber," Mike quipped.

"Any chance he'll get a chopper to swoop down and whisk him away?" Jason didn't seem to be joking.

"Doubtful. And Spider-man isn't likely to come save him, either."

"Do you have any federal back-up coming?" Mike asked, "or are we dependent on the local uniforms?"

"We're it," Perkins answered. "This wasn't an operation; it was just your hunch. We figured we were a protection detail, not a hostage team. When we get some more uniforms here, we'll set up a perimeter and see what our guys do."

They didn't have long to wait before a group of four cops in uniforms hustled down the lane and asked for Rickenbacker. Agent Perkins took charge and gave instructions while Rickenbacker was on his cell phone, presumably trying to get some support from his superiors. Mike mumbled to Jason that waking your Captain at 1:00 a.m., even on a Saturday night in Vegas, was always a tricky proposition.

Mike's cell buzzed in his pocket. "Stoneman," he used his usual answer. He expected it to be Michelle, asking where he and Jason were. Instead it was a voice he thought he recognized, but couldn't place.

"Stoneman. Listen quick. You want your little bitch boy back, you tell the cops to get back. Now. We're going to walk out with the fag and you are all going to stand back or he's a dead queen."

By the time the voice stopped talking, Mike recognized him as the tall man with the giraffe neck from the meeting with Costanzo. "Why not put down your gun and surrender? You can't win here. Right now you're only in for assault. You add murder to the mix and you're done."

"Why don't you go fuck yourself?" Rick shot back.

Agent Perkins looked quizzically at Mike, realizing he was talking to The Neck. "What does he want?"

Mike tapped the mute button. "He wants us to pull back and let him leave. You want to let him get somebody to drive in there and take him out if he lets Jackie go first?"

"That's not in the hostage negotiation manual."

Mike shrugged. "The manual says to protect the hostage. You know who this guy is, right? So, he's not going to disappear."

"He might take Jackie with him; then we lose them both.

But he's your friend. You think The Neck will give up his hostage?"

Mike unmuted his phone and engaged the speaker. "I tell you what, Rick, you call for a car and have one of your boys drive it up here by our position. You come up and leave Jackie when you get in the car and the cops will let you take off. You can trust the local cops, right?"

The line went silent. Mike figured Rick was on another phone with the boss, trying for instructions. He saw that Rickenbacker was on his cell and wondered if they were talking to each other. Then Rick's voice blared from the speaker. "Fine. I'm calling in a car. Should be about five minutes. Make sure the cops let him in."

Mike muted again and turned to Perkins. Perkins looked at Rickenbacker, who quickly shut down his phone call. "He's bringing in a car. Tell your boys out front to let the guy in. I assume you're good with that?"

Rickenbacker ignored Perkins and held out his hand so Burkhart could give him a radio, which he used to relay the instructions to the cop who had the car lane blocked off out at Las Vegas Boulevard.

After six tense minutes, a dark SUV rumbled over the cobblestones down the little road. Two of the uniformed officers approached with guns drawn and motioned to the driver to turn around and face back out toward the main street. They also inspected the interior and verified that nobody else, nor any weapons, were inside.

"We're coming out!" Rick's voice called out through Mike's phone. "Tell them to put down their guns and clear me a path, and nobody needs to die today."

The line went dead. Mike looked at Agent Perkins. "If I had a gun, I'd put it down."

The agent holstered his gun and motioned to Agents Shields and Dumm to do the same. Rickenbacker, who had heard the end of the conversation, yelled to the local cops to pull back and not shoot. As the six cops backed away, Rickenbacker called for two of them to take up a position on the far side of the access road. Mike noticed that Rickenbacker did not put his gun away.

"We're coming out," Rick called from the dim reaches of the carport as he and Eddie inched around the bend in the lane. Rick had Belle pinned in front of him with a thick arm around her neck as he shuffled forward, keeping the silver dress between him and the cops. His black handgun was pushed into Belle's side. Eddie was right behind Rick, stretching his arm around Rick's waist, his own gun in his right hand. The FBI agents, the two New York detectives, and the six Las Vegas cops all watched in silence. As he and Belle got closer, Rick waved his gun toward Rickenbacker, motioning him to move toward the other side of the SUV. "Open the back door on the driver's side."

Mike saw what he was doing – trying to put the big SUV between himself and the bulk of the gathered cops. There were two uniformed officers on that side of the lane, making sure their suspects didn't try to bolt toward the Wax Museum. But, when the SUV door opened, it would be a barrier blocking those cops from Rick – and Belle.

As Rick waved the pistol, he momentarily removed it from Belle's side. Belle saw Mike and Jason standing less than ten feet away. As Rick made a final motion with his gun hand and Rickenbacker reached for the door handle, Belle took matters into her own heels. In one motion, she raised her right foot and lowered her chin. Rick screamed in pain as Belle sank her teeth into his hairy forearm. At the same moment, Belle's four-inch stiletto heel ripped through the polyester mesh of Rick's New Balance sneaker and dug deeply into his right instep with a crunch.

The pain caused Rick to loosen his neck lock. Eddie, taken by surprise, stepped back as Rick jumped, trying to lift his injured foot but only driving Belle's heel further into the fresh wound. Belle went limp, slithering past Rick's relaxed grip and down his body. Rick lashed out with his bleeding arm, smashing the back of his fist into the side of her face. Belle slumped sideways and continued to fall toward the pavement. Her foot pulled away from the silver pump, leaving the heel still stuck in Rick's sneaker.

Mike and Jason both moved the moment they saw Belle start to slide down. Mike went toward Belle, reaching to grab a limp arm and pull her away. Jason rushed toward the two men and launched himself into a tackle, driving his shoulder into Rick's side and pushing the injured man over into Eddie. Eddie fired his gun wildly, realizing what was happening a second too late. Rick pulled his trigger, sending a bullet into the cobbled pavement that ricocheted away.

Agents Perkins and Dumm reached for their weapons as they watched the scene unfold. The local cops did the same, then ducked as the two shots blasted out. Rick and Eddie both toppled under Jason's weight. Perkins sprang forward toward the three men, who were now on the ground in a pile. He stopped when he heard another shot echo through the dark space, coming from his right, next to the SUV. When he spun his head in the direction of the blast, he saw Rickenbacker's gun barrel still smoking. The open passenger door blocked him from the two cops on that side of the street. The big vehicle would have blocked everyone's view, except that Perkins was already in the middle of the road.

The silence following Rickenbacker's shot was broken by Rick's anguished moan. Jason had one hand on Eddie's wrist, preventing him from raising his gun. His other hand was grasping Belle's silver stiletto pump, which he was twisting and grinding down into Rick's foot. The Neck had dropped his pistol. Agent Shields rushed to help Jason as four uniformed officers sprinted toward the scene.

Agent Perkins stepped toward Mike and Belle, placing himself between them and Rickenbacker, who was moving toward the scrum on the ground. Belle was lying on the cobblestones. A dark gash marred the chest of her silver gown. Mike, still grasping Belle's arm, released his grip, allowing her to roll backwards onto the rust-colored stones. A red stain and another gash marked the side of the gown opposite the bullet's entry hole. Belle's face was blank, eyes closed.

"Call 9-1-1!" Mike barked, as if he were in charge. The one uniformed officer who was not working with Jason to handcuff Rick and Eddie obediently whipped out his radio microphone and called in the second request for an ambulance. Mike removed his jacket and stuffed it under Belle's unconscious head.

Jason got to his feet and dusted off his pants. Leaving Rick and Eddie in the apparently capable hands of the local uniforms, he looked around for Mike and Belle. When he saw Belle on the ground, he took a step in that direction, but felt a solid hand grab his elbow and tug. He spun and saw the sneering face of Buzz Rickenbacker, who had traded his service pistol for a pair of handcuffs. "You're under arrest, tough guy."

"What the hell?" Jason tried to wrench his arm away to get to Belle, but Rickenbacker held fast. He pulled Jason off balance, then lifted his knee and planted it into Jason's groin. Jason let out a groan and doubled over with Rickenbacker still holding his arm.

"What do you think you're doing?" Agent Perkins bellowed, reaching out and gripping Rickenbacker's wrist.

"Back off, Fibbie!"

Perkins removed his hand. "Fine. It's your town." He stepped back, making a show of holding out his arms as if surrendering the situation to the Vegas cop. "Dickson, don't resist. You hear me?"

Jason, still gasping, nodded his head. He turned around, bent over at the waist, and held his hands behind his back.

Rickenbacker cuffed Jason more roughly than necessary. As he slapped the second cuff onto Jason, Rickenbacker felt cold metal snap onto his right wrist. "What the—"

Before Rickenbacker could react, Agent Perkins twisted the big man's arm, reached around his body, and snapped a cuff on his other hand.

"I'll fucking bury you!" Rickenbacker roared.

"Sure you will, Asshole. As soon as you get out of prison. I saw you target the hostage."

When Burkhart tried to come to Rickenbacker's aid, Agent Dumm stepped in and put a finger in his chest. "Careful. You're about an inch away from joining your partner in cuffs. I'd advise you to step back."

Burkhart did. Perkins reached into Rickenbacker's jacket pocket and extracted the keys to his handcuffs, while Rickenbacker continued to spew a free flow of expletives toward the federal agents.

Once freed from his bonds, Jason rushed to Belle. Mike, who had watched the activity with great interest said, "She's breathing."

"But she's bleeding." Jason reached out with both hands and grabbed the front of the silver dress. He ripped the fragile fabric, exposing Belle's chest, where a well of blood seeped into the thin nylon wrap holding her impressive fake breasts. The left boob was slightly flattened, pierced by Rickenbacker's bullet on both sides. After exiting the latex mound, the hot slug had grazed across Belle's skin under the right breast, leaving a gash that was bleeding but did not look life-threatening. Jason extracted a white handkerchief from his jacket and applied it to the bloody scene.

As Jason pressed gently, Belle winced. "Ow! What the—"

"You're alright," Jason soothed.

"Then why are you—" Belle lifted her head, wincing again. She looked down toward the pain, then cried out, "What did you do to my dress!?"

Jason and Mike both burst out laughing.

A few minutes later, the EMT crew arrived. Right behind them, Michelle rushed to Mike and threw her arms around him. "How'd you get past the cops?" Mike asked when they concluded a lengthy kiss.

"I told them I'm a doctor and followed the EMTs."

"Good move," Mike chuckled.

"Mike, when those gunshots – and you don't have a gun . . ."

"We're all fine. Even Jackie." Mike hugged Michelle tightly and rocked her gently.

The emergency crew spent ten minutes going through their paces checking out Belle, who kept assuring them that the wound was superficial and did not warrant an ambulance ride. Jason advocated following the EMT's suggestion, but admitted that they always suggested getting checked out at the hospital by a doctor. It was their protocol and intended to cover their liability when a victim ended up with internal bleeding or some other hidden injury that didn't get properly treated. Michelle stepped in and assured the paramedics that she was a doctor and would keep an eye on Belle.

Agent Perkins organized a quick conference call with the Las Vegas police chief. After confiscating his pistol, Perkins released Rickenbacker and told him to expect a federal arrest warrant, so he should not skip town. Rickenbacker and Burkhart were escorted out of the now-crowded lane by a cohort of uniformed officers.

Jason and Mike gave statements to a different pair of local detectives who arrived on the scene. Mike promised that Belle would come in to give a statement and identify Rick and Eddie the next morning.

Belle emerged from under the police tape next to the fountain in the Venetian plaza, leaning on Jason. Lizzy, April, and Cleo ran forward and assumed the chore of supporting their friend. Belle was barefoot. The silver dress was ripped down the front; Michelle had secured it temporarily with a safety pin from her purse, but it was ruined. The bloody silver stiletto had been bagged as evidence and Belle had abandoned its orphaned mate. Between the blood on the dress, the bullet holes, and the welt on Belle's cheek where Rick had hit her, she looked like the hostage standoff had lasted a week rather than an hour.

It was 2:30 a.m., but a sizeable crowd was still gathered in the plaza, most of whom had no idea that there had been a shooting an hour earlier. As the group slowly moved back toward the overpass leading to the Mardi Gras, Belle stumbled and nearly fell. Jason stepped in and swept her into his arms, carrying his future brother-in-law up the escalator.

"You're lighter than Rachel," Jason commented playfully.

"I hope so. The girl's bigger than me, and she's pregnant!"

Michelle was walking arm-in-arm with Mike, trailing the

bedraggled drag queens, who were not generating as much attention this time from the passing pedestrians. She said, "Exactly what are we going to tell the bride about all this?"

"Don't worry." Mike squeezed Michelle's arm gently with his. "I'm sure Jason will handle it with his usual aplomb."

Michelle laughed and leaned her head toward Mike's shoulder. "Is it always like this in Vegas?"

"Always. But the real question isn't what Jason tells Rachel. It's what he tells her parents."

Chapter 50 — Wedding Bells

Sunday, January 12
Las Vegas, NV

JASON'S PLAN WAS TO GENTLY EXPLAIN THE EVENTS of the previous night to Rachel. He didn't want to upset the bride on her wedding day. But Rachel had gone to bed three hours before Jason, and was up before him. When Jason finally forced his eyes open and staggered out into the sitting room, Rachel motioned him to the sofa, where she was watching the morning news on the local network affiliate.

"This is so crazy. There was a big shootout on the Venetian plaza last night. Did you guys see it?"

Jason watched the story, featuring long cuts from a slightly jumpy cell phone video that captured people running across the plaza, the sound of gunshots, and then images of Rick and Eddie being brought out in handcuffs. The producers of the show had opted to keep Jackie's face off the air, and none of the clips they selected for the story showed Mike, Jason, or any other member of their party. At the conclusion of almost five minutes of coverage, including a live remote from the Venetian plaza (mostly empty at 9:00 a.m. on a Sunday morning), the female anchor came on with a perky smile.

Jason reached out and took Rachel's hands in his, then told her the entire story. Later, after Rachel's frantic call,

Jackie came to the suite and described what had happened from his point of view. Rachel hugged Jackie so hard she aggravated the still-sensitive area around the bullet wound. She had some experience with such non-lethal bullet scars and fussed over Jackie's bandage, insisting on changing it and disinfecting it. Jason smartly stepped back and gave his soon-to-be bride plenty of space.

At 10:00 a.m., Jackie, Mike, and Jason met Jerry at the police station to give statements. Jerry remarked that their little party had kept him busy, but he was happy to tell the reporters gathered outside the station that he was the lawyer for the hostage, Jackie Robinson, who had been wrongfully arrested by the LVPD earlier in the week. Based on Mike's briefing, he predicted that local detective Buzz Rickenbacker would soon be arrested and charged with attempting to kill Jackie. It was the first the reporters had heard about this aspect of the story, and kept Jerry in front of the cameras for fifteen minutes.

The group gathered again at their pool-side table for lunch. The mood was relieved and excited. Everyone had their own version of the events on the Venetian plaza for Rachel. She said over and over how much she wished she had been there. Jason was happy she had been safe in her bed during all the excitement.

After their late lunch, Rachel adjourned to her suite with Michelle to start preparing for the wedding. Mike and Jason headed off to Mike's suite. Jason had other business to attend to, but Mike had two final hours to hit the poker room before he was due to meet Michelle and get dressed. As he approached the podium where the floor manager assigned seats to new players, Mike passed by a table where a short man in a baseball cap with a large diamond ring on his finger and a tumbler of scotch in his hand was shouting about how stupid one of the other players was. When he arrived at the assignment desk, Mike made a point to avoid the table where Lenny Dkystra was seated.

Ninety minutes later, Mike was up $300 and feeling good about himself. In six days in Las Vegas, he had managed less than three hours at the poker tables. This was going to be difficult to explain back at the precinct. At least he would be able to say he didn't lose money.

Michelle wasn't in their room when Mike arrived, so he knocked on Rachel's door. Michelle greeted him with a kiss and invited him inside. Rachel was wearing the dress.

"Wow!" Mike exclaimed as soon as he saw her. "The last time I saw that dress it was hanging in Michelle's closet. That seems like months ago."

"It was three weeks," Michelle said. "It's just that this week has felt so long."

Lizzy and Jackie arrived, wearing matching suits with pink satin bowties. Michelle had already changed into her outfit as the maid of honor, a black cocktail dress that showed off her legs. She was happy not to have to compete with Jackie's at the wedding.

"Where'd you two get those suits?" Mike asked.

"There's a wedding chapel number we do in some of our shows. We figured the theater wouldn't miss the costumes for an evening," Jackie explained.

"Well," Mike admired the assembled bridal party, "I think everyone at the wedding is going to be very impressed with how great you all look."

♦♦♦

At 5:00, Mike and Jason arrived at The Little Jewel Chapel. Rachel had decided at the last minute that she didn't want Jason to see her in the dress before the ceremony. It was not part of the original plan, but whatever the bride wanted. So, Mike and Jason went alone, with Rachel and her entourage slated to arrive later.

As soon as they walked through the door, Mike recognized a distinguished-looking Black man wearing a light gray suit, and a woman with gray hair in a peach-colored dress and a matching hat. The newcomers got up from a plush sofa in the area outside the inner chapel doors and hurried toward Jason. Olivia Robinson hugged him. Ernie Robinson waited for his wife to detach before extending his hand toward his imminent son-in-law.

"Thanks again for bringing us out for this, Jason. That was a class move. Does Rachel know we're here yet?"

"No," Jason said, glancing over his shoulder toward the door. "I expect her in a few minutes, along with Michelle and the rest of her wedding party."

"Does that mean Jackie?" Olivia asked.

Jason grimaced and hesitated, so Mike jumped in to support his partner. "Mr. Robinson, this is Rachel's day. And Jason's. It's a happy day. I'm sure you both agree?"

"Sure," Ernie replied.

"Well, I think we can all agree that making Rachel happy is the most important thing."

Olivia said in a soft but authoritative tone. "Of course. Plus, since Rachel is pregnant, we don't want to do anything to upset her. She's already nervous enough, I'm sure, and her hormones are probably running rampant. We'll make sure everything remains calm. Won't we, Dear?" She directed a steely stare toward her husband.

"Right," Ernie agreed.

"How did you know she's pregnant?" Jason asked Olivia.

"Oh, please. We were making plans for a wedding in June. Now, suddenly, you're getting married here with no notice? Of course she's pregnant. And we're thrilled about it. Aren't we, Dear?"

"Absolutely," Ernie again agreed readily, slipping his arm around his wife's waist. "Another grandchild is something we're looking forward to. No matter what the circumstances." The sincerity level in Ernie's voice diminished toward the end of his statement.

"Well, let me tell you, Sir, that you could never want a better man for a son-in-law than Jason."

"We know, Mike," Olivia said. "We adore Jason." She reached out and squeezed his hand.

"Did you guess that Jackie was going to be here?"

"Jason told us before we left that he and Rachel had been catching up with Jackie. We're so happy that he'll be here. Aren't we, Dear?"

This time, Ernie's response was not as quick nor as enthusiastic. "Yes. We're both excited about seeing Jackie."

Jason stepped in, ready to take any heat. "Sir, let me tell you about what's been going on here this week."

During the ten-minute explanation, Jason minimized his own role in the final confrontation with Rick "The Neck" Garetti. He accurately explained how Jackie had stomped the kidnapper and single-handedly created the situation that led to the arrest of the two assailants. He left out any mention of the FBI photo or the dead senator. Before either Ernie or Olivia could emerge from their stunned state, Michelle burst through the door of the chapel, took one look at the situation, and ordered Jason to remove himself. The bride was ready to come in, and the groom needed to not be there.

"But, I haven't—" Jason stopped when he saw the daggers coming from the eyes of both Michelle and Olivia. "Fine. I'll go into the chapel. Mike – can you explain—"

"There's nothing to explain," Michelle said. "Now, scoot!"

Jason turned, motioning for Mike to accompany him through the inner door. As they exited the outer reception area, Mike said, "That was a great use of your craps winnings. I think Rachel will be thrilled you brought out her folks for this. Definitely got it in good there."

Chapter 51 — Loose Ends

Sunday, January 12
Las Vegas, NV

WHILE THE WEDDING PARTY WAS ARRIVING at The Little Jewel Chapel, Freddy Costanzo was waiting in his office. He was expecting a report on recent events. Freddy was not accustomed to losing. It wasn't so much the hundred thousand dollars, which was not significant money. It was the blow to his ego that some lightweight asshole had shaken him down twice and gotten away with it. With The Neck out of commission, sitting in the Clark County lockup with Eddie, awaiting an arraignment, and with his personal detective likely to be arrested, Freddy was frustrated beyond words. He paced the room like a tiger in a cage.

A knock on his door caused him to stop and call out, "Come!"

Through the door walked Stephen Balaban, known as "Stevie the Blade," carrying a small athletic bag. He took a seat and crossed his legs casually.

"You have something to tell me?" the boss asked.

"I do. The dude was stupid. He stayed in town."

Freddy leaned against his desk. "How'd you find him?"

"The magician gave him up."

"How'd you find the magician?"

Stevie shrugged. "There aren't that many magicians. The Neck got a photo of him. He did one particular trick with a Lucite cube. I asked around. I had to drive to Reno, but I found him. It didn't take much persuasion."

"So, who was Shithead?" Freddy reached for the crystal cigar box on his desk and extracted a Cubano. He held it between two fingers, but did not light up.

"Dude named Alexander Lewbowski. He's a booking agent. Calls himself The Big Lewbowski. He's got a whole stable of talent, including the magician. When The Neck needed the girls for the sting, he called Lewbowski and asked for one girl and two Black queens. The Lewbowski dude got the money, then hung around outside long enough to see you and your mark arrive. Turns out one of the bitches told him what went down inside. Somebody named Mimi. She told him you were there. When the mark turned up dead, he was just smart enough to put it together. He figured he could make a big score, but then he didn't skip town. Idiot. He also made the mistake of having too many accomplices who could rat him out. Maybe if he got more dough, he could have paid them off better. The magician didn't seem very loyal. Whatever."

"Am I safe from further blackmail attempts?"

"Oh yeah." Stevie reached down, unzipped his bag, and pulled out a wrinkled, brownish lump inside a zip-lock bag. He deposited his trophy into an ashtray on the coffee table. Black hairs protruded from the puddle of flesh.

"That's disgusting," Freddy deadpanned.

"I know. I hated doing it. I really hated making his girlfriend watch. But I thought it was important that word get around town about what happens to somebody who crosses Freddy Costanzo. You want me to take her out, too?"

"No," Freddy said, reaching for his cutter and snipping off the bottom of his cigar. "Let her be. Like you said, somebody needs to tell the tale. You sure she can't finger you?"

"I don't think so. And I'm pretty certain she wouldn't try, after what she saw. What about the magician?"

"Does he know anything?"

"Nah. He only knows that Lewbowski wanted him to make some backpack disappear and then deliver it. He didn't know why."

"OK. That figures. He can't hurt us." Freddy held the cigar to his nose and sniffed the pungent aroma from the snipped end. "You did good, Stevie."

"What about that last drag bitch? You want that loose end taken care of?"

"No." Freddy pulled open the top drawer of his massive desk and extracted a lighter. "That one's no threat. I got insurance. I'm more concerned about The Neck and Eddie. I'd prefer it if they don't have a chance to start making deals."

"I'll take care of it," Stevie said, standing up.

Freddy lit his Cubano and took several quick puffs to get it going. "Stevie."

"Yeah, Boss?"

"Take that limp dick with you."

"Right." Stevie picked up the ashtray and dumped its contents back into the athletic bag. "You can count on me, boss." The man walked confidently to the door and let himself out.

When the door latched behind Stevie, Freddy turned to his window, put the cigar in his mouth, and looked out at the sparkling Las Vegas Strip.

Chapter 52 — I Do

Sunday, January 12
Las Vegas, Nevada

WHEN RACHEL STEPPED INTO the exterior lobby of The Little Jewel Chapel and saw her mother and father, she lost all emotional control and burst into tears of joy. She was shocked to learn that Jason had used his winnings at the craps table to buy plane tickets and made the last-minute arrangements for her parents to come to Las Vegas. It was the sweetest thing he had ever done. Even better than taking a bullet to protect her.

The initial euphoria was interrupted when Jackie stepped up next to Rachel to greet their parents. Olivia opened her arms and embraced Jackie. Then, Olivia looked over at her husband with a pleading expression.

Ernie held out his hand and Jackie gave him a firm shake. "Jason told us what you went through this week, and how you fought off that thug. He also told us how great you and Rachel have been together this week." He paused, glancing at Olivia for a moment. "I'm proud of you, Jackie."

He extended both arms toward his son. Jackie hesitantly moved forward and gave his father a hug. Not as long or as tight as with Olivia, but a genuinely affectionate embrace. When they separated, Jackie wiped a tear away, while Rachel rushed in to join the embrace, careful about not messing up the dress.

None of the Robinsons noticed when the door to the inner chapel opened and Helene DiVito-Rosen stepped into the outer lobby. She wore a layered peach skirt and jacket combination with a matching wide-brimmed hat. Her blouse revealed only a tiny peek of cleavage. "Oh, this is so wonderful!" she held back her own tears as she approached the bride. "Rachel, you look so gorgeous! I'm so glad you and Jason are here to be my first couple."

"Really?" Olivia was surprised.

"Oh, well, yeah. We just opened up. I'm so happy. Oh!" Helene reached into a white handbag hanging on a chain from her shoulder. "Here. I want you to wear this." She held out a diamond-encrusted tiara that sparkled in the overhead lights.

"Oh, my. No – really, I couldn't accept this," Rachel said, pushing away the fabulous bauble.

"It's not a gift, Sweetie," Helene said with a chuckle, "it's a loan for the ceremony and the pictures after. You have to give it back. It's your something borrowed!"

Rachel laughed and accepted the loaner diamonds. "Thank you. Michelle loaned me a bracelet, but this is so much . . . flashier."

"Well, take them both. You can't have too much good luck on your wedding day."

Helene helped Rachel arrange the tiara, and her photographer appeared and arranged the bridal party for pre-ceremony photos. Rachel was glowing. Ernie and Olivia watched proudly, and even allowed themselves to be dragged into the final few shots.

At 5:55, Helene went into the chapel, leaving the bride in the care of her entourage. Lizzy leaned over to Rachel and said,

"She needs those huge boobs to hold in her big heart." They both sniffed back tears and laughed at the same time.

When the music started and the chapel doors opened, the wedding party processed down the aisle toward Jason and Mike, who were standing at the altar, waiting. Ernie walked Rachel to the front before giving her a kiss and then sitting in the front row next to Olivia. Helene sat next to them. On her lap she held a sparkling tissue-box cozy covered with rhinestones. She pulled out a tissue and dabbed her leaking eyes even before the reverend began the ceremony.

Olivia stared at the box, asked for a tissue, and said, "Where can I get one of those box covers?"

Helene smiled. "We sell them in the jewelry store. I'll show you after the wedding."

As they stood in a line next to Michelle, Lizzy and Jackie nudged each other. Lizzy whispered in the direction of the reverend, who stood in a flowing red-and-gold robe holding a large bible. "April? What are you doing here? You never told us you were a preacher."

The reverend, whom they had last seen wearing fishnet stockings while walking away from the Venetian plaza, gave them a wink. "Hey, everybody needs a side hustle."

The music stopped. The reverend recited the formalities, then turned to Jason. "I understand that the couple has written their own vows. Jason, please face your bride."

Jason and Rachel faced each other. He reached out and took her hand. "Rachel, you are my queen, the glimmering spotlight of joy in my life. Your smile melts away all my stress and you bring me a sense of calm and peace that I have never known before. I love you with all my heart and promise to do whatever I can to keep that spotlight glowing for the rest of our lives." He took a delicate ring from Mike's hand and placed it on Rachel's finger.

The reverend turned to Rachel and nodded. Rachel cleared her throat, wiped a tear from her eye, and said, "You are my hero, Jason. I know now, more than ever, that you know me and you see me and I can depend on you to be there for me. You deliver me to my destiny, to infinity and beyond. I am so blessed to have you in my life and I promise to do my best to be as strong and supportive for you as you always are for me. I love you, Babe, now and always." She slid a thick gold band onto Jason's finger.

Helene pulled another tissue from her bejeweled box, then handed one to Olivia.

"With the power vested in me by the State of Nevada, I now declare you to be married. You may kiss each other."

Jason and Rachel kissed, then kissed again before Jackie reached out to pull Rachel away. "Save some of that for us, girl!"

Everyone laughed as Rachel and Jason raced back down the aisle toward the doors to the outer lobby. Helene had arranged for a very tasteful reception with champagne and a lovely little wedding cake. On the top, the bride carried a first aid kit and the groom had a policeman's hat.

With a half-consumed glass in his hand, Jason approached Ernie. "Sir, I hope you're not too disappointed that we couldn't do this back home in June like we planned."

"I'm not," Ernie said gruffly. "This was terrific. And I'm happy Jackie could be here. Rachel and Jackie have always been really close, so this was great. And—" Rachel's father held up his glass toward Jason. "—You can call me Ernie." Then Ernie walked over to his son and put a hand on his shoulder. "Jackie, after what I've heard about how you handled yourself this week, I guess wearing a dress doesn't make you a pussy."

Everyone who heard raised their glasses to salute Jackie.

When the reverend came by, Jason offered to give him a tip. He declined, without clueing Jason in to his drag identity. "This one was a labor of love. Plus, Helene already took care of me."

Ernie and Olivia walked over to shake the reverend's hand. "Let me tell you how much I enjoyed the way you officiated today. It's so nice to see a normal, conservative young person in this crazy town."

April said, "Ain't that the truth." He thanked Ernie for his kind words and gracefully walked to the exit.

A few minutes later, the glasses were put down and the wedding party went outside in the Vegas twilight. A white limo was waiting to take the bride and groom back to the Mardi Gras. Mike had spoken to the hotel manager and explained that Jason was the hero cop who had saved their star performer from being murdered. The manager upgraded the happy couple to the Bridal Suite and comped the bride's parents' room for both Sunday night and Monday. He also provided meal vouchers and $100 in slot machine credits. Ernie and Olivia were thrilled. Mike told Michelle that the behavior was pretty standard for Vegas.

Lizzy, Jackie, Ernie, and Olivia took a waiting Lyft car and followed the limo.

Helene came over and put her arms around Mike and Michelle. "I just knew those two were really in love. I could tell all along. It makes me believe in happily ever after." She sniffed and reached for another tissue.

"We agree," Michelle said. "They're a great couple. All they need to do is keep out of the way of stray bullets for a while." Michelle reached a hand and laid it on Helene's shoulder. "And thank you so much for making it all happen. Congratulations on opening the chapel. I hope you have great success here."

"Thanks," Helene sniffed. "It was terrific to have you here for this. I'd been thinking about opening my own jewelry store, but I never thought I'd have a wedding chapel. How's that for financial feminism?"

"It's great." Michelle gave her a hug. "Oh, rats. I meant to ask Rachel to tell me what Jason had engraved on her ring."

"Oh, I can tell you that!" Helene leaned in toward Michelle, as if there were anybody else there who might overhear. "Rachel's ring has today's date and says *My Queen Forever*."

"Aw. That's so sweet. Well, we'd better get going so you can set up for your next wedding. Do you have another one today?"

"No. I'm working on getting more bookings. I'm hoping I'll have a nice niche with the jewelry store and the chapel together. I'm sure it will work out. Where is there more love in the air than in Las Vegas, right?"

"You'll be successful," Mike said encouragingly. "You've got a lot of heart. If I were going to have a Vegas wedding, I'd definitely come here."

Michelle took Mike's hand and gave it a squeeze.

Chapter 53 — Homeward Bound

Monday, January 13
United Airlines Flight 2427

WHEN THEIR PLANE reached cruising altitude en route from McCarran International Airport to Newark Liberty, Mike and Michelle both put their seats back and settled in for the flight home. After eight days of vacation, they were exhausted.

Mike had sent a message back to New York about the events in Las Vegas and asked Berkowitz to let Captain Sullivan know to expect a call from the Vegas cops. He had also sent a message to Agent Forrest, to thank him for his help in protecting Jackie.

Jerry Garcia had waived his fee as a wedding present to Jason and Rachel. Michelle and Mike agreed this was generous of him, but they also knew that his interviews with two of the three network affiliate TV stations had already resulted in a flurry of new business for him. It turned out he had been working on a book on the history of the Vegas Mob. Now, his unique knowledge about what had instantly become known locally as the *Drag Disgrace* was going to make a great chapter.

Although Jackie and Lizzy never revealed the full background about what led to the shootout on the Venetian plaza, the gutsy actions of Belle de la Pomme generated considerable positive publicity, and solidified Jackie's status as the new star of the drag revue at *The Birdcage*.

Before takeoff, Mike had received an email from Agent Perkins, letting him know that Buzz Rickenbacker was in federal custody. Mike should expect a subpoena to testify if the case ever got to trial, but he expected that the cop would work out a plea agreement. The FBI hoped to leverage the charges to put pressure on Rickenbacker to flip on Freddy Costanzo. It was a long shot, but they were keeping him locked up where Freddy couldn't take him out before he had a chance to fully appreciate the benefits of the witness protection program. Mike was surprised to learn that the program included paying child support on behalf of a federal witness, which Perkins thought might be another pressure point for Rickenbacker.

Michelle, who had the window seat, leaned to her left and rested her head on Mike's shoulder. "Despite everything, you have to admit the wedding was romantic."

"I agree completely," Mike said, reaching his right hand and gently entwining his fingers with Michelle's.

"Do you think we'll ever be able to take a vacation where we get to rest and relax?"

Mike chuckled. "I certainly hope so, although our track record isn't great at this point. But I'd say we're due."

"We still have a credit for a free cruise, you know."

"That's true. Maybe when we get back home we'll book one for this August or September. Maybe the *Colossus of the Ocean* will be sailing to Bermuda again."

"That would be great. I'm sure we'll have better luck this time around."

Mike turned his head and gazed into Michelle's eyes. "I feel like I've been pretty lucky already." He leaned in for a lingering kiss. When they parted lips, Mike leaned back in his seat and closed his eyes.

Michelle looked down at her left hand, still entwined with Mike's right. She smiled and admired the delicate gold band on her ring finger. It had been a very romantic wedding, indeed.

Rachel and Jason's nuptials had also been lovely.

The End

Thank you for reading *Perilous Gambit*. I truly enjoy hearing from readers about their reactions to my characters and stories. I welcome critical comments and suggestions that can help me improve my writing and urge every reader to **please leave a review**. Even a few words will go a long way and I will be grateful. Post on Amazon, Goodreads and/or BookBub to let other readers know what you think. And feel free to send me an email directly at www.kevingchapman.com to tell me your thoughts about this book.

And please tell your friends (and book club leaders) about this book. As an independent author, I need all the word-of-mouth plugs I can get. Keep reading books by indie authors; there are a lot of great writers out there just waiting for you.

Kevin G. Chapman
November 2021

About the Author

Kevin G. Chapman is, by profession, an attorney specializing in labor and employment law. He is a past Chair of the Labor & Employment Law Network of the Association of Corporate Counsel, leading a group of 6800 in-house employment lawyers. Kevin is a frequent speaker at Continuing Legal Education seminars and enjoys teaching management training courses.

Kevin's second novel, *A Legacy of One*, originally published in 2016, was a finalist for the Chanticleer Book Review's Somerset Award for Literary Fiction. *A Legacy of One* is a serious book, filled with political and social commentary and a plot involving personal identity, self-determination, and the struggle to make the right life decisions. *A Legacy of One* has been significantly revised and updated and was re-published in 2021. It's available on Amazon.com if you're looking for something very different from Mike Stoneman's world.

Kevin has also written several short stories, including *Fool Me Twice*, the winner of the New Jersey Corporate Counsel Association's 2012 Legal Fiction Writing Competition, which was the genesis of Mike Stoneman. *Fool Me Twice* is available as a stand-alone short story and is <u>FREE on Amazon</u>, <u>Kobo</u>, <u>Nook</u>, and other ebook retailers, or you can get it directly from <u>Kevin's website</u>, where you can also interact with the author. Find him on Facebook and <u>KevinGChapman.com</u>

Book Club discussion questions for *Perilous Gambit*

1. What was your impression of the drag performer community before reading this book? Did it change at all based on this read?
2. Did your impressions about Jackie change over the course of the story? How?
3. How long did it take you to figure out that Jackie was one of the drag queens in the FBI photo?
4. Were you surprised by Mike's gambit?
5. Did you guess (be honest) who was blackmailing Freddy?
6. What was your impression of how Drew Maulgray handled his interactions with Buzz, his senior partner? Did you expect more from him? What did you think he should have done?
7. Did you think the wedding would happen?
8. For readers of the whole series, were you surprised how Helene DiVito-Rosen showed up in Vegas? Were you amused?
9. How did you feel about Rachel's parents showing up at the wedding and the reunion between Jackie and Ernie?
10. Who predicted the ending? (Really?)

AUTHOR'S NOTE & ACKNOWLEDGEMENTS

As always, I must credit my insightful wife, Sharon, for keeping all the subplots on track. She's a great wedding planner. Sharon has a fantastic vision for where my characters are going. She brought Helene DiVito-Rosen from nowhere, and made sure the romance was where it needed to be. She understands these characters sometimes better than I do.

I also thank my brilliant editor-daughter, Samantha (Samanthachapmanediting.com) whose careful reads, sensitivity, and great ideas helped put the book over the top. She's the editor that every author wants. And kudos to my cover designer, Peter from bespokebookcovers.com. Peter outdid himself with this eye-catching cover. Also kudos to Jiawie "Peter" Hsu from Fotolux in Princeton Junction, NJ (my local photo shop) for making me beautiful prints for my publicity posters.

My beta readers provided me with invaluable perspectives and ideas as the book was in development. Thanks so much to Matt (M.C.) Thomas, Barbara Daniels Dena, Roxx, Gayle Wilson, Buzz and Beth Baradyn, Mimi Bailey, Kay Barton, Fred Casiello, Amy Knarr, Kay Hagan-Haller, and Joanna Joseph. Everyone contributed something to the final product.

I owe a particular debt of gratitude to Rían O'Ceárta, who treated me with dignity and compassion while guiding me gently into their world and giving me excellent guidance and suggestions for how I could better understand the drag characters in my story. Rían helped me immeasurably and I can only hope that my characters contain a hint of their insight and courage.

I also thank Taryn Cooper and Chuck Monsanto for being sensitivity readers. I was dipping into some treacherous water here, and without much prior understanding. I sincerely thank them, along with Rían for steering me in the right direction. Any remaining flaws, errors, mischaracterizations, or lack of sensitivity is entirely my own.

I also pay tribute to Amy Vansant at AuthorsXP.com and her band of Typokillers, who combed over the finished manuscript and rooted out the last few errors, large and small, to make the final text as clean as it can be. (But, if you find a flaw, please let me know so I can fix it.) All authors should use the typokillers. Thanks to Kim Hine, Susan Bock, Deena Guptil, Aicha Traore, and Adele Maree.

If you're a Mike Stoneman fan, join me on Facebook (Mike Stoneman Thriller Group) and send me a note to get on my newsletter distribution list or onto the Whiteboard Squad (my social media army). Find me at www.KevinGChapman.com

Other novels and stories by Kevin G. Chapman

The Mike Stoneman Thriller Series

Righteous Assassin (Mike Stoneman #1)
Deadly Enterprise (Mike Stoneman #2)
Lethal Voyage (Mike Stoneman #3)
Fatal Infraction (Mike Stoneman #4)
Perilous Gambit (Mike Stoneman #5)
Fool Me Twice (A Mike Stoneman Short Story)

Stand-alone Novels

The Other Murder
Dead Winner
A Legacy of One
Identity Crisis: A Rick LaBlonde Mystery

Short Stories & Novellas

The Car, the Dog & the Girl
Ghost Creek (a romantic mystery novella)

Visit me at www.KevinGChapman.com

Connect with Kevin:

Kevin's website: https://www.KevinGChapman.com

Facebook page: Mike Stoneman Thriller Group
https://www.amazon.com/gp/product/B08BZMDSVT

Email: Kevin@KevinGChapman.com

Preview of Double Takedown
(Mike Stoneman #6)

The trip to Las Vegas and the two weddings took Mike, Michelle, Jason, and Rachel to January of 2020. As you may recall, a few months later the world pretty much stopped while we all dealt with the Covid-19 pandemic. I decided that I did not want to write a Mike Stoneman story where my detectives would have to interrogate suspects while wearing masks and dealing with all the other pandemic protocols.

So, instead, I wrote two books that are stand-alone stories set in the present day, but without any specific date. In *Dead Winner* and *The Other Murder*, I was able to ignore the pandemic. I'm very proud of both my non-Mike Stoneman books. *Dead Winner* was a Blue Ribbon winner in the 2022 CLUE Award (best in category). *The Other Murder* was the Grand Prize Winner in the 2023 CLUE Award (best overall suspense/thriller novel) and a finalist for the National Indie Excellence Award.

Now, it's time to return to the Mike Stoneman storyline. My next book, *Double Takedown*, book #6 in the series, picks up briefly in May of 2022, then continues the story in the late summer of 2023. By then, the pandemic is over and things are back to mostly "normal" in the world of homicide detectives. Keep reading for a preview of Chapter 1 of *Double Takedown*. The book will be available in the fall of 2024.

Double Takedown

Mike Stoneman Mystery/Thriller #6

Chapter 1 -- A Night at the Ballet

May 23, 2022

NEW YORK HOMICIDE DETECTIVE Mike Stoneman was decidedly out of his element. The David H. Koch Theater's palatial lobby resembled the red carpet outside the Academy Awards. Bejeweled women sipped champagne under crystal chandeliers while celebrities mingled and posed for pictures. *What's a cop doing in this crowd?* he thought, not for the first time.

Mike's black tuxedo pants were annoyingly snug. Standing in a crowd of people, only a few of whom were wearing face masks, exacerbated his discomfort. Every one of the glamourous members of the Broadway community swirling through the room was either taller, thinner, or younger than him. Most were all three.

Jason Dickson, Mike's partner, on the other hand, was happy to show off his tall, fit physique in a perfectly tailored tux. His dark skin contrasted with the snowy white collar of his dress shirt. Mike was used to being the older, shorter, and paunchier member of his team. His only solace was that all the other homicide detectives in their Manhattan precinct looked more like Mike. He had overcome the jealousy years ago, but at a formal occasion like this, he felt a tiny pang.

Mike was also not a fan of ballet, which was the upcoming performance following the cocktail reception. He appreciated the dancers' physical prowess and the fluid beauty of the performances. But the story that others claimed they saw within the dance eluded his perception. This was supposed to be the first big post-pandemic event for Mike and Michelle. Time to get back to something approaching normal after more than two years of social distancing. Mike felt like an old war horse at the Kentucky Derby.

Michelle, by contrast, was smiling, laughing, and having the time of her life alongside Jason's wife, Rachel. For Rachel, one of the most outgoing and people-loving individuals Mike knew, the pandemic had been torture. Tonight, Rachel was resplendent in her sparkling purple gown. Jason had quietly revealed to Mike that she had not fit into it since the baby. A solid month of near-starvation and workouts yielded the eye-catching results before them.

These musings were interrupted by the clinking of silverware on crystal. The crowd hushed and all eyes turned to a white-haired man standing on the red-carpeted stairway leading to the theater. Once he had everyone's attention, Albert Edward Gooday the Third thanked everyone for coming and for donating to the Broadway Cares / Equity Fights Aids foundation. In a three-minute speech, Mr. Gooday gave his personal thanks to a list of people who made the event possible. Mike paid little attention until their host encouraged everyone to drink the wine and enjoy the hors d'oeuvres before the performance began in thirty minutes.

Michelle's soft voice penetrated the growing murmur of the crowd. "Thank you, Mike."

Turning to his left and looking down at Michelle's beaming face, most of Mike's discomfort melted away. Four inches shorter than Mike, Michelle's smooth skin and dark eyes produced the illusion of being much younger. Passing men admired her soft curves and slim legs and neck, wrapped in a black, sequined cocktail dress. He often marveled that Michelle was his wife. When he started dating the Manhattan county medical examiner during the Righteous Assassin investigation, Mike never imagined that, five years later, they would be together at a Lincoln Center charity ballet.

"I didn't do anything."

"You agreed to come, and you dressed up for me. I appreciate it. I'm having a wonderful time. I hope you don't hate this too much."

"I'm fine. Looks like Jason and Rachel are loving it." He tilted his head toward their companions, who were deep in conversation with three women in progressively more revealing gowns and one tall man with perfectly groomed hair. An actor, of course, but Mike did not recognize him.

"I'm sure they are. Thank you for agreeing to spend the money."

"Yeah, well, it's a good cause, right?"

A booming voice caused Mike to swing his attention to his left. "Detectives Stoneman and Dickson!"

"Well, I'll be damned," Mike lowered his voice, hoping only Michelle would hear.

"Shhh! Be nice," Michelle whispered back.

A rotund man accompanied by a glamourous blonde advanced toward Mike, extended his meaty hand, and gave Mike's an enthusiastic shake. "Victoria, allow me to present two of New York's finest homicide detectives, Mike Stoneman and Jason Dickson. I can truthfully say I owe these men my life."

"Well, I guess we shouldn't be surprised to see the great Max Bloom at an event like this," Mike said.

"Allow me to present one of my protégés, Miss Victoria Franklin, an up-and-coming actress," Bloom gushed.

"Actor, Max. Please." Victoria extended her manicured hand toward Mike. Her ears dripped with a three-tiered cascade of diamonds, matching a necklace dangling between her exposed cleavage.

Michelle said, "Are you one of Max's clients?"

"One of my cast members," Max crooned, placing an arm around Victoria's slim waist. "Since the tragic death of my wife, Sheila, I'm happy to say that I'm now a producer of one of this year's biggest shows, *Godfather: The Musical.* It's up for eight Tony Awards. Sheila always loved the theater. It's what she would have wanted." Max patted his companion's hand, as if grieving deeply over his loss.

"You're producing *that* show?" Rachel blurted. "I should introduce you to my brother, Jackie. He's a brilliant performer. You should give him an audition."

"Oh, I'd be happy to, Miss Robinson. Anything for my favorite detectives." Max held out his business card, which Rachel placed into her purple clutch.

"And it's now *Mrs. Dickson.*" Rachel flashed a satisfied smile at Jason and extended her left hand, displaying her own diamond ring.

"Wonderful!" Max bellowed. "Congratulations. I owe your husband everything I have. You can have your brother call me anytime." Max then squeezed his date's shoulder, pulling her gently. "Come, my dear. There are many other people who need to meet you." Without a glance back, Max and Victoria disappeared into the crowd like Shoeless Joe Jackson melting into an Iowa cornfield.

Michelle clutched Mike's forearm, pulling him forward. "We don't have much time before the performance. I want to meet Alex Bishop. I saw him over this way. He's the lead in Max's show, so now we can tell him we know his producer."

"I'm not sure I want to be associated with Max Bloom," Mike grimaced. "He's probably here playing some angle."

Jason, who had been listening, said, "I'll bet you ten bucks Max got somebody else to buy his ticket for this shindig." Mike laughed, but did not take the bet.

When the lights dimmed and the guests made their way toward the stairs, Mike and Michelle walked past a large placard listing the names of major donors. She pointed out that Maximillian Bloom was listed as a $50,000 benefactor.

Mike looked over his shoulder at Jason. "Well, I guess you were wrong."

* * *

FORTY-FIVE MINUTES INTO THE FIRST ACT of the ballet, Rachel pulled down her sparkling purple facemask and whispered into Jason's ear, "What's going on down there?"

They were seated in the next-to-last row of the orchestra level. At the front of the house, partially illuminated by the stage lights, someone was standing. Rachel could not see who it was, but could hear the buzz of people talking. Then, a woman's scream attracted everyone's attention. Necks strained to see. More people stood.

The music stopped in the middle of the piece. The performers continued dancing for several seconds on a silent stage. The conductor, standing on a raised podium so she could see the stage and the orchestra pit, turned toward the audience. She was talking into her headset microphone. There was another scream. Then the conductor's voice boomed over the sound system.

"Ladies and gentlemen, please remain in your seats. We have a medical emergency in the front row. If there are any doctors in the house, we need assistance right away."

Rachel's EMT training kicked in before the conductor finished saying "emergency." She leapt over Jason's lap, then kicked off her heels as she sprinted barefoot down the long, sloping path toward the stage. Dozens of people began filming on their phones. Despite the conductor's instruction, half the house seemed to be standing.

Mike jumped up as soon as he saw Rachel leave her seat. He grabbed Jason's sleeve. "Let's go, we need to work crowd control down there. Michelle, call 9-1-1."

Jason and Mike were forty feet behind Rachel. When they reached the front of the theater, a small group of gawkers had already gathered in the aisle.

"NYPD! Please take your seats and keep this aisle clear for emergency services!" Jason shouted, his baritone carrying throughout the auditorium.

Mike gently eased several men in formalwear away from the space between the front row and the orchestra pit. Jason did the same. The two detectives took up positions on either side of the aisle, casting authoritative glares at anyone who seemed interested in venturing toward the commotion in front of the stage.

Jason glanced down the front row and saw Rachel's bare back hunched over someone lying on the floor. The straps of her purple dress flashed in the house lights, which had come on. Rachel and two men worked together to drag a figure on the floor toward more open space. Jason saw black shoes and pants, but could not see the man's face. An usher ran down the aisle, holding a small red case that Mike assumed was an automated external defibrillator. He dashed past the two cops and handed the device to Rachel, who had taken charge of the emergency situation.

Rachel barked instructions while prepping the AED, then administered an electric charge to the victim's now-bare chest. On the elevated stage, twenty dancers leaned over the edge to watch.

One minute later, an actual EMT team barreled down the aisle with a gurney on wheels carrying their own equipment. Rachel remained on her knees, working on the supine man, while the two tuxedoed doctors stepped back. The public address system announced that there would be an intermission in the performance due to the medical emergency and asked everyone to calmly return to the lobby. As the crowd slowly rose and meandered to the exit, those still filming remained standing until Mike, Jason, and several ushers shouted them into submission and herded them toward the doors.

On the floor, the EMT crew loaded the unconscious man onto their gurney, then hustled out an emergency exit door at the left corner of the stage. As soon as the crew passed them, Jason and Mike rushed toward Rachel. Jason gently pulled her to a standing position. She hugged Jason in her bare feet as Mike stood back. Before Jason and Rachel disengaged, a tap on Mike's back caused him to spin around. Michelle held out Rachel's sparkling heels with a concerned expression.

"Don't like following instructions, huh?" Mike said.

Michelle flashed a tiny smile. "I told the usher I'm a doctor and he let me stay."

"Thanks," Rachel said, slumping into a front-row seat and working to slide back into her shoes.

"Do you know who that was on the floor?" Michelle asked.

Rachel stood. "Oh my God. You couldn't see, could you? It was Alex Bishop."

"The lead in *Godfather?* He was just nominated for a Tony!" Michelle grabbed Mike's sleeve.

"He was," Rachel said, "but unless the EMT crew works a miracle, he won't be there to win it."

* * *

Read the rest of *Double Takedown* – available fall 2024.